The Mistress of Longbourn

by

Jann Rowland

One Good Sonnet Publishing

By Jann Rowland
Published by One Good Sonnet Publishing:

PRIDE AND PREJUDICE VARIATIONS

Acting on Faith
A Life from the Ashes (Sequel to *Acting on Faith*)
Open Your Eyes
Implacable Resentment
An Unlikely Friendship
Bound by Love
Cassandra
Obsession
Shadows Over Longbourn
The Mistress of Longbourn

PRIDE AND PREJUDICE VARIATIONS
Co-Authored with Lelia Eye

WAITING FOR AN ECHO

Waiting for an Echo Volume One: Words in the Darkness
Waiting for an Echo Volume Two: Echoes at Dawn
Waiting for an Echo Two Volume Set

A Summer in Brighton
A Bevy of Suitors
Love and Laughter: A Pride and Prejudice Short Stories Anthology

THE EARTH AND SKY TRILOGY
Co-Authored with Lelia Eye

On Wings of Air
*On Lonely Paths**
*On Tides of Fate**

*Forthcoming

This is a work of fiction based on the works of Jane Austen. All of the characters and events portrayed in this novel are products of Jane Austen's original novel or the authors' imaginations.

THE MISTRESS OF LONGBOURN

Copyright © 2016 Jann Rowland

Cover Design by Marina Willis

Published by One Good Sonnet Publishing

ISBN: 1987929500
ISBN-13: 978-1987929508

To my family who have, as always, shown
their unconditional love and encouragement.

ACKNOWLEDGEMENTS

Libertines abound;
Our heroes, though, are found,
Not where one would think,
Good friends shall never shrink.
Backing always says,
Our love which never strays.
Ultimate gratitude,
Resolute attitude,
Now, unto all who viewed.

Prologue

$\mathcal{L}$ ife has often been compared to a journey, a voyage through time and space, and one which takes the traveler through every kind of terrain imaginable. Indeed, the succession of rolling hills and gentle valleys are matched by the appearance of tall cliffs of jagged rocks, steep paths carved into high mountains, and the depths of the sea, cold, lost, and lonely. It is also often compared to a never-ending, ever-changing emotion, where one can experience a sublime happiness, only to become a crushing sadness, all within the blink of an eye. So great is the variance that it is a wonder that anyone makes it through the journey of his life — or perhaps it is more proper to say that it is a surprise that people do not succumb earlier than they do, for it is clear that the blows life deals take as much toll as age or infirmity.

Life also has a way of sneaking up on one, of showing how fragile it is, and how it can be taken away when least expected, gone before one knows it. And though the one who passes on is freed from the cares of the world, freed to continue his journey to his reward — or punishment — earned in his lifetime, it is the ones left behind who suffer loss and heartache, especially the young, just setting forth on the paths of their own sojourns.

Such were the thoughts running through the minds of two young women kneeling in a small churchyard in Hertfordshire. Before them were five freshly dug graves, the earth still turned and barren, without any covering of the foliage which would, undoubtedly, cover them as time wore on. Or perhaps such weighty thoughts were the province of one sister, for the other was not much given to thoughts of philosophy or matters of an eternal nature. Indeed, her thoughts tended toward bewilderment and loss, such as she had never expected to experience.

It had been a hard winter in the small market town of Meryton. The season had begun much as any other winter had, with the slow decline of autumn, the leaves turning golden, red, and yellow in all their glory before falling to the ground, the temperature gradually decreasing until the colder weather held sway over the land. As usual, the residents of the area had hunkered down to wait out the cold months, relying on the promise of the coming spring when all would be brought back to life.

The trouble had begun with a few reported cases of a cold, in which aching muscles and congested noses were the most common complaint. Those, however, had rapidly turned into an epidemic accompanied by a vicious fever, a splitting headache, and a dry, hacking cough, which slowly sapped the life of those caught in its grasp. It was not long before the icy tendrils of death stretched forth to claim its first victims. From there it had only multiplied, not discriminating between either the young and hale or the old and infirm.

Few families in the district had emerged unscathed, almost all losing a member or two. But it had been the Bennets of Longbourn who had been dealt the worst blow, as evidenced by the five new graves in the cemetery of their ancestors.

In a bit of irony, it had been Elizabeth who had exhibited the first signs of sickness which had led to her confinement to her bed. But of those members of the family who had contracted the disease, she was also the only one who had proven to be hardy enough to fight it off and survive. Even while kneeling beside the graves of her family, more than a month after the onset of the sickness, Elizabeth still felt weak and a little dizzy, though she knew she would eventually recover.

Her recovery, she felt, was in no small part due to the loving care of her angelic sister Jane, who had nursed her unceasingly from the time she had fallen ill, until Elizabeth had begun to make her recovery. Of course, by that time, Jane had begun to feel the effects of the illness herself and had been confined to the bed from which she was not destined to arise, being the first of the Bennets to succumb to the illness. From there, it had spread to the other members of the family one by one, claiming them all in succession. And even when they had finally thought themselves free of the curse, with three sisters remaining from a family of seven, Mary had fallen ill, and had finally passed from it, the newest of the five graves.

Only Kitty had escaped the illness altogether, through some measure of providence which could not be understood. Still, Elizabeth was grateful for it—though she had never been close with her two youngest sisters, both of whom were a little too frivolous and silly for her tastes. Kitty was still a link to the rest of her family, however. At least Elizabeth was not alone. Conversely, if Kitty had been the only one left, Elizabeth did not know how she would possibly have managed, so ignorant to the ways of the world was she.

Women of the time were not allowed to attend funerals; it was deemed too demanding for the delicate sex, too harsh for their sensibilities. Thus, neither Elizabeth nor Kitty had been permitted to witness the final progression of farewells to the members of their family as they were laid to rest. Their uncles—Mr. Gardiner from London and Mr. Phillips from Meryton—had spent the past months traveling to and from their homes, a requirement more difficult for the more distant Mr. Gardiner, but neither had complained, though the marks of loss were on both their countenances, much as those Elizabeth and Kitty bore themselves.

"Lizzy," the small voice of her sister penetrated the fog of Elizabeth's grief.

Elizabeth looked up and beheld her sister staring at her. Kitty looked as if she was lost at sea, with neither sail nor rudder to assist her in making her way to shore. Lydia's death in particular had been difficult for Kitty, as Lydia was the one in the family with whom she had been the closest. The two youngest girls had been thick as proverbial thieves from the time they had both been in leading strings. And now they were sundered, one passed on to the next life, while the other was left to navigate the river of life alone.

"What shall become of us, Lizzy? How shall we manage to carry on?"

It was the naked pain in her sister's eyes and voice which allowed Elizabeth to force her own pain down into a dark corner of her mind, not forgotten, but suppressed until she was able to give it rein. And allow it out she knew she must if she were ever to heal.

Shifting her weight, Elizabeth scooted closer to her sister, heedless of the ground underneath her and what it would do to her dress, and took her trembling sister into her arms. Though Kitty shook with suppressed sobs for several moments, soon she calmed a little, though Elizabeth could still hear her sister's sniffles. For herself, Elizabeth felt as much comfort in the near presence of her sister as she was giving.

"We shall survive," said Elizabeth, though she was not truly certain of it herself. Physically, they would be well, but the emotional blows . . . She was not certain how they could possibly recover from them.

"Longbourn has been left to me, and it will always be our home. Should neither of us ever marry, we will be comfortable in our home. It can never be taken from us."

A watery chuckle met Elizabeth's reassurance. "For that, at least, we may be grateful."

"We will be well again, Kitty," said Elizabeth. She pushed herself away from her a little, looking into Kitty's eyes, which were swimming with those tears which had not yet cascaded down her cheeks to dampen her dress. "Though it does not seem possible now, though the sorrow which will pervade our home seems like it will never depart, one day we will feel whole again."

"We will 'feel' whole," echoed Kitty.

The inference in Kitty's bitter tone was clear to Elizabeth, and in fact, she wholeheartedly agreed with it.

"There will always be a void where the members of our family, now passed on to the Lord's embrace, once dwelt. I do not deny that. Inasmuch as you will always miss Lydia's presence in your life and I will forever yearn for Jane, and Mama and Papa and Mary, who each had their own places in our lives, one day we will be able to think of them with fondness and happiness at the joy they brought to our lives. One day, and I pray it will not be too far distant, we will remember them with fondness and a hint of melancholy, rather than this debilitating sadness. We will heal. We will continue to live."

"I shall hold you to that promise, Lizzy," said Kitty, as she rested her head once more on Elizabeth's shoulder.

And Elizabeth, as she held her sister, rocking her slightly as if she were naught but a small child, thought back on her own sorrow, allowing it to well up within her, to bring tears once more to her eyes. For she knew that the promised recovery would not be swift in coming, not with so many blows dealt them within such a short period of time.

But eventually they would heal. They would carry on. For such was life.

Indeed, time heals all wounds, or at the very least, it blunts the pain. Though Elizabeth and Kitty spent many months sorrowing for their departed family, slowly, the immediacy of loss departed, replaced by a softer, gentler sort of melancholy, a quiet longing for those who were no longer there, a dull ache rather than the sharp stab of a knife.

Throughout the next year of their lives, the two remaining Bennet sisters lived primarily at home, spending their season of mourning at Longbourn in quiet and solitude, coming to terms with their losses, becoming accustomed to their new situation in life, taking to new routines and new activities. For Elizabeth, this meant accustoming herself to her new role as the proprietor of Longbourn and to her responsibility for the care and upkeep of the estate. For Kitty, it meant learning to live without her younger sister, without the frivolity and mischief into which Lydia had constantly dragged her. Kitty was forced to find other employment, quieter pastimes, which she did, though not always without complaint. Elizabeth was careful to ensure that Kitty was always given the greater part of her attention, and Kitty's desire to make her only remaining sister happy ensured that her improvement, though not always steady, was still noticeable.

Mr. Gardiner, who had been named the girls' guardian in their father's will, visited as frequently as his business allowed. Though technically his role was to direct Longbourn's enterprise, in reality Elizabeth, who had shown an astuteness for the management of the estate that her father had never quite possessed, made the decisions, which were ratified by her uncle almost as a matter of course. Thus, when Elizabeth decided to introduce new techniques designed to improve the yields of their fields, Mr. Gardiner was content to leave it in her hands, knowing that her management skills had quickly surpassed his, he who had never attended to the needs of an estate himself. And when Elizabeth purchased several prized horses to embark upon a new business venture of horse breeding, Mr. Gardiner, once he had listened to her ideas, was quick to agree. She was even able to purchase a few small parcels of land to add to Longbourn's burgeoning wealth, increasing the income of the estate even further. In Mr. Gardiner's own province, that of business and investment, he advised them with an astuteness borne of years of experience. With a yearly budget, which was necessarily reduced due to a smaller number of people to feed and clothe, Elizabeth found there was extra money which could be invested. Soon Longbourn's wealth was increased further in concordance with Mr. Gardiner's handling of their investments.

At times, Elizabeth wondered if she was truly meant to act as the estate's master. Many women who inherited estates from their deceased husbands, or only daughters who never married, operated their own homes with little difficulty. But Elizabeth was of tender years, less than twenty when her family had passed on, which led to some difficulty amongst the tenants.

Mr. Gardiner's largest contribution to the estate, therefore, was the selection of a steward who was added to the staff within a few months of Mr. Bennet's passing. Mr. Bennet had never used a steward, not believing the addition of such a servant warranted the additional expense. But as Mr. Gardiner explained to Elizabeth, she could only benefit from a male servant in a position of authority to deal with the more obdurate tenants, and furthermore, to watch after the sisters themselves, in Mr. Gardiner's place. And as the new steward—Mr. Whitmore—came highly recommended, having trained at the feet of an experienced steward of a great estate in the north, though he was himself a young man, Mr. Gardiner felt it fortunate they were able to secure his services. He made certain that Mr. Whitmore was compensated well, hoping he would never feel the need to seek a higher paying position at a larger estate.

The other major change at Longbourn was the need for a new housekeeper, for the previous woman—Mrs. Hill—had perished along with her mistress and the other members of the family. Though Elizabeth had interviewed several women for the position, in the end she had decided to give it to Susan Chambers, the most senior maid in their employ. Not only was Susan intelligent and industrious, but Elizabeth was familiar with her, Susan having lived at Longbourn for the past ten years. She was older than Elizabeth, but young enough that Elizabeth thought she was able to relate to her on a friendly basis.

Of course, it was not long before the young woman caught the eye of the young steward, and Miss Susan Chambers became Mrs. Susan Whitmore. She kept her position, however, as by that time she and Elizabeth had formed a true friendship and confidence between them, and though Elizabeth knew she would need to find a replacement when Susan eventually became a mother, for the present she was happy to continue the arrangement without any alteration.

Their life ordered and Longbourn thriving, the two girls were at least able to live without the fear of their physical needs not being met. And when the year of their mourning ended, they began to take part in the neighborhood once again. For the spring the year after they were left alone in the world came and with it, a hint of new life, of new purpose. They had become much closer as a result of their need to rely on each other, and they were united in the bonds of love and family. This allowed them to further heal.

Chapter I

"*L*izzy! Lizzy!"

Looking up from her desk in her study, Elizabeth looked out the door toward the sound of the voice of her sister crying her name. Kitty, Elizabeth noted with a wryness of affection, had improved her behavior much over the past eighteen months, but she had never completely outgrown the tendency to speak loudly or to occasionally laugh more than she should, not to mention a penchant for making comments which were not strictly proper.

Still, she was a good girl, and Elizabeth knew her life would be much more difficult if she did not have such a bright and effervescent sister present to carry her away from her constant cares.

The sound of her footsteps striking the tiles of the hallway preceded her, and soon Kitty rushed into the study, panting due to her exertions. She wore an expression of excitement as Elizabeth had seen many times before, and her eyes were alight with happiness.

"Hello, Kitty," said Elizabeth, her smile accompanied by a pointed look, which suggested that her sister should settle herself before she attempted to speak.

Kitty received the message instantly, taking a seat in front of Elizabeth's desk while attempting to catch her breath. Kitty had been visiting her friend Maria Lucas at Lucas Lodge that morning, and it appeared like she had run all the way back, eager to impart whatever gossip she had heard there.

"Lizzy, you will never guess what I have heard," said Kitty when she had tolerably composed herself.

"No, I suppose I have little chance of actually guessing," replied Elizabeth, flashing her sister an amused smile. "Perhaps you should not keep me in suspense."

"Oh, Lizzy!" exclaimed Kitty. "You do sometimes take the fun out of my efforts to surprise you!"

"As I have no notion of what has made you so excited, I dare say you shall still have your fun. Now, what is the news you bear?"

"Only that Netherfield has been let at last. I had almost thought I would never see the day!"

In fact, Elizabeth had already heard the momentous news. Though Lady Lucas and their Aunt Phillips were notorious gossips, renowned for their ability to ferret out secrets and receive the news of the district almost invariably before any others, in matters of local properties, they were often outmatched by the gentlemen. Elizabeth, though not one of the men, was still friendly enough with most of them—especially her closest neighbors—to hear most of the news of the local estates before it was disseminated to the rest of the community. In this particular case, her Uncle Phillips had informed Elizabeth of the potential buyer for the estate, knowing she might be required to deal with the new master.

Of course Elizabeth would not inform Kitty of this fact—let the girl have her fun by imparting such news. Elizabeth would not suspend her sister's pleasure, and she doubted Kitty was perceptive enough to detect Elizabeth's earlier knowledge.

"That is very good," replied Elizabeth. "It is beneficial for the district too, as Netherfield has remained empty far too long."

"And do you not wish to hear of those who shall take residence?"

"I have no object to your stating it," replied Elizabeth, "I only caution you not to put too much stock in the gossip of others. Those who ultimately take residence might not resemble what you have been told."

It appeared that Kitty was far too excited to pay heed to Elizabeth's words. "It has been taken by a Mr. Bingley, a man of good fortune from the north. According to Lady Lucas, he and a longstanding friend came to view the estate on Monday last, and he signed the papers the very next day."

"And when is he to take possession?" asked Elizabeth with some interest, as she had as yet heard nothing more than generalities.

"Lady Lucas is not certain. But she believes it likely that he will come before Michaelmas." Kitty's eyes positively shone with anticipation. "And do you not know that it is rumored he will come with a large party of friends and relations! Hopefully, he will bring with him many handsome gentlemen, for gentlemen in the district are scarce and new dance partners would be welcome."

Elizabeth smiled with indulgence at her sister. Though Kitty's improvement had been great, she still took pleasure in simple things — shopping, gossiping, and especially dancing were enough to render Kitty content. Elizabeth had attempted to teach her to play the pianoforte, and though Kitty would never be a virtuoso, she had taken to it with tolerable ease and could now play some simpler pieces. Interesting Kitty in literature had been a more difficult proposition, for she was not of a disposition that lent itself easily to quiet activities. Still she had broadened her horizons sufficiently that Elizabeth was able to interest her in the occasional book which was not a novel. On the whole, Elizabeth was happy that her sister now found more meaning in life than the superficial activities which had dominated her doings in the past.

"New dance partners would be welcome indeed," observed Elizabeth.

"Yes, they would. But perhaps the most important part of this news is that Mr. Bingley is a single man of fortune." Kitty was alight with excitement and hope. "What a wonderful thing it is for us."

"How so?" asked Elizabeth, slipping into a slightly teasing tone, one for which her father had been infamous. "How can it possibly affect us?"

"Oh, Lizzy!" exclaimed Kitty. "Are you not inclined to romance? Why, if this Mr. Bingley is a handsome and amiable man, he might fall in love with one of us, whisk us off to Netherfield in his chaise and four, love one of us as if we were his most precious possession."

"Yes, Kitty, I do understand your meaning. But while I know nothing of this Mr. Bingley and acknowledge that he may be the handsomest, most amiable man in the world, still, I believe we should allow the man to settle into his estate before throwing ourselves at him as potential marriage candidates. Do you not agree?"

"Of course I do not mean to throw myself at him. But I think it would be a good joke indeed if he were to choose me, and if the younger were to be married before the elder."

Elizabeth only smiled indulgently at her sister. Soon, however, she noted a hint of melancholy which fell over Kitty's face.

"I only wish Papa were still alive so he could go and visit Mr. Bingley. We shall have to rely on Sir William for our introduction."

Standing, Elizabeth moved to the other side of the desk and sat close to her sister, grasping one of her hands. "I am sure that Sir William will perform his duties adequately. Besides," continued Elizabeth, showing her sister a hint of a mischievous smile, "can you imagine our father visiting Mr. Bingley without teasing Mama about it?"

A laugh escaped Kitty's lips and the gloom was dispelled. "He would, would he not?"

"Indeed, I believe he would feel it his duty to do so. I can see him refusing to go, claiming it was not necessary, while she badgered and cajoled, and eventually called for her salts, claiming ill use of her nerves."

"No doubt Lydia would exclaim about handsome men and her desire to dance while Jane would only watch serenely."

"And Mary would have some homily or another to share with the family."

The two sisters laughed together. It was always thus—when thoughts of their lost loved ones intruded and threatened to bring them pain, the other would interject with a quip, bringing some happy thought to mind, allowing them to remember with fondness, to laugh instead of cry.

"Is there any suggestion that Mr. Bingley will attend the next assembly?" asked Elizabeth when their mirth had settled.

"No, but as it will be after Michaelmas, meaning Mr. Bingley should be in residence, I cannot imagine Sir William neglecting to extend an invitation to him and all of his party."

"Such a thing would be inconceivable, it is true. We shall have to wait for the assembly to become acquainted with him."

"And a long wait it shall be," said Kitty with a huff. "I can scarcely wait. It shall be so exciting to meet new people."

In reality, Elizabeth was more concerned than excited, knowing that a neighbor with whom one did not get on could be a curse, rather than a blessing, and Longbourn's border with Netherfield was its longest. With most of the rest of their neighbors, Elizabeth got on quite well, though they tended to be a little condescending with her as a general rule. Only Sir William, who had been a close friend of her father's, treated her with respect and deference, though he was congenial with all.

With Elizabeth's northern neighbor, a Mr. Pearce, she possessed no more than a cordial relationship, but as the border was small, it truly did not bother her over much. Of course, that relationship had been soured by what had passed between them during the late spring and early summer. Unfortunately, this Mr. Pearce, perhaps sensing an opportunity, had begun to involve himself in the society of Meryton, though traditionally he was a member of society in Stevenage to the north, and it had not been long before his purpose had been revealed when he had begun to call on her.

It was not the man himself to whom Elizabeth objected. In fact, Mr. Pearce, while somewhat older than Elizabeth wished for in a husband, was quite tall, passably handsome, and possessed of good manners and an intelligence Elizabeth had always wished for in a husband. He was also acceptable as a suitor for the most part, treating her with respect, though she had noted a certain distance in his manner which she thought to be part of his character. No, to the man himself there was not much objection. It was in his plans and his utter disregard for her wishes in conjunction with those plans for which she had not cared.

Elizabeth could remember the latest conversation between them as if it had occurred only the day before. Mr. Pearce had called on her, and though he could not sit with them, given the lack of a male guardian in the house, they had walked out along the lanes close to Longbourn village, which was situated just outside the estate.

Their conversation, as it often did, consisted of subjects of a slightly banal nature, for though Mr. Pearce was an intelligent man, he had little interest in the kind of literature Elizabeth preferred, cared nothing for her new venture into horse breeding—he rode but little himself, and only when absolutely necessary—and possessed few interests in common with Elizabeth.

"Longbourn appears to be a good piece of land," observed he, as they strolled around the perimeter of the gardens at the back of the property. "I can see you and your sister have done much to make this an idyllic spot, especially with your tending of the flowers in behind the house."

"Yes, Kitty especially enjoys such work," replied Elizabeth. Previously, it had been Jane who had taken the most interest in the gardens, but Kitty, perhaps finding an activity in which she was interested, one which, more importantly, did not consist of forcing herself to read through the "dusty old tomes" preferred by her sister, had taken to them with willingness, if not enthusiasm.

"She has done well with them. It lends beauty to your home. I commend her diligence. I also understand you have introduced new techniques, which have allowed the income of the property to rise."

"Yes," replied Elizabeth. She was happy with his interest, as he had never mentioned Longbourn before in their discussions. "My breeding operations, while still in their fledgling state, will one day be a ready source of income."

"That is good," said Mr. Pearce, though his tone was offhand. "It shall make it much easier to sell the property when the time comes."

"Sell the property?" asked Elizabeth, shocked that he would even suggest such a thing. "Whatever do you mean?"

"Of course it will become necessary to sell it," replied Mr. Pearce, seemingly unconcerned with Elizabeth's shock and displeasure. "You cannot expect me to care for an estate so distant from my own, one which is bisected by a mile or more by the prominence of Oakham Mount. It would be difficult in the extreme to care for it properly, you understand. Besides, there are several fields adjacent to my own lands on which I have my eye. The proceeds from the sale of Longbourn will allow their purchase and allow my wealth to increase by means of new investments. We will even be able to put some money aside for any eventual daughters' dowries to ensure they are able to find good partners in marriage."

"You seem to have forgotten that I have not yet accepted any proposal, sir. We are not even officially courting."

Mr. Pearce only waved off her testy tone. "All in good time, my dear. I have only begun calling on you; we cannot rush these things, you understand."

"Then I would wonder why you would even make such statements," snapped Elizabeth, now thoroughly displeased.

It seemed like the fact of her displeasure finally penetrated the man's consciousness, and he looked at her, a hint of question appearing in his eyes.

"I am sorry, Miss Bennet; are you unhappy about something?"

"How astute of you to have noticed," murmured Elizabeth. She firmly forced away her asperity so as to speak with perfect composure.

"I only wish to inform you, sir, that I could never countenance any sale of Longbourn, for whatever reason. It has been in my family's possession for generations, and I am not willing to part with it for any price."

Cocking his head to the side, Mr. Pearce regarded her. "I am sorry, Miss Bennet, but once we are married, the choice will not be yours. I am certain you well understand that marriage puts the possessions of the woman in her husband's hands."

"Your thinking is laced with fallacy, sir. For I have not consented to become your wife, nor will I ever do so, if your express purpose in calling on me is to obtain Longbourn in order to sell it, so as to fund your dynastic ambitions."

A startled and confused expression settled over his face. "For what other reason would I call on you? You are a comely young woman—it cannot be denied—but members of our class marry for reasons of prudence, which consist of connections or fortune. While your connections are unfortunate, it is true, the possession of an estate and the means to enhance your future husband's fortune make up for that lack. Did you, perhaps, have another view of our relationship?"

"I apologize for leading you astray, sir," said Elizabeth, "though I will inform you I had not the least intention of doing so. For you see, I am convinced that only the deepest love will induce me into matrimony. To reasons of prudence, I am perfectly indifferent."

"With an attitude such as this, I doubt you will ever find a man willing to marry you."

"Perhaps, but as you know, I have no need to marry. If I should remain unmarried, I might pass the estate down through Kitty's children, and if she does not marry also, to my uncle's eldest son. I need not worry for my future."

"Will it not be an empty life?" asked Mr. Pearce. Elizabeth was heartened by the fact that his tone suggested he was not offended by her assertions, little though he seemed to understand them.

"I believe it would be preferable to spending my life with a man I cannot love."

"Then you allowed me to call, hoping to achieve that love."

"More, I wished to understand if it was possible. But I will inform you now, sir, that I will not be induced to respond to a proposal in the affirmative if my future husband's intention is to sell the home I love. I will reiterate—I will not part with Longbourn for any money. It is the home of my ancestors, and while I understand that marriage might necessarily take me to other climes, still, I will have my future husband's solemn promise that Longbourn will be retained before an engagement will be entered into."

Mr. Pearce regarded her for several moments, his mien impassive. He did not appear angry or annoyed, but Elizabeth could almost feel the calculating quality in his gaze. She was certain he was attempting to discern how adamant she was about her statements.

Eventually, he came to the correct conclusion. "In that case, I must conclude we are not compatible, Miss Bennet. As I stated before, I have no desire to see to an estate at such a distance from my own, and since you do not wish to part with it, there appears to be no way to cross the impasse."

Elizabeth noted with interest that Mr. Pearce did not say anything regarding her stated wish for love in a marriage, but she was not about to concern herself on that score.

"I understand, sir. I am happy we have had this conversation now, ere we proceeded further in this relationship. I wish you all the happiness in your future life."

"Thank you," replied Mr. Pearce, and with a tip of his hat, he strode away. From that day forward, he was but rarely seen in Meryton.

Looking back on the matter, Elizabeth realized she had learned several lessons from the event. The first was that great care must be taken in choosing a man to become her husband, if, indeed, she were ultimately to marry. If she chose a man who already possessed his own estate, he would need to understand her intention to retain Longbourn, which meant she would need to ensure that he was a man of integrity, not that she would wish to marry a man who was not, regardless. Mr. Pearce's sentiments would not be unusual, but in this matter, Elizabeth wished for someone who would put her wishes before his own.

The second lesson Elizabeth learned was that it would possibly be more difficult to find a marriage partner than she had previously thought. With the deaths of her parents and sisters, Elizabeth had arranged to have her mother's dowry of five thousand pounds reallocated so that it became Kitty's dowry. Elizabeth was busy putting as much away as possible, hoping to increase Kitty's dowry to a respectable level. She hoped that it would be at least ten thousand pounds by the time Kitty was ready to marry.

For Elizabeth, her dowry consisted of Longbourn itself, and she knew that it was worth much more than Kitty's. And though Elizabeth had thought on the matter for some time, even speaking with Kitty about it, they were both agreed that Longbourn was not to be parted with for any price. Kitty claimed she was content with what Elizabeth had been able to do for her, and in the sunny optimism of youth, she was certain she would find a man who would love her, rendering her dowry nothing more than an additional benefit.

Elizabeth was not quite certain this would be the case, but she allowed her sister to maintain her optimism. For herself, Elizabeth knew that the qualities she desired in a future husband might well be impossible to find. Since Mr. Pearce had withdrawn, several others of the area had called on her, but none of these gentlemen had paid her any more attention than simple mild flirting. She had been certain to inform them of her desires from the beginning, but in the end it had not mattered.

Ever philosophical, Elizabeth had decided it did not signify. If her family's passing had taught her one thing only, it was that life was fragile, and it did not do to worry excessively concerning the future. She would marry or she would not—it was in the hands of the divine, and there was nothing she could do. Better to enjoy those precious days with Kitty and live her life with hope and happiness than to fret about that which she could not control.

Though Longbourn's longest border was with the much greater estate of Netherfield, their closest neighbor was, in fact, Lucas Lodge, the manor houses being situated no more than a mile apart. Sir William was new to the ranks of the gentry, having saved enough to purchase the small estate where his family now made their home. He was a bluff, kind soul who, though not especially intelligent, was happy and solicitous toward all. His wife, Lady Lucas, was a mothering sort of woman, delighting in gossip and all manner of news.

There were two of the family who were particularly important to Elizabeth and Kitty. Charlotte Lucas, Sir William's oldest child, was of age with Elizabeth, being only two years older, and Maria, his second daughter, was of an age with Kitty. Through the dark months of their loss, these two stalwart friends had often been the means of pulling Elizabeth and Kitty from the brink of despair, showing them friendship and, above all, love. Elizabeth did not know what they would have done had they not had such wonderful friends on whom to lean.

It was customary for the friends to gather together often to enjoy one another's society and listen to Lady Lucas's news of the area. No two families could be closer, especially since the epidemic, which had claimed the lives of most of the Bennet family. The Lucases had also lost a younger son, a sorrow which they shared with the two remaining Bennets.

"Are you as excited as your sister concerning the new arrivals?" asked Lady Lucas. It was some days after Kitty had first informed Elizabeth of the news, and the Bennets were visiting Lucas Lodge.

Elizabeth shot an affectionate glance at her sister, who was seated next to Maria, their heads close together as they giggled about some matter or another.

"I cannot imagine anyone could be *that* excited. But I will own I am eager to see some new faces in our gatherings."

"As am I," said Charlotte. She coughed daintily into her hand, her propensity to catching frequent chills and coughs a legacy of her own bout of sickness the year before. Elizabeth thought that she herself, though she had always been a robust sort of girl, was also more prone to them than she had been before, regardless of her continued active style of life.

"Have you heard anything more of the composition of the new family?" asked Elizabeth, knowing if anyone had been able to gather such intelligence, it was Lady Lucas.

"Perhaps a little," replied the lady in question. "It appears Mr. Bingley first viewed the place in the company of a close friend, and there is some suggestion that this man will be staying with him for at least some time. As for Mr. Bingley's immediate family, I believe he has two sisters. Whether they will accompany him or not remains to be seen."

"And Mr. Bingley is indeed still single as Kitty suggests?"

"I believe so," said Sir William, speaking up for the first time. "I visited him yesterday, you see, as he has just taken up residence, though the rest of his party was not yet present."

"And is he a handsome man?" asked Elizabeth, as she favored Charlotte with an expressive smile.

Sir William laughed. "I do not know that I am qualified to speak to what young ladies consider handsome in a man, but I found him very well favored, congenial, happy, and energetic. I dare say he will be a charming addition to our neighborhood."

It was, perhaps, not quite the ringing endorsement that Sir William intended it to be, due to the simple fact that the man giving it was disposed to be civil to one and all and possessed hardly a cynical bone in his body. Still, Elizabeth thought that, with such statements, Mr. Bingley would turn out to be, at the very least, tolerable enough to tempt most romantic young maidens of the neighborhood.

"And can we assume that Mr. Bingley has received an invitation to the upcoming assembly for himself and whoever joins him at the estate?"

"Of course!" cried Sir William with expansive enthusiasm. "For there is nothing like a country dance to introduce newcomers to the neighborhood. Of course, they must attend. And I should inform you that Mr. Bingley told me there is nothing he loves better than a country dance, so I am certain he will oblige the company."

"Hopefully he knows the steps," said Elizabeth as an aside to Charlotte. "For there is nothing so disagreeable as a man who cannot refrain from treading on his partner's toes!"

"Oh, Lizzy!" said Charlotte, her eyes shining with affection. "I am certain Mr. Bingley will be a delight on the dance floor. For what young man is not eager to dance with pretty young women?"

"Well, if he only dances with the pretty ones, I believe I shall dislike him exceedingly; for the plain young ladies also desire a dance on occasion."

Charlotte shook her head and regarded Elizabeth with amusement writ upon her brow. "I know what you are saying, Elizabeth, and you are aware that I consider you to be daft. You are no more a plain young woman than I am a general in His Majesty's army!"

The two girls laughed together, enjoying each other's company. It truly was wonderful to have as good a friend as Charlotte. Together with Jane, they had been close since the earliest days of the Lucases' arrival at the newly christened Lucas Lodge, and though they both felt the same measure of loss at the absence of the third member of their triumvirate, Charlotte and Elizabeth had grown much closer as a result.

"There is another piece of news which you will find interesting," said Lady Lucas, eagerly attempting to regain the focus of the company on her newest piece of gossip, "for I have recently discovered that a company of militia will be quartered in Meryton for the winter. I have been told that we can expect their arrival within the next two weeks."

"Indeed," said Elizabeth, all interest at this latest piece of news. "That is welcome news, for even if a soldier is not precisely the kind of man to make a good husband, further additions to our society must be welcome."

"Not make a good husband?" asked Kitty, perplexed. "I think it would be romantic to marry a soldier."

"Perhaps, but you must know that you would not live the life to which you are accustomed now."

A shadow crossed Kitty's face. "I do not understand."

"Soldiers are not wealthy men, Kitty," said Elizabeth, smiling at her sister. "Though your dowry will, hopefully, be substantial by the time you are ready to marry, still, you would be required to economize, as a soldier's pay is not large."

Kitty thought about that for a moment before she nodded her head slowly. "So you believe I should marry a man who is wealthy."

"Not necessarily, Kitty. If you loved a red coat, then perhaps you would be happy in that kind of life, and I would think it acceptable. But you must take some thought for prudence. I would suggest your ultimate goal should be a man who will love you as you deserve and do his utmost to provide for you."

"I believe if I could find a man who could provide for me, that would be enough to induce me to accept a proposal," said Charlotte. "We are not all blessed with the ability to choose our marriage partner with such prejudice."

"I have not espoused any such opinion," replied Elizabeth. "I merely suggested that felicity in marriage is as desirable as security."

"And I am not surprised to hear you say it. It is exactly what I would have expected to hear from you."

"Then we can claim to know each other very well!" exclaimed Elizabeth.

The Bennet sisters returned to Longbourn soon after that exchange, and while Kitty went to her room, Elizabeth entered the vestibule with the intention of going to her study. It was there that she encountered Mrs. Whitmore exiting the sitting-room. Greetings were exchanged, and Mrs. Whitmore passed on a request from her husband to meet with Elizabeth at any time convenient.

"Of course, Mrs. Whitmore," replied Elizabeth. "Please have your husband join me in the study at any time he finds convenient."

"Very well," said Mrs. Whitmore with a curtsey. "Also, while you were away, a letter came in the post. I put it on your desk."

"Thank you," replied Elizabeth, and she repaired to the library.

The letter in question was indeed sitting on the desk before the chair, and when Elizabeth picked it up, expecting it to be from her Uncle Gardiner, she immediately noted that it was not in her uncle's hand. In fact, the hand was a patchwork of flowery, flowing script, obviously intended to be a work of art in its own right. But the hand was also somewhat unsteady, as if the direction had been written in a perturbation of spirit, or perhaps the author simply possessed an unsteadiness of the hand. Regardless, it was from no one that Elizabeth knew.

Curious, Elizabeth opened it and began reading, and its contents soon astonished her.

Hunsford, near Westerham, Kent, 15th October.

Dear Cousin,

The disagreement subsisting between our late honored fathers has always given me much uneasiness, and I have often thought to heal the breach between our two families. My mind is now made up on the subject, for I have recently been ordained and received the single honor of being preferred to the valuable living at Hunsford parsonage, connected to the estate of the honorable Lady Catherine de Bourgh. Her ladyship is most attentive to all concerns within the reach of her influence, and most recently when we were discussing the situation of my family and, more particularly, of you, my distant cousins, she was forthright enough to share her opinions on the particulars of your situation.

Though you have recently been bereaved and have received the estate from your father, and, while from a certain perspective, your situation can be compared to that of my patroness – for she is widowed and in control of her own estate – in actuality, your situations cannot be more different. In her usual condescension, she informed me that it is not proper for a young woman such as yourself to control an estate without the help and support of a man to guide you. Though her ladyship does not scruple to point out when others have not done their duties, it was, nevertheless, clear to me that I have not done my duty as head of the family.

Thus, I propose that we heal the breach between our two branches of the family, a sentiment which is, I flatter myself, highly commendable. In the furtherance of this goal, I suggest a visit, by myself, to your estate, so that I may advise you on those matters which you, as a woman of tender years, cannot possibly understand or perform to any reasonable degree. While I am there, we may speak of certain other matters, which must be mutually beneficial, for having no protector immediately to hand, I am certain you must long for the gentle guidance and support of a gentleman.

Thus, you may expect me on the afternoon of Monday, November 18th, by four o'clock. The exact length of my stay we may determine upon my arrival, but if events play out as I expect they will, I believe my initial stay in the area will be no less than a se'ennight the following Saturday. Lady Catherine, in her gracious beneficence, has granted me leave from the matters of the parsonage since I have engaged another pastor to see to the needs of the flock in my absence.

I can only say that I am anticipating our meeting with eagerness, for I know that we shall be the closest of family.

William Collins.

For a moment, Elizabeth could only stare at the letter, wondering at the character of a man who could compose lines so replete with contradiction, so arrogant on the one hand, while evoking an image of a dog groveling on the floor on the other. Then, of course, she was forced to laugh at the absurdity. It was thus that Mr. Whitmore found her.

"Miss Bennet," said he with a bow as he entered the study. "I am happy to see you in such good spirits."

"I know not if it is good spirits," replied Elizabeth gesturing toward the letter, "or merely a response to absurdity of the kind I have never before experienced."

At Mr. Whitmore's questioning look, Elizabeth handed him the letter, wiping her eyes with her handkerchief. "If you are in need of a laugh, this letter will surely oblige!"

"He is an oddity to be sure," said Mr. Whitmore once he had read the letter. He turned his attention to her and quirked an eyebrow. "Can I assume you mean to decline?"

"Though he has not given me much of an opportunity to do so, I see no other option. My papa would have found his brand of the ridiculous diverting indeed, but we cannot have him stay here. It would not be proper."

Mr. Whitmore nodded. "I knew you would see it that way. As you are aware, your uncle has tasked me with your safety, as well as the maintenance of the estate, and I do not think having this Mr. . . ." he looked down at the letter, "Collins staying here would be at all advisable."

"I cannot agree more. I will compose a letter informing him of our refusal. No doubt I will be peppered with entreaties to change my mind, but I shall be firm."

"You do not intend to begin a correspondence?"

Elizabeth looked down at the letter he handed back to her. "No doubt Father would have been eager to savor the delights of his regular communications, but I am certain I would find that a little of his inanity would go a long way. I think I will direct him toward Uncle Gardiner and allow him to decide if he wishes to allow it. For myself, I believe I would prefer not to open a correspondence with Mr. Collins."

"Very good," said Mr. Whitmore with a smile of approval. "Now, I wished to bring a matter of the east pasture to your attention."

"The furthest one we purchased from Netherfield last year?" asked Elizabeth.

"Yes. As you know, we have not relocated the boundary fence as of yet, as the estate stood vacant for some years. I believe that with a man taking the lease on the estate, we must address that issue so that there is no confusion."

Elizabeth cocked her head at her steward. "Do you expect the new master of Netherfield to dispute it?"

With a smile, Mr. Whitmore shook his head. "By all accounts, he is a good man and a friendly one. Even if he did take issue, we possess all the proper papers which detail your ownership of the land, though I do not expect to be required to use them.

"But these things should be handled with care to avoid any misunderstanding. What if, for example, the new master decided that was a good location for his cattle to graze, without realizing he does not own the land?"

"The cattle could do damage to the field," said Elizabeth slowly, understanding his concerns.

"And given the plans we have for that field, it would be time-consuming and expensive to repair the damage."

A quick nod and Elizabeth turned the discussion. "Then what is the effort required, and what would the expense be?"

The discussion lasted for about fifteen minutes, and by the end, they had a firm plan decided for uprooting the final remains of the existing fence—most of it had already been cleared away—and the erection of the new fence. Once again Elizabeth was grateful for the steward's foresight and experience. Though Elizabeth considered herself competent and capable enough to manage her father's estate, she knew she was as of yet inexperienced. Mr. Whitmore had prevented her from making mistakes several times since she had come into her inheritance.

When they had completed her discussion, Elizabeth left the study, intent upon finding her sister. Though Kitty was not so prone to enjoying the follies of others as was Elizabeth, she thought her sister would be amused by Mr. Collins's letter.

Kitty was to be found in the front sitting-room, trimming a bonnet by the window. When she entered the room, Elizabeth stopped to watch her sister for a moment, bestowing a fond smile on her. Though Kitty's interests were much more wide-ranging than they had been, there were times when she took pleasure in those activities in which she had been so immersed before. Elizabeth remembered many times when Kitty and Lydia, amid the sounds of whispered confidences and giggles, had sat in that very spot, trimming, pulling apart, and redoing all of their work over and over. The thought brought a poignant bit of nostalgia into Elizabeth's breast, and she wished for what seemed like the millionth time that the rest of her family were still with them.

Shaking off such thoughts, Elizabeth approached her sister, noting Kitty's smile as she looked up.

"It is not uncommon for you to stop and watch me as I am doing something," said Kitty. "Can I correctly deduce that you are remembering our family?"

"Of course," said Elizabeth. "It often strikes me, especially when you are engaged in something you used to do with Lydia."

"As I often remember Jane or Papa when I see you."

The two sisters shared a melancholy, wistful smile, before Elizabeth turned her attention to the letter in her hand, knowing well how quickly such talk could become maudlin.

"I have received a letter today from a relation and thought you would be interested in reading it."

Something in Elizabeth's countenance must have informed Kitty that this was not a normal piece of correspondence, and she took it, curiosity etched on her face. It was not long before that curiosity turned to an expression of distaste.

"I remember Papa speaking of Mr. Collins."

"I believe he was speaking of Mr. Collins's father," reminded Elizabeth. "Unless I am very much mistaken, I do not think Papa ever met Mr. William Collins."

"A great pity, indeed," murmured Kitty. She turned a searching look on Elizabeth. "I am certain I do not find this so diverting as you obviously do. Can I assume you do not intend for him to stay here?"

Elizabeth shook her head. "It would not be proper."

"I doubt this . . ." Kitty slapped the letter with her free hand, obviously not impressed with what she was seeing. "This *man* will understand or will give credence to it if he does."

For a brief moment the two young ladies shared and expressive look before they broke down into giggles. Elizabeth gathered her sister into a warm embrace, grateful for Kitty's sunny outlook and happy demeanor.

"Be that as it may," said Elizabeth, "I shall write to him to inform him that he cannot stay, and I will ask Uncle Gardiner to do likewise. That should put any pretensions the man may possess to rest."

"Then you had best do so at once. I suspect it might take Mr. Collins some time to understand the significance of what you are to tell him."

Laughing, Elizabeth did just that.

Longbourn Estate, Hertfordshire, 19th October

Mr. Collins,

I must own that I was surprised to receive your letter, sir, though the contents are not unwelcome. It is commendable indeed to wish to mend the break in our family, and I applaud you for making the attempt.

Unfortunately, there is no possible way my sister and I can receive you at Longbourn. As you must be well aware as a clergyman, it would be improper in the extreme should you stay here with my sister and me, and as my guardian in London is much occupied with his business, he will not be able to be here during the time you propose to visit. I offer my apologies, but I respectfully decline your attendance here at Longbourn.

However, we are happy to maintain our correspondence in the hopes of furthering our understanding and bringing our families closer together. For any future correspondence, you may write to my uncle, for he, as my guardian, possesses the proper authority to respond on our behalf. I have enclosed his directions in this letter.

I can only add my cordial wishes for your health and happiness.

Elizabeth Bennet

Chapter II

*A*s was always the case when an assembly approached, the talk between the sisters consisted of little but the upcoming event, due to Kitty's excitement. Their return to society had only been of a few months' duration, and during their mourning, Elizabeth had found herself happy to be relieved of Kitty's propensity to speak of nothing else. That October's event was no different, though this time Kitty's chatter about dances and partners was interspersed with speculation concerning the newcomers, what the ladies would be wearing, and how handsome the gentlemen would be.

When Elizabeth and Kitty arrived, they were among the first in attendance, partially because Elizabeth preferred to arrive early, and partly because Kitty could not retain her excitement, necessitating an early departure. They spent some time sitting by the side of the room, watching as the residents of the nearby estates slowly trickled in, greeting those who arrived, and speaking in low tones about dresses, hair styles, or whatever subjects popped into Kitty's head.

At length, however, a few of Kitty's closest friends of the neighborhood arrived, and she left Elizabeth for their company. In order to pass the time, Elizabeth spoke with those nearby, and at length, fell into conversation with some of the local gentlemen.

"I know the methods you employ are tested and true," said Elizabeth, a familiar argument amongst the gentlemen of the area. "But the new techniques of crop rotation have been proven to increase yields substantially. Mr. Whitmore has seen them in use at the estate at which he was an assistant, and he tells me that the results were remarkable."

"I am well aware of the fact that you think very highly of your steward," said Mr. Goulding, "but I wonder at his competence. He is very young, you know, and cannot have the experience necessary to manage an estate properly."

What Mr. Goulding left unsaid—what they *all* left unsaid—was how Elizabeth herself, as a young woman, could not possibly see to the estate properly herself. At first, when she had come into her inheritance, Elizabeth had been annoyed over the local gentlemen's presumption. But she soon realized that they were set in their ways and there was little harm in them, and though perhaps their words were condescending and their actions dismissive, they truly did not mean to appear to censure her. In fact, she knew that she was respected for her intelligence and tenacity, even while most of the men did not think it possible for her to manage Longbourn half so well as they managed their own lands.

In spite of the provocation, Elizabeth kept her temper and kept her own counsel. They might dismiss Mr. Whitmore as a man too young to have any true experience and condescend to Elizabeth because she was of the wrong sex, but eventually, when the income of Longbourn rose due to the changes Mr. Whitmore was instituting, they would clamor to learn the secrets which would improve their own situations. Then, she imagined, the last laugh would be hers, though she doubted any of them would appreciate the joke.

When the Lucases entered the room, Elizabeth was happy to give up the company of the men for that of her dearest friend and confidante. The two ladies exchanged greetings and quickly fell into an animated conversation.

"When will the illustrious new members of our community make their appearance?" asked Elizabeth.

Charlotte smiled at Elizabeth's teasing tone. "You know the foibles of the higher members of society. No doubt they will arrive some time after the first dance begins, fashionably late."

"I have no doubt you are correct. I suppose we shall simply have to do without them."

As it turned out, Charlotte's prediction about the coming of the Netherfield party was borne out, as some half an hour after the first dancers took their places, the newcomers arrived and filed into the room.

As it occurred during a lull between the dances—Elizabeth had been asked to dance the first by Charlotte's brother Samuel—Elizabeth was able to see them as they entered and to form some basic impressions of them.

There were five members of the party in total—three men and two women. Two of the men were tall and slender, one with slightly reddish hair, while the other's was coal black, and the third man was portly and much shorter with his own dark hair, which showed a slight hint of grey at the temples. Elizabeth noted that his eyes sought out—and found—the refreshment table almost immediately. The two ladies were both tall—standing several inches taller than the diminutive Elizabeth—with handsome features, hair a slightly darker version of the first man's reddish locks—marking their kinship—and dressed in fine gowns with elaborate feathered headdresses completing the ensemble. Elizabeth was forced to disguise a smile; undoubtedly, these two ladies thought rather highly of themselves, for their dresses were intended to show those of the neighborhood just how high in society they were.

The expressions on their faces were, however, the most telling. The portly man was easiest to read, for it was clear that he cared for nothing more than obtaining a glass of port and sampling the sweetmeats laid out for the attendees. The two women both had their noses raised as they looked down haughtily on those assembled, further lowering Elizabeth's opinion of them. As for the final two men, the man with red hair appeared to gaze around with interest and enthusiasm, marking him as an amiable man, while his darker-haired friend showed little emotion, though Elizabeth thought she detected a wish to be anywhere but in that room at that moment. The cut of his clothes suggested wealth, so it was possible he was used to far finer entertainments than what he saw before him. As such, Elizabeth decided to excuse his reaction.

"Lizzy!"

Elizabeth turned, noting the approach of her sister, at whom she smiled with indulgent affection.

"They are frightfully handsome, are they not, Lizzy?" exclaimed Kitty as she approached. Luckily, she had modulated her voice so that it was not audible across the entire room.

"I dare say they are." Elizabeth turned back to Charlotte. "Perhaps Charlotte has some knowledge of the newest members of our community?"

"A little," replied Charlotte. "Though I have not met them, my father has given me some news of them.

"The tall man there," said Charlotte, pointing at the man with reddish hair, "is Mr. Bingley, and the two ladies are his sisters, Miss Bingley and Mrs. Hurst. Mr. Hurst is the shorter man to the side."

"Oh, that is fortunate," whispered Kitty with a giggle.

The other two laughed along with her, though Elizabeth shot her sister a mock glare, which Kitty proceeded to ignore.

"And the other man?" asked Elizabeth.

"That is Mr. Bingley's oldest friend, Mr. Darcy."

"He is frightfully handsome, is he not?" asked Kitty.

"In fact I have rarely seen a man so handsome," replied Elizabeth. It was only the truth, though Elizabeth thought the man's smile, should he deign to offer it, would set ladies swooning all around the room.

It would be some time before Elizabeth and Kitty were to be introduced to the newcomers, which was a source of frustration for Kitty, who had been caught by dreams of handsome and dashing young men. Sir William escorted them around to the various families, making introductions where necessary, a process which was often interrupted when Mr. Bingley asked some young lady or another for a dance. As for Mr. Darcy, he talked with the gentlemen, and he danced once each with Mrs. Hurst and Miss Bingley. He asked no other young lady to dance, and when his friend was dancing and he was not, he stood to the side of the room, watching with a steady gaze and an air about him which seemed almost impatient.

When they finally made their way to where the Bennet sisters were standing to the side of the dance floor after a particularly energetic dance, the introductions took place, offered by a still jovial Sir William.

"Ah, there you are, my dears," said Sir William as they approached. "Our guests have indicated a desire to be introduced to you."

"Of course, sir," said Elizabeth.

"Then allow me to present Miss Elizabeth Bennet and Miss Catherine Bennet to your acquaintance. Lizzy, Kitty, please allow me to introduce Mr. Charles Bingley and Mr. Fitzwilliam Darcy."

"I am delighted to make your acquaintance," enthused Mr. Bingley when the gentlemen and ladies had exchanged bows and curtseys. "I thank you and your neighbors for making us feel so welcome here tonight. It is almost as if we have lived here all our lives."

"You are certainly welcome, Mr. Bingley," said Elizabeth. "What are new members to the community but an opportunity to make new acquaintances and study new characters? I fear that we are in your debt, for in a society as small as ours, we do not have much opportunity to make such engaging new acquaintances often."

"So you consider yourself a proficient in the field of character study,

Miss Bennet?" asked Mr. Darcy suddenly.

"I do not know that I can consider myself a proficient," said Elizabeth, "but I will own it is an amusement of mine."

"In that case, you shall have to inform us of how you get on at a later date."

Elizabeth directed an impish smile at him. "And what if I determine yours is not an estimable character, sir? You would put me in a difficult position, for at that point I must tell an untruth, which would render me a liar, or forthrightly state my opinion, which might lead to offense."

The smile which Elizabeth felt would improve his countenance was, in fact, greatly underestimated, as it lit up his entire face and made him uncommonly handsome. By her side, Elizabeth could see that Kitty was in awe of the man, though she had the wit to refrain from saying anything.

"Then we shall be required to be on our best behavior. It would not do to burden you with either of those two fates."

"I thank you, indeed, sir," said Elizabeth. "It is truly gentlemanly for you to ignore my foibles and not expose me before all of the company."

"That should hardly be the case," said Sir William, his voice jovial, but slightly censuring. "You are well regarded in Meryton and should never doubt it."

"I am certain you are," said Mr. Bingley. "Is your father present? I do not remember him visiting Netherfield, and I would wish to make his acquaintance."

"I am sorry, sir," said Elizabeth, again feeling the pain of her lost family. Kitty, by her side, was experiencing the same emotions, Elizabeth thought. "But our father is passed."

Mr. Bingley paused awkwardly, seemingly uncertain of how to respond, when Sir William interjected. "There was an epidemic which swept through the area two years ago." The normally ebullient man was far more serious than usual. "Mr. Bennet, along with the rest of the Bennet family—as well as my own second son—were victims of the illness. Miss Bennet and Miss Kitty are the only members of their family left."

"I beg your pardon," said Mr. Bingley, seeming embarrassed. "I should not have asked such a question."

"You could not have known, Mr. Bingley," said Elizabeth, attempting to put the man at ease. "We are not offended."

"Thank you," said Mr. Bingley, clearly relieved. "If Miss Kitty is not otherwise engaged, might I request the next two dances?"

"I am not engaged, sir," said Kitty, her tone filled with the excitement of dancing with such a handsome man.

As the next dance was starting, Mr. Bingley extended his arm and escorted Kitty to the dance floor, leaving Elizabeth standing close by Mr. Darcy. Sir William had excused himself to attend to some other matter only he thought important.

Feeling the need for some conversation, Elizabeth turned an arch look on her companion. "I see you have chosen not to dance much this evening, Mr. Darcy. Might I assume that a dance is not a favorite way to pass the time?"

"Oh, my apologies, Miss Bennet," said Mr. Darcy. "But you are correct. Unless I am closely acquainted with my partner, I find dancing to be a punishment more than a pleasure."

"I fully understand, sir. And do not suppose I commented to induce you to dance with me. I fully understand that everyone has different tastes when it comes to amusements."

And so began a stilted conversation, punctuated by long silences and, for the most part, banal utterances. It was puzzling to Elizabeth, for she remembered their banter upon first making each other's acquaintance, and knew that he was intelligent, could be personable when he chose, and was not deficient when it came to conversation. But the moment his friend left, it seemed he had little to say. Elizabeth was not certain of this man, but perhaps further acquaintance would teach her what simple observation had failed thus far.

Fitzwilliam Darcy was not enjoying the assembly. His words to Miss Bennet were nothing more than the simple truth—he was not at his best in a ballroom, and recent events had made him short tempered, not that any of these people would ever know of *that* matter. Furthermore, though he knew that those in attendance were simple people, much as could be found in any other corner of the kingdom, still he could not feel comfortable among them. Their interests were decidedly plain, and there was not much fashion and precious little intelligence to be had. Except for . . .

As they had been doing all evening, Darcy's eyes moved, almost of their own accord, to where Miss Elizabeth Bennet was dancing with one of the local men, her eyes alight with that delightful intelligence he had seen when first making her acquaintance. In a location which was decidedly mundane, she was a character different from all the others, and one of whom he had no trouble confessing he would like to know more.

So his eyes followed her throughout the evening, and he spoke to her on occasion, discovering little tidbits of information concerning her. He had learned that she was now the owner of her father's estate, left to her in his will, and that her uncle served as her guardian. And all this he had learned from her own mouth.

"We were fortunate, Mr. Darcy." The woman had looked at him through beautifully expressive eyes, speaking of the matter with perfect composure, though he could easily discern that the subject of her family still gave her pain.

"For you see, my father's estate was entailed until he became the master of the estate. Had the entail lasted one more generation, the estate would have devolved to a distant cousin, leaving us homeless."

"You have no other relations upon whom to appeal for support?"

"I do have an uncle in London, sir, as well as an uncle in Meryton. My London uncle is, in fact, charged with our care, and serves as our legal guardian, or at least he will until I reach my majority next summer."

Darcy turned and eyed her with surprise. "So, you and your sister live on the estate by yourselves?"

"We do, sir," said Miss Bennet. Darcy could see the challenge in her eyes, noting that he had somehow managed to offend her.

"I am sorry, Miss Bennet; I did not mean to imply anything. I would have thought your uncle would join you at the estate, if he was made your guardian, or that you would go to live with him until you were of age."

"But my uncle cannot be spared from his business, and I did not wish for the estate to be left without the guidance of a member of the family in residence. My uncle has hired a good man to be the steward of Longbourn and to provide us with protection, and Sir William is good enough to assist. Between them and the other manservants, we are adequately protected."

Nodding, though not precisely agreeing, and filing the information she had revealed about her relations for further contemplation later, Darcy said: "I understand your concern. I am uneasy myself when I am away from my estate for a long period of time."

She was independent, Darcy decided, and though independence was not a quality which the greater part of society prized, to Darcy it was a sign of an intelligent woman who knew her own mind and was able to care for herself. If only Georgiana had the same confidence . . . .

Later in the evening Darcy began to feel even more uncomfortable as he overheard whispers concerning his situation. He wished for this interminable night to end, so that he could return to his room at

Netherfield and brood in peace. Of course, Netherfield was not the restful location he had hoped it would be. Not with Miss Bingley in residence.

"Has the society in Meryton quite charmed you, Mr. Darcy?" asked Miss Bingley. She had come upon him as he was walking around one side of the room, and Darcy was certain she wished to hear him disparage her brother's neighbors, no doubt in order to bask in her own supposed superiority. But Darcy was not about to play her game.

"The society here is adequate, Miss Bingley. There are fewer people than you will find at an event in London, of course, but they are good people."

Miss Bingley sniffed with disdain. "There is not a person worth knowing amongst them." She had sidled closer to him in order to speak more quietly. No doubt, she also wished to give the appearance of intimacy with the company. "There is little fashion, no breeding, and little but noise when they open their mouths."

"Pray, excuse me, Miss Bingley," said Darcy, and he turned away.

Looking back on the exchange, Darcy was uncertain why the woman had thought that speaking in such a manner would endear her to him. He had certainly never been so unguarded as to share his opinions with her, whether he agreed with her or not. She had set her cap for him, and he knew she was determined to have him for a husband. Unfortunately for Miss Bingley, Darcy was equally determined that she would not catch him in her web.

It was a little later, when Darcy was beginning to feel like a caged lion, that Bingley approached him. Darcy almost groaned aloud when he saw the man, for he was certain Bingley would importune him to dance, a scene which had played out many times during their acquaintance. For some reason, the man seemed unable to understand that Darcy was not one who could feel comfortable in any company other than family and close friends. It was frustrating, but there was no way out, as to flee from Bingley would be to draw attention.

"Come, Darcy!" said Bingley, confirming Darcy's conjecture. "You must dance. I hate to see you standing around in this stupid manner. You had much better dance."

It was only by force of will that Darcy refrained from rolling his eyes. Bingley was nothing if not predictable.

"I certainly shall not. You know how I detest the activity unless I am previously acquainted with my partner."

"I know you protest as much," replied Bingley, "but I suspect it has more to do with your fastidious nature, which I declare, is a rival for the

Prince Regent himself."

"You may think what you like, Bingley. You still shall not induce me to dance."

"Not even with a young woman who is quite pretty, in addition to being someone with whom you conversed quite cordially?"

"Whom do you mean?"

"Miss Elizabeth Bennet," said Bingley, gesturing behind Darcy and a little to his right. Darcy turned and noted the young woman sitting by the side of the room, obviously close enough to overhear their conversation.

"Miss Bennet has been sitting there for some time, having sat out this dance, no doubt due to the fact that gentlemen are scarce. Why, I have even seen her standing up with her sister tonight, as some of the other young ladies have done. I know you think that I do not listen when you drone on about gentlemanly behavior, but would it not be the epitome of such behavior to ask a young woman who does not have a partner to dance?"

"Aye, Miss Bennet is pretty enough to tempt any man," replied Darcy. Then he turned his head slightly and when he was certain Miss Bennet was the only one who could see, he winked at her before turning his attention back to Bingley. "But though she is indeed handsome, I have the distinct impression that she is a bluestocking, and you know it would not do for a Darcy to be seen with one such as she."

Bingley's face fell, and he looked at Darcy with a hint of consternation evident in his mien. Darcy, for his part, felt a savage glee for being able to turn the tables on his friend; perhaps Bingley would think twice before approaching him in this manner in the future.

"Uh . . . Darcy, I believe Miss Bennet is close enough to hear us," said Bingley, shifting from side to side and sneaking glances at Miss Bennet.

"Then perhaps she has received her just desserts for listening to a private conversation. One never overhears anything good about oneself, after all."

"But—"

"Bingley, you are wasting your time with me. Return to your partners and enjoy their flirtatious attentions. I do not intend to dance again tonight."

Though obviously reluctant, Bingley grimaced and walked away, but not without sneaking another glance at Miss Bennet. When he had left and Darcy could see Bingley standing across the room, speaking with several people of the area, he turned and regarded Miss Bennet, allowing a hint of challenge to enter his expression.

* * *

For her part, it was all Elizabeth could do to refrain from bursting out laughing, and when she saw Mr. Darcy turn around and look at her, she could do nothing other than rise and move to confront him. As she did so, she noticed his steady expression, the slight upturn of his lips, and the hint of a challenge on his face, and she was forced to acknowledge again how handsome he was. He had played the scene with his friend in a masterful way.

"I may be a bit of a bluestocking, sir, but I assure you that I will not embarrass anyone with my pert opinions and impertinent ways."

Mr. Darcy cocked his head to the side. "Oh, so you do not deny it?"

"No, sir. In fact, my father ensured that I was as educated as he could make me, and when he was alive, we enjoyed many discussions of literature, philosophy, and world events. I owe what I am today to his patient tutelage."

"That is unusual, Miss Bennet."

Shrugging, Elizabeth said: "My father was a lone man in a house of six women, sir. Of all my sisters, I was the only one to take an interest in such subjects, and when I was old enough, I became his intellectual partner." A hint of pain which, even after all this time, was never far away, settled over Elizabeth, and she directed a tremulous smile at him. "I miss them, sir. I miss all of my family, but particularly my father and my eldest sister. Jane was an angel, the best person I have ever met. She was my rock in this world. I cannot tell you how much I miss her."

It was easy to discern the compassion in Mr. Darcy's eyes. "I fully understand, Miss Bennet. My mother is deceased these past fifteen years, but my father only for the last five. I still long for their presence, I assure you. I cannot even imagine the feeling of loss brought about by losing so many at once."

"Thank you, sir," replied Elizabeth quietly. Then, not wishing for their interaction to become mawkish, she regarded him, willing a bright smile to come over her countenance, as she said: "And may I commend you for the adept way in which you put your friend off just now? I thought poor Mr. Bingley would expire from shame when you seemingly insulted me."

This time Mr. Darcy chuckled. "It is a scene which has played out many times, Miss Bennet, as I am sure you have been able to detect. Perhaps next time he will decide it is not worth it to approach me."

Elizabeth regarded him, her curiosity coming to the fore. "Do you truly despise dancing that much?"

"Only when I am unacquainted with my partner. When I know my partner, I am much more willing, I assure you."

"Then perhaps we should ensure that you are acquainted with some of the local ladies, so that in the future you may dance without hesitation."

"I believe I should much rather talk. You have claimed to be a bluestocking, but I have had little evidence of such a thing thus far. Shall we not speak for a time?"

And speak they did, and for most of the rest of the evening. When Elizabeth returned to Longbourn that night, while she listened with half an ear to Kitty's chattering regarding the evening, her thoughts turned back to Mr. Darcy time and again. And she reflected that she had enjoyed her conversation with him. She had enjoyed it a great deal.

Chapter III

$\mathcal{A}$s the next several days passed, Elizabeth found herself thinking of Mr. Darcy quite often. It was the oddest thing. She would be working in her study, dealing with matters of the estate, when she would wonder about his diligence in caring for his own estate. She attended to matters of the tenants, thinking on how she thought he would likely treat his tenants or on any number of other things a gentleman would need to consider. Reading would lead her to speculate on his views, and she would try to determine if his opinions would match hers.

Elizabeth determined that it was due to the discussions they had indulged in the night of the assembly. Quite simply, he was unlike any other man she had ever met. Though she could confess that she did not yet know him well, she felt that even after their short conversation that she already had something of a measure of him. He was a liberal man, she decided, not opposed to new ideas, and yet she thought he was a good master, one who was involved with the care of his estate. He confessed to having only one younger sister, and the pride and affection in his voice when he spoke of her told Elizabeth that he loved her a great deal.

At the same time, however, he was full of contradictions, a truly complex man, and one it would take almost a lifetime to truly take the measure of. He was clearly uncomfortable with new acquaintances, yet he spoke with confidence when he did speak. He also listened to her opinions intently, never disparaging her when he disagreed, which was more than Elizabeth could say about most of the gentlemen in the neighborhood. He was clearly a superior dancer, but he would not dance with those only newly acquainted. And he seemed to possess a streak of pride and arrogance which could be offensive, if one did not know of his reticence. But then he showed a more tender side when he spoke of his own losses and made his comforting comments about hers. A complex man indeed.

For the next several days, however, Elizabeth was to have no further opportunity to study the enigma which was Mr. Darcy, for there were few events of society in the area. She thought her opinions of the Bingley sisters were well founded, as no visits were undertaken between them, and as Mr. Darcy, who was clearly of higher society, was a resident at Netherfield, Elizabeth felt that it was up to the Netherfield party to initiate visits, if that was what they desired to do.

So Elizabeth concentrated on the operation of the estate, visiting those of the area with whom they had been acquainted all of their lives, and spending time with her younger sister. An invitation to Lucas Lodge for an evening of society changed this.

That evening was the first time the good people of Meryton were treated to the presence of the company of militia which had arrived in the interim. As Kitty and Elizabeth stepped into Lucas Lodge that evening, they were confronted with a veritable sea of red, as it seemed that every officer who could be spared from his duties was present. Sir William was in his element, his genial voice ringing out in welcome, as he played his role of host as one long accustomed to it.

It seemed there were some interesting young gentlemen attached to the regiment. Colonel Forster, the commanding officer, was newly married, and his young wife was a woman much like Lydia had been in essentials. They no doubt would have been famous friends. In the present, however, Elizabeth endeavored to steer Kitty away from the young woman, knowing that she tended toward silliness, given the chance.

Captain Carter, Lieutenants Denny, Chamberlayne, and Pratt were all good men, though the lower ranked officers were all little more than boys. But they were great fun to converse with, and Elizabeth soon found herself enjoying their banter.

"We are happy to have been invited by Sir William tonight," said

Captain Carter at one point during their conversation.

Elizabeth only laughed. "I do not think you could find a man more eager to accept any and all society into his home than Sir William."

"That is fortunate indeed, for our commanding officer is of the opinion that his officers are in great need of society."

"I do not think we are all as inept as Colonel Forster seems to believe," said Mr. Denny, who was standing in the group.

"I think you mistake the matter, Denny," replied the captain. "It seems to me that the rest of you lot are all green with little experience. Society can only be to your benefit!"

Several of the lieutenants raised their voices, protesting this portrayal of them, but Carter only smiled at them, and Elizabeth laughed.

"Well, society is one thing we can provide, though much of it shall consist of silly young girls, as my father used to say."

"And do you count yourself as one of them?"

"Oh, no, sir!" cried Elizabeth. "I assure you that I am intelligent, rational, and always in control of my giggles."

Captain Carter laughed at that and lifted his glass in salute.

"My friend Lizzy is an erudite young woman," said Charlotte with a mischievous smile directed at Elizabeth. "She must operate her estate with soberness and forethought, and if she was prone to giggles like the younger ladies, her tenants would not take her seriously."

Though she attempted a glare at Charlotte for spilling such news to a group of young, unattached males, she was forced to laugh at Charlotte's innocent expression and the impish twinkle in her eyes. It would have come out eventually, though Elizabeth thought she would have preferred it remain hidden for the time being.

As she could have predicted, the eyes of every man in their small group turned to Elizabeth, their interest written upon their brows.

"You own your own estate, Miss Bennet?" asked Chamberlayne, a little too eagerly for Elizabeth's taste.

"I do," replied Elizabeth. "It was left to me by my father, who has passed these last eighteen months. My sister and I are the only members of my family remaining."

Several of the young men made comments of condolence, which Elizabeth had intended. Surely, with such a communication made, they would not pursue further information concerning her situation or estate. Or at least they would not for the present.

A little later, the Netherfield party arrived — fashionably late as they had before — and Elizabeth noted the looks on the faces of the sisters, the stony expression on the countenance of Mr. Darcy, and the eager look which graced the face of Mr. Bingley. This was clearly not an event the likes of which they had attended frequently, and Elizabeth was certain that Mrs. Hurst and Miss Bingley, at the very least, wished themselves miles away.

Greetings were exchanged and the newcomers welcomed, and Elizabeth soon had the relief of being separated from the officers, who were still looking on her with some interest. She would need to make it clear in the next few days that she was not interested in a suitor at present. As it was Mr. Darcy who approached her, she was quick to express her gratitude.

Mr. Darcy only looked at her, puzzled as to her words. "You are quite welcome, Miss Bennet, but I am afraid I am unaware of the reason for your thanks."

"Why, for rescuing me from the officers," replied Elizabeth in a low tone. There were none nearby, but she did not wish for them to overhear her making fun at their expense.

Mr. Darcy's gaze roamed over the room before he turned his attention back to Elizabeth. "Were some of them giving you trouble?"

"Oh, no, sir!" replied Elizabeth. "In fact, it was nothing more than a discovery of my single status, coupled with my possession of an estate. Regardless of how willing these men are to do their duty and serve their king, I have no doubt that the life of a gentleman farmer would be much more to their tastes, even if my estate is not large."

"One of the officers has caught your eye, has he?" interjected a new voice.

Turning, Elizabeth noted the approach of Miss Bingley, who had apparently overheard her comments. The woman was watching her, a hint of a condescending sort of glee etched upon her face.

"Such a man would be good for you, and not much more than you could expect in your *position*."

"And what position might that be?" asked Elizabeth. "The daughter of a gentleman? Or a gentlewoman in my own right, now in possession of my own estate?"

"If I have offended, I apologize most heartily," replied Miss Bingley, feigning remorse. "I meant only that your little neighborhood cannot boast the highest society has to offer. I dare say that many of these officers are second sons to gentlemen and can therefore be a good catch for you. If you have your sights set on one of Mr. Darcy's stature, I am certain you are destined to be disappointed."

"Indeed, I have not 'set my sights' on anyone, Miss Bingley." Elizabeth focused on the woman, eyes narrowed. "But just so we set the matter straight, regardless of my father's lack of sons, the Bennets are an old and respected family, having lived at Longbourn for centuries."

"But you have never been a member of higher society."

The challenge in Miss Bingley's tone made Elizabeth wish she could indulge in a shake of her head, but she decided that she would not stoop to the woman's level.

"No, that much is true. But we *are* a gentle family. Furthermore, should I ever decide to marry, the content of my husband's character will be more important to me than his level of society."

The arched eyebrow the other woman directed at her was insolent, and Elizabeth longed to knock it off her face with a well-earned slap.

"Then you would marry a shopkeeper? Or perhaps a stable boy would do."

"I have said no such thing. I merely suggested that I have more integrity than to attempt to attach myself to the highest ranked man I can find for nothing more than access to his fortune and position. I am content at Longbourn, and should I never leave it—should I marry a younger son, as you suggested—I shall be quite content, indeed, as long as I respect and love my partner and have his love in return."

The condescension was almost dripping from the woman's long nose, which had risen higher in the air. "Such quaint ideas. I wish you well in them." She then turned to Mr. Darcy, seemingly content to ignore Elizabeth. "My sister and I had wished to speak to you, Mr. Darcy, if you will consent to join us."

"I believe you have ample opportunity to speak to me at Netherfield, Miss Bingley," replied Mr. Darcy. "At present, I am quite happy where I am."

Though obviously frustrated at her inability to pull the man away, Miss Bingley nevertheless kept her countenance and curtseyed before she moved away. Elizabeth watched her go, annoyed at the woman's presumption. It appeared that a little of Miss Bingley's company was more than enough to satisfy for a very long time.

When Elizabeth turned her eyes back to her companion, she noted his attention was fixed on her. Feeling the heaviness which had accompanied Miss Bingley's presence and departure, and thinking that Mr. Darcy was no great friend of hers, Elizabeth attempted levity.

"What a charming hostess you have, Mr. Darcy. Of course, I rather suspect that she wishes to be your hostess on a more permanent basis."

A slight smile was her reward. "You may very well be correct, Miss Bennet. Her desires, however, have very little effect on me."

"Poor Miss Bingley," said Elizabeth, not feeling sorry for the woman in the least.

"I did want to say, however, that you should take great care. Miss Bingley is right about one thing—men such as these are often younger sons, but there may also be more unsavory characters among them. I have no doubt your independence would be an irresistible temptation for many, and they may not always resort to proper means to obtain that which they desire."

Elizabeth felt a stab of irritation enter her mind, but she quickly forced it away. Mr. Darcy was not being officious with his warning.

"I do understand, Mr. Darcy, though I appreciate the warning. I will not give them any encouragement and will take care to protect myself. To be honest, I have seen little harm in the men I have met tonight, but it would be prudent to be cautious."

Bowing slightly, Mr. Darcy said: "I am happy to hear it."

Miss Elizabeth Bennet was quite unlike any other woman Darcy had ever met, and though he had been thinking something similar since the night they met at the assembly, Darcy was forced to acknowledge it yet again. She had been part of his frequent thoughts since that night, his mind reluctantly returning to the words they had exchanged and what he had learned of her.

It was not her knowledge and the fact that she was learned about many subjects. It was not her beautiful dark eyes and pretty countenance, devoid of any hint of a blemish. It was not her manners, which were lively, sometimes bordering on impertinence. Indeed, Darcy had met many other women who had possessed similar attributes. But none of them had seemed to possess *all* of these traits, and the fullness of her character intrigued and attracted him. She attracted him far more than he would like to confess, and this after only knowing her for a few weeks and having met her only twice!

That evening at Lucas Lodge, Darcy found himself occupied in two primary activities—avoiding Miss Caroline Bingley and watching Miss Elizabeth Bennet. Mindful of her reputation in society and knowing rumors could be started with little provocation, he attempted to mask his interest, watching her surreptitiously. There were others with whom he spoke as he mingled with the locals, but his eyes and his mind were never far from Miss Bennet.

Later in the evening, he chanced to overhear a conversation between herself and Miss Lucas which put to rest any concerns he might have had about her character, if any such still existed, given her exchange with Miss Bingley. The two, who appeared to be great friends, stood to the side of the room, when the topic of their conversation turned to Miss Bennet's younger sister.

"I must own that I am prodigiously proud of Kitty," said Miss Bennet. "She has improved greatly."

"She does still tend to an exuberance of spirits," noted Miss Lucas.

Darcy followed her gaze and saw that Miss Kitty was, indeed, still possessed of high spirits, as she was in a group of several officers, speaking animatedly and laughing occasionally. She was, Darcy thought, a pretty girl, though not the equal of her elder sister. Her laughter was perhaps a little louder than he would wish if it had been Georgiana in her position, but then again, he would give much to see Georgiana laugh at all when in the company of others. Perhaps a girl of Kitty's liveliness would be good for his shy and reticent younger sister.

"She does," replied Miss Bennet, "and I would not wish to extinguish that spark she possesses. She is a good girl, and as long as she acts with restraint and good judgment, I shall not censure her."

"Someday you will be required to allow her to leave and find her own destiny."

Miss Bennet sighed, a gloomy sort of sound. "And well am I aware of it. I am certain it shall be hard, as she is the last of my sisters. But I would not dream of holding her back. Hopefully, with her increased dowry, she will be able to attract some attention, though it is not likely she will find a partner here."

"A larger dowry invites fortune hunters."

"Perhaps. But it also makes it easier to excite a man's interest. I will stay with her, and I think she will become adept at spotting fortune hunters herself. If I could see her cared for by a good man, I would be well pleased indeed."

The discussion continued on for some time, and Darcy was forced to acknowledge that he felt a measure of warmth for this young woman. The care she showed for her younger sister was not out of the common way, but to be burdened with such things at so tender an age was, and Darcy could not help but be impressed by her poise and confidence and the way she performed her duties.

He was reminded of his own situation. Fitzwilliam Darcy had been left with the care of a much younger sister at the tender age of only two and twenty, which was in many ways a much more difficult task than the management of a great estate. With an estate, even if a mistake should be made, the consequences might be a loss of income, business, or a temporary setback in the estate's fortunes. Pemberley had been left to him by his father in a state more than capable of withstanding such a blow. With a much younger sister, however, a misstep could be of much greater significance, as he had found out the previous summer. People were not so easy to fix. And had he failed to rescue his sister when he had, he had no doubt her life would have been ruined.

But though Darcy could see the parallels between his own life and Miss Bennet's, the differences were profound, leading to a much greater level of difficulty for the young woman. For one thing, she had inherited four years earlier than he had—if Darcy had inherited when he was eighteen as had she, he did not think he would have been able to survive. But more than that, Miss Bennet's gender would have been a far greater detriment than any tenderness of youth. She would likely have encountered difficulties with the tenants and would not have been received well by the other estate owners; cordial relations with those nearby was a critical element to the success of an estate.

In short, Darcy was astounded and humbled that she had been able to weather such storms as well as she had. This was a woman who was as determined as anyone he had ever met, more intelligent than most of his acquaintances, and still retained her sweetness of temper—though it was not displayed without that archness he had found so intriguing!

The conversation between the two women had continued while Darcy was thinking, and soon after he heard Miss Lucas make the suggestion that Miss Bennet play for the company.

"You have the most talent of anyone in attendance, Lizzy," said the woman, fixing Miss Bennet with an amused smile. "It would not do to refuse to delight us all when you know how much we enjoy it."

"You are a strange sort of friend, Charlotte," said Miss Bennet, her eyes shining with amusement. Darcy had the distinct impression that this conversation had played out between the two young women many times. "If my vanities included music, your insistence on hearing me exhibit before the company would have been invaluable. As it is, I would really rather not."

At that moment, Miss Lucas seemed to realize that Darcy was standing close enough to hear their conversation, and she turned to him, pulling him into the debate.

"Mr. Darcy, you must assist me in convincing Elizabeth to play for us. Surely you would wish to be treated to her performance."

"I would be happy to hear you play, Miss Bennet," said Mr. Darcy.

"Charlotte!" exclaimed Miss Bennet. "Surely you do not need to pull others into your wicked schemes!"

A laugh escaped Miss Lucas's lips. "I hardly consider my efforts to be wicked, Lizzy."

"Perhaps not, but now that you have asked one of the newly arrived members of our society, I cannot refuse without seeming churlish."

"The thought had occurred to me." Miss Lucas's tone was positively smug.

"Then I suppose I have no choice."

"Do not think you must," said Darcy, feeling it incumbent upon himself to reassure her that it had not been his intention to back her into a corner. "I believe we are perfectly content should the prospect be too onerous."

"I thank you for your words, Mr. Darcy," said Miss Bennet, and she reached forward to touch his hand. "I have no true objection, in all honesty. It is simply a little game Charlotte and I often play."

"Then you had best get to it, Lizzy," said Miss Lucas. She was already walking away toward the pianoforte situated in a corner of the room.

Miss Bennet's eyes followed her friend's retreating form, a half smile gracing her lips. Then she turned to regard Darcy once again.

"If you will excuse me, sir, I should go and do my duty."

"I am all anticipation, Miss Bennet," replied Darcy with a bow.

As she departed, Darcy followed her at a leisurely pace, so as to obtain a good vantage from which to listen to her performance. Inside he was curious. Miss Lucas had intimated that Miss Bennet was the most talented of those in attendance, and while that did not necessarily mean anything in a small neighborhood such as this, on some level he wondered if he was about to hear the performance of a virtuoso. She sat at the instrument and limbered her fingers, playing through a few scales.

When she began to play, Darcy knew he was listening to a talented performer, and when her voice rose to accompany the instrument, he was impressed all over again. Her voice was a light and airy soprano, hitting the higher notes with ease, and the lower notes with a sultry richness which was rarely heard. The performance, when all taken together, informed Darcy that she was not a professional in the theater, but she was talented and sang and played without pretense and with far more feeling than most others. Miss Bingley herself was perhaps more technically proficient, though her voice was not nearly so pretty, and the overall effect of her performance was not nearly so enjoyable as that of Miss Bennet.

This woman was a rare find, he decided. One day, he was certain that she would make some man an admirable wife. Surely such a woman could not go through life without *someone* realizing her worth. And the man who earned her love would be fortunate indeed.

* * *

There was, however, another in the room who was not disposed to think kindly of Mr. Darcy's attentions to Miss Bennet. Since she had schemed and dreamed to become the mistress of Pemberley from the first time she had met the man four years earlier, the appearance of an upstart who had captured his attention seemingly without effort was an affront. The woman had no connections, her fortune was tied up in her small and pitiful estate, and regardless of her boasts concerning her ancestors, Caroline knew that Elizabeth Bennet was nothing more than a country bumpkin, a woman with naught to recommend her.

As the night progressed, Caroline watched Mr. Darcy as his own eyes followed Miss Bennet wherever she went. She was encouraged that when they conversed, their words thus far seemed to be innocuous, focused on estates, literature, and other such nonsense, but she was alarmed at how quickly they seemed to have become easy in each other's company. It would not do, Caroline decided, and she would not stand for it.

"Perhaps we simply need to investigate her background," mused Caroline in a low tone to Louisa. "There must be something Mr. Darcy would find objectionable."

"I believe you are overreacting," returned Louisa. "Mr. Darcy has met Miss Bennet all of twice, and though he has spoken with her at times, I can detect no admiration in his looks."

"Nor can I, but his countenance is infuriatingly difficult to read."

Louisa only shrugged; it was nothing more than the truth.

"Anyway, I cannot allow some country upstart to charm him without responding. I have staked my reputation on securing a marriage proposal from the man. I must protect my interests."

"If only you had controlled your tongue and not bragged of our acquaintance, you would not be in this predicament."

"I had to, for us to rise in society. You know that."

"A boast concerning our friendship with him is one thing, but you insinuated that he was on the precipice of making you an offer. You know that is patently untrue."

Caroline grimaced as her sister referenced the incident in question. It had been the previous month in London, when Caroline had been visiting some friends. Unfortunately, a woman she detested — Lady Marion Lampley — had also visited at the same time, and as the daughter of an earl, she was not shy in expressing her contempt for those of lower social strata. The Bingley sisters, in her mind, fell into that category.

Before Caroline had known it, a boast of Mr. Darcy coming to the country as their guest had turned into a suggestion that he would propose soon, and though many of the ladies had looked on her with awe, Lady Marion had been openly disdainful. Even now, Caroline had difficulty in getting the woman's words from her mind.

"If you are successful in affecting a proposal from Mr. Darcy, Miss Bingley, then you are to be commended. But given the man is reticent, is a close friend of *your brother*, and has never looked on you twice, you will forgive my skepticism."

"You may believe what you wish," Caroline had replied with a dismissive gesture. "When I return to London, it will be as an engaged woman."

The expression on the woman's face had been amused, displaying for all the world to know that she knew of Caroline's bluff and could not wait for it to be proven false. Caroline only sneered at her and turned to another nearby lady, speaking to her and ignoring her tormentor.

"All we need to do," said Caroline to her sister, pushing her unpleasant memories to the side, "is to ensure he understands what a wonderful hostess I would be."

"I am not sure that is what he wishes for in a wife."

Caroline only waved her off. "All men wish for that in a wife, and Mr. Darcy is no different. And you must help me, Louisa. We must ensure Mr. Darcy does not leave Netherfield without proposing to me."

The level look that Louisa directed at her spoke to her displeasure, and Caroline wished to wipe it from her sister's face. Louisa had always possessed an independent streak, one which Caroline had often wished her sister devoid of. Louisa kept her own counsel and would not be induced to support Caroline without due thought. It was vexing.

"I will assist you to an extent, but I will not compromise my principles in doing so. And I will only do so because it would reflect badly on our family for you to be revealed as delusional."

"I am certain it is not delusion, Louisa," said Caroline, maintaining her composure, though she was seething inside. "All we must do is allow him to see my better qualities."

Caroline turned a lazy eye back toward her quarry, noting he was standing near to the pianoforte listening to Miss Bennet as she played. A critical ear turned toward the music emanating from that end of the room revealed that Miss Bennet's talents were not capital, and by no means the equal of Caroline's own. Perhaps if Mr. Darcy enjoyed music, a display of her own talents would be helpful in showing the disparity between her and the upstart.

"I require more information," said Caroline as she tapped a finger to her lips in thought. "I think we should invite the Bennet ladies to dinner some night. There, it would not be strange if we should ask them about themselves. There might be something I can use to dissuade Mr. Darcy's interest."

"If you are so convinced of his interest, would it be wise to put her in his company any more than necessary?"

"No, it would not," decided Miss Bingley. "But if there is some opportunity to do so when Mr. Darcy will not be present, we will take it."

The matter decided, Miss Bingley sat back and watched the man she meant to have, thoughts and machinations playing around in her mind. She meant to have him, and she meant to do it, regardless of the cost.

Chapter IV

*I*t was only a few days after the gathering at Lucas Lodge when Elizabeth received a note from Netherfield. The contents surprised her very much.

Miss Elizabeth Bennet,

Dine with Louisa and me tonight, for the gentlemen are to dine with the officers, leaving us to our own devices. As a woman who lives alone with one sister, I am certain you can understand that a night's tête-à-tête between sisters is a perilous thing and can likely end up in arguments and hurt feelings. Please save us such a fate, and indicate your acceptance of our invitation. Your sister is, of course, invited to come as well.

Caroline Bingley

All bemusement, Elizabeth tapped the letter against her lips for a few moments, wondering what the woman could be about. Mrs. Hurst had been cordial though rather uncommunicative the times they had been in her company, but Miss Bingley had been nothing short of hostile, taking every opportunity to flaunt her perceived superiority. Why they should be asking her to come for dinner was something Elizabeth could not understand.

With a sigh, Elizabeth rose and went to find Kitty. It was a beautiful autumn morning, as Elizabeth was well aware, having returned from her morning constitutional to the sounds of birds chirping and the wind rustling through the trees, which were mostly bare of their summer mantle. It had been a pleasant autumn for the most part, with little inclement weather to disrupt their lives, but with November upon them, Elizabeth knew that it was only a matter of time before winter settled in.

As she passed a window, Elizabeth looked out on the grounds, and her thoughts were drawn to years past. Her mother had never understood Elizabeth's penchant for walking, nor had Elizabeth ever made any attempt to explain it—a large part of the reason she had walked so often, after all, was to escape a house which was always in the midst of some tumult or another, most often caused by her mother's unrestrained ways. Now Elizabeth could look fondly back on her mother, but the woman had often mortified her with her behavior.

Unfortunately, Elizabeth's long walks were a thing of the past. Not only was she more engaged in the operation of the estate and the house—though Kitty had taken much of the work of the mistress of the house, with Elizabeth's patient training—but it was not proper for a young woman, whose guardian was four hours away in London, to walk the hills of her home with impunity. Elizabeth could still remember the conversation with her uncle which had resulted in her giving up her walks.

She had gone out one morning not long after her family's deaths, eager to retreat from the world and think about her changed circumstances in the peace of her own company. She had walked further than was usually her wont, and when she had returned, her uncle—who had been visiting, as he often had in those days—was waiting for her. Without his speaking a word, Elizabeth had known that he was not pleased with her, though she had not understood why until he drew her into the study.

"Where have you been this morning?" Elizabeth had felt his displeasure with her, where she had rarely ever heard the like from him.

"Out walking, Uncle. I needed to think things through and I have always been best able to do so in solitude."

Uncle Gardiner regarded her for some moments before he spoke again, but while his words were gentle, his tone was more censuring in nature. "Elizabeth, I am sorry, but these walks of yours, at least in their present incarnation, must stop."

Nonplused, Elizabeth said: "Must stop? Whatever for?"

Sighing, her uncle drew her to a pair of chairs and sat her down, and when he spoke, it was with the authority of a guardian, rather than the affection of a loving uncle.

"Because, Lizzy, your circumstances have changed. You are not a carefree child any longer. Though you are not yet of age, you are a young woman who is on the cusp of receiving the inheritance of an estate, and with that comes responsibility. As you know, you will be alone with Kitty in this house for the most part, as I cannot leave my business in London to live with you here. Thus, much of the operation of Longbourn will fall on your shoulders." Mr. Gardiner smiled. "In fact, I believe that to be a good thing, for my aptitude is for business, not the running of estates."

"I am certain you could learn, if you put your mind to it."

"Perhaps, but I am content where I am." Uncle Gardiner's countenance grew stern again. "Furthermore, as the owner of this estate, you must see that you will become a target for every fortune hunter who chances to come this way. If you do not think that they will utilize an opportunity to find you alone and force you into marriage, you are not thinking properly. Your father was negligent in this matter — you should never have been allowed to wander so far or so frequently. I am sorry, Lizzy, but it must stop."

Not having truly thought of the matter to any great extent, Elizabeth could understand his point, though she was loath to give up something that was such a benefit to her. "Surely you do not think that our neighbors are so lacking in common decency."

"I do not *know* your neighbors, Lizzy. For all they appear like good people, one can never be certain, as a vicious character may be hidden by pretty manners. Even a good man might be tempted by the lure of even such modest wealth as you possess." Mr. Gardiner paused for a moment and regarded Elizabeth sternly. "I must insist upon this."

So, though Elizabeth had been reluctant at first, she gave her promise that she would not walk far, and if she was to go further than the grounds, she would take a footman for an escort. And though Elizabeth at times still did walk, she now mostly confined herself to those areas nearby, though sometimes Oakham Mount, her favorite walk, was an irresistible lure. Now, however, she would often go on horseback, for learning to ride had become a necessity. It was not possible to walk to all the locations of the estate, and sometimes such travel in their small gig was not feasible, especially after a rain when the ground was soft and muddy. And her uncle had been right; most days there were many tasks to complete, and she simply did not have the time to walk as she had walked before.

It was not long before Elizabeth found Kitty in the sitting-room, and there she was, making use of the outside light to assist with her sketching. Elizabeth smiled when she saw her sister. In the past, when their family had been alive, she and Lydia had been loud, uncouth, vain, and idle, always intent upon having fun, living their lives in an unserious manner. But in the past eighteen months, Kitty had changed until she was almost unrecognizable from the girl she had been before. Sketching was only one of her new interests.

"Kitty, I have received a note this morning, and I do not quite know what to make of it."

Turning, Kitty regarded Elizabeth, saying: "Not another letter from Mr. Collins, is it?"

A laugh escaped Elizabeth's lips and she shook her head. "No, indeed. He has not written to Uncle Gardiner, as of our uncle's last letter, so I suspect we have heard the last from our esteemed cousin. Actually, this note was delivered from Netherfield."

At the mention of the neighboring estate, Kitty looked up, her eyes bright. "Oh? And what does it say?"

"It is from Caroline Bingley, inviting us to dine with them tonight. The gentlemen are to dine with the officers."

A brief look of disappointment came over Kitty's face, but it was soon gone, and she gestured toward the letter. "May I see?"

Elizabeth handed the letter over, and Kitty read it briefly, smiling as she handed it back. "They must not be very close if a single night can cause them to hate each other forever."

"Oh, Kitty," said Elizabeth, though she laughed at her sister's quip. "Miss Bingley makes no such statement."

"Well, I can believe it, at least of Mrs. Hurst. Miss Bingley would drive anyone to bedlam." Kitty looked at Elizabeth. "So we are to dine at Netherfield tonight?"

"I had thought to decline."

"Oh, Lizzy, do let us go. It will be more fun than staying at home all evening."

Surprised, Elizabeth regarded her sister. "I would have thought you would be more eager than me to forgo the pleasure of Miss Bingley's company."

"Of Miss Bingley's company, I can cheerfully do without. But they *are* our neighbors, are they not? Perhaps we should give them the chance to prove themselves to be our friends."

Elizabeth watched her sister dubiously. It seemed out of character for Kitty to wish to go to Netherfield and put herself in the company of the Bingley sisters, with whom she had actually had relatively little contact. In fact, most of what she had heard had come from Elizabeth herself, though Elizabeth had attempted to avoid poisoning Kitty against the sisters too much. There was something else at play here, though Elizabeth could not quite determine what it was.

"Are you certain, Kitty? I expect that Miss Bingley, at the very least, has some ulterior motive for inviting us. You will have to be on your guard, for I would not put it past her to ask impertinent questions and make veiled statements."

"I am able to withstand her barbs, sister," said Kitty. "And if I am uncertain, I shall simply look to you for guidance."

Nodding slowly, Elizabeth turned her eyes back to the letter in her hands. Though she was not eager to spend the evening in the company of the two sisters, she supposed no true harm could come of it. Besides, she was curious, not only of Miss Bingley's purpose for the invitation, but also concerning Kitty's eagerness to attend.

"Very well. I shall pen a response."

"Thank you, Lizzy!" said Kitty, and she embraced her sister before turning back to her sketchbook.

But though Elizabeth made to leave the room, she looked back at her sister and noted that though Kitty's eyes were on the sketch in front of her, she did not appear to see it.

A response was dispatched to Netherfield, and an offer to send the Bingley carriage was soon received. Elizabeth, shaking her head, replied, saying they were well able to traverse the distance in the Bennet carriage, and politely declining the offer.

At the appointed time the two Bennet sisters entered their carriage for the short journey to Netherfield, and when they arrived, they were welcomed enthusiastically by Miss Bingley, but with more reserve by her sister. Elizabeth, who had no great opinion of either of them, resolved to watch them carefully in order to determine the motive for the invitation. It was not long before they were called in to dinner, which was where the true inquisition started.

It began innocuously, with Miss Bingley telling them some anecdotes about her family, and asking questions concerning theirs. However, it was not long before the questions became probing, designed to ferret information out, and though Elizabeth wondered why the woman felt it necessary to query her at such length, she decided that she had nothing to hide.

"It is singular that you live at your estate without the benefit of a guardian," said Miss Bingley after the soup had arrived. "You *are* still underage, are you not, Miss Bennet?"

"Indeed, I am, Miss Bingley, though I shall obtain my majority next summer."

"Then should your guardian not live with you?"

"That is not possible. Uncle Gardiner lives in London and is involved in his own concerns. We have a steward who runs the estate and provides us with protection, as well as several manservants. Furthermore, Sir William has been delegated with the responsibility of watching over us, and as his estate is just down the lane, we are adequately cared for."

"And it is beautiful country indeed," said Mrs. Hurst. The look Miss Bingley directed at her suggested that the interruption was unwelcome. "I will own, however, that I am partial to our home near York. That is where Hurst's family estate is located as well."

Interested in the change in topic, Elizabeth pursued it for a time, and some pleasant moments were spent discussing the various differences between Hertfordshire and Yorkshire. Miss Bingley listened attentively, but she said relatively little. At the first opportunity, she turned their attention back to the previous subject.

"I am curious of your arrangements, Miss Bennet. If your uncle is not able to live in Hertfordshire, would it not be more prudent to live with him in London?"

"There is nothing wrong with our living arrangements, Miss Bingley," replied Elizabeth. Though she was beginning to become annoyed with the woman for her insistence in challenging her, Elizabeth kept her temper. "Our situation has been approved by our guardian, and we have many friends nearby should their assistance become required. In another nine months, even that will become unnecessary, as I will be one and twenty and will have complete control over Longbourn."

Though skeptical, Miss Bingley evidently decided it was not worth it to pursue that line of questioning, so she changed tack.

"You mentioned an uncle in London. Is he your only living relation?"

"No, indeed," replied Kitty. "Uncle Gardiner is my mother's brother, and my mother's sister also lives in Meryton."

"In addition, we have a distant cousin of my father's who has been in contact recently," said Elizabeth, taking over the explanation. "We are a small family, it is true."

Miss Bingley and Mrs. Hurst exchanged glances, but it was Mrs.

Hurst who responded. "That is quite unfathomable to us. For you see, my father had eight siblings, and my mother six. We are quite the large family with uncles, cousins, nephews, nieces, and all manner of more distant relations clamoring for attention."

Elizabeth smiled. "That sounds heavenly, Mrs. Hurst. I have always wished for a larger family."

"It comes with its own drawbacks and benefits, to be sure. On the whole, however, I suppose I cannot repine. Hurst's side of the family is much smaller, and I think that sometimes the Bingleys almost overwhelm him."

Laughter rang out over the table. "Yes, I can see how that might happen," replied Elizabeth.

"Where are your uncles' estates?" asked Miss Bingley, after their laughter died down. "You mentioned your uncle in Meryton, but I have not been introduced, to the best of my knowledge, to a man who claims kinship to you."

"That is because neither of my uncles own estates," said Elizabeth. "Uncle Gardiner is an importer, and he does very well at it, while my Uncle Phillips is the local solicitor. Uncle Phillips is now the proprietor of my grandfather's practice, as his own son chose to pursue a different living."

"A businessman?" asked Miss Bingley, her face reflecting her astonishment. "I must own that I am surprised. Though mingling of the trade and landowner classes has become more widespread, still marriages between the two are peculiar."

Knowing exactly to what the woman was referring, Elizabeth smiled brightly at her. "That is indeed so, for if it was not, Mr. Darcy and your brother would not be friends. I had understood your fortune came from trade—is that not correct?"

"Our father owned a business making carriages," supplied Mrs. Hurst helpfully. "The business was inherited from his father, and had been in the family for generations."

"But we do not have anything to do with the business any longer," said Miss Bingley as she directed a barely concealed glare at her sister. "Charles wishes to purchase an estate, which he will do once he has gained some experience. It was our father's favorite wish."

"Then you are moving up in the world," replied Elizabeth, ignoring the woman's tone. "Your brother is to be commended for his diligence."

The look Miss Bingley shot at Elizabeth suggested that she suspected her of making sport with her, but she said nothing further. Throughout the rest of the evening, Miss Bingley continued to make probing comments, but Elizabeth, by now quite annoyed with the woman, refused to take the bait. Instead, she put her off, changing the subject when required, and not allowing the woman to make an issue of their connections and fortune. Before long, the dinner conversation was being carried mostly by Elizabeth and Mrs. Hurst, with some assistance from Kitty; Miss Bingley had largely lapsed into silence.

After dinner the woman seemed to rally a little, but she confined her comments to the banal, and for the first time in their acquaintance, Elizabeth thought her company was actually tolerable. It was fortunate for all concerned that the tone between the ladies remained cordial for the rest of the evening, for after the original inquest, Elizabeth was little disposed to endure Miss Bingley's impertinent questions.

As the hour was becoming late, however, their conversation was interrupted by the loud rumbling of thunder, accompanied by a flash of lightning. Soon they could hear the sound of the rain beating down on the window panes.

Rising, the ladies crowded around the closest window, and within a few moments, the landscape outside was lit up by a flash of lightning, revealing the heavy rain, the trees swaying in the wind, and the rapidly accumulating water on the footpaths outside.

"Oh, dear," said Mrs. Hurst. "That is a storm not often seen. I do hope it will not persist for long."

"I am certain it will blow itself out before long," said Miss Bingley. "Come, let us return to our tea and our conversation."

And return they did. However, it quickly became apparent that the storm would not let up any time soon. Indeed, though the rumble of thunder eventually grew distant and then ceased altogether, subsequent queries of the household staff revealed that the roads had become difficult to navigate and the rain was not expected to lessen any time soon. It soon became apparent that the Bennet sisters would not be leaving that night, little though Miss Bingley appeared to wish to bow to the inevitable.

When the invitation was finally given, Elizabeth accepted it on behalf of herself and her sister graciously, and soon after the sisters were ensconced in their own rooms, each with a nightgown from Mrs. Hurst—who was more of a size with the Bennet sisters than her taller sibling. Elizabeth went to sleep that evening, wishing to be back at Longbourn, but amused at Miss Bingley's antics. What she could not determine was why Miss Bingley wished to know the details of their situation. It was not as if Mr. Bingley had paid either Bennet sister any attention, after all.

* * *

"So, do you believe me now?"

Louisa glanced at her sister and restrained the impulse to shake her head. Such occurrences were becoming more common when confronted with her sister's brand of absurdity.

"I hardly believe Miss Bennet used witchcraft to bring the rains so she could stay at Netherfield for the night."

"Of course she did not!" snapped Caroline. "But she was most eager to accept the invitation to stay, you must concede."

Louisa sighed and motioned to the maid to finish with her hair for the night. Louisa had been happy to retire and wait for her husband to return, but Caroline had obviously hurried her maid through her own preparations so that she could accost Louisa in her room and complain over the Bennets' continued presence, as if she, Caroline Bingley, had not invited them.

"I believe she was not given any other choice," replied Louisa. "You heard the butler—the heavy rains have made travel inadvisable. There was no other choice than for them to remain the night."

"I am certain this is all a ploy to ensure she does not return to her insignificant estate without putting herself in the path of Mr. Darcy." Caroline almost seemed manic in her displeasure. "The improper chit has her eyes on him, mark my words."

"Then I suppose you must increase your efforts. But if you will excuse me, I am tired and wish to sleep. I am certain in the morning all will be better.

Though she was obviously annoyed and unwilling to leave, Caroline huffed and stalked from the room. Louisa breathed a sigh of relief; Caroline was difficult to manage at the best of times, and now was certainly not the best of times. Her obsession with Mr. Darcy was problematic, but she would not hear any censure concerning her behavior, insisting that she was in the right and that Mr. Darcy was only waiting for the right moment to approach her. Louisa did not understand how she could think that, for if he was, Louisa had no doubt he, as a man of action, would have asked for her hand many weeks, or even months, ago.

But Caroline could not be reasoned with. Louisa could only hope that she would not do something to make their family seem foolish. With their roots in trade, it would not do to make their situation in society even more tenuous.

* * *

The following morning, Elizabeth was confronted by a problem. She had parted with Kitty the night before, and though Kitty had given every indication of health, Elizabeth had found out from the maid assigned to her care that she was not well. While Kitty had sometimes been prone to coughs and fevers and other such agues since the time she was a child, she had largely outgrown that problem in the past few years.

Furthermore, Elizabeth could not shake the suspicions she had espoused before they left Longbourn the previous day, and she wondered what was truly bothering her sister. As she felt it improper to impose upon their guests for any longer than was necessary, Elizabeth decided she must speak with Kitty before she knew how to act.

A query directed to Kitty's maid revealed that her sister was awake, though still abed, and Elizabeth requested the girl refrain from speaking to the housekeeper while Elizabeth attempted to determine the seriousness of Kitty's condition. The maid agreed, and soon Elizabeth had entered her sister's chambers. Kitty was lying on the bed looking out the window, and when she saw Elizabeth enter she looked away for only a brief moment, informing Elizabeth that there was something else at play than simply an illness.

Elizabeth took a seat on the edge of the bed next to her sister. She fussed with Kitty's blankets and pillows and put her hand against her sister's forehead, noting that it was cool to the touch. A cough, delicately covered by her hand, told Elizabeth that at least some of her sister's distress was real, but she was now more certain than ever that there was some other reason why Kitty wished to stay. Elizabeth was determined to discover the truth.

"You have a cold do you? I do not feel a fever, but it seems you have a hint of a cough."

"Indeed, I feel dreadful! I have such pains in my head, and my chest aches. I do not think I can return home today."

A raised eyebrow prompted Kitty to look away, her face flushed a little. That had always been Kitty's problem when she had tried to lie—she was a little too melodramatic to be able to do it convincingly. That and the fact that her attempt at a straight face was typically doomed to failure when Elizabeth—or anyone else—looked on her with the least bit of suspicion.

"Kitty, I know you are not being completely forthright with me," said Elizabeth, noting Kitty's responding blush. "You know I will not be severe upon you. Will you not tell me why you feel it imperative to trespass upon our hosts in such a manner?"

"I . . . I simply feel it would be . . . beneficial if I were to rest today and then return home tomorrow. Maybe I will be well enough to join you all in the sitting-room this evening."

Sighing, Elizabeth said: "No, we shall not stay, Kitty, especially when I am convinced that there is little wrong with you. If you will not divulge the reason for your behavior, then I suppose that is what it shall be. But we will not stay here and be a burden on our hosts when there is no reason for it."

Elizabeth rose, intending to call the maid to assist Kitty to dress, but before she had moved away from the bed, Kitty reached out and caught her hand, her expression beseeching.

"I love Mr. Bingley," blurted she. "I do not wish to leave without seeing him."

Turning, Elizabeth looked at her sister, astonished by her words. But then the hints and clues she had put together over the past few days suddenly fit together in her mind, and she knew that her sister was telling her the truth. Elizabeth allowed herself a smile, though she did not show her amusement to her sister, who she was certain would not appreciate it. Kitty, it seemed, still retained a little of her mother in her character.

But what she was suggesting was not proper, so Elizabeth allowed a little displeasure to come over her face, though she spoke in a soft and sympathetic voice.

"You love Mr. Bingley?"

"I do," replied Kitty, a sigh escaping with her words, her eyes unfocused. "He is the most handsome and amiable man of my acquaintance. How could I not love him?" Kitty's eyes turned to Elizabeth, and she continued, again in an imploring tone. "You must allow us to stay, Lizzy. I am certain, if I attempt it, that Mr. Bingley will fall as much in love with me as I am with him."

"Kitty," said Elizabeth, choosing her words carefully, "I know that you think you feel a deep and abiding love for Mr. Bingley at present, but I doubt it is anything more than a strong infatuation."

When Kitty tried to protest, Elizabeth put up a hand to forestall her words, and she subsided, though not without a sulk.

"You have not known him long enough to know anything of his character, other than that he is amiable and kind. Furthermore, at your tender age, it is difficult for you to know what you desire in a man. You see a man who dances with you and laughs with you, and you misconstrue it for love."

Though Kitty was shaking her head, she also seemed a little thoughtful, which was all Elizabeth wished for.

"Now, if Mr. Bingley is to fall in love with you, I believe there are other ways to encourage it. But imposing upon him in order to be close to him is not proper, and I will not allow it. We will return home today as planned."

It was apparent Kitty was upset with Elizabeth's decree, but it seemed all the fight had gone out of her, and she nodded, albeit a trifle sullenly. Elizabeth smiled.

"Let us get you prepared to depart. And Kitty, remember that you have many years to search for a husband. Though I dare say Mr. Bingley is a good man, an amiable man, and one who would seem to be the ideal for any woman desiring a husband, I believe it would be beneficial to take the time to learn more of his character. 'til death do us part is a very long time, Kitty. It is best to know as much of the character of your husband as possible before he leads you to the altar, for if you choose incorrectly, you may condemn yourself to a life of misery."

A smile and a nod of the head was Kitty's answer, and Elizabeth left to call the maid to assist her to dress. In fact, Elizabeth was anticipating their departure. This new development must be handled with care, and Elizabeth wanted nothing more than to retreat to Longbourn to think on the matter.

Within half an hour, the sisters descended the stairs to the main floor and were directed to the small, family dining room where the residents of Netherfield were gathered. It was later than Elizabeth had hoped to depart, and as such, they were all in attendance, though she suspected that most of the party had kept to town hours, even though they had been resident in the country for some time.

"Miss Bennet, Miss Kitty," said Miss Bingley as they entered. She rose and crossed to them, searching their faces as they approached. "We understood that Miss Kitty was suffering from some indisposition this morning and wondered if you would need to stay another day."

Though she truly could not blame the maid, still Elizabeth was a little annoyed that Miss Bingley had been informed of the matter. It would be another reason for the woman to despise them.

"It is only a slight cough, Miss Bingley. We are well able to return to Longbourn today, where I have no doubt Kitty will recover quickly in the comforts of her own bedchamber."

"Miss Bennet," said Mr. Bingley. He and the other two gentlemen had risen upon their entrance, and he was now striding toward them, his manner all concern for their wellbeing. "If there is any question of her continued health, I would ask that you stay another day at the very least and have her seen by the apothecary. Do not concern yourself for an instant that we would not welcome you with open arms."

Kitty's eyes were positively shining with admiration for the gentleman, but Elizabeth, though feeling a little amused, was not about to be swayed.

"I thank you, Mr. Bingley. You are very kind to offer your home to us. But Kitty will be very well at home. There is no need to delay our departure."

Taken aback, Mr. Bingley looked at her closely. "Are you certain? I would not wish for your sister to suffer unduly because she made an ill-advised journey when prudence would suggest she rest here."

"I am quite certain, Mr. Bingley. We shall depart after breakfast as we had originally planned."

It was apparent that Mr. Bingley wished to contest the matter further, but it seemed that he possessed the discretion to allow it to drop, now that Elizabeth had made her sentiments known. In a short amount of time, the sisters were seated at the table, breaking their fast with the family. And if Kitty sat beside Mr. Bingley and they conversed together for most of the time they were present, Elizabeth contented herself with watching them closely. Kitty would see sense, Elizabeth was certain.

Darcy lifted his cup to his lips, sipping his tea as he considered the Bennet sisters. It was very difficult to impress Darcy — he had seen much in the world, had endured the machinations of young women whose only goal in life was to catch a wealthy husband, and he was well aware of the fact that it had jaded him over the years. Now his first inclination was to regard those with whom he met with suspicion, to assume that they meant to ensure their wishes superseded his own.

But though the Miss Bennets had a perfect opportunity to play the part of the fortune hunter, they had declined to do so. There were not many in London who would not use the excuse of a nonexistent indisposition to impose themselves upon their hosts. Even Bingley was enough of a catch for the young women of the Bennets' status that he had almost expected only Miss Bennet to come down and weave some tale of her sister's deadly illness.

But she had not. Instead, she had marched her sister down the stairs to the breakfast room and announced their imminent departure, ignoring even Miss Bingley's suspicious questions and Bingley's earnest entreaties that they stay. And she did this without artifice and without displaying any of the normal clues which would have led Darcy to believe her set on capturing a rich husband for herself or her sister. And though Darcy thought none of the others had noticed it, he suspected that Miss Kitty had been reluctant to agree to leave the estate.

It showed Miss Bennet to be a woman of conviction. And her sister, if she had indeed wished to stay, was still a young girl being taught by a wise elder sibling. Thus, she could be excused from wishing to use such machinations. At least her sister was on hand to rein her in and teach her how to behave properly.

It was not long after the Bennet sisters sat down to break their fast that Miss Bennet rose and announced their departure. "I thank you, Miss Bingley, not only for dinner, but also for your hospitality in providing us with shelter for the night. It was greatly appreciated, I assure you."

Miss Bingley, it seemed, had espoused the same expectations as had Darcy himself, but whereas Darcy had discerned the reason for their departure, it seemed Miss Bingley was confused by it. In Miss Bingley's eyes, every other woman was a rival, and she could not understand why they would leave, when she herself would have behaved in a much different manner.

"Good bye, Miss Bennet, Miss Kitty," said Darcy as they stood to leave. "I hope Miss Kitty's indisposition is not serious."

Miss Bennet bestowed a soft smile on him, which made Darcy feel warm all over. "Thank you, Mr. Darcy. I am certain she will be well with a little rest. I will ensure she receives the proper care."

"I am sure you shall. I can see that you take prodigious care of your family."

"I must, Mr. Darcy, for she is my only remaining sister."

With another curtsey, Miss Bennet led her sister from the room, in the company of the Bingley sisters, but they did not disappear before Darcy was witness to a sharp look from Miss Bingley at the elder sister. Clearly she had not been amused by the words they had exchanged.

My dear Miss Bingley, thought Darcy, stifling his amusement, *though I have no inclination to grant Miss Bennet my favor, any more than I wish to extend it to you, I shall not allow you to disparage them when they are not deserving of your censure.*

Darcy waited in the dining room while the ladies of the house saw the Bennet sisters on their way, patiently sipping on his tea, refilling his cup while he waited. At the head of the table, Bingley ate his breakfast and looked through the morning paper, little interested though he seemed in what was contained within its pages. As for Hurst, he was concentrating on his breakfast to the exclusion of all other concerns. Of course, Darcy never expected anything else from the man.

When the Bingley sisters finally returned, Miss Bingley did not disappoint. Almost the first words from her mouth disparaged the recently departed guests.

"How wonderful it is to have one's home back to oneself," declared she as she sank down into a chair dramatically.

Bingley took note of her comment and put his paper down. "Did you not invite them? I am certain you must have for I do not think it is likely they would have come to our door without an invitation."

"Of course I invited them, Charles," snapped his sister. "I had no idea they would be required to spend the night."

"It is a good thing they did," grunted Hurst. "The weather outside last evening was not fit for man nor beast."

"I find it interesting that you invited them on a night when we would not be present," said Bingley, speaking as if his brother had remained silent. "Furthermore, I wonder why you did not think to inform us of the fact that you were to have guests."

Miss Bingley only waved him off. "Must I tell you of all my plans?"

A shrug was Bingley's only response, and he turned away. Darcy looked on the man with some exasperation. It was not as if Bingley was incapable of standing up to his sister; rather, he simply could not be bothered. Bingley's interest was quickly lost in favor of something else — the discussion between siblings was perfect evidence. As the matter truly did not concern him, Bingley said his piece and his mind quickly turned to something else.

But Miss Bingley was not about to lose this opportunity to make her case. "We had an interesting discussion with the Bennet sisters last night, Charles." Bingley did not make a response, which was all the encouragement Miss Bingley needed. "Their uncles, of which they have two, are nothing less than the country solicitor in Meryton and a man of trade in London. Their only other relation is a distant cousin on their father's side, and I had the distinct impression that they possessed little knowledge of the man."

"I have often thought it must be nice to have a small family, as Darcy here does," said Bingley in a musing tone. "We have so many relations that it is difficult to keep them all straight."

Darcy said nothing, content to watch the scene play out until it was time for him to intervene. Miss Bingley, of course, was not finished.

"Once again you have missed the point, Charles. Their relations are decidedly inferior, and they have not much fortune to recommend them. I was not able to discover that they had any other connections worth mentioning."

"And what is that to us?" asked Bingley lazily. "How can it possibly affect us?"

"It cannot, of course," replied Miss Bingley. "I merely mention it to illustrate what a backward part of the kingdom you have stranded us in, Brother. How I long to return to town!"

"They are descended from a long line of gentlemen, Caroline," said Hurst. "For all your airs, that is one thing that you cannot boast, no matter how much you wish you could. Perhaps you should think of that, before you attempt to disparage them."

"I, for one, consider them to be dear girls," declared Bingley, as Miss Bingley was glaring at Hurst. "To me, their connections do not matter a jot. I should be happy to continue our acquaintance with them, should they have uncles in trade in every town between here and London."

"Once again, you are not seeing the point, Charles," said Miss Bingley. She had evidently decided that debating with Hurst was a waste of her time. "The material point is that their situation makes them desperate for social advancement, as it does all in this insignificant speck of a town. You would do well to remember that and endeavor to avoid their machinations."

"I do not believe they are desperate about anything, Miss Bingley," said Darcy, deciding that it was time to speak up. "They are financially secure, with the support of an estate, one whose revenues are increasing, from what I understand. Absent the burden of financial trouble, I cannot imagine to what you refer."

The smile Miss Bingley directed at him was sickly sweet, and he instantly saw through it as false. "I am sorry, Mr. Darcy, but as a woman, I am much better able to understand the motivations of those of my sex. I can assure you that Miss Bennet means to have either you or my brother, and if she can manage it, I believe she would entrap you *and* my brother for herself and her insipid sister. You had both better take care."

"Then why did they not take the opportunity to stay here for at least a day or two longer when it presented itself?"

"Whatever can you mean?" asked Miss Bingley, wide-eyed with feigned confusion.

"Come now, Miss Bingley, surely you saw that Miss Kitty was, in fact, inflicted with a mild cough this morning. I know many women who might have parlayed a slight indisposition into a weeklong stay, if not more. And yet the Miss Bennets did nothing of the sort. Instead, they remained determined to depart so as to avoid giving us any more trouble than they must, resisting all entreaties to keep them here. Such behavior suggests they are anything but fortune hunters."

When Miss Bingley did not respond, Hurst chuckled. "I believe he has you there, Caroline." Then Hurst drummed his fingertips on the table as he thought, and a sly smile came over his face. "In fact, I believe I remember a time last summer when we all visited Pemberley. Our departure was delayed by an indisposition you suffered on the day before our originally scheduled departure. Did it not take you three days to make your recovery?"

Cheeks blooming, Miss Bingley regarded her sister's husband with barely veiled fury. Darcy only looked on—he had considered that incident when he had made his comments, and given the antipathy which existed between Hurst and Caroline, coupled with Hurst's love of tweaking his sister's nose, Darcy had known he could count on the man to bring it up.

Rising, Darcy bowed to the ladies, stating his intention to work for a time in his sitting room. But he was not able to depart without directing one further barb at his friend's sister.

"As for their situation and the state of their connections, I can assure you that, should they desire it, they will have no trouble in attracting suitors. Birth trumps fortune, Miss Bingley. And as Longbourn appears to be a profitable estate, I do not doubt Miss Bennet's situation would be a desirable one. Given her attention to detail, I believe her sister will be well looked after too, and though Miss Kitty's dowry might not be a vast fortune, I am certain that it will not be a pittance either."

And with those words, Darcy left the room. He had enjoyed Miss Bingley's expression of consternation far too much, he knew, but though it was ungentlemanly, he took satisfaction in her set down. She was eminently deserving.

Chapter V

By the next morning, Darcy was frustrated with Miss Bingley. Whatever she had seen in his interactions with Miss Bennet had given her enough cause to be suspicious, and she spared no opportunity to disparage the young woman whenever possible. If it was not their deportment, it was comments about their relations, and when that did not seem to move him, she spoke at length concerning the state of their common origins and their lack of an acceptable dowry.

Darcy snorted at the mere thought. Though Longbourn was not a large estate, even one of two thousand pounds a year was a valuable asset, especially if the man she ultimately married did not possess his own!

Clearly Miss Bingley did nothing more than compare the annual income of the estate to her own twenty-thousand pound dowry and assumed her money was a far greater prize. This did not even take into account how absurd her statements concerning the Bennet sisters' status in society, as if she, the daughter of a tradesman, were higher than they. What a silly creature Miss Bingley was!

Soon Darcy was desperate to escape the house. It was fortunate that Miss Bingley, disdainful as she was about the country, kept to town hours and could be counted on not to awake and descend before ten o'clock, and sometimes not before eleven. Darcy thought she had completely missed the fact that he was up early every day, which he was prepared to use to his advantage. Thus, two days after the Bennet sisters' departure, Darcy called for his horse to be saddled, and he rode away from Netherfield.

It was a pleasant day, common to early November, where the chill in the air carried a hint of the winter to come, but was still warm enough to enjoy. For a time, Darcy rode hard, heedless of everything but the need to escape, and without taking any thought for his direction. He was certain his horse, who had been cooped up in the stables for some time, enjoyed the exercise as much as Darcy did himself.

At length, however, he allowed his mount to slow its pace gradually until he was moving at a walk. Darcy looked down at the sleek and powerful animal, grateful for his efforts that morning.

"Good boy," he said, slapping him on the shoulder. The horse whickered eagerly, letting Darcy know that he could easily have run for many more miles.

Now at his ease, Darcy glanced about the area. He knew he had traveled west from Netherfield initially, but as he had followed paths and in some cases the contours of the land, he was not certain exactly where he had ended up. Some way in the distance he saw a fence which marked Netherfield's boundary with the neighboring estate, but he was not certain whose estate it was.

Slowly, Darcy allowed his mount to wander toward the fence, as he looked around with some interest. The other side of the fence appeared to be a field which had been left fallow the previous summer, with woods beyond. It was somewhat incongruous, Darcy decided, as he approached the fence. The field on the other side of the fence appeared to be more naturally a part of Netherfield than whatever estate lay on the other side. He noted that the fence itself appeared to be new.

It was not long before a pair of riders appeared on the other side of the fence, along the far line of trees. It was easy for Darcy to see that the first was a woman, riding side-saddle as she was, with her riding habit flowing down her legs and behind her in the wind. As Darcy watched her, she turned her head toward him, and in the distance, he could just make out the smiling countenance of Miss Bennet.

Without thinking, Darcy heeled his horse around, and turned, approaching the fence at a gallop, and urging his horse, sailed over without hesitation. A moment later he was in front of her, tipping his hat with a smile.

"Miss Bennet, I am happy to see you today. I had no notion of what direction I had traveled, but I am happy to see you."

"Mr. Darcy," replied she, her voice filled with laughter. "I can see a measure of impulsivity in your character, though your companion appears to be capable."

"I am surprised to see you out so early. I was also not aware of the fact that you ride."

A brilliant smile came over the woman's face, and she patted her mount which nickered in response. "I will own that I only recently started riding, Mr. Darcy. When I was younger, I walked a great deal. But it is difficult to walk everywhere when dealing with tenants."

"You have a fine animal."

"Yes, she is. She is one of the cornerstones of the breeding program we have begun. The stallion, of course, is too large for me to ride, and far too spirited. My steward rides him, so that he might get his own exercise."

"That is prudent, Miss Bennet. A stallion can become unruly if left for long periods of time."

Miss Bennet turned her horse and began walking it on their way again, and Darcy heeled his own mount to accompany her.

"In fact, I am not riding for pleasure today, sir. I am to visit a tenant family on the northern edge of the estate."

Darcy looked at her, noting the ease with which she led her horse, noting her erect posture and loose grip with which she held the reins. If she had learned to ride only within the last year, then she was a quick study indeed.

"In that case, I hope it is agreeable if I accompany you."

A laugh escaped her mouth and she turned to him. "I had understood you were on something of a holiday, sir. Would you attend to matters of an estate which is not even your own?"

"Do I not already do so for Netherfield?"

A curious gaze met his statement. "Is not Mr. Bingley's purpose to learn estate management? I had understood you were teaching him."

"That is true, but it is still work, and I enjoy sharing whatever knowledge I possess. Of course I would not dream of intruding, but I would like to accompany you if you would allow it."

"Of course, sir. I have no objection."

Nodding to the other rider—likely a footman, given his deference and attention—Darcy settled his horse in beside Miss Bennet's to her left, so he could face her and more easily converse, the other man following in behind. Darcy had not visited Longbourn yet, but as they rode, he could tell that it was a neat and well maintained estate. As it was now early November and the harvest was in, he could not see what it would look like in summer, but the fields had been properly prepared for the winter season, and he could see no lack therein. They spent their time speaking of the estate, Miss Bennet speaking of their crop rotation strategy, of which he held an interest, as he had adopted a similar method only a few years before. And in every word and every look, Darcy could see Miss Bennet's love for the estate shining through.

"I had wondered, Miss Bennet," said Darcy, their conversation of Longbourn's fields reminding him of the strange field he had seen earlier. "The location where we met; it seems to me that geographically speaking, that field would belong to Netherfield rather than Longbourn."

"That is because until six months ago it *was* a part of Netherfield," replied Miss Bennet with some smugness.

"The owner sold it to you?"

"We made him an offer he could not refuse," replied Miss Bennet. "Since the current owner has not lived at Netherfield for some years, the estate has suffered to a certain extent. The steward is a good man, but as the owner takes little interest in its operation, there are times when matters are not decided and work cannot commence. Historically, that field was one of Netherfield's best producing. But a few years ago there was a dispute among several of the tenants, which led to the man who worked that field leaving Netherfield entirely. It has sat fallow since then."

Darcy nodded his head, knowing that she was correct. Indifferent management always led to the diminution in an estate's producing power and there was only so much that a steward could do. Darcy himself own three such satellite estates, in addition to Pemberley, and he attempted to be diligent in seeing to each estate's needs. He also tried to visit each one every year or two, though that was sometimes difficult. In the upheaval during the summer, he had not been able to journey to Scotland to see to his estate near Kircaldy, and he had not been there for more than two years. It was a location he would have to make time to visit next year.

"So you purchased the field with the expectation that it would increase your income."

Miss Bennet nodded. "If my steward is at all correct, it should pay handsomely, allowing us to make back the expenditure in only a few years."

It was something he would have done—his father had done a time or two. An astute landowner was always looking for the means to improve his income and ensure the solvency of the estate. Darcy found himself impressed all over again.

"What do you produce, Miss Bennet?"

"We grow grains and herd cattle, of course," replied Miss Bennet. "We also have many vegetables, mostly on the tenant farms, though we do produce enough for the manor house on the home farm. I have lately purchased a number of horses for breeding purposes, though we are still a number of years from making a profit in that endeavor. And we have a herd of sheep in the rockier sections of the far northeast of the estate."

"A diverse enterprise, then."

"It has always been thus," replied Miss Bennet. "Though I have grown the estate by the field you saw, plus another one on the other side of the estate, the only thing I have truly changed is the addition of the stud farm, and like I said, it will not begin to profit for some time yet."

"But you have maintained what your father left you, expanding it when possible. I am very impressed, indeed." Miss Bennet blushed under the force of his praise. "Do not think that I am slighting you when I say that many men would not expect a woman to manage her estate with such flair, especially when she is so young. Though I have not yet seen much, it seems likely to me that Longbourn operates better than many estates whose owners have been managing them for years."

"Thank you, Mr. Darcy," said Miss Bennet, still shy in the face of his commendation.

As they continued on, their conversation became lighter in tone, and while Darcy attended her, another part of his mind was ruminating upon an entirely different subject. For Darcy was aware of another lady who was in a similar situation to that Miss Bennet found herself in, and though the circumstances were different, still there was enough commonality to make a comparison.

His aunt, Lady Catherine de Bourgh, was a widow, having managed her estate at Rosings Park for the past fifteen years. It was true that Rosings was a much larger estate, providing some eight thousand pounds per annum in income. But when Darcy compared the two—even taking into account what he did not know about Longbourn—he was forced to concede that Longbourn was the much healthier of the two enterprises. Darcy was in a perfect position to know Rosings' finances, as he visited his aunt every spring to go over her books and smooth whatever ill feelings had risen due to his aunt's authoritative dominance over the estate.

Lady Catherine was a woman not easily gainsaid, and she was also not a woman given to new ideas and new techniques used in modern times for the purpose of increasing an estate's income. Many times Darcy had attempted to impress upon her the importance of diversifying her income or trying new methods, but she was stubborn in her refusal. That, coupled with her tendency to spend too much, ensured that Rosings' income never increased. In fact, in the past several years, it had actually decreased.

At length, they reached their destination, a small but neat cottage in the furthest reaches of the estate, and they dismounted, Miss Bennet taking hold of a basket which had been fastened to her saddle on the other side. She alighted on the ground lightly and with the grace of a well-bred woman and approached the cottage.

They had crossed perhaps half the distance when the door suddenly swung open, and a young girl of approximately five years escaped from the house and approached at a run. Miss Bennet only had enough time to pass the basket off to Darcy before the child was upon her, and to Darcy's complete surprise, she threw herself into Miss Bennet's arms.

"Miss Lizzy, Miss Lizzy!" exclaimed the child, hugging her closely like one would a favorite aunt. "You have come today!"

"Indeed, I have, you naughty child," said Miss Bennet, though her fond smile belied any censure her words might have implied. "Have you been minding your mama?"

"I have," said the child solemnly. "Mama does not have as much time for me as she used to, so I must occupy myself and help with the chores."

"That is good, Miss Jenny. I dare say that you are well on your way to becoming a lady." Miss Bennet put the child down, and she reached down to lift the child's dress slightly, revealing a pair of soft boots, which were handsome, yet sturdy, protecting the child's feet against the autumn weather. "I see you are wearing the boots I brought you."

"I am," said Jenny. "Mama has told me that since they are special boots, that I must care for them and ensure they last for the next several years."

"Your mama is very wise, Jenny. As I ensured the boots were too large on your little feet, I am certain you shall be able to wear them for at least the next two years, and if you take good care of them, your sister might be able to wear them when she is a similar age."

"Oh, Miss Bennet," a voice called, drawing their attention.

A young woman, perhaps five and twenty years of age had followed the little girl out of the cottage. In her arms she carried a swaddled bundle which Darcy immediately realized was a young child, only a few months of age. And on her face she wore a look of consternation, tinged with annoyance.

"I am sorry for Jenny's exuberance. I have tried to tell her not to jump on you in such a fashion, but she becomes so excited, I am afraid she cannot control herself."

"It is no problem, Mrs. Miller," replied Miss Bennet. "I quite enjoy her exuberance, I assure you. According to my dearly departed father, I was much the same at her age. The least I can do is allow your daughter her own high spirits."

"You are too kind, I am sure."

Miss Bennet quickly introduced Mr. Darcy to the woman's acquaintance and asked after her husband.

"Mr. Miller is off inspecting the northern field. I am certain he will return before long."

"That is fine, Mrs. Miller. In fact, my errand today is with you, rather than your husband. I have brought some dresses my sister and I have sewn for your daughters."

The basket was opened and several small dresses, most sized for an infant—though there were one or two which would fit Jenny included as well. They had been finely sewn and beautifully designed, and Darcy was certain the two women had worked on them for some time. In addition to these, the basket contained several pieces of fruit, as well as a freshly baked loaf of bread and a jar of preserves.

"These are almost the last of the apples from the orchard," said Miss Bennet. "The rest have all been put up for the winter." She turned her smile upon the young girl, who was bouncing up and down in her excitement. "I have also included a jar of Mrs. Hill's famous apple butter."

The young girl let out a whoop at hearing of the treasures contained in the jar and she clutched it to her breast, clearly not intending to let it go.

"Oh, Miss Bennet, you spoil us so," said Mrs. Miller, a beaming smile setting over her face. "I do thank you for the gifts, though. And Jenny thanks you for her new dresses."

"Thank you, Miss Bennet," chimed in the girl. "They are very pretty!"

"And will do you much credit, I am sure," replied Miss Bennet. She turned back to the mother. "How is the little one?"

"Over the bout of cold and on the mend," said the young mother, clearly relieved. "I thank you for sending the apothecary to our aid."

"It is no trouble," said Miss Bennet. "I am only happy that it has worked out for the best. May I see her?"

Nodding, the young mother took the child and settled her in Miss Bennet's arms, and she looked down at the child, cooing softly. The girl yawned and looked up at her, and within moments she was responding to Miss Bennet's ministrations, cooing back at her, carrying on the kind of conversation between child and adult which had been repeated endless times over the centuries. Though Darcy could not see into the future and could not know at the time, it was an image which would stay with him for the rest of his life. Miss Bennet stood there, an infant in her arms, speaking with it as a mother would to her child, looking so very desirable in her long, flowing riding dress, with the pale warmth of the autumn sun shining down on her. In later years, Darcy would look back on that day as the time when he had first begun to love her.

Later, when they had exchanged further words with the woman — and many more with the daughter, who was not about to be ignored — the pair rejoined the footman and left the farm for the return journey to their separate estates. Darcy rode alongside Miss Bennet, thinking about what he had witnessed, thinking all over again how impressed he was with this young woman.

His mind returned to thoughts of his Aunt Catherine, and though she ruled over her domain and cared for those in her purview, her care was more the authoritative kind, and her decrees were expected to be instantly obeyed. Darcy could not imagine his aunt cooing over a child, though he supposed that she must have done something similar with her own daughter. Then again, considering the way she spoke for Anne, thought for Anne, and ruled Anne's life, Darcy supposed she might have simply demanded that Anne stop crying when she was an infant, with every expectation of being obeyed. It was as likely as any other scenario.

It was Miss Bennet's caring, he decided. Many women throughout the kingdom served as mistresses of their estates, whether as a man's wife, or as the proprietor in their own right, but though there were undoubtedly good woman among them, Miss Bennet's effortless charity touched him like he had never been touched before. She served these people, brought them assistance and succor, and was clearly well known among them, if Jenny's reaction to her coming was any indication. And the child's boots were another thing — Darcy thought they had probably been purchased at some expense. Miss Bennet could have simply provided something of adequate protection and no one could have faulted her, but instead, she had thoughtfully provided a gift which would benefit the family for years. She was much to be admired, he decided.

However, when Darcy made these observations, the woman merely deflected them. "You did not see the tattered remnants she was wearing this summer, Mr. Darcy. The rains were heavier than normal this spring, and as such, Mr. Miller's harvest was affected. He would never have been able to afford her appropriate footwear for the coming winter. With those boots, they will not have to worry about the matter for some time."

"And the infant? You had mentioned she had been ill?"

Miss Bennet nodded, though solemnly. "You have to understand, Mr. Darcy, that after the events of the winter two years ago, any little ague, every cold, is scrutinized carefully and worried over excessively. The Millers lost their son to the illness that swept through the area that year. The last time I saw Mrs. Miller, she was almost frantic with concern over her daughter. My heart is eased that the child has recovered so well."

"The apple butter was also welcome, I noted."

Miss Bennet laughed, and Darcy noticed, like he never had before, how musical and beautiful a sound it was. "Yes, it was indeed. Our former housekeeper owned the recipe, which she made sure to leave us when she was struck with the illness that claimed her life. It is well known and prized throughout the district, and Jenny's particular favorite."

"And might the newcomers to your neighborhood be so bold as to request a taste of this famous concoction?"

"Of course, sir!" said Miss Bennet. "You cannot truly be called a member of Meryton society until you have tasted Longbourn's famous apple butter."

When they parted later as they approached Elizabeth's home, Darcy turned his mount toward Netherfield. He had been given much on which to think, and though the return to his friend's estate also meant a return to Miss Bingley's cloying attentions, he thought himself much more able to bear them.

Darcy was not surprised when, the very next day, one of Longbourn's footmen arrived with a small package, compliments of Longbourn's kitchens to the family at Netherfield. And Darcy was ready to concede that the apple butter contained in the jar was as fine as any he had ever tasted.

There was little congress between the estates of Longbourn and Netherfield for the next few days, and though Elizabeth visited other tenants during those days and she watched the countryside assiduously for some sign of the gentleman, she did not see him again. Something had struck her as she had ridden and spoken with him, something which altered her perception of him ever so slightly.

He was a good man, she decided, intelligent, kind, attentive, and though he was sometimes aloof, at least the trait did not rule him. His knowledge of the matters of an estate spoke to his understanding of what it meant to be a landlord, and his insights, as they spoke, pointed to a diligence which could only be termed as admirable.

At church that Sunday, Elizabeth, who sat in the Bennet family pew with her sister, watched him as unobtrusively as she was able from where he sat across the aisle. He had, she decided, a beautiful baritone voice, and his knowledge of the hymns which he sang, only occasionally looking at the words, suggested a familiarity with them which could not be feigned. He listened attentively to the sermon, spoke the words from the prayer book with equal familiarity, and prayed with the rest of the congregation without hesitation. His entire demeanor suggested that he was a true believer and adherent, rather than one who simply paid lip service to the forms, without ever thinking of the substance.

One point of concern for Elizabeth was the behavior of her younger sister. Though Kitty's actions were not overt, Elizabeth noted that her sister rarely turned her attention away from the person of Mr. Darcy's friend. She watched him as he sat beside his friend, though Elizabeth noted that while Mr. Bingley acquitted himself well, his knowledge of the forms was not as profound as Mr. Darcy's. But as Kitty did not make a fool out of herself, Elizabeth decided that it was simply best to let it be.

After church, the congregation made its way outside the chapel doors and stood mingling for some minutes in the light of the morning sun, weak though it was. There, Elizabeth once again had the opportunity to speak to Mr. Darcy.

"I would like to thank you for the gift you so graciously sent us the other day, Miss Bennet. It was much appreciated and quite delicious, I assure you. Longbourn's reputation for fine apple butter was, if anything, completely understated."

"As I said, Mr. Darcy. I am happy you are able to recognize true genius when you taste it."

Mr. Darcy laughed, but Miss Bingley, who was standing nearby, looked on him with exasperation, and then Elizabeth with condescension. "The apple butter was from your kitchens?"

"Yes, indeed it was, Miss Bingley," replied Elizabeth. "Longbourn's apple butter is known throughout the district and sought after by many. We are happy to provide as much as we possibly can, though the demand is such that most families will see no more than a single jar every year."

If possible, Miss Bingley's countenance grew even haughtier. "It was adequate, I suppose."

"The finest I have ever had," stated Mr. Darcy, his tone brooking no opposition.

"Quite," was all Miss Bingley could say.

"And young Miss Jenny?" inquired Mr. Darcy. "Can I assume she is wearing her new dresses with distinction?"

"I can only assume. Unfortunately, as the babe is still recovering, they are not here today. The Millers usually attend church with us, though it is some distance for them to come."

"Then perhaps we shall see them anon."

The discussion turned to one of the business of the estate, and though Miss Bingley attempted to interject her own comments wherever possible, it was mostly carried by Mr. Darcy and Elizabeth. Several times Elizabeth was forced to contain her laughter, as Miss Bingley, in her attempts to draw Mr. Darcy's attention to her, made comments to which he listened politely, and then he turned back to Elizabeth to continue on with what they were previously speaking.

Of much greater amusement was the way in which he seemed to find her presence and conversation a trial. Though his reactions were never overt and he always maintained control over his emotions, still she could sense an exasperation with Miss Bingley, and even once Elizabeth thought he had barely restrained himself from rolling his eyes. It was all very diverting to Elizabeth, and she wondered at the woman's inability to see Mr. Darcy's disinclination for her company.

"You have seen the eastern pasture we recently purchased from Netherfield, Mr. Darcy," said Elizabeth. "To what use do you think we should put it?"

Mr. Darcy looked at her thoughtfully. "There are any number of ways you could put it to good use. Might I ask if you intend to pass it to a tenant, or will it be part of the home farm?"

"Oh, the home farm without a doubt, sir. Our home farm is situated to the south and east of the manor, and though the field is separated from the rest by a strand of trees, still it is most logically put to use as part of the home farm."

"In that case," said Mr. Darcy, "it could be put to the same use as the rest of the land used by your farm, though staggered to ensure a similar income from one year to the next. I would suggest a standard crop rotation to take full advantage of the field, which, if my assumption concerning the quality of soil is correct, will provide a handsome profit. Row crops, followed by legumes such as alfalfa or clover, and grains such as wheat or barley. In addition, you may leave it fallow one year, and encourage your cattle to graze there, to provide manure to replenish the nutrients removed by the different crops."

As Mr. Darcy was speaking, Elizabeth noted that Miss Bingley looked on him with barely concealed astonishment. Elizabeth resisted shaking her head; did the woman not know that as a landowner he would be conversant with such things?

"Your advice is similar to my steward's, Mr. Darcy. It is excellent advice indeed. As the land had been somewhat misused when it was in production, and had been left fallow for several years, we left it this year, at times driving our cattle there to graze, as you suggested. Besides, it was quite late in the planting season by the time we were able to pry it from its previous owner."

"Excuse me, Miss Bennet," interjected Miss Bingley, "but given the conversation, might I be correct in assuming this field, of which you speak, is one you purchased from Netherfield?"

"Indeed, it is, Miss Bingley," replied Elizabeth. "We were able to purchase it at a good price from Netherfield's owner last spring."

"I am all astonishment. I had no idea that you were so conversant in matters of business." The way Miss Bingley looked down her nose at Elizabeth, she almost thought the woman considered it a personal affront that Elizabeth had actually possessed the audacity to buy a parcel of land previously owned by the estate her brother was leasing.

"I do not claim to be an expert, Miss Bingley. However, some familiarity is necessary, else the estate becomes vulnerable, either to mismanagement or to an unscrupulous steward."

"And do you employ such a man?" Miss Bingley's tone was all insolence, but rather than be offended, Elizabeth was, in fact, amused.

"No, indeed, Miss Bingley. In fact, my steward is a very good man whom I trust completely."

"Then I cannot imagine why you would take such an interest. Is that not what a steward's job entails? Why should you—a woman—dirty your hands in such a manner?"

"Because I love the estate, Miss Bingley. It has been in my family for generations, and I will not do anything to compromise its solvency. All the people who work the land depend upon the estate's smooth operation for their livelihoods. There is more to owning an estate than simply living off the proceeds."

"There is nothing wrong with seeing to one's property, Miss Bingley," added Mr. Darcy. "I myself oversee my steward. He is a good man, very capable, and eminently trustworthy, but he is also not the master. Some decisions must be made by the master, as his must be the ultimate authority."

At first Miss Bingley looked on Mr. Darcy with some consternation, but it soon turned to fawning. "Of course you may take an interest in your own lands, Mr. Darcy. I dare say your knowledge is so profound that a steward, regardless of his experience, will have little to add that you do not already know." Miss Bingley's eyes once again found Elizabeth, and the pleasant warmth she had been trying to present to Mr. Darcy turned to a bitter winter chill. "But there can be no occasion for a woman to engage herself in such unladylike activities. Better to allow the steward to do his work, or allow her guardian to become involved, rather than lose one's gentility and femininity."

"I am not all knowledgeable, Miss Bingley," murmured Mr. Darcy.

At the same time, Elizabeth said: "So you believe there is never any call for a woman to concern herself for her property, Miss Bingley? I should leave everything in the hands of the steward and content myself with the pianoforte, drawing, painting, netting screens, embroidery, and all those things on which society puts great stock?"

"Of course, unless you wish to be considered worse than a bluestocking."

Out of the corner of her eye, Elizabeth saw Mr. Darcy stifle a laugh, no doubt remembering the night of their first meeting. Though she supposed she ought to be offended, Elizabeth was in fact amused. To consider that a woman, not of gentle birth herself, having no knowledge of the function of an estate, would attempt to school her in the proper behavior of her class was not so much insulting as it was absurd.

"That is a very interesting point of view, Miss Bingley," was all Elizabeth said in reply to the woman.

She then turned her attention back to Mr. Darcy. "Might I ask after your aunt, Mr. Darcy? Have you heard from her since you came to Hertfordshire?"

Though Elizabeth knew it was not precisely polite to ask after a woman to whom she had never before been introduced, Mr. Darcy immediately understood the reason for her question, if the hand he brought to his mouth to stifle a smile was any indication.

"Very well, indeed, Miss Bennet," said he, not missing a beat. "In fact, I heard from her only last week. She and my cousin are very well indeed."

"You have told me so much about her, I feel as if I already know her." It was all Elizabeth could do not to laugh at the presumption in her words, but she was determined to make her point, so she continued on. "And how is her *estate*? I understand that she is heavily involved in its operation and takes a prodigious amount of care of everyone within reach of her influence."

In fact, Elizabeth knew no such thing. Mr. Darcy had only mentioned a widowed aunt in passing, but given his few comments, she sounded like a forthright sort of person who would not suffer others to look after her interests without interference.

"Indeed, it seems as if you already know her, Miss Bennet. Aunt Catherine is, indeed, a woman of frank opinions and an independent spirit. It is not so much that she cares for those of her estate; it is more like she . . . demands harmony and will not suffer want."

"Then perhaps you should introduce me to her when the opportunity presents itself, for we *independent* and *forthright* women who are determined to manage our own properties must remain unified. I should like to make her acquaintance."

Miss Bingley, who had watched their conversation with growing horror, interjected that moment, her manner almost desperate. "Surely your aunt, given her position in society, does not manage the affairs of the estate by herself, Mr. Darcy."

"Oh, I assure you she does," replied Mr. Darcy, "though I must dispute your words concerning her position in society. She has lived most of the past fifteen years of her life at her estate, and as such, whatever influence in society she once possessed has largely dissipated, for all that she *is* the daughter of an earl. In matters of her estate, my aunt does not suffer fools, and she is quite capable of managing her own affairs. I also have a great aunt, a spinster who has never married, who inherited her estate from an elderly relation. She manages her own estate as well, and when she dies, she plans to leave it to my cousin Colonel Fitzwilliam."

"Then it seems as if this *unladylike* practice of caring for one's own estate is more widespread than you had thought, Miss Bingley." Elizabeth smiled pleasantly at her. "As it seems to have done neither of Mr. Darcy's relations any harm, and I doubt either of them have suffered enough to have lost their *gentility* or *femininity*, I feel myself confident enough to continue as I have."

Elizabeth turned to Mr. Darcy and smiled. "Thank you both for this interesting conversation, but I believe Kitty and I should return to our home."

"Of course, Miss Bennet," said Mr. Darcy, bowing over her hand. "I believe Bingley wishes to return to Netherfield presently."

"Then I anticipate our next meeting."

And with a curtsey—and the barest hint of a nod for the still dumbfounded Miss Bingley—Elizabeth turned and, calling to Kitty, who was speaking with Maria Lucas, she departed. Perhaps it was not proper to toy with the woman and expose her for a fool, but it had been satisfactory indeed. Elizabeth did not think she had ever met a woman more absurd than Miss Bingley.

Chapter VI

*O*ne day more than a week later, Elizabeth and Kitty were ensconced in Longbourn's front sitting room when they received a most unexpected visitor. To that point it had been a typical day; Elizabeth had woken early, taking care of some business of the estate, while Kitty had gone to visit some of the tenants, carrying baskets of much needed food and other items to help see them through the winter. Elizabeth had bid her a fond farewell when she left, happy at her sister's continued progress toward becoming a truly genteel young woman.

They had come together again for a light luncheon and spent the afternoon in companionable pursuits, reading together, after which Kitty drew while Elizabeth played the pianoforte for some time, interspersed with conversation between the two. It was not much more than another hour before dinner when they were interrupted.

The first indication they had of the impending arrival was the sound of a small carriage proceeding down Longbourn's driveway. Kitty, curious about the sound, went to the front window and peered out, turning to Elizabeth.

"Lizzy, were we expecting a visitor today?"

Engrossed in a book she had picked up to pass the time, Elizabeth shook her head. "I am certain it is nothing more than a delivery for cook or, perhaps, someone to see Mr. Whitmore."

"I do not think so, Lizzy. It is a small carriage, and a man is alighting. He looks to be a clergyman."

Surprised, Elizabeth looked up at her sister. "A clergyman?"

"Yes. He is not very handsome and appears a little heavyset, but he is wearing the high collar of a parson."

Suddenly suspicious of the identity of their visitor, Elizabeth rose and looked out the window. The man was, indeed, quite tall, but he also possessed a portly frame, and around the brim of his wide black hat a shock of dark hair appeared.

Annoyed, Elizabeth crossed to the bell pull to summon a maid, who appeared only moments later.

"Please send for Mr. Whitmore and have him join us on the front drive," instructed Elizabeth.

The girl curtseyed and left to do her bidding. Knowing there was little else to do, Elizabeth beckoned to Kitty to follow her.

"Do you know who it is?" asked her sister, confused at Elizabeth's hard countenance.

"Perhaps," replied Elizabeth shortly. "If you recall, we received a letter some time ago informing us of our cousin's wish to visit us."

Eyes wide in sudden comprehension, Kitty turned an uncertain eye on Elizabeth. "But you responded to that missive declining his wish, did you not?"

"I did. But it appears like my words were ignored and he invited himself nonetheless."

Kitty frowned. Such a breach of etiquette was beyond the pale, and Elizabeth knew Kitty wondered if she was incorrect in her supposition. For that matter, if their cousin was the kind of man she expected, she rather hoped that she was mistaken herself.

The sisters crossed the entranceway and exited the estate through the front doors, arriving just in time to witness the man supervising the last of his trunks being removed from the vehicle. The parson paid the carriage driver for his services and then turned to the sisters as the carriage began to move away.

"Miss Bennet, Miss Catherine," said he, as he bowed low before them.

Kitty and Elizabeth looked at one another, Elizabeth noting the amusement on her sister's face, which she knew was mirrored on her own. Such an obeisance could only be reserved for a reigning monarch, not for a pair of young woman, neither of whom were even of age.

When he straightened, Elizabeth was able to obtain her first true look at the man. As Kitty had averred, he was not handsome. His face was rather pudgy, with a large, bulbous nose and beady black eyes peering out from under his broad brimmed hat. When he removed that hat, Elizabeth could see that his hair, while still black and not speckled with gray, was thinning in the center, still visible though he had grown his hair on one side long, and had attempted to hide the unfortunate bald area by brushing the longer hair over. Furthermore, his hair stood out on all sides, likely from the effects of the hat, and was lank and greasy, seeming like he had not washed it in more than a month. All of these unfortunate traits gathered together depicted a man who was about as far from handsome as Elizabeth had ever seen.

"My delightful young cousins," began he, his tone overflowing with a sort of unctuous eagerness, "I am most happy to finally meet you. I cannot tell you how much of an honor it is to finally make your acquaintance, and I am confident that our previously strained family relations will be repaired to the extent that we shall once again be bound by the closest of ties, ones as unbreakable . . ."

Mr. Collins seemed to realize he was rambling on, making little sense, when he finally caught himself and put a hand up before his mouth.

"But of such matters, it would perhaps be best for nature to take its course. I will say nothing of it for the moment, but I assure you that we will speak of it anon. For the present, let me repeat, in the most animated fashion at my disposal, how happy I am to be here with you, where I greatly anticipate our opportunity to once again bask in the beauteous benefits of the society of close relations. For, as my noble patroness would say, 'there is nothing so noble and so pure as the bonds of family, for no other link is so profound.' Since I have had the poor fortune to lose my excellent father, I have not had another member of my family in whom to confide. Our meeting is fortuitous indeed."

Out of the corner of her eye, Elizabeth noted Kitty's astonishment as she listened to the man's long-winded and convoluted — not to mention repetitious — greeting. For herself, Elizabeth felt slightly bemused and saddened at the same time — bemused over the fact that Mr. Collins was perhaps even more ridiculous than she had expected and saddened at the thought that her father, who delighted in absurdity, had never had the opportunity to meet his cousin. Her father would have savored the delight of meeting Mr. Collins for certain!

"Mr. Collins," replied Elizabeth, dropping into a shallow curtsey, noting that Kitty had mirrored her. "I am confused, though, sir. Why are you here?"

It seemed the simple question was beyond Mr. Collins's modest capabilities as, first, he stared at her in seeming stupefaction for several moments, mouth moving with no sound proceeding forth, and then stammering incoherently for several moments. Presently, however, he seemed to master himself, and he replied, little though Elizabeth appreciated the response.

"Did you not receive the letter I sent you? In it I specified the date and time I would grace your abode with my presence. Surely you must recall it."

"I do recall it, Mr. Collins. But do you not recall that I replied, expressly declining to issue an invitation?"

The dullard before her gaped at her again, and Elizabeth allowed him to work through it on his own. Her tolerance for the follies of others was not nearly so developed as her father's had been. Elizabeth thought only of being rid of this man as soon as possible.

"My dear cousin," said Mr. Collins at last, his face etched with a most unpleasantly condescending leer, "I did receive your letter. However, I knew you could not be serious, so I accepted the invitation you could not, in your feminine delicacy, bear to issue. I see now that I was right to come."

"By what convoluted bit of reasoning do you assume I would not issue an invitation for nothing more than 'feminine delicacy?' An invitation must be issued for a stay to be approved, and since I declined to invite you, you should have believed me and remained at your parish."

"I am well aware of the hesitance of young ladies," replied Mr. Collins, though his manner was not nearly so self-assured as it had been before. "But you need not fear. I have come, as head of the family, to visit you. I offer my protection, as well as my affection and assistance. You need not fear again."

"Mr. Collins," said Elizabeth, by now feeling annoyed, "we are quite well here, I thank you. I was not hesitant about inviting you. Rather, I was well aware of the impropriety of the mere suggestion, and not only would I never consider risking my reputation and that of my sister, but I would never put a parson, such as yourself, in such an untenable situation."

"Whatever can you mean?" cried Mr. Collins. "Your father is, sorrowfully, passed from this life to journey to the courts on high for his just reward, and as I am the last remaining man of your family, it is my responsibility to provide you the guidance of a guardian. There is nothing improper about a guardian staying with his female relations.

"Now, if you will, I should like to refresh myself after my long journey. If you would lead me to the master's suite, I shall change and bathe and return to you as soon as may be."

"On the contrary, Mr. Collins," said Elizabeth, her voice unyielding, "I do not know where you will rest and refresh yourself, but it will not be in Longbourn's master suite, nor will it be in any of our other rooms. As you should already know, the role of guardian is filled by my uncle in London. When he stays here, he, of course, does so without the issue of propriety. You, however, are a cousin, and you are most certainly *not* my guardian, and as such, it would be improper in the extreme for you to stay here. I apologize that I cannot accommodate you, but you cannot stay at Longbourn."

A hard expression came over the man's fatuous face, but before he could vent his frustration for her recalcitrance, Mr. Whitmore appeared from the front doors.

"Miss Bennet? Do you require assistance?"

"Thank you, Mr. Whitmore, but I think we have everything in hand."

"My dear cousin," began Mr. Collins, his tone almost insulting in its condescending quality, "I am afraid you have quite mistaken the matter. As a member of the clergy, it is no more improper for me to stay with you than it is for you to live together as sisters, and as I am a close relation, there can be no fault to be found with my proposed residence here. Please discontinue this argument, and let us go inside the house."

"Pardon me, Miss Bennet," said Mr. Whitmore, "but will you do me the honor of introducing me to this gentleman?"

"Of course, Mr. Whitmore." Elizabeth turned to Mr. Collins. "Mr. Collins, this is Mr. Whitmore, my steward, and my *guardian's* surrogate here at Longbourn. Mr. Whitmore, my late father's cousin, Mr. Collins."

"A pleasure to meet you, sir," said Mr. Collins, a hint of testiness appearing in his tone. "Now, if you would be so good as to lead the way, I wish to wash the dust of the road from my person."

"I am sorry, Miss Bennet, but I do not understand," said Mr. Whitmore. "Did you invite Mr. Collins to stay at Longbourn? If you did, you should have consulted with me first, because I cannot permit it, nor would your uncle have agreed, should his opinion have been canvassed."

"It appears we have had a misunderstanding, Mr. Whitmore," said Elizabeth. "I did not invite Mr. Collins to stay with us."

"But . . . but . . ." Mr. Collins hesitated. "But I am a clergyman!"

"Perhaps you are, sir," said Mr. Whitmore, turning a hard eye on the unfortunate parson, "but parsons are not exempt from the rules of proper behavior."

"And what would you, a common steward, know of the matter?"

"I have never been a parson, if that is what you are asking. But I have uncles in the church, who have provided an example. Besides, it is well understood that young ladies cannot stay in the same house with men who are not their guardians without a chaperone present. If Miss Bennet's father were still alive, he might, at his discretion, invite you to stay here. But with only Miss Bennet and Miss Kitty in residence, it would be improper to allow you entrance."

"But where shall I go?" demanded Mr. Collins. "You have brought me here under false pretenses. My home is a day's journey away, and I am tired and dirty from my travels. Surely you cannot mean to turn me away, to make my own way back to my home."

Though Elizabeth bristled at the suggestion that it was *her* fault the man had arrived when he did, and she was annoyed at the presumption which had led him to her door, she could not simply force him to walk to Meryton on his own.

"Perhaps we can ask Sir William if he can offer Mr. Collins shelter for the night."

Mr. Whitmore eyed Elizabeth for a moment before he nodded tightly. "I will send John to Lucas Lodge at once, Miss Bennet."

A beatific smile appeared on the parson's ugly face and he nodded once, though his expression soon turned to distaste when he looked at the steward. "This Sir William, he is a gentleman?"

"Yes, and our nearest neighbor. He also stands as a surrogate for my uncle when necessary."

"Very well, that is acceptable." But though Mr. Collins appeared content, still he looked longingly at Longbourn. It was clear he was only appeased for the moment. "Shall we not sit while we wait for this Sir William to arrive?"

"Mr. Whitmore," said Elizabeth, noting that John was now making his way down the drive toward the village, and Lucas Lodge beyond, "will you escort Mr. Collins into the house? I believe Kitty and I will take a constitutional behind the house while we wait."

"Of course, Miss Bennet."

And Mr. Whitmore gathered the unfortunate parson and directed him toward the house, while Mr. Collins looked back at the sisters. It seemed to Elizabeth that the man was only capable of showing three faces to the world: consternation, confusion, and smug superiority. He truly was the oddest mix of parts that Elizabeth had ever met.

"It is a little cold, Lizzy," said Kitty, rubbing her arms through her thin dress. "Shall we not return to the house for our outer wear?"

"No need," said Elizabeth, noting the approach of Mrs. Whitmore. "I see you have anticipated us."

"There is no call for you to catch a cold while that interloper enjoys your sitting-room," said Mrs. Whitmore as she helped Elizabeth and Kitty into their pelisses. "Enjoy your walk—I will tell cook to hold dinner for half an hour until we can be rid of your cousin."

Thanking her, Elizabeth directed Kitty toward the back of the house. It was fortunate the day was mild, though she supposed that had not it been so, they could easily have slipped into the study with no one being the wiser. No one of any consequence, anyway.

"What can he mean by coming here after you declined to invite him?" asked Kitty.

"I do not know," replied Elizabeth. "And I am not sure I wish to know."

At length, Sir William arrived, and once the matter was explained to him, he was happy to extend an invitation to stay at Lucas Lodge. Sir William was perhaps the only man in the district who would be able to tolerate Mr. Collins. Their characters were not precisely similar, but Sir William put great stock in being civil to all, and as he was not from a gentle background himself, it would likely be easier for him to either ignore Mr. Collins or simply not understand in what manner he was being improper.

The two gentleman bid the Bennet sisters a good day, Mr. Collins with the same flowery verbosity with which he had greeted them, and soon Mr. Collins's possessions were loaded onto Longbourn's wagon for the short journey to Lucas Lodge. His intention to visit the following day Elizabeth discounted; hopefully Sir William would have him on his way back to his parsonage on the morrow, and even if he was not, Elizabeth knew Sir William, given his responsibility for them, would not allow it without his presence.

Once they had gone, Mr. Whitmore approached Elizabeth, a graveness which was not usually part of his character, displayed for Elizabeth to see.

"Miss Bennet, I think you should know that while we were waiting for Sir William to arrive, Mr. Collins made several statements which inferred that I could expect to be released without reference when he became master of the estate."

Elizabeth could only sigh. "So that is the way the wind blows."

"Mr. Collins means to marry you?" squeaked Kitty with horror.

"It appears to be so," replied Mr. Whitmore. "I fully expect him to attempt to induce Sir William to allow him to stay longer."

"And Sir William will not be able to refuse."

"Exactly. It would behoove you, therefore, to take care while he is in residence. I have no doubt he will see encouragement where you mean none and see favor where you are repulsed. Your uncle, of course, will never consent unless it is your will, but you should avoid any hint of impropriety, for he has not the least understanding of it. I do not think he is vicious, but there seems to be some . . ."

Mr. Whitmore paused, looking into the distance, attempting to find the words.

"I am not certain that I know exactly what I sensed, but he almost seems desperate, and I do not know what he will attempt. At the very least, he might compromise you without realizing it, so lacking is his understanding of even the rudiments of propriety."

"Thank you for your warning, Mr. Whitmore. I have no desire to be shackled to Mr. Collins for the rest of my life. I will take care."

Nodding, Mr. Whitmore excused himself, leaving the two sisters alone. Kitty turned to Elizabeth, and in a low voice, said: "I think I would almost rather wed Uncle Phillips's crotchety old manservant, rather than Mr. Collins."

"I do not disagree with you, Kitty," said Elizabeth.

It would be a long two weeks, Elizabeth decided, for she doubted Mr. Collins would be leaving before the end of them.

The next day, Elizabeth was forced to own to some curiosity. There had been no word from Lucas Lodge concerning Mr. Collins, and though she hoped he had departed that morning to return to his home, she thought it likely that was not the case. Therefore, she determined to walk there and see for herself.

"Are you certain that is wise, Lizzy?" asked Kitty when Elizabeth stated her intention.

"Perhaps not," conceded Elizabeth. "But I believe it would be best to know if Mr. Collins will remain in the area."

It was clear that Kitty did not quite agree with Elizabeth's assessment, but she readily agreed to accompany her. After Elizabeth's morning tasks were complete, they made ready to depart. Mr. Whitmore, though he did not say anything, looked at Elizabeth as if to remind her of their conversation from the day before, and though Elizabeth appreciated his care, she truly did not require the reminder.

It was a bit of a blustery morning, and the girls' skirts were whipped about as they walked, winding in among their legs, blowing at their hair in an attempt to remove it from its confinements. Though Kitty muttered at the inclement weather, annoyed at the way it treated them as they walked, Elizabeth, who had rarely gone more than a day or two without walking, rather enjoyed the bracing winds. It was evidence of the continuance of life, the ability to go on, to better herself and make her father proud of her.

As it was not a great distance to walk, the sisters soon arrived at Lucas Lodge. As they entered the entrance hall, they passed their outer wear to the waiting housekeeper, and it was there that any residual hope Elizabeth had for Mr. Collins's early departure were proven to be unfounded. For as soon as they entered they could hear the sonorous tones of Mr. Collins's voice pontificating on some matter or another. The two sisters shared a look and a grimace before they allowed themselves to be led to Lady Lucas's parlor.

There they found, as Elizabeth had expected, Mr. Collins sitting with the Lucas family. Charlotte and Maria were gazing at the man with, it seemed, perpetual expressions of shock, while the oldest son, Samuel, watched him with sardonic amusement. Sir William appeared almost confused, while Lady Lucas seemed hopeful. Elizabeth grimaced; clearly she regarded the man as a prospect for her eldest daughter who, though not yet on the shelf, was two years older than Elizabeth. Charlotte's obvious disinclination for him encouraged Elizabeth, but she could not know for certain what would happen should a proposal be offered.

"Miss Bennet, Miss Catherine!" exclaimed Mr. Collins when he espied them entering the room. Quickly he was on his feet, honoring them with another low bow. Then he straightened and leered at Elizabeth, seemingly pleased with himself. "How kind of you to join us this fine morning. Shall you not sit down?"

The man offered his arm to Elizabeth, but she was not about to allow him to see any encouragement—real, or imagined—in his supposed interest in her. So, she curtseyed to him and murmured a greeting, and sat beside Charlotte, noting that Kitty had sat next to Maria, striving to be as far away from the parson as she could contrive. Mr. Collins, though seeming confused for a moment, returned to his seat, already speaking of some nonsense.

"I must own to some confusion, Mr. Collins," said Elizabeth when the man paused to take a breath. "I had thought you would be off to return to your home by now."

"Indeed, no," said Mr. Collins, casting a pleased smile at his host. "Sir William graciously extended an invitation to host me until it is time for me to return to Kent, since you could not be induced to receive me at Longbourn." Mr. Collins paused, seemingly still annoyed at being banished to Lucas Lodge. "Thus, I shall remain steady to my purpose."

"That is . . . fortunate, indeed."

The variety of responses to the man's statement was fascinating to Elizabeth, but the most interesting was the one from Sir William. Given his grimace, Elizabeth thought he had already learned to regret his decision to allow the man to stay, which was no less than astonishing, considering his prodigious talent for civility.

Even though the parlor was full, Mr. Collins spoke more than the rest combined. No subject seemed too dull for his attention, and he flitted from one to the next as fancy took him, often without any evident correlation. His favorite topic was, of course, his patroness, Lady Catherine de Bourgh, and he seemed to believe that the woman could do no wrong. To Elizabeth, she sounded like a rank dullard, and a meddlesome one, if stories of her condescension and advice were any indication.

"It was Lady Catherine's express wish that I repair to Hertfordshire in order to repair the breach between our families," pontificated Mr. Collins at one point. "'Mr. Collins,' said she, 'there can be nothing so odious as strife within families. My brother, the earl, will not tolerate it, and I myself insist on peace and harmony. You must repair the rift as soon as may be, for if you do not, how will you be able to stand as an example before your parish?'

"Lady Catherine is so wise, and her munificence so boundless, that I instantly determined to make the attempt, for though my cousin Bennet cared not to mend what lay between us during his life, I was certain that now that he has passed on it is possible. And if there are other . . . benefits to be had for taking this step," Mr. Collins paused and leered at Elizabeth, "then I can only be thankful that God has put forth a plan for my life."

By this time, Elizabeth had had enough of the odious man, and as visiting time had sufficiently passed, she decided it was time to leave him to the Lucases.

"You are fortunate, indeed. But if you would excuse us, I believe Kitty and I must depart for town."

"Oh, you are to walk to Meryton?" asked Mr. Collins. He clapped his hands and nodded vigorously. "Perhaps we should make an outing of it, for I would dearly love to hear more of your home. Accompanying you to the town would be agreeable indeed."

Realizing she should have best remained silent, Elizabeth tried to dissuade him, but he would not be gainsaid. To town, he was determined to follow them.

"Then Maria and I will accompany you," said Charlotte, looking on them with compassion. "I believe Mama has an errand or two for us anyway."

Grateful for Charlotte's perception, Elizabeth accepted the offer, and soon the two Bennet sisters, in the company of the two Lucas sisters and the ponderous Mr. Collins, departed for Meryton. If Elizabeth had expected the man to walk silently or divide his attentions between the four young ladies, she was destined to be disappointed, for Mr. Collins did nothing of the sort. Instead, he attached himself to Elizabeth and refused to leave her side, allowing her to talk to no one else and continuing on with his monologue the entire distance. By the time they reached the town, less than a mile from the Lucas estate, Elizabeth was considering the benefits of acquiring a muzzle for the ever-loquacious Mr. Collins!

In town they walked from shop to shop, stopping in a few. Kitty wished to enter the haberdashery to obtain a length of ribbon for a bonnet she wished to re-trim, while the Lucas sisters stopped to have a word with the butcher regarding an order their mother had commissioned. They stopped at the confectioners for a few sweet treats so adored by the younger girls; they would have been even merrier had Mr. Collins and his droning voice not been present.

When they had been there for some time and were about to turn back for Lucas Lodge, they happened to meet an acquaintance. Mr. Denny was a member of the militia quartered there and a great favorite among the ladies, not only for his good looks, but also for his happy manners and his ability to induce laughter with a quick quip or a compliment. To Elizabeth, he was one of the more sensible officers, and one whom she thought the members of the small community could trust not to misbehave.

Mr. Denny had been away recently, apparently on business in London, and as a result, it had been some days since they had last seen him. On this particular day, he was accompanied by a tall gentleman, with dark wavy hair and kind brown eyes. The man walked with an erect bearing, almost aristocratic, and he carried himself as if he was no stranger to the sitting-rooms of the quality. Every eye seemed to follow him as he walked along the street, and it was no surprise to Elizabeth that both Maria and Kitty watched his coming with giggles of anticipation.

"Have you ever seen such a handsome gentleman?" asked Maria to Kitty, their heads close together. The only reason Elizabeth could hear their discussion was because she was standing close behind them.

"Very handsome," replied Kitty. "But I cannot think him anything to

Mr. Bingley."

Maria looked at Kitty and giggled. "Of course *you* would think so. You are madly in love with him, after all."

"I am not!" replied Kitty hotly. Then she smiled tentatively. "But I do think him to be the most handsome and amiable man of my acquaintance. Besides, Mr. Bingley is wealthy and able to afford a wife."

"But you have a dowry which could be used to tempt a man to marry you. He does not even have to be rich."

"Perhaps not," replied Kitty. "But my dowry is not exorbitant. The interest on a dowry might help keep us in comfort, if used prudently, but it would be difficult to continue to live in the style to which I am accustomed at Longbourn"

"Aye, then a man such as Mr. Bingley might be for the best. Lizzy may marry where she likes, with Longbourn as her dowry."

Kitty glanced back at Elizabeth, who was studiously ignoring them, watching the gentlemen approaching. She was curious as to this conversation and wished to know how it would play out.

"And I am very happy for her. She has always wished to marry for love, you know, and now she has the means to do so. I also wish to marry for love, but I will be required to be a little more judicious."

As the young men had almost reached them, the two girls ceased their whispering, but Elizabeth, rather than focus on them, thought about the girls' conversation, deciding that she was excessively proud of Kitty. Her feelings for Mr. Bingley were, Elizabeth thought, nothing more than an infatuation at present, but at least Kitty looked on him with favor for the proper reasons. Her comments about prudence were also a welcome indication of Kitty's continued growth.

By then the two men had joined them and greetings were shared by all with the lieutenant.

"Will you not introduce us to your friend?" asked Maria, almost speaking over the greetings in her eagerness.

Mr. Denny laughed and motioned to his companion. "This is my friend, George Wickham. Wickham, this is Miss Lucas and Miss Maria Lucas, and Miss Bennet and Miss Kitty Bennet.

"And this is our cousin, Mr. Collins," said Elizabeth, stepping forward to complete the office.

Mr. Collins bowed in response, though Elizabeth noted that it was not so low as was his wont. Apparently he considered himself above these men and thought he had no reason to impress them.

"Wickham and I have been acquainted for some years, and met by chance when I was in London," continued Mr. Denny. "He accompanied me here to see about an open commission in the regiment."

"I dare say you will do your regimentals much distinction, Mr. Wickham," said Maria.

"Maria," said Charlotte in an undertone, admonishing her sister for her forwardness.

"I thank you," said Mr. Wickham, ignoring the girl's less than proper behavior. "I must own that I am happy to be here, as those that I have met so far have been kind and obliging."

Mr. Denny turned and teased his friend. "As of yet, these people are the *only* ones you have met!"

"Exactly," replied Mr. Wickham to the sound of general laughter.

The group stood there for some minutes speaking, and Elizabeth watched the newcomer curiously. It was clear that he was an amiable man, as he spoke with all and sundry with ease and gentlemanly comportment. Elizabeth wondered at his background—with such manners she thought it likely that he must be the son of a gentleman, though he did not offer any information concerning his origins.

Conversation was fluid for the most part, and soon Elizabeth found herself the sole recipient of Mr. Wickham's attention, as the other three ladies were clustered around Mr. Denny, hearing about his recent journey to London.

"Do you live nearby, Miss Bennet?"

"Just a mile up the road," replied Elizabeth, gesturing toward the lane which led toward Lucas Lodge and Longbourn.

"Excellent! Then I am certain we shall be seeing much of each other, as Denny tells me that the regiment is often invited to the events of the area."

"Indeed, they are. We are happy to have them winter with us, for they provide new conversation partners and interesting people to meet."

"Dare I assume that I am one of those interesting people?"

Elizabeth laughed. "I suppose only time will tell, Mr. Wickham. I believe you are off to a charming start."

"And I have never met such pleasant girls in my life. I believe that we shall be great friends."

"Perhaps it would be best not to speak in such flirtatious tones."

The sound of a voice directly behind her startled Elizabeth, and she stepped to the side quickly. Having forgotten about Mr. Collins, his interruption—and especially the way in which he startled her—was not at all welcome.

"It was nothing more than casual conversation between newly acquainted people," replied Mr. Wickham easily.

Elizabeth looked at him gratefully for allowing her to collect herself. But Mr. Collins was not finished speaking.

"Perhaps so, but as my benevolent patroness, Lady Catherine de Bourgh, always says, one cannot be too careful of one's behavior, lest one be seen as improper. For a woman in your position, Cousin Elizabeth, you must take great care. I would not wish for others to misconstrue our relationship."

"There *is* nothing to misconstrue, Mr. Collins," said Elizabeth irritably. "And I will thank you not to speak in such a way."

"Lady Catherine de Bourgh?" said Mr. Wickham, just as Mr. Collins was about to make some response. "That great lady is your patroness?"

Mr. Collins looked on Mr. Wickham with astonishment. "You know Lady Catherine?"

"I do indeed, Mr. Collins, though not well, you understand. She is the aunt of a . . . friend of mine, and though I have not seen her in many years, I recall her as a busy, forthright sort of person."

"She is, indeed!" exclaimed Mr. Collins. He stepped toward Mr. Wickham eagerly, his sudden change in demeanor amusing. "What a fortunate coincidence, sir. I had not thought to meet anyone this far from Kent who was familiar with my patroness, though I suppose it should not be surprising. Her wisdom must be known throughout the land, so great and benevolent is she."

"Indeed, sir. I could not have said it better myself."

As Mr. Collins attempted to speak again, Mr. Wickham held up his hand. "While I would like nothing better than to compare our remembrances of Lady Catherine, I believe I must depart, for I am scheduled to meet with my new commanding officer."

"And we should be returning to our homes," said Elizabeth. "I thank you for your conversation, sir. I hope we will meet again."

"As do I, Miss Bennet. As do I."

There was some quality in Mr. Wickham's voice which brought Elizabeth up short, though she was not certain at all what disturbed her. He was still the same amiable gentleman he had been the whole time they had been speaking, but his words now seemed to convey some deeper meaning which Elizabeth could not quite fathom.

The ensuing farewells put the matter from Elizabeth's mind, and within moments, the ladies—in the unwanted company of Mr. Collins—had started down the street, headed for their homes. As they departed, Elizabeth chanced a look back and she noted Mr. Wickham, standing beside Mr. Denny, watching them. And though she could not be certain, she thought that his eyes were fixed upon her particularly. Though Elizabeth did not quite know why, she shivered.

Chapter VII

"*L*ovely ladies abound! Did I not tell you, Wickham?" A nudge in the ribs accompanied the jovial statement.

Wickham turned to his friend and smiled. "You did, indeed. I dare say that I have never seen so many who were so handsome."

"Aye, that is true. And you have been fortunate to have met the jewels of the bunch. The Miss Bennets are the loveliest ladies in the district, though I dare say the two Lucas girls are very pretty in their own right."

"Particularly Miss Bennet," replied Wickham. "Such dark, expressive eyes, such beautiful dark hair. A man could be lost looking into such a pretty face for a lifetime."

Denny slapped Wickham on the back. "Trust you to choose the prettiest girl to receive your attentions, eh, Wickham? For myself, though I will grant that Miss Bennet is very pretty, she is also very intelligent and well-read, and apparently manages her estate as well as any man. In truth, some of the men find her a little intimidating, though she in no way attempts to alarm.

"Her sister, on the other hand." Denny stopped and smiled. "Miss Kitty is like a breath of fresh air. She is happy and eager to laugh, and her blonde hair and dark eyes are more than a match for her sister's beauty, in my opinion."

"I could not agree more, my friend," murmured Wickham in response.

They watched the group as they departed, and when they had disappeared from sight, Wickham followed Denny away toward the colonel's headquarters, his mind full of thoughts of the people that they had just met. As they walked, Denny chattered on, speaking of the wonders of local society, and though Wickham might have preferred that he be silent, he could only look on with amusement. Denny was a good fellow, if a bit of a simple soul. He was invaluable as a friend, as Wickham had cause to appreciate at present, even if it meant he must don a red coat for the occasion.

The truth was that Wickham had nearly depleted his available funds, and though he was certain that military life would not agree with him, he thought he could put up with it for a time. Opportunities did not fall into one's lap—over the years, Wickham had learned this truth over and over again. It sometimes required bold action and the willingness to put oneself out to affect a change in one's fortunes. Wickham had no doubt that his time in Meryton would be profitable indeed. He had only to play his part and allow the rest to fall into place.

Caroline Bingley was not a happy woman. She had come to Hertfordshire with great reluctance, knowing, even as she had agreed to act as hostess for her brother at his leased estate, that the local society would be savage, the fashion would be out of date and that there would be no one worth seeing, or to be seen by, and precious little conversation which would interest her. She fully expected a sense of ennui to come over her, leave her snappish and irritable within days of arriving.

In fact, the only reason Caroline had agreed to it at all was that her brother had invited Mr. Darcy to accompany him to the estate, ostensibly to assist him in matters of the estate and school him in those things he needed to know in preparation for his own purchase at a later date. The fact that Charles had, as yet, taken little interest in the estate and had left everything to Mr. Darcy only fueled Caroline's contempt for him. He had no ambition other than the next dance with the next pretty girl and was content to do nothing but live off the interest of his inheritance from their father. Mr. Darcy, on the other hand . . .

It was for Mr. Darcy and no other that Caroline was currently residing at Netherfield. The man was handsome, tall, broad-shouldered, intelligent, and in possession of seemingly every virtue. In Caroline's eyes, his most important virtues were the possession of a fine estate in Derbyshire, several satellite estates scattered throughout the country, a grand house in town, and connections to the highest echelons of society. He was all Caroline had ever craved in a husband, and she meant to have him.

This stay in the hinterlands of Hertfordshire, therefore, was to be Caroline's crowning achievement. Caroline had never forgotten her family's despised roots in trade, and she had always known that it would be difficult to attract Mr. Darcy's exclusive attention. On the other hand, such marriages were becoming more common, and the longer Mr. Darcy remained unattached — and perhaps more importantly, the longer he continued without showing even the slightest hint of interest in *any* other young woman — the more confident Caroline became that he would ultimately choose her for his future wife.

As long as she had been watching him, following his every move, analyzing his every interaction with every available woman, she had never seen him pay anything more than the most basic civility to anyone. He was invariably polite, unfailingly proper, and unstintingly kind, but his manners never went beyond these basic qualities. Once she had learned that she would have a captive audience the entire time of their stay in Hertfordshire, Caroline had been certain that she would finally succeed.

She knew she must succeed, for that blasted Lady Marion had goaded her, and she knew that she would be a laughing stock if she did not succeed. The gossips of society were merciless, a fact Caroline knew well, as she had often taken part in tearing another's reputation apart. She had no desire to become a victim of the same behavior.

And Caroline was certain she would not fail. At least, she had been certain until meeting Miss Elizabeth Bennet.

To be fair, Mr. Darcy's behavior when in company with Miss Bennet was no different from that he displayed with any other young woman. But for someone who had watched Mr. Darcy for so long and had attempted to catalogue all of his interactions with the intensity that Caroline Bingley had, the slightest deviation from his typical behavior was certain to attract attention, and his interactions with Miss Bennet had done so. Caroline could not put her finger on it, but she knew that on some level, whether he even knew it yet himself, Mr. Darcy admired Miss Elizabeth Bennet. It might lead to nothing, but Caroline was not inclined to take that chance.

Something must be done. Caroline simply did not know what, just yet.

Two days after they had seen the chits at church, her brother had declared his intention to visit Longbourn. It appeared that he was concerned because of Mr. Darcy's comments of the girl's cough, though Caroline was certain it had been nothing more than feigned.

"It is good manners to visit and inquire after her health," said Charles as he ate his breakfast.

"Indeed, it is," added Mr. Darcy. "Though the affliction was slight and I expect her to be fully recovered, still it is the proper thing to do."

Inside Caroline seethed. Mr. Darcy's words effectively negated her desire to object to her brother's design. Though Caroline wished for nothing less than to go visit them, it seemed she had no choice.

Her first impression of the Bennet estate was not positive. The park in which it sat was pretty enough, but it was dreadfully small and nothing compared to even Netherfield, which itself had little to recommend it. The manor house was made of red brick, with ivy climbing the walls, but it was a small building, only two stories, and gave a cramped, inferior sort of feeling. The inside was not much better, as the furnishings were dreadfully out of fashion, and the sitting-room was small.

And there, inside, sitting there waiting, like a queen about to hold court, sat Miss Eliza Bennet. For the first time since coming to the insignificant neighborhood, Caroline realized that she absolutely despised the woman. She would remain watchful, and should anything present itself as a means to discredit the woman, Caroline would take it. She did not mean to lose to such a woman as Miss Bennet.

Darcy's reaction to his first sight of Longbourn could not have been more different from Miss Bingley's. The estate was not large, it was true, but the house and grounds were well maintained, the workmanship obviously fine, and the décor was simple, yet tastefully done. In fact, it reminded him greatly of a property he owned in Staffordshire, an estate whose annual income was similar to what he suspected Longbourn's to be.

"Miss Bennet, Miss Kitty," said Bingley, leading the way into the sitting-room to greet the two ladies waiting there. "We thought we would come to inquire after Miss Kitty's health. Might we hope that you are recovered?"

Miss Kitty blushed, confirming Darcy's suspicion that she fancied herself in love with his friend, but she replied with perfect composure.

"Thank you, Mr. Bingley, I am very well, thank you. It was nothing more than a bit of a cough."

"I am happy to hear it. One can never be too careful with one's health."

The company sat down and began to speak, and though Darcy was situated near Miss Bennet and fell into conversation with her, he could see that Bingley had sat beside Miss Kitty. Mrs. Hurst and Miss Bingley were situated on a sofa on the other side of a long table, but though Mrs. Hurst took part in Darcy's conversation with Miss Bennet, Miss Bingley stayed silent, looking about the room—and especially at the Bennet sisters, he noted—with a hint of disdain.

"I trust all is well at Longbourn," said Darcy to Miss Bennet.

"Yes, Mr. Darcy, I thank you. As the work of the summer months has been completed, we are quite settled in for the winter, awaiting spring. I am indeed anticipating the coming year, for I shall then be of age, free to manage Longbourn as I please."

Darcy regarded her with amusement. "And you do not enjoy that privilege at present?"

Blushing slightly, Miss Bennet nevertheless returned his look with one of her own. "Well, I will own that my uncle leaves the details to me, but as I am not of age, my uncle is required to ratify any major decisions. After my birthday in early July, that will no longer be required."

"Then I am happy for you. I can well remember my own coming of age. But you should consider that being an adult does not necessarily mean that you are completely free."

"Of course not!" replied Miss Bennet with a laugh. "There will always be responsibilities and demands on our time, no matter how old we are. I am grateful to my uncle for the assistance he has provided, but I believe I would much rather do as I will. It takes time to help him understand what I wish to do, and as he is a man of business—and not a gentleman farmer—it is sometimes difficult. I am certain he is as eager as I for his responsibility to end!"

"I am certain he cannot but be happy to assist."

"We are in a similar position," said Mrs. Hurst, joining the conversation for the first time. "Our uncle—father's eldest brother—is the one who actually manages the family business. It is this that allows my brother the leisure to lease an estate in preparation for when he eventually purchases."

"But we have nothing to do with the business any longer," said Miss Bingley, quick to disavow her family's history. "We are firmly of the ranks of the landed now. Or we will be, should Charles ever get around to finally making a purchase."

"There is nothing wrong with making a living through trade, Miss Bingley," said Miss Bennet. "My own uncle has built his business himself, and now he makes more in a year than Longbourn produces.

Your own father must be an example of this, considering your brother's intentions for the future."

"I agree," added Darcy. "Business and trade are the wave of the future, and though land ownership will always have its place, already many of the tradesman class have made large fortunes and obtained fabulous wealth through their own tenacity and hard work. They are to be commended."

Rather than respond to what was, after all, a compliment of the highest order, Miss Bingley only sniffed and turned away. Her withdrawal from the conversation was no great loss, as those remaining were happy to continue without her.

The visit went on apace, and as the time progressed, Darcy became aware of two things. The first was that his admiration Miss Bennet continued to grow the more he knew of her. She was a young woman yet, still not even of age, and yet she had risen to the challenge of managing her father's estate and had by all accounts increased its income. She was intelligent and quick, always ready with a response or a humorous quip, and though she sometimes teased, her tone made it evident she did so with affection, and her manner disarmed reproof.

The second thing he noted was the return of Bingley as he had known the man before coming to Hertfordshire. Bingley was, by nature, an open, jovial sort of man, happy in company, and at ease with anyone. He was also, however, a man whose head was easily turned by a pretty face, not to mention long, blonde tresses.

Darcy had not seen a hint of infatuation with any of the local girls since they had arrived in Meryton, and Darcy had begun to think that they might finally have found a place where he would *not* fall in and out of love in the space of a few weeks. It was a welcome change, for to Darcy, serious minded as he was, Bingley's habit was unseemly. He never set out to break hearts, but Darcy had sure knowledge of more than one woman injured by the cessation of his attentions.

Until now, that is. For Bingley had sat beside Miss Kitty the entire time of their visit, speaking animatedly with her, laughing, talking, and jesting. And by the time the half hour of their visit had expired, and Bingley rose, bowing over Miss Kitty's hand, Darcy was once again concerned for his friend's actions. Miss Kitty had already shown an infatuation with him. Darcy did not wish for her to be hurt if he should withdraw his attentions which, given Bingley's history, he almost certainly would.

This was further evidenced by Bingley's behavior when they rose to depart. Darcy had seen the exact same scene unfold many times—too many for him to mistake what he saw. Bingley rose with Miss Kitty, bowed over her hand, and flashed her his most winsome smile.

"I thank you for a wonderful time, Miss Kitty. I enjoyed speaking with you."

Miss Kitty, though she was clearly aflutter with his actions, nevertheless responded with all the appearance of calm. "I thank *you*, Mr. Bingley. I have enjoyed this opportunity to come to know you as well."

The visitors soon made their way from the room, and Darcy, though he took leave of the Bennets with every civility, he was in fact considering his friend. Not for the first time, he wished that Bingley was a little more serious of mind and careful in forming his attachments. He was a good man and a good friend, but sometimes his judgment was overwhelmed by a pretty face, and he was always impetuous.

They made their way out to the front drive of the house, the Bennets accompanying them, when Darcy saw the approach of someone he thought he knew.

"Adam Whitmore?" asked he, incredulous at the sight of the man.

"Mr. Darcy," replied Whitmore, bowing low.

"I never thought to see you here," said Darcy with pleasure, stepping forward to shake the other man's hand. "So this is the estate that lured you away from Snowlock?"

"It is indeed, Mr. Darcy," replied Whitmore. "Miss Bennet's uncle does business with your uncle, and when he was searching for a steward to manage the estate, your uncle put me forward as a candidate."

"Yes, my uncle mentioned something of that nature. But you were in line to take over as steward at Snowlock, and though Longbourn is a worthy estate, you must confess that Snowlock is much larger, and potentially would have paid much more."

"That is true," said Whitmore. "But old Dawkins is unlikely to release his iron grip on your uncle's estate for another decade or two."

Darcy laughed at Whitmore's portrayal and allowed it to be so.

"I decided I would rather be the steward of an estate than the understudy for God alone knew how long. And with the improvements Miss Bennet has been making, Longbourn might be the rival of Snowlock someday."

"I do not doubt it, my friend."

"Besides," continued Whitmore with a shrug, "taking over the stewardship of Longbourn has had its own benefits. I am now married; my wife is the housekeeper of Longbourn."

"That is excellent news, my friend," replied Darcy, happy for the man he had always known was an exceptional one. "I wish you every joy."

"Excuse me, Mr. Darcy," said Miss Bennet, stepping forward to stand next to them. She was watching them both, clearly confused at their having known each other. "I was not aware that you were acquainted with my steward."

"Your uncle hired me from my position as an assistant to the steward at Snowlock, the Earl of Matlock's estate," said Whitmore. "As Mr. Darcy is quite close to his Fitzwilliam relations and had occasion to visit many times, I have had dealings with him."

"Whitmore is an excellent steward, Miss Bennet. Your uncle did well in hiring him. I do not doubt your estate is in good hands with Whitmore."

"Thank you, Mr. Darcy," said Miss Bennet. "I can make no dispute to that claim. Mr. Whitmore has been invaluable since his arrival here." Miss Bennet turned to Mr. Whitmore, regarding him with a raised eyebrow. "You never mentioned that you were familiar with Mr. Darcy, though his name has come up between us."

"I did not think it signified, Miss Bennet. My acquaintance with Mr. Darcy is a slight one. I would never had dreamt to impose upon him or claim an acquaintance which was not warranted."

"Now you exaggerate, Whitmore. I am quite familiar with your work."

"Thank you, sir."

"Mr. Darcy, we are fatigued." Miss Bingley stepped up beside him and looked at him with what she must have thought was beguiling eyes. "Shall we not depart?"

"Of course, Miss Bingley." Darcy turned back to Miss Bennet and Mr. Whitmore. "Miss Bennet, thank you for receiving us. Whitmore, it was a pleasure to see you again."

The final few words were exchanged and soon the Netherfield party was ensconced in the carriage, and the driver was given the command to depart. Darcy, amused at finding a familiar face at Longbourn, spent much of the return journey thinking of the matter. If Whitmore was the man entrusted with Longbourn's management and the protection of the Miss Bennets, then Darcy felt easier about their situation. Certainly Whitmore was an excellent man, and as he was now tied to the estate via a marriage with the housekeeper, Darcy knew he would not soon leave.

An additional benefit to Darcy's preoccupation was his ability to ignore Miss Bingley's words about their visit to Longbourn. He had heard her speak on the subject before, so there was nothing new that he wished to hear.

* * *

At Longbourn, the discussion was much different, though, the same as in the carriage, it did center about those with whom they had just been in company. But rather than speak of the faults of those recently departed, Elizabeth was treated to a constant commentary about Mr. Bingley, his amiability his handsome countenance, and his ability to make Kitty laugh.

"I have never seen such happy manners, Lizzy," said Kitty for about the third time since the Netherfield party had departed. "He is everything one could wish for in a young man, and so particularly well situated."

"Yes, he is that, indeed," murmured Elizabeth.

Luckily, Kitty was so lost in her thoughts and reminiscences that she had no ability to listen to her sister. Elizabeth watched her for some moments, thinking about the situation, wondering if she should say something to Kitty. In the time since their family had passed on, leaving them together, Elizabeth had undertaken the care of her sister, who was three years younger than Elizabeth herself. Though Elizabeth had attempted to be an elder sister and confidante, there were times when, inevitably, their relationship more approximated one between a mother and her daughter. This was due not only to the fact that Elizabeth was the one who led while Kitty followed, but also because Kitty's behavior had often not been the best, and Elizabeth felt it incumbent upon her to make sure Kitty learned how to conduct herself properly.

As Kitty had improved, Elizabeth had taken care to turn their relationship more to the one normally shared by sisters, and while there were still times when Kitty required instruction rather than sisterly companionship, they had settled into a closer relationship than they had ever shared before. Elizabeth had perhaps been closer with Jane, and Kitty, with Lydia, but now, having been alone for more than a year and a half, Elizabeth thought that those relationships were paling compared to the one Kitty and Elizabeth shared now. Then, they had had the other members of their family for support—now, in a large part, they relied upon each other.

As she thought on the matter for some little time, Elizabeth decided that she would speak to Kitty on the subject of Mr. Bingley, but that she would attempt to speak more like a sister than a guardian.

"Kitty," said Elizabeth when her sister had paused, a dreamy sort of smile fixed upon her face. "I am happy that you are pleased with Mr. Bingley's attentions."

"As am I, Sister," replied Kitty shyly. "Would it not be a good joke if

I, the younger sister, were married before you?"

Elizabeth laughed. "I believe that is something Lydia might have said."

Though she had not intended her words to be an insult, Kitty's cheeks bloomed. "I . . . I am s-sorry, Lizzy," stammered Kitty. "I had not meant to offend."

"And you did not offend me, dearest," said Elizabeth. She moved a little closer to her sister and caught Kitty's hands in her own. "I was not intending to censure; rather it was a fond remembrance of Lydia, who, as you recall, was obsessed with being married — before the rest of her sisters, if she could manage it."

"She was," said Kitty. "She talked about it constantly."

Nodding, Elizabeth said: "I shall not become angry for your outburst as it did not injure me. But please remember that others might be offended by such a statement."

"I shall. I believe I am much better about holding my tongue on such occasions."

"So you are." Elizabeth paused, looking at her sister, projecting concern, rather than sternness, which she thought would help Kitty accept her words rather than becoming hurt.

"As for Mr. Bingley, he is a handsome and amiable man, and I give you leave to like him." The sisters laughed together. "Just remember to respond to his overtures with composure and dignity, and do not expect too much from him at present."

A frown fell over Kitty's face. "You do not think he likes me? He spoke exclusively to me, and was ever so polite and interested in what I had to say."

"I do not think that way at all, Kitty. But you have not known each other long, and we still know relatively little of Mr. Bingley's character."

When Kitty still frowned, Elizabeth squeezed her hands and favored her with an affectionate smile.

"I am not casting any aspersions at Mr. Bingley's character, nor am I suggesting that you are not behaving properly. I only advise that you enjoy his attentions and conversation without espousing any particular expectations at this time. You are still very young, Kitty, and there is no need for you to hurry to find your companion in life. Have fun and enjoy your time with him. If your relationship does become a loving one in which you wish to join your lives together, I will be the first to congratulate you and wish you well. But do not expect anything from Mr. Bingley that he may be unwilling to give. If it does not turn out the way you wish, you will be disappointed, and I would not wish that for you."

Kitty was silent for a few moments, thinking about Elizabeth's words. In time, however, a tentative smile came over her face, and she looked at Elizabeth shyly.

"I understand what you are trying to tell me. I shall try to keep my heart under good regulation."

"I am happy to hear it."

The sisters embraced and then separated until luncheon. Elizabeth repaired to the study to complete some tasks which awaited her there, while Kitty gathered her outer wear for a walk about the grounds. Elizabeth was happy to see her sister looking so thoughtful and loath to see her hurt, should she expect too much from Mr. Bingley.

Chapter VIII

For the next few days, Elizabeth existed in an almost constant state of exasperation, and it was all due to the unwanted attentions of her obsequious cousin, Mr. Collins. Elizabeth made a conscious decision to avoid Lucas Lodge those days, knowing her cousin would be there, and wishing to refrain from putting herself in his presence as much as possible.

But she had not counted on the fact that Collins would do everything in his power to put *himself* into her company and would visit her at Longbourn every day. Although for a man to visit a young woman alone was far from proper, and Elizabeth thought she could simply bar him from the house, she was frustrated in this design, as he seemed to have a willing accomplice.

The first time he arrived at Longbourn in the company of Elizabeth's closest friend, she frowned at Charlotte. The only answer she received, however, was a shrug and a smile, with an eyebrow raised in Mr. Collins's direction. Needless to say, Elizabeth was not amused. She decided to let the matter pass in favor of keeping cordial relations with Charlotte.

When they once again arrived at Longbourn the very next morning, Elizabeth was not in a very charitable mood, a fact which her friend seemed to sense. Fortunately, it was easy to have a quick word with her friend, as Mr. Collins could drone on about nothing for hours without ever requiring a response. It was while Mr. Collins was thus engaged that Elizabeth eased close to her friend and fixed her with a stern glare.

"What do you mean by bringing Mr. Collins to Longbourn, Charlotte?" hissed she.

Charlotte's innocent expression did not cool Elizabeth's temper, and neither did her words. "Should you not share in the joy of your cousin's attentions?"

"I would truly prefer to defer the pleasure," said Elizabeth, "if I can manage it, indefinitely."

"But he is your guest, in a roundabout way."

"He would not be, if your father had simply sent him on his way."

Far from being offended by Elizabeth's words, Charlotte appeared amused. "I am sure you are correct, but you know it is not in my father's nature to simply ship him back to Kent. The moment you contacted my father about housing for the night, his residence in Hertfordshire was assured."

"Perhaps," said Elizabeth, a sour taste entering her mouth in large part because she knew her friend was correct. "I would hope you would assist in keeping him away from me. After all, it is not *you* he is pursuing so assiduously."

"No, but my mother wishes it was."

"Your mother has been pushing you at Mr. Collins?"

Charlotte shook her head with rueful exasperation. "She has not been nearly so overt as that, but she has made it clear that it would be agreeable to her should Mr. Collins turn his attentions on me, as it is obvious that you do not welcome them."

"Then why do you and Mr. Collins come here?"

"Because Mr. Collins is intent upon visiting you, and he will do so regardless of our words to the contrary. You may not admit him to the estate, but we both know that he will force you to meet him outside, attempt to court you in the paths behind Longbourn."

"Lady Lucas underestimates me," muttered Elizabeth. "I would much prefer to force him to stay outside and hope he caught a cold. Then, at least, he would be bedridden, and I would not be forced to put up with him."

Charlotte could not stifle a laugh, which drew Mr. Collins's attention. He fixed a beatific smile upon them, though it was clear he had no notion of what was so amusing. Within moments, he was once again speaking, leaving Elizabeth and Charlotte to their conversation.

"Mayhap my mother does underestimate you, but she does not want to take the chance of leaving you alone with him. After all, he might eventually wear you down."

"You may tell your mother that she has nothing to fear from me."

This time Charlotte disguised her laughter and avoided drawing Mr. Collins's attention. "I had not expected anything less of you. But my mother does not know you as well as I do."

Elizabeth nodded, but she decided that there was nothing to be done on the matter. Instead, she turned her attention to her friend's predicament.

"And what is your opinion concerning Mr. Collins?"

A shaken head was Charlotte's reply, confirming Elizabeth's suspicion. "I am almost three and twenty, but I am not yet desperate enough to accept such objectionable attentions. It is clear that Mr. Collins has his sights set upon an estate, and not a relatively dowerless girl to take back to his parsonage. My mother seems to have her heart set on the match, but as I am of age, I may choose to refuse him, and my father will support me."

"Then I wish you luck, if such an eventuality does come about. As for myself, there is nothing that will induce me to accept him. If it were not so improper for me to bring the matter up myself, I would make it clear to him myself."

"I have no doubt you would, Eliza."

And thus, Elizabeth was forced to bear with the attentions of the ridiculous man. She made some attempt to inform him that she was not interested, but Mr. Collins was as dense as the day was long. Nothing she said had any effect on him, and it seemed like their every interaction convinced the man that she was madly in love with him.

And even worse, he had little to say which did not refer to their "close" relationship as cousins, his pride at his ability to rise so quickly to be the pastor of a valuable living, and the beneficence of his patroness. Of the last subject, there was comparably more than the first two, and thus, the subject irritated Elizabeth far more. She heartily wished that Mr. Collins would feel bereft at the distance from the woman and speedily return to Kent.

"Lady Catherine is all that is condescending and attentive," said Mr. Collins, forgetting that he had already told them of the woman's instructing him to come to Hertfordshire. His voice had risen when he turned the subject to his patroness, infused by the manic quality which always entered it whenever he spoke of the woman. Though it was only the third day of the man's visits, it already seemed like he had been in residence for a month.

"There is nothing which is beyond her attention, and her suggestions are all so intelligent, her thoughts so profound, that I cannot but follow them. She is aware of everything that happens in the parish and will not allow any to live in disharmony. In fact, she is the arbiter who brings about peaceful relations and prosperity for everyone. All those who live within the reach of her influence must, necessarily, give thanks to her for our very livelihoods. I cannot imagine there to be any greater or wiser lady in all the land."

Though she had already heard much of the woman, Mr. Collins's words only strengthened Elizabeth opinion that Lady Catherine was a busybody, one who pried into the affairs of others and browbeat them until they did what she instructed them to do. Furthermore, her supposed knowledge of everything in the district smacked of her questioning even those matters which were disclosed in the confessional. If true, that would be a serious breach of canon law.

"Furthermore, it was at Lady Catherine's behest that we find ourselves in our current happy . . . situation. For as she most graciously told me, a pastor must set the example of marriage in his parish, for if he does not, who will? When I informed her of my perfect willingness to follow her directives, she abjured me to find a woman most expediently, which I believe I have done, and though her Ladyship did not expect that I would look this far afield for the companion of my future life, when she understood the particulars of our close kinship, she was by no means displeased, even should it result in her loss of her clergyman. 'I may replace you without issue, Mr. Collins,' said she, 'so you may conduct your wooing without reference to your duty to me.'

"I am very grateful for her gracious forgiveness, and so soon after I was preferred to be the parson of Hunsford! I owe everything to her Ladyship and mean to do everything in my power to demean myself with the greatest respect for her advice and support. When we are married, you may expect her to visit, for I do not doubt that she will have many gracious suggestions concerning the arrangements here at Longbourn, and I am convinced it would be to our benefit to follow her instructions to the letter."

Though Elizabeth had already known it, his interminable speech confirmed without any doubt that the man was attempting, in his own ineffectual way, to court her. Not only could she not imagine ever accepting him, but the insulting thought that this Lady Catherine, having never laid eyes on Longbourn, would presume to tell her how to make the arrangements in her own house did not produce nearly the reaction that Mr. Collins was hoping.

"For my part," replied Elizabeth, "should Lady Catherine ever visit me, I will welcome her with respect for her position, but the arrangements at Longbourn date back to when my parents presided at my home. I cannot imagine ever changing them."

Mr. Collins looked at her with astonishment. "But-but, Miss Bennet!" He paused to assert control over his emotions. "At that point, I believe it will be your husband's prerogative to mandate your acceptance of her Ladyship's suggestions. I am confident that, given the proper young lady you are, you will not attempt to go against your husband's wishes."

"I would think my husband would respect my intelligence and my authority over my own home." Though she had attempted to keep the edge out of her tone, Elizabeth realized that she had snapped at him, prompting him to frown. "Regardless, I do not mean to be married any time in the near future, so it truly does not signify. I shall continue on as I have."

Elizabeth thought that Mr. Collins's eyes would bulge out of their sockets at her words, but before he could say anything, Charlotte distracted him by changing the subject. The man obliged readily, but for some time after, he peered at Elizabeth carefully, a frown etched upon his homely face, as if he was trying to make her out. Eventually, he shook his head and continued on as he had before, either ignoring Elizabeth's words or deciding she had meant something other than what she had said.

It did not signify to Elizabeth one way or another. Since she would never be induced to accept a proposal from Mr. Collins, he could say and do as he wished. It would have no effect on her.

In those days, another man was constantly present, though he could not visit her at Longbourn for obvious reasons. Mr. Wickham had, indeed, taken the scarlet, and within days of his purchase of his new commission, he was in evidence in almost every other forum in which he could conceivably insert himself. When they went into Meryton, he was there with a cheerful greeting and a few friendly words; once, when Elizabeth and Kitty visited Lucas Lodge, their visit had coincided with Mr. Wickham and Mr. Denny's; and he had even been invited to Mrs. Phillips's card party—along with many of the other officers—and he spent most of his time there, conversing with her.

When Mr. Collins and Mr. Wickham were both in company with Elizabeth, it seemed to be sort of a contest to determine who could command her attention, for Mr. Collins instantly saw the other man as a rival. But though Mr. Wickham was friendly and spoke to her a great deal, he did not press her like she might have expected a suitor to do. Elizabeth could not even be certain what his purpose was, but as he was friendly and engaging, she decided it did not signify.

But though she was not certain of Mr. Wickham's intentions and though she thought him to be an interesting man with happy manners and an engaging way of speaking, Elizabeth found that she did not truly consider him to be a potential suitor. It was nothing she could put her finger on. He was essentially penniless as he was a militia officer, which was certainly a point not in his favor, but then again, if she loved a man and was certain of his love, her dowry consisted of Longbourn, so there would be no reason to worry on that score.

Furthermore, though he was charming and handsome, Elizabeth found that his manners were a little too glib, his words a little too smooth for her tastes. Elizabeth determined to simply enjoy his conversation and inform him of her disinclination for anything more from him, should he ever make such attentions known. It was interesting, but given the fact that the entire district of young maidens appeared to be instantly smitten by the man, the ladies of Longbourn remained largely impervious to his charms, Elizabeth because of her suspicions of his lack of substance, and Kitty because she was focused on Mr. Bingley. Charlotte also was not impressed by him, and though she said nothing to Elizabeth concerning the man, Elizabeth also noticed that Charlotte steered well clear of him.

After Charlotte and Mr. Collins had departed from Longbourn one day once the visiting time had expired, Elizabeth spent some time in her study and then went searching for Kitty. She found her sister situated in the sitting-room with a book in her hands, and she smiled—it had not been long ago when Kitty had rarely been seen in such an attitude, and though she would never be the reader Elizabeth was, and had not the taste for the deeper works Elizabeth often preferred, still she had learned to take joy in a book's pages. Shakespeare had become an especial favorite of Kitty's, and Elizabeth noted the book in her hand was a compendium of sonnets.

"Kitty," said Elizabeth, "I had thought to canvass your opinion on something which has been on my mind."

Smiling, Kitty put down her book and waited expectantly.

"Since Miss Bingley and Mrs. Hurst invited us to dine at Netherfield, I believe it would be only proper for us to return the favor. What do you think about inviting the Netherfield party to Longbourn?"

"The entire party?" asked Kitty. She was clearly excited about the possibility of once again spending an evening in Mr. Bingley's company, but Elizabeth was pleased at how she controlled her reaction.

"Unless you wish to have Miss Bingley all to yourself," teased Elizabeth.

Kitty chuckled. "I am certain Miss Bingley would wish for that as little as I would myself." Kitty paused and regarded Elizabeth with a frown. "Of course, if we invited the entire party, that would necessitate the attendance of the Lucases."

"And Mr. Collins," said Elizabeth with a nod. "I know. I would like to avoid the man, but it is necessary if the gentlemen are to come."

Pausing, and clearly considering her words carefully, Kitty said: "Though you know that I would like to speak with Mr. Bingley again, I would not wish for you to be uncomfortable, which you almost certainly would be if Mr. Collins should attend. If you prefer, I am happy with inviting only the Netherfield ladies."

"Thank you, Kitty," said Elizabeth, giving her sister an affectionate embrace. "But you need not fear for me. I am well able to fend off Mr. Collins."

"Then I would love to have the Netherfield party join us for dinner."

"I was also thinking that we should invite some of the officers, make it a true dinner party."

"Oh, like Mama used to have!" exclaimed Kitty, excited at the prospect. "That would be so much fun!"

"Exactly. Longbourn has not entertained in such a fashion in almost two years, and I think the old house would love to hear the sounds of guests and laughter once again."

"But who shall we invite?" asked Kitty.

"The colonel and his wife, certainly, and perhaps several of the officers we know best," replied Elizabeth.

Kitty nodded, saying: "Denny, Carter, Sanderson, and perhaps Wickham, then."

Though she paused at the last name, Elizabeth did not say anything, instead contenting herself with nodding her agreement. She could find no fault with Wickham, though his true character was still a mystery. She had never told Kitty about her feelings about Wickham's smoothness, as it did not seem to matter. There was no reason to exclude him, and he had been much in evidence lately.

"Then it is decided," replied Elizabeth. "I shall dispatch the invitations immediately. Would you like to put together a menu for the evening?"

It was clear that Kitty was flattered that Elizabeth had put such faith in her abilities, but she eagerly agreed. Thus decided, Elizabeth left to prepare the invitations. Though the presence of Mr. Collins was objectionable, she was happy to once again entertain at Longbourn. It had been a very long time since that had happened.

"What do you think of this?" asked Caroline, brandishing the invitation from Longbourn.

"It seems to me to be what it purports to be," replied Louisa.

Instantly annoyed by Louisa's bland tone, Caroline scowled. Louisa had been recalcitrant the entire time of their residence at Netherfield, and she was only becoming worse as time passed.

"I am thinking we should reject it. I have no desire to spend any more time at Longbourn than necessary."

"I do not think that would be wise," replied Louisa.

"And why should that be?"

Louisa shook her head with exasperation, and Caroline glared at her sister because of it. "Because, Caroline, the Bennets are returning the favor of our invitation to them, and it would not be good manners to reject the overture. Charles, for good or ill, has leased this estate, and he requires the goodwill of his neighbors. Besides, you know how much Charles enjoys society. If he were to discover that we declined an invitation for an evening in company, he would not be pleased."

"I find that I am not disposed to concern myself with Charles's displeasure."

"Well, you should. He *does* control your dowry, and you live with him at his sufferance, regardless of his disinclination to use the power he possesses."

Scowling, Caroline glared at her sister, becoming even more annoyed when Louisa just looked back at her mildly.

"The fact of the matter," said Caroline, trying a different tack, "is that I do not wish for either Charles or Mr. Darcy to be in company with those artful little chits. I am certain the Bennets have our brother and Mr. Darcy in their sights."

"Oh, Caroline, how can you be so tiresome?"

"It is not being tiresome," cried Caroline, resisting the urge to stamp her foot in frustration. "You saw Kitty Bennet when we visited Longbourn, how she monopolized our brother's attention. And I am absolutely certain Miss Bennet has set her cap at Mr. Darcy."

"She has shown him no such attention, Caroline. And Miss Kitty could hardly be impolite and refuse to speak with Charles. I will own that she appears to be infatuated with him, but I can see nothing artful in her manners, contrary to what you suggest."

The two sisters glared at each other for a long moment. Caroline, little though she wished to concede the point, knew her sister was right. It would be rude to refuse such an invitation, despite how she wished to reject it and give no attention to either of the little adventuresses.

But she would watch them carefully so that their schemes might be foiled. Charles was meant to marry an heiress; Miss Darcy would be best, as she was not only shy and malleable, but it would forward Caroline's own ambitions quite nicely. And Mr. Darcy could not be allowed to consider anyone other than Caroline herself as a potential marriage partner.

So Caroline acquiesced, though not without making it clear to her sister that she was not pleased at the necessity of it.

When the night of the dinner party arrived, Kitty and Elizabeth waited anxiously for their guests, feeling all the nervousness of young ladies who were, after all, accepting visitors into their home for the first time as the only residents of Longbourn. It was true the Lucases had dined at Longbourn in the past year and a half, but Elizabeth had hot hosted a general dinner party since she had become mistress of Longbourn. Thus, she felt it only understandable that she should be nervous.

The Lucas party had been invited to arrive about fifteen minutes before the other attendees, and when they entered the room, they were greeted with pleasure. Lady Lucas particularly came forward and embraced Elizabeth.

"It does my heart good to see Longbourn once again entertaining, my dear. Your mother would be proud of you both."

Elizabeth's eyes misted over, and she thanked Lady Lucas for her kind words, but the tender moment was broken by the loud voice of Mr. Collins who, it seemed, had a knack for speaking when he should be silent.

"Indeed, it is unfortunate that you should have lost your dear family. But it is brave of you both to put your bereavement in the past and attempt to push on. The mistress of Longbourn must, necessarily, be active in this small community, and I cannot be happier that you are willing to put your duties before your personal feelings and welcome your neighbors into your home. I believe that once you are married, your husband will be most appreciative of your fortitude."

In that moment, Charlotte's assertions concerning her mother's desire for a union between her and Mr. Collins were proven correct, as the woman's eyes narrowed a little. She was wise enough not to say anything, but Elizabeth did not miss Lady Lucas's attempts to draw Mr. Collins's attention back to her daughter.

"The Bennet girls are dear girls and so very resilient," said she, "but Charlotte has been trained to run a household as well, and I am certain she would do very well for any man."

"Indeed, she would, Lady Lucas," replied Mr. Collins, "and a wonderful girl she is. It is only a shame how she possesses so little dowry as to make an offer of marriage so unlikely."

Elizabeth could not believe her ears, and for a moment she gaped at Mr. Collins's rudeness, noting that Charlotte must be inured to it, as she did not so much as blush. Lady Lucas, however, certainly did notice, and she glared at the oblivious parson. Evidently she decided that the prospect of having a daughter married outweighed the parson's thoughtless statements and lack of social graces, for she steered the man toward a conversation with Charlotte, little though he appeared to wish for it. Charlotte and Elizabeth exchanged amused glances. Elizabeth, remembering the character of her own mother, knew it likely would have been little different had Mrs. Bennet still been alive to direct the man to her daughters.

The second party to arrive was the one from Netherfield, which brought a new group of characters to the party. Though the Lucases were already acquainted with those from Netherfield, Mr. Collins was not, and Sir William, his happiness at being in the position to be useful plain for all to see, performed the office. Mr. Collins was polite and regaled the new arrivals with flowery compliments which he thought necessary to any situation, but he did not pay them any particular notice, as he soon sought to turn his attentions back to Elizabeth. Lady Lucas, however, anticipated him, and directed him back to Charlotte, much to both the gentleman and Charlotte's chagrin.

"I thank you for your kind invitation to our party," said Mr. Bingley, greeting Elizabeth with his customary cheerfulness. "Though you would have been within your rights to ask only the ladies, I am happy you have chosen to include us."

"It is no trouble, Mr. Bingley," replied Elizabeth. "Kitty and I love the company, and we have not entertained in the past year and a half, so we were happy to have you here."

Mr. Bingley bowed, but it seemed he was eager to be elsewhere, and he retreated as soon as he could politely withdraw. Soon, he had taken up his position beside Kitty, and they were engaged in conversation. Elizabeth watched carefully, but Kitty appeared to be demure and to maintain control of her emotions, so Elizabeth let them be.

"You have not entertained since your family's passing, Miss Bennet?"

Elizabeth, having forgotten of Mr. Darcy's presence, turned back to him and shook her head. "We have had the Lucases here in the past but no others. This will be the first time entertaining more than just them. We also expect some members of the militia to join us."

Nodding, Mr. Darcy said: "The officers seem like good men, for the most part. It seems that many find their presence agreeable."

A laugh escaped Elizabeth's lips. "Indeed they do. It is nice to have new characters and new people to speak to, though I will own that many of the young ladies find their presence acceptable for other reasons."

"But you do not?"

"I am not young enough to find the thought of a red coat romantic, Mr. Darcy. I like to think that I have more sense than to lose my mind at the mere sight of an officer."

"I am glad to hear it," murmured Mr. Darcy.

When the officers arrived, Mrs. Whitmore escorted them into the room to the general greetings of all. As Elizabeth was still speaking with Mr. Darcy, she was witness to the exact moment that he became aware of Mr. Wickham's presence. The sight of the man caused Mr. Darcy to start, and his face was overset with a red hue.

For his part, Mr. Wickham did not notice Mr. Darcy's presence for several moments, but his reaction when he did espy Mr. Darcy could not have been more different. Whereas Mr. Darcy had turned red, Mr. Wickham turned an unhealthy shade of white, and, for a moment, Elizabeth thought the man might swoon. He soon recovered his equilibrium, and though he inclined his head in Mr. Darcy's direction, the other man did not deign to respond.

Soon, however, Mr. Darcy seemed to think better of ignoring Mr. Wickham, and he excused himself, approaching the man with a hard look in his eye, his jaw seemingly chiseled from granite. When he spoke, his voice was just loud enough that Elizabeth could overhear.

"I trust you will not be up to your usual tricks here in Meryton?"

"Come, Darcy!" said Wickham, attempting a jovial response. "I am a member of the militia now. I am an upstanding member of society. You have nothing to fear."

Mr. Darcy was not amused, and he leaned forward and hissed something at Mr. Wickham, something which clearly made the man uneasy, but as his voice was low, Elizabeth could not overhear him. Then Mr. Darcy shot one final glare at Mr. Wickham and stepped away, taking himself to a corner away from the rest of the party, where he stood and watched, his countenance thunderous and brooding.

Though she could not help but be curious, Elizabeth decided that it would be best not to know. She would not put herself in the middle of a dispute between the two men. Thus, she put the matter from her mind and moved about the room, ensuring that her guests felt welcome at her home.

On the other side of the room, Darcy watched Miss Bennet as she mingled with her guests, showing herself to be the consummate hostess he had always thought she was. For a woman who had not entertained in more than a year — and never as the hostess in her own right — she was certainly practiced at it. Darcy felt she would be comfortable in the presence of the quality, should she ever have the opportunity to keep such exalted company.

Then Darcy's eyes turned to Wickham, and he almost scowled at the sight. That the libertine should be present in this, of all locations, was enough to make Darcy's blood boil! Wickham was a blight, a disgusting, filthy cretin who did not deserve the loyalty with which Darcy's father had always favored him. And after his actions with respect to Georgiana, he deserved to pay for his crimes to the fullest extent Darcy could arrange.

But Darcy would not make a scene, not in a neighborhood drawing room, where others could see, nor would he embarrass his hostess, who was one of the finest women Darcy had ever met. Thus, he controlled his temper, only imparting a warning to Wickham to behave himself or face the consequences. Darcy had little hope that the man would actually heed his warning, but he could not expose him for fear of how his retaliation would affect Georgiana.

As the night went on, however, Darcy noted that Wickham seemed to be plying his trade with Miss Bennet, and though Darcy wished that she would see through Wickham's pretty manners, he could not be certain. She spoke to him with the same easy politeness with which she spoke to everyone, though Darcy did not see any interest out of the common way.

And this was his dilemma. Darcy esteemed Miss Bennet enough that he did not wish for her to fall prey to the likes of Wickham — her life would no doubt become extremely uncomfortable should Wickham actually succeed. But Darcy did not wish to jeopardize Georgiana's reputation. It was a fine kettle of fish and one he would need to think upon before he came to any resolution.

It was when the party was called into the dining room that the evening began to fall apart. It was not any one thing that caused the guests to be uncomfortable, nor did Mr. Darcy suddenly rise to his feet and call Mr.

Wickham out, but a number of things all conspired to put the family at Longbourn in the worst possible light. Elizabeth had thought that with the passing of her mother the worst of her mortification caused by her relations was over. It appeared she was incorrect.

The first minutes of the dinner proceeded relatively smoothly. Mr. Collins, as was his usual wont, spoke in a loud and obnoxious voice, making comments of his patroness and speaking to all and sundry of his happiness to be there, making veiled—in his own small mind—comments of his happy situation and his willingness to be at Longbourn indefinitely. Elizabeth ignored him, as was *her* wont, and she spoke with Mr. Darcy, who, being the highest ranked man in the room, had escorted her in and sat beside her. It was not long, however, before Mr. Collins's soliloquies caught Mr. Darcy's attention.

"The estate is most perfectly situated, I assure you," said Mr. Collins to one of the officers, who was seated by his side. "My cousin has done wonders, considering she has naught but her own abilities to guide her. But I am certain that when she is married, her husband will take matters into his hands and set course on the estate with a firm hand on the rudder. It is unfortunate, but a woman cannot possibly maintain an estate as well as a man."

Mr. Collins paused and a queasy sort of expression came over his face. "Of course," said he, hastily, as though desperate to get the words out of his mouth, "I do not include my own gracious and intelligent patroness in such censure, for she is all that is capable and experienced.

"But I am convinced my cousin," he directed a sickly sort of smile at Elizabeth, which he undoubtedly intended to be affectionate, "requires a guiding hand."

As the man droned on, Elizabeth found herself wishing she could stuff a roll into his mouth to silence him. The two most likely to censure, Mrs. Hurst and Miss Bingley, were staring at Mr. Collins with barely concealed astonishment, and though Mrs. Hurst kept her countenance, Miss Bingley seemed to think that she had triumphed due to the man's behavior. She kept sneaking sly glances at Mr. Darcy, which the gentleman in question ignored. Instead, his countenance was hard, and he glared at Mr. Collins.

"I am sorry," said Miss Bingley from her position down the table, "I was not aware that you had a suitor, Miss Bennet. May I wish you joy?"

"No," said Elizabeth shortly.

At the same time, Mr. Collins preened like he was a peacock and said: "Not yet, though I dare say that I have the greatest hope that my fondest wishes will soon come to fruition. For you see, I have been sent to

Hertfordshire to find a wife, at the behest of my most excellent patroness, and I believe I have unearthed a jewel of the first order. I could search the length and breadth of the land and not find one so uniquely suited for me. I am certain ours shall be a great union."

"Wonderful," replied Miss Bingley. "I do so love a wedding."

Elizabeth glared daggers at the man, but he remained oblivious. As for Miss Bingley, she appeared akin to the cat who had got into the cream, though Elizabeth could not understand why she would give three straws concerning the matter. Elizabeth's salvation came from a most unexpected source.

"Can I assume that nothing has been decided yet?" asked Mr. Darcy.

"Nothing official," simpered Mr. Collins, "but I have great hope that it will all be resolved before long."

"Then if it *has not* been resolved yet, it is not proper to discuss it in company. Please be silent and leave Miss Bennet in peace."

Though Elizabeth could not have believed the man could provide her with amusement, she was indeed almost forced to laugh at the sight of Mr. Collins's countenance warring between his natural obsequious veneration of anyone above his social sphere, and his affront that anyone would question him as to his intentions toward Elizabeth. Eventually, his affront finally won.

"Far be it for me to suggest that you are incorrect, sir, but I am a clergyman, and as such, I believe I am better able to determine proper behavior than you are."

Mr. Darcy was relentless. "Given your performance here tonight, sir, I must wonder if you have any knowledge of propriety whatsoever. Speaking of such things openly, and especially when Miss Bennet clearly does not welcome them, is beyond the pale. I must ask you to desist."

"And who are you, sir, that you might censure me thus?"

"Did you not know?" asked Mr. Wickham with a sly smile at Mr. Darcy. "He is Fitzwilliam Darcy, master of Pemberley estate in Derbyshire, and nephew to your own patroness, Lady Catherine de Bourgh."

Whatever reaction Elizabeth had expected from the man, she had not expected utter stupefied silence. She glanced at Mr. Darcy, noting the way his jaw was working, and the glare of utter loathing with which he pierced Mr. Wickham, and she knew that Mr. Wickham's words were true. For Mr. Wickham's part, he seemed to be unconcerned and unmoved by Mr. Darcy's displeasure, and Elizabeth immediately knew he had made the connection known for some purpose of his own, likely to throw fuel onto the fire and embarrass Mr. Darcy. The hostess in

Elizabeth could only glare at him for making one of her guests uncomfortable.

"Is it true?" said Mr. Collins, his voice almost pleading. "Are you indeed my patroness's nephew, Mr. Darcy?"

Though Elizabeth could instantly see that Mr. Darcy wished for anything other than to answer the question in the affirmative, he nodded once in a clipped motion.

"I had no idea, sir! To imagine that I would be so blessed as to meet the nephew of my most gracious patroness is not a boon I would have expected to receive in my wildest dreams. How fortunate, how . . ."

Suddenly, Mr. Collins turned an unhealthy shade of white, and he began stammering apologies at Mr. Darcy. "A thousand times, I apologize, sir. I would never have said such things if I had known who you are. I should never have dreamed to push aside your wise advice, knowing, as I do, that your relationship with her Ladyship means that your own wisdom must be akin to her own. I apologize most humbly, I assure you."

"You need not apologize to me," replied Mr. Darcy. "I believe you should direct your apologies at Miss Bennet, for it is she who has borne the offense of your loud and unguarded statements.

"And rather than speak," said Mr. Darcy, his voice rising to drown out the profuse apologies that Mr. Collins had already begun to direct at Elizabeth, "I think it would be best if you apologize by ceasing to speak of the matter which has so consumed your thoughts tonight. I cannot say what Miss Bennet thinks about your suit, but it is clear that she does not welcome your words."

Poor Mr. Collins, if he could indeed be termed as such, seemed he did not know what to do. He made to speak to Elizabeth, and then he seemed to recall what Mr. Darcy had said about apologizing by ceasing to speak, and though it was not in his nature to be silent, even for a moment, he made a credible attempt at it, though Elizabeth noted that his mouth opened several times.

Or, at least he remained silent until Mr. Wickham threw more fuel on the fire.

"I am certain you must have much news for Darcy. Perhaps you might inform him of how his aunt and cousin fare?"

"Oh, yes, of course!" cried Mr. Collins. "How thoughtless of me to have forgotten. If I could change seats I would sit beside you and tell you all!"

Mr. Darcy once again glared at Mr. Wickham, but he directed his comments to Mr. Collins. "Not now, Mr. Collins. It would not be proper, nor would speaking across the room in a loud voice. If you wish to speak after the meal, then I may spare some time for you."

Mr. Collins's thanks and praises of Mr. Darcy's person were long, loud, and not in keeping with Mr. Darcy's rebuke. Elizabeth, however, was not of mind to comment on the matter, as she was simply glad that Mr. Collins had been diverted from his topic. She looked around the table, noting that the officers were looking at Mr. Collins with wonder — not to mention at her with pity — the Hursts were largely focusing on their own meals, though they were whispering with each other, while the Lucases, having already been quite aware of Mr. Collins's character, looked with sympathy at Elizabeth. Lady Lucas was watching the parson with an expression akin to contempt, but Elizabeth was certain she had not yet given up on the man for the sake of her daughter.

When Elizabeth caught sight of Kitty, she noted another issue — her sister's countenance had taken on a rosy hue, and she was sipping from her wine glass with great frequency, giggling at something Mr. Bingley was saying. Elizabeth almost put her head into her hands and groaned. Kitty, on the few occasions when she had consumed too much wine, became sillier than she had been following Lydia, and Elizabeth was certain she was more than a little tipsy.

And so the evening progressed. If it was not Mr. Wickham's sly comments, directing the fool Mr. Collins toward Mr. Darcy, then it was Kitty's improper giggling. Mr. Collins's inanities were well understood and would not cease, regardless of how much Elizabeth wished they would, but Elizabeth was disappointed with her sister. Though Elizabeth wished the evening would end, it seemed interminable, like it was destined to continue, feeding her mortification.

But though Elizabeth was annoyed, primarily with the three who had conspired to make the evening a mess, she felt a warmth for Mr. Darcy. He had deflected Mr. Collins's statements, and after dinner, he willingly put up with the man, blunting his excesses and turning his attention away from Elizabeth. She did not know if Mr. Darcy did it on purpose to spare her, but she was grateful nonetheless.

Chapter IX

$\mathcal{I}$t was a dilemma, to be sure, and one that Darcy was not certain how he should resolve.

The dinner party the previous evening had been difficult, and though it was ultimately the hostess's responsibility to make certain her guests were happy and comfortable, Darcy could not fault Miss Bennet. Perhaps it was not the best judgment to invite Wickham, but having just met the man, she could have no suspicion about Wickham's character.

The very thought of George Wickham caused Darcy's fists to clench. Something clearly must be done, but Darcy was not certain what. He would not cause injury to his sister for anything, especially for someone who was not in any way connected with him. But to simply leave Miss Bennet to Wickham's machinations was also unthinkable. Darcy had, over the years, avoided thinking about Wickham whenever possible, certain that his own character would speak for itself and that anyone with a modicum of sense would see through Wickham's tales of ill use. Since Wickham had not been aware of his presence in the area before the previous evening, Darcy doubted he had said anything yet, but he knew that it was now only a matter of time.

"What do you think, Sister? Shall we send a card to Longbourn to wish Miss Bennet joy?"

The grating tones of Miss Bingley's voice penetrated Darcy's thoughts, and he noted the woman stealing sly glances at him. Her words, though spoken to her sister, were really for Darcy's benefit, and though they were improper, Darcy knew she did not care. Her only concern was to ensure he saw her perceived rival in the worst possible light. Little did the woman know that he had difficulty seeing anyone in a worse light than Caroline Bingley. Wickham, of course, was an exception.

"Oh, Caroline," said Mrs. Hurst, her exasperation plain in her voice. "I wish you would not carry on so."

Darcy wished the same. Caroline, from the time they had entered the carriage the previous evening, had only ceased making her comments when they had parted for the night, and even then, Darcy was not certain she had not continued to speak in her sleep.

"It seems that Mr. Collins *is* fixed on her as a future bride. I would have thought you would wish to congratulate her for her good fortune."

"I doubt she favors his attentions."

"Perhaps not, but it does make sense. He is her cousin, he seems to ardently admire her, and she cannot help but see the benefit of a man in residence at Longbourn to see to matters of the estate. If Mr. Collins took up residence, he would be able to handle such matters, allowing her to return to more womanly pursuits.

"Besides, he is the best the woman can expect."

Darcy watched as Mrs. Hurst sighed and shook her head in resignation. How he wished he could indulge in such an action himself!

"I must say," said Bingley, "that I can find nothing wrong with Miss Bennet's behavior. It is as Darcy said—she owns her estate, so she must care for it. There is nothing improper about that."

A sniff of disdain met Bingley's declaration. "Everything is wrong with her behavior. She is a bluestocking, she prattles and chatters about her estate, she makes clever comments, seeming to revel in her supposed intelligence, and she takes on a man's work as if she was born to do it. A little delicacy would not hurt her, and I believe she might find it if she were married."

"Or perhaps she would be miserable," said Darcy. "In matters of understanding, it cannot be an equal match, as Mr. Collins is not precisely gifted."

"Neither is Miss Bennet, if you will excuse my saying so," replied Miss Bingley, seemingly determined to make her point. "For all her clever comments and attempts to be learned, I am positive she knows little of the world and memorizes such things to make herself appear to be more intelligent. Her sister is insipid and her behavior last night was deplorable. In fact, this entire village is intolerable. How I long to be back in town!"

"Then perhaps you should go there," said Bingley. Though Darcy had rarely seen his friend angry, it seemed his sister's harping on the subject of the Bennets had finally pierced his perpetually sunny disposition. "I will not object to it, as Louisa may serve as my hostess if you wish to be in town."

"Do not be stupid, Charles!" snapped Miss Bingley. "You are well aware of my inability to go to town by myself."

"Then I suggest you temper your comments, as I am quite fixed at Netherfield, and I believe Hurst and Louisa are quite happy to be here as well. If you simply must go to town, I am certain you can apply to one of your friends to host you for a time."

Eyes narrowed, Miss Bingley glared at her brother, but she made no further comment.

"Besides, as we have discussed, I mean to hold a ball at Netherfield, and I shall not depart before that event. After that, I believe I will have some business in town, but I intend to return as soon as it is completed. Thus, I will be fixed here for some time. You should become accustomed to Netherfield, Caroline, because unless you leave alone, you will be in residence here for some time."

Deciding that he had experienced enough of the siblings' squabbling, Darcy rose to leave, excusing himself from their company, citing some business letters which required his attention. As he walked through the hallways, Darcy chewed on the matter which had been on his mind since the previous night. A warning concerning Wickham's usual behavior would not go amiss, he thought. If he did it properly, Wickham would never even know that he had warned Miss Bennet against him. He would not say anything of Georgiana, of course, but he could not leave Miss Bennet at Wickham's mercy. It would be unconscionable.

The following morning, Elizabeth found she had a headache, no doubt induced by the events of the previous evening. Not wishing to put up with Mr. Collins that morning, she instructed Mrs. Whitmore to turn away all visitors to the estate, and most especially Mr. Collins. Then with a cool, wet cloth pressed to her forehead, Elizabeth retreated to the study in order to complete some work. She thought she heard the sound of raised voices soon thereafter, and was certain that Mr. Collins had not been happy to learn that Elizabeth would not accept visitors. But it soon quieted, and Elizabeth could not be anything but grateful.

Though Elizabeth attempted to concentrate on her work, she found her mind continually returning to the previous evening. The Lucases were not a problem, as they had known the Bennets for many years and were not inclined to judge them harshly. Besides, they were hosting the buffoon at present, so she knew that they were well aware of Mr. Collins's character. The officers had typically been well-behaved, and Elizabeth did not worry about their opinions either. They were young men, and they could be counted on to focus more on pretty women, than to censure others for their behavior.

But it galled Elizabeth that Miss Bingley in particular had witnessed the spectacle. Elizabeth had no doubt Miss Bingley would attempt to work on her brother, to dissuade him from his attentions to Kitty, and though Elizabeth was not certain the burgeoning relationship would lead to anything more permanent, she did not wish Kitty to be hurt. And she knew very well that Kitty would be hurt if Mr. Bingley went away, for at the very least, she was infatuated by the man. Better for her to determine for herself that she would not suit with Mr. Bingley, should their current relationship not lead to marriage.

The thought of Kitty and her behavior the previous night caused Elizabeth to sigh and set her quill down on the desk. The girl had been doing so well and improving her behavior by leaps and bounds, but she still slid back from time to time. Elizabeth knew that Kitty had not set out to drink so much wine, but she had probably done so out of nervousness and excitement. Elizabeth did not wish to censure her, but she knew that she should at least bring it to Kitty's attention and remind her to keep herself under better regulation the next time.

Knowing it would not do to allow the matter to remain as it was for long, Elizabeth rose to go to her sister.

In the end, it seemed Elizabeth might not have bothered. She found Kitty in her own room, and though she was awake and dressed, it was clear that Kitty had been dealing with her own demons that morning. The shades were drawn in the window keeping as much light as possible from the room, and Kitty was sitting, facing away from what little light still filtered in. She sat on her chair, a book held in one hand, while the other hand was propping her head up, and her fingers occasionally massaged her temples. She was clearly feeling the effects of the wine from the previous evening, a lesson Elizabeth felt would be much more effective than any admonishment she might make.

"You do not need to speak of it, Lizzy," said Kitty, as her fingers once again moved against her temples. "I am fully aware of my folly, I assure you."

"So it appears you are," said Elizabeth. She moved a chair, situating it beside her sister's, and sat close to her, coaxing Kitty to rest her head on her shoulder.

Kitty sighed when Elizabeth embraced her close. "I did not mean to consume so much wine, Lizzy. In fact, I am not certain how I managed it. But I was nervous that Mr. Bingley was paying me so much attention, and it impaired my judgment."

"I know, dearest. I had intended to have words about it, but it seems you have understood the consequences of your actions."

"I do," declared Kitty fervently. "I think I may promise never to indulge in such a manner again."

"Good." Elizabeth paused and then laughed. "Perhaps now that our first dinner party is over, the next one might be more successful."

"More successful?" asked Kitty, sitting up again and looking at Elizabeth with confusion. "I was unaware that there were problems other than my overindulgence."

Elizabeth shook her head. "It was mostly perpetrated by Mr. Collins, though Mr. Wickham and Miss Bingley both had their hands in the soup. I believe that this is the last time Mr. Wickham will be invited to Longbourn, and I sincerely hope that Mr. Collins will return to Kent as soon as may be. As for Miss Bingley," Elizabeth paused and smiled at her sister, "I will endure the woman for Mr. Bingley's sake."

Kitty laughed and put her head back on Elizabeth's shoulder. "Tell me what happened, for I believe I dearly need a laugh."

And so Elizabeth did, and she found that by the light of the day, what had happened did not seem so particularly bad. A pleasant time was had by the sisters, speaking of the eccentricities and silliness of others, much as their father might have done.

Two days after the dinner party at Longbourn, Mr. Bingley, in company with Mr. Darcy and Miss Bingley, once again visited the estate. Elizabeth welcomed the gentlemen, but she detested the sight of the woman, though, mindful of Kitty's feelings, she put on a brave face and drew on her innate sense of propriety to behave with cordiality. It did not help that Miss Bingley watched her with a sort of smug satisfaction, as if she knew something no one else did. Elizabeth could have cheerfully slapped the woman.

"Miss Bennet, Miss Kitty," said Mr. Bingley as he and his companions sat with them, "we have come this morning for a particular purpose."

"Particular purpose or not, you know you are always welcome at Longbourn," replied Elizabeth.

The man fairly beamed at them before he produced a card and handed it to Elizabeth. "My sisters and I are planning to host a ball at Netherfield on the evening of the twenty-sixth of November, and we would be happy if you would consent to join us."

Elizabeth did not miss the significance of this invitation. Generally, when inviting one's neighbors to a function one meant to host, the invitations were delivered by servants. It was only the closest and most intimate of acquaintances who were invited in person. Elizabeth avoided looking at Kitty, knowing it was most likely Mr. Bingley's interest in her which prompted such attention.

It appeared, however, that Miss Bingley also did not misunderstand the significance, and if her scowl was any indication, it seemed the woman had argued strenuously against his delivering the invitation in person. Though Elizabeth was still of two minds about his attentions to Kitty, she was heartened to see evidence of his resolve. Miss Bingley could go hang for all Elizabeth cared—regardless of Miss Bingley's opinion, socially, Kitty was a step up for Mr. Bingley. Elizabeth was more concerned with Kitty's happiness, than with Miss Bingley's ambitions.

"Thank you, Mr. Bingley," said Elizabeth. "Kitty and I would be happy to attend your ball. In fact, I am certain we would like nothing better."

"It would not be the same if you did not come," replied the man jovially.

Then he turned to Kitty and, after bestowing a smile of utmost affection upon her, said: "Miss Kitty, I would like to solicit your hand for the first two dances of the evening, if I might be so bold."

Elizabeth, who knew her sister well, thought Kitty might jump up and down for the excitement. But she managed to control her enthusiasm, and she responded demurely: "I would be very happy to cede those dances to you. I thank you for your consideration, sir."

"It is my pleasure," was Mr. Bingley's warm reply. "I would not wish for anything else."

The visit continued for some minutes after Mr. Bingley's request to Kitty, but it was clear that while Mr. Bingley spoke with Kitty with the same amiable easiness which usually characterized his interactions, Miss Bingley sat and fumed and said relatively little. As for Mr. Darcy, he sat between Miss Bingley and Elizabeth and carried on a banal conversation, in which Elizabeth readily partook.

It was not many more moments before Miss Bingley seemed to pull herself from her dark thoughts and addressed her brother: "We should depart, Charles, for we have other tasks which must be completed today."

Mr. Bingley allowed it to be so, and the pair rose to depart. But then a most curious thing happened—Mr. Darcy, though he rose along with the siblings, turned to Elizabeth and said:

"If I might impose, Miss Bennet, would you give me a moment of your time? I have something which I must share with you."

Though surprised, Elizabeth was not at all inclined to deny him his application, but she looked around, wondering if he meant to stay in the sitting-room with her, which would not at all be proper. Mr. Darcy seemed to recognize her concern.

"We could walk outside, Miss Bennet. I will not take much of your time."

"Perhaps we should accompany you," said Miss Bingley, her consternation clear for all to see.

"No, indeed, Miss Bingley," said Mr. Darcy. "Since I rode here, I am very capable of making my way back to Netherfield, and as I know that you have many things which must be accomplished, I would not dream of keeping you from your tasks."

There was no way for Miss Bingley to insist they stay, so she conceded, though with ill grace. She then shot a poisonous look at Elizabeth, as if Elizabeth had contrived some way to keep Mr. Darcy at Longbourn, and allowed her brother to lead her from the room.

"Shall we?" asked Mr. Darcy, gesturing toward the door.

They made their way to the vestibule, and Elizabeth accepted her gloves and pelisse from Mrs. Whitmore. They exited the house, just in time to see the Bingley carriage pull away from the house, and though Elizabeth could not see within the depths of the vehicle, she was quite certain Miss Bingley was watching her, likely wishing her the worst.

"I am at your disposal, Mr. Darcy," said Elizabeth.

Mr. Darcy smiled and offered her his arm, and they made their way around toward the back of the house. For the first few minutes of their walk, they spoke little, he confining his comments to what he could see of the estate's park, and Elizabeth making some small comments about their arrangements, the rose garden in the back, now bereft of blooms due to the lateness of the season, as well as the orchard off in the distance. Mr. Darcy seemed impressed by what he could see; Longbourn was not a large estate to make its owners wealthy, but Elizabeth was quite proud of what she and her forebears had been able to accomplish.

Finally, they reached a small bench set on Longbourn's grounds, and Mr. Darcy suggested they stop, saw her seated on the bench, before he turned and addressed her as she sat.

"Miss Bennet, I have some information that I believe you require in order to take steps to protect yourself, and I could not rest until I communicated it to you."

Though astonished, Elizabeth nodded. "That does sound serious, Mr. Darcy. I will listen to you."

"Not long ago, a man arrived in Meryton, and though I was not aware of his coming until the night of your invitation to dine at Longbourn, I am intimately familiar with his ways and know his character to be lacking."

Comprehension dawned on Elizabeth. "Do you perhaps refer to Mr. Wickham?"

"I do," replied Mr. Darcy, though he looked on her, curiosity written upon his brow. "I am surprised you have divined his identity."

"I happened to witness your first sight of the man, as well as his response. It seemed likely to me, given his paleness versus your obvious anger, that you were the offended party, rather than the reverse. Can I assume this man has injured you in the past?"

A slight smile came over Mr. Darcy's face. "I suppose I should not be surprised, Miss Bennet, given how perspicacious I know you to be. Yes, you are correct that he has caused my family injury, but though I would tell you all, some of it must remain confidential, for I would not further injure others of whom he has taken advantage."

"Then please tell me what you can, sir. I am listening."

Mr. Darcy paused, obviously thinking of how best to approach the subject, and then he sighed and spoke, his tone filled with resignation.

"You may be surprised to hear it, Miss Bennet, but Mr. Wickham has actually been known to me from my earliest childhood." Mr. Darcy smiled at her reaction to this news. "Yes, Miss Bennet, I know him intimately, am familiar with his ways and his vices, and have been witness to many of them, I assure you.

"Mr. Wickham is, in fact, the son of a very respectable man. Old Mr. Wickham was my father's steward and had, for many years, been entrusted with the management of Pemberley. He was a good man, one who was much like his son in essentials, with impeccable manners and a charming countenance. Mr. Wickham the elder, had he wished it, could have passed himself off as a gentleman with ease, had he possessed the character which made such deception desirable.

"Unfortunately, his son, while possessing the same traits as the father, was not given even a speck of the morality of the father and has chosen to use his gifts for ill, rather than for good."

"I have always found his manners to be too smooth," murmured Elizabeth, "but I had never thought him to be this bad."

Mr. Darcy paced a little, his head bowed in thought. "I assure you, Miss Bennet, that his sins are of a much greater degree than this. My father was attached to Mr. Wickham, but he could not know what Mr. Wickham was, as he was always careful to hide his ways when in the presence of my father."

"And you chose not to speak of the matter?"

Sighing, Mr. Darcy stopped pacing and sat down on the bench at a respectable distance. "I did not, for various reasons, most of which I will not speak of. You have to understand, Miss Bennet, that though my father was a good man, he was often harsh, one who put duty and honor above all else. I was often the recipient of this harshness, as he attempted to mold me into a man who would care for his beloved estate when he was gone. Though we dealt with each other with respect, we were not close, and on some level, I feared that my father would not believe me should I speak to him concerning Wickham's ways. It would have been better for all had I been able to make that communication and induced him to believe me."

Elizabeth nodded, though slowly. "I understand your reticence, sir. I was always close to my father, but my mother was a flighty woman who never understood me. Had I tried to speak to her of my youngest sister — who was her favorite — and inform her of any unflattering aspects of her character, she would have accused me of jealousy."

Smiling, Mr. Darcy said: "That is exactly it, Miss Bennet. However, I should tell you the particulars, as thus far I have only told you he is not to be trusted, and not why.

"Simply put, Mr. Wickham is a spendthrift. Money flows through his fingers as though it were water. He is a gamester and a debaucher, and though he has often attempted to make his fortune through high stakes gaming, his talents in no way approach his opinion of them, and his luck is abysmal.

"What particularly concerns me on the matter is your situation." When Elizabeth turned to look at him, a question on the tip of her tongue, Mr. Darcy continued: "You are a young woman, having inherited your father's estate, and you are pretty and friendly. I feared that you would have no suspicion of his motives until it was much too late."

"On the contrary, Mr. Darcy, there is something about him which disquiets me. He is smooth — far too smooth, I think — and I had already intended to avoid inviting him to Longbourn again."

Mr. Darcy nodded. "That is likely for the best. Should he somehow succeed in marrying you and gain control over the estate, I have no doubt he would bankrupt it in no time, all in order to fuel his habits. When he had wrung every last drop from you, I have no doubt he would have left you penniless."

When Elizabeth nodded, but did not speak, Mr. Darcy continued speaking.

"He is also known to defame my character whenever he can. One of his favorite tales concerns a living under my gift. After my father died, he left a legacy of one thousand pounds and recommended in his will that I assist Wickham in his future occupation. Though the living was never mentioned by my father, apparently they had spoken of it in the past, and Wickham, not having any interest in acting as a parson ought, came to me and demanded ten thousand pounds in exchange for his renouncing any claim on the living."

"Ten thousand pounds?" exclaimed Elizabeth. "That must be a very large and handsome living indeed, for him to think he could extort that much out of you."

"It is a valuable living, Miss Bennet," replied Mr. Darcy, "but it is by no means worth such a princely sum. Mr. Wickham knew this; it was his way of opening negotiations, hoping to wring as much as he possibly could from me.

"Unfortunately, I reacted badly." Mr. Darcy paused and looked skyward. "Much might have been changed if I had spoken to him in a more temperate manner. I told him, in as insulting language as I could muster, that not only would he not get the living, that he would not see a penny from me in lieu of it, and when he argued the matter, I showed him my father's will, pointing out—quite smugly, I might add—that I was by no means obligated to do anything other than assist him in finding his vocation in life. I am certain you can understand how he reacted to my words."

"Oh, dear," said Elizabeth. "What a man to have come among us."

"Indeed. He might have become violent if I had not thought to have my largest footman in attendance, a man who has certain matters to hold against him. When Wickham started yelling, Thompson picked him up, deposited him in a chair, and then stood over him, informing him that he would be thrown from the estate should he raise his voice again." Mr. Darcy laughed. "To be honest, I had thought Wickham might soil himself."

Elizabeth laughed along with him. "This Mr. Thompson is a large man?"

"At least a hand taller than myself, and about twice as wide," said Mr. Darcy. "He also does not like Wickham since Wickham attempted to seduce his fiancée."

"Then this Mr. Wickham is a womanizer too," said Elizabeth.

"I have known him to father several children, and he cares not that he leaves them with child and without means to support themselves. Thus, I am concerned, given your youth, your beauty, which he would find more than enough to tempt him, and the estate which you own."

Blushing, and feeling rather flattered at the man's praise, Elizabeth nodded.

"But to continue," said Mr. Darcy, "negotiations were quieter from that point on, but Wickham did not like the outcome any better. He noted my father's instructions regarding his future endeavors, and I informed him that I was completely willing to fulfill the terms my father had left in his will. I proposed that I purchase Wickham a commission in the army, but Wickham was not disposed to serve therein. When he suggested the law as a career, I told him that I would see to a fund set up for him which would pay for his lodgings, his books, whatever money was required to pay for his learning, and a small monthly stipend besides. As you can well imagine, he was not impressed, and resisted all suggestion of anything other than receiving a sum of money which he would control himself.

"I refused. I told him I knew what he was, and that I would not allow him to waste my family's funds indiscriminately. He accused me of breaking the spirit of my father's wishes, and I reminded him that had I informed my father of his ways, he likely would have received nothing. We ended at an impasse, and Wickham left the estate with his bequest of one thousand pounds, but nothing else. I have not seen him since, but I have heard tales of how he has conducted himself. I do not know for certain, Miss Bennet, but I suspect the deficiencies he had previously betrayed to me are the least of his sins now."

Mr. Darcy fell silent, and Elizabeth considered what she had been told. Elizabeth did not, even for an instant, think to disbelieve what he told her. It mirrored her own opinions of Mr. Wickham far too closely to consider such a thing.

"I thank you for this, Mr. Darcy," said Elizabeth. "I shall, indeed, take care in my dealings with Mr. Wickham. I would not wish to end as you described, with my family's legacy reduced to nothing more than a means for a man to enjoy a dissipative lifestyle."

Mr. Darcy bowed and after a few more words between them, he rose to his feet and made to depart. A sudden thought seemed to come to him, however, and he turned and looked at her, regarding her with a strangely intense expression.

"Miss Bennet," said he, "I was wondering—would you do the honor of dancing the first with me at Bingley's ball?"

Had Mr. Darcy asked her to sprout wings and fly to the moon, Elizabeth could not have been more surprised. However, the proper young lady in her came to the fore and allowed her to respond with composure.

"Certainly, Mr. Darcy. I look forward to it."

With a smile and a tip of his hat, Mr. Darcy bowed to her and excused himself, leaving Elizabeth to think about what had just passed between them. She surprised herself by thinking that though he was a serious, severe sort of man, there was much to admire in the person of Mr. Darcy.

Chapter X

*I*t was perhaps too much to ask that Elizabeth be left in peace. She had much to think on after being the recipient of Mr. Darcy's communications, and she wished to do it in peace. However, on the same day as the Bingley party had delivered their invitations to the ball, Elizabeth had two unwelcome visitors which disturbed her peace and made her long for their absence.

The first was, of course, Mr. Collins. He arrived, clearly excited, and proceeded to demand from the housekeeper that Elizabeth attend him, and Elizabeth, though she would like nothing less, decided it was best to see him, lest he make a commotion and expose them all to ridicule.

He was more than usually unkempt that day, his hair blown askew, betraying more of his balding pate than had ever before been the case. His words soon made his errand — and his less than impeccable state — clear.

"Miss Bennet, I have received the most remarkable news, and I hastened to Longbourn to pay my respects and to ask a most particular question of you."

"Mr. Collins!" cried Elizabeth, fearful the man would do the unthinkable, but he simply continued speaking over her consternation.

"Indeed, the Lucas family has been invited to a ball at Netherfield, and as I am in residence at Lucas Lodge, it was made clear that I was *particularly* invited to attend. I am humbled by the gracious kindness of those at Netherfield and happy to accept, I assure you, for I consider dancing to be a pleasurable diversion and not at all out of keeping with my role as a clergyman."

A scowl settled over Elizabeth's face. She could well imagine what the invitation had said, considering Miss Bingley's words from the night of the dinner party. Why, Elizabeth could not understand, but she seemed eager to forward a match with Mr. Collins.

"I am gratified, I assure you," continued Mr. Collins, almost without pausing to take a breath. "The significance of this event is not lost on me, nor, I am certain, have you missed it. Given her words from the previous evening, I am convinced that Miss Bingley means to honor us, for, it will be our first function as a couple. I am all anticipation!"

"Mr. Collins!" scolded Elizabeth. "I would ask you to cease this unseemly display! There is nothing between us, and under no stretch of anyone's imagination could we be called 'a couple.'"

"But, Miss Bennet—"

"Not another word, Mr. Collins!"

Though the man gaped at her for several moments, soon Mr. Collins's alarm turned to cunning. "Of course, Miss Bennet, I fully understand. It is not proper to make such statements until we come to a formal understanding. You may be certain that such words will never pass my lips until the matter is completely decided!"

Then you will never say them, thought Elizabeth, though she doubted his ability to hold his tongue. *I would much rather marry one of the carriage horses than you, Mr. Collins.*

"In that case, I shall return to the house," said Elizabeth. "You did not need to come here to inform me of the ball, for I already knew of it myself."

"You misunderstand me, Miss Bennet! I have not come here only to inform you of the ball, but to request your hand for the opening sets! I cannot think it anything but proper for us to open the ball, especially since Miss Bingley has made it very clear it shall be held in our honor."

While Elizabeth wished to gnash her teeth in frustration, she could not help but give thanks to Mr. Darcy, most fervently, for already requesting those particular dances. She could not imagine that dancing with Mr. Collins could be in any way pleasurable!

"I am sorry, Mr. Collins, but I cannot accept your offer."

"Cannot accept?" cried Mr. Collins before Elizabeth had a chance to explain further. "Whatever can you mean? Of course you may, and if you do not, you must eschew dancing the entire evening."

"No, Mr. Collins, I shall not. The reason I am not at liberty to accept is because I have already accepted a request for those dances. My apologies, sir, but you are too late."

That bit of intelligence seemed to be almost more than Mr. Collins could process, for he stared stupidly for several moments. Unfortunately, he was eventually able to find his tongue.

"Already accepted them? But the invitations have only just been dispatched. You cannot already have been solicited for those dances."

"Am I not worthy or pretty enough to tempt another man?" said Elizabeth crossly. "I assure you, sir, that I am already engaged for those dances, and I shall not recant."

A suspicious scowl came over Mr. Collins's face. "And who, might I ask, has pre-empted my request?"

"Mr. Darcy," replied Elizabeth, though she would have preferred to remain silent. "So you see, it is not only possible, it has actually happened. Mr. Bingley delivered the invitation to us personally, and as Mr. Darcy was also here, he took the opportunity to request my first sets."

Mr. Collins's scowl deepened. "This is unseemly, Miss Bennet. How can you have induced a man of the consequence of Mr. Darcy to ask you to dance?"

"Is it not typical for young men to ask young women to dance? Perhaps you should apply to Mr. Darcy to explain his reasons."

A paleness came over Mr. Collins's countenance, as Elizabeth had expected—it seemed the very thought of requiring so great a man to account for his actions frightened Mr. Collins excessively. On the heels of his paleness, Mr. Collins's countenance suddenly turned suspicious.

"Perhaps you have not heard, Miss Bennet, but Mr. Darcy is all but betrothed to his cousin, Anne de Bourgh, who is the only daughter of my own patroness, Lady Catherine de Bourgh. What do you have to say to that?"

Though Elizabeth felt an unexpected and undefinable pang of loss at hearing such a statement, she composed herself and filed the emotion away for further reflection later. For now, she was forced to deal with a buffoon.

"Then I wish Mr. Darcy well, but it does not change the fact that he has asked me to dance, and I have accepted."

Mr. Collins's suspicious glare never wavered. "Are you certain you have not induced him, with your arts and allurements, to forget himself?"

With utmost patience, Elizabeth refrained from slapping the man. "Mr. Collins, I am a woman, and Mr. Darcy is a man. It is up to the man to ask the woman, who may then accept or reject, though rejection bears its own consequences."

But Mr. Collins was shaking his head, and she did not think he heard a word she had said. "No, Miss Bennet, it shall not be. You must speak to Mr. Darcy and inform him that you have reconsidered."

"I shall not," replied Elizabeth. "Not only have I given my word, but should I refuse to dance, I will not be able to dance at all that night. That would defeat your purpose completely, would it not?"

Though the man was caught with indecision, he soon nodded, though slowly. "You do not have any intentions with respect to Mr. Darcy?"

"It is none of your concern, sir," replied Elizabeth, by now affronted by the man's temerity. "As I have stated, Mr. Darcy asked me and I accepted. That is all there is to the matter. I will not say anymore."

"Then you must dance the second with me."

Much though Elizabeth would have wished to refuse the man and sit out the rest of the night, she knew she could not. So she nodded once abruptly and returned to the house without looking back. Later, Mrs. Whitmore informed her that Mr. Collins had stood outside gazing at the doors for some time, as if deep in contemplation. Elizabeth did not care—she only wished he would return from whence he came, the more expeditiously the better.

The second visitor arrived almost on the heels of the first, and was, perhaps, even less welcome, for if Mr. Collins was a dullard of the first order, he was not vicious in character. Given what she had heard of Mr. Wickham, Elizabeth suspected that viciousness was an essential part of *his* character.

"Miss Bennet," called he, as he strode in from the front of the house. Elizabeth, as she had decided to walk after Mr. Collins's departure, was just about to return to the house when he saw her.

Resisting the urge to order him from her lands—he had not actually done anything to *her* yet—Elizabeth greeted him with a curtsey and far less pleasure than he likely would have wished.

"How fortunate I am to see you, Miss Bennet, for I wished to ask you a particular question."

"Oh?" asked Elizabeth. "I will confess I am intrigued, sir, for I was not aware that we were at all acquainted enough for a 'particular question' to be proper."

It appeared like the man did not quite know how to respond to her words. He looked at her, an appraising sort of scrutiny, and Elizabeth instantly felt uncomfortable. She had the distinct impression that Mr. Wickham expected all young women to swoon due to nothing more than the sight of his smile, and he was perplexed when she did not behave as he had expected. It made Elizabeth wonder if the man had only attempted to ply his trade with sixteen-year-old girls.

"Perhaps we do not know each other . . . *intimately*," said Mr. Wickham, "but I believe we are well on the way to becoming good friends."

Not if I have anything to say on the matter, my dear Mr. Wickham.

Out loud, the only thing Elizabeth said was: "That remains to be seen, Mr. Wickham. I believe you had a question you wished to ask?"

"Indeed, I do," replied Mr. Wickham, continuing on smoothly. "For you see, I was present this morning when a general invitation to Mr. Bingley's ball was delivered to the militia headquarters, and when I thought of the delights of attending such an event, I knew it would not be complete if I did not have you as my partner to open it. Thus, I would like to petition your hand for your first sets, if you please."

Elizabeth regarded the man, thinking of what Mr. Darcy had told her. He was confident, practiced, and adept at his trade, and Elizabeth was certain that for him, that is exactly what it was—a way of life for a scoundrel. Furthermore, she noted his eyes as they raked over her form, recognized the lascivious look in the depths of his eyes. His smile at her reminded her of a cat her family had once had, which took particular pleasure in toying with a mouse before it made the kill. Perhaps the man was after her estate, and she was only a fringe benefit, but she would not fall prey to him. She would not allow Longbourn to be used as the fuel for his habits.

"It is very interesting that you have asked for those dances, sir," said Elizabeth. "It seems that I am quite in demand for the first sets at Mr. Bingley's ball. You have my apologies, but I am afraid I cannot accept. Your evening will have to remain incomplete."

The smile ran away from Mr. Wickham's face, but he kept control of his countenance. "You have already been asked for those dances?"

"Indeed, I have," replied Elizabeth pleasantly. "And as I received a second request for those sets, my second sets have already been secured. So you see, it is impossible for me to accept your gracious offer."

"I am all astonishment!" said Mr. Wickham. "I had not dreamed you were so popular with the gentlemen."

"Come, Mr. Wickham. Am I so ill-favored that it is a wonder that any man should wish to dance with me?"

"I beg your pardon," said Mr. Wickham, bending in an elegant bow. "I spoke without thinking. I think no such thing, as my application must prove." He paused, a suspicious gleam in his eye, and he said: "Might I ask who is the lucky man who has secured your favor?"

"You may not," replied Elizabeth, glaring at him. "That is an impertinent question, and I shall not answer it."

"Of course not! You have my apologies. But I must insist upon your third set, if the first two are taken."

Elizabeth resisted the urge to sigh. It appeared the man was determined to favor her with his attentions, though it should be clear by now that she did not wish for them. Whether he was so completely confident in his own charms or was simply obtuse she did not know, but she heartily wished he would leave her alone.

When she had given her acceptance, though displaying the greatest of reluctance, hoping he would get the hint, she curtseyed and turned toward the house. Mr. Wickham, it appeared was not about to allow her to escape so quickly.

"I had hoped, Miss Bennet, that you would allow me a further moment of your time," said Mr. Wickham, holding a hand out to forestall her departure. "I have some information which might be of interest to you."

"Mr. Wickham," said Elizabeth, displaying her annoyance in her folded arms and the tapping of her foot on the ground, "I cannot imagine to what you refer. Please step aside so that I might return to my home."

"It will only take a moment," said Mr. Wickham in a soothing tone. "For you see, I understand that you have been keeping company with Mr. Darcy of late."

"Again, that is none of your business," said Elizabeth, her anger flaring. "I would ask you to desist."

"But you must not know much of him, as he has not been in residence long. In fact, I have known Darcy all my life. He is not what he seems, Miss Bennet. He takes great pleasure in playing the ever proper gentlemen, but then he seduces young girls and ruins them, knowing his standing in society will protect him from any repercussions. I advise you to take care."

"Is that so?"

Startled by the sound of a new voice, Mr. Wickham stepped to the side, his eyes widening as he saw Mr. Whitmore standing there, watching him. Elizabeth found the situation to be quite amusing, as Mr. Wickham's heart appeared to be pounding in his surprise. Served the man right.

"By what means to you impugn a good man's character, sir? And what proof do you offer to substantiate your claims?"

By that time, Mr. Wickham had regained his composure. He shot Mr. Whitmore an insolent glare and turned his attention back on Elizabeth. "I will not be questioned by a servant."

"You are rather prideful for a lieutenant in the army, are you not?" jibed Mr. Whitmore. Wickham turned back toward him, anger rising in his eyes, but Mr. Whitmore was merciless. "Given the fact that I judge you to be at least five and twenty, and you are yet a newly commissioned lieutenant, I suspect a lack of serious consideration for your occupation at best, or a gamester at worst. In fact, I do not need suspicion for I recognize your name, given how many times I heard the son of my previous employer, the Earl of Matlock, speak of you. It is amusing that you label me as a servant, sir, for I am well aware that you are nothing more than the son of one. Your father was a good man. It is truly unfortunate that the apple fell far from the tree in this instance."

As Mr. Whitmore continued his assault, Mr. Wickham's eyes widened, betraying complete astonishment. It was clear to Elizabeth that Mr. Wickham was accustomed to others believing his tales without the necessary burden of proof.

"I believe you should leave, Mr. Wickham," said Elizabeth. "As I have promised to stand up with you for the third dance at Mr. Bingley's ball, I will not renege on that agreement. If, that is, you choose to attend, rather than tucking your tail between your legs and avoid it like you should. I will also ensure that Mr. Darcy knows that you are attempting to malign his good name."

Mr. Wickham looked at her, seemingly astonished at her words. For a moment Elizabeth thought he might say something, attempt to redeem himself from the indignities he had suffered, but apparently he knew when to retreat from the battlefield, as he sketched a quick bow and walked away.

"A bad apple indeed," murmured Mr. Whitmore, as he watched Mr. Wickham walk away. "I heard much of him at Snowlock, I assure you."

"And Mr. Darcy told me of his dealings with the man this very morning," said Elizabeth. "I was already inclined to distrust him, but I appreciate Mr. Darcy's willingness to lay his private matters open for me to see, in order that I might protect myself."

Mr. Whitmore turned and regarded her, approval evident in his nod. "I am happy to hear it."

Nodding, Elizabeth turned to enter the house. With any luck, Mr. Wickham would decide that the dangers of trying to pay court to her far outweighed the benefits, and leave her in peace. She suspected, however, that he would consider the disappointment he had suffered that day to be nothing more than a mild setback.

The remaining days before the ball were filled with laughter and camaraderie, as the two sisters prepared for the night in company. Though Elizabeth looked on the ball with a certain level of ambivalence, Kitty was excited, and she rarely thought—or spoke—of anything else. Rather than be vexed with her sister, Elizabeth allowed herself to be caught up in Kitty's excitement, and though she did not anticipate it as much as Kitty did, still she found that she could look forward to an evening in company all the same.

When Elizabeth examined her feelings, she could not state with any surety why this particular entertainment was to be looked upon with such indifference. It seemed a mixture of circumstances, when mixed together, brought about her ennui. Certainly the second and third dances—with an idiot and a libertine, respectively—did not excite any particular excitement, and the hostess, whom Elizabeth actively detested, would attempt to stir up trouble. On the other hand, Mr. Darcy was a good man, so dancing with him would be no punishment, and Mr. Bingley was happy and outgoing and had paid particular attention to her sister.

A sly remark by her sister also led to an addition to their wardrobes. When they examined their dresses, there was some discussion about what dresses would most suit or best show them to advantage, and it was not long before Kitty took matters into her own hands.

"All these dresses are out of style and old," complained Kitty. "We have not had new ball gowns since we came out of mourning. Shall we not purchase new gowns, Lizzy?"

Elizabeth looked at her sister fondly. In truth, she was not opposed to Kitty's request, but she was curious if Kitty could put forward a better argument. "But we have many serviceable gowns right here."

"Oh, but, Lizzy, I should so wish to make the best impression," replied Kitty, warming to her subject. "Though we have been back in society these months, we have not attended an event like this for ages. I would like to show all of Meryton that the Bennet sisters are back."

Elizabeth could not stifle a giggle at her sister's words.

"Besides," continued Kitty in a coy voice, "I think you would have a beau too, if you would only put some effort into it. Mr. Darcy seems to favor you above all other ladies, and he did request your first."

"Surely you are seeing something which does not exist!" cried

Elizabeth. "Yes, I am friendly with Mr. Darcy, but I believe he has requested my dance because he is reticent and not at all comfortable with most of our neighbors."

"Then why did he not ask Miss Bingley to open the ball with him?"

It was all Elizabeth could do not to roll her eyes. "Because he detests the very sight of her?"

The sisters collapsed against each other giggling. "I do not claim to understand Mr. Darcy to any great degree, but his disinclination for the lady is plain to see. I imagine he will do his duty and stand up with her, but I cannot imagine him enjoying it."

"Nor can I. But then why ask you at all? If his disinclination for dancing is as strong as you suggest, why not avoid dancing the first altogether?"

"Kitty . . ."

"I will not tease you, Lizzy," said Kitty. "In all seriousness, I will bid you to truly watch Mr. Darcy's behavior. He watches you a great deal. A gentleman does not watch a woman unless he admires her."

Though she was not at all convinced of Mr. Darcy's interest, Elizabeth agreed, as much to prevent her sister from continuing to speak of the matter as anything else. A niggling thought suggested that Kitty might be right, but her sister's next words soon put the matter from her mind.

"Now, what about that new dress?"

Laughing, Elizabeth leaned forward and embraced her. "I have no objection, Kitty. A new ball gown you shall have."

Kitty squealed and thanked her, and their discussion turned to patterns, styles, fabrics, lace, and all manner of other such subjects. Kitty quickly dragged her out to the local dressmakers where they spent a pleasurable afternoon discussing those selfsame items, and though it seemed like several of the ladies of the area had likewise commissioned new dresses for the upcoming ball, the dressmaker assured them their gowns would be ready on time.

At length the night of the ball arrived, and the sisters entered the carriage for the short journey to Netherfield. The moon was bright that night, lending a cool glow to the surrounding landscape which, though no snow had fallen as of yet, fairly gleamed and glittered. The coachman had much light to see by, and as the sisters knew he was experienced and careful, they merely enjoyed the ride, speaking animatedly as was their wont. Soon, nostalgia set in, and they were speaking of their absent family.

"Do you think Papa would have been induced to leave his bookroom for a ball?" asked Kitty.

Elizabeth, caught in the throes of reminiscence, smiled and nodded. "Papa would not have missed it. He did prefer the company of his books to that of other people, but a ball such as this would have provided much entertainment for our dear Papa. He was a connoisseur of human folly, after all."

Making a face, Kitty could only agree. "I am sure you are correct, though I never understood the fascination."

"Papa did have a sardonic outlook on life. But he was a good father who loved us all. I am certain he would have put his disinclination for company aside for our sakes."

"But Mama would have been all aflutter with excitement. And I dare say she would have been pushing us all toward Mr. Bingley and Mr. Darcy, and likely Mr. Collins and the officers too!"

There was no way to refute such a statement, though the thought that Mr. Bingley might be paying attention to Jane rather than Kitty, were she still with them, entered Elizabeth's mind. Of course, she would never say such a thing to Kitty.

"Jane would be serene while Lydia's excitement would surpass even yours," replied Elizabeth.

"And Mary would have brought a book with her!" exclaimed Kitty.

"That is true. But I have always thought that had Mary allowed a more flattering hairstyle and clothes, and if she had not assumed such a severe countenance all the time, I think she might have appeared more to advantage and secured more dances."

"That is possible," said Kitty.

Pausing for a moment, Kitty seemed to be in the midst of some great emotion, and when she spoke again, her voice was rough, confirming Elizabeth's supposition.

"I miss them." Kitty's voice was so quiet that Elizabeth was almost unable to hear her, though she was seated by Kitty's side.

"As do I," said Elizabeth, putting an arm around Kitty's shoulders. "But I believe they would all wish us to be happy."

"All except Lydia," said Kitty with rolled eyes, though her tone was more affectionate than unkind. "She would be angry that she is missing the fun."

Elizabeth shook her head; Lydia had always been selfish and a little spoiled, and Elizabeth had no doubt that Kitty's was an accurate portrayal.

"Even Lydia would not have begrudged us happy lives. We will always miss them, but I believe we can take solace in the notion that they are looking down on us, happy that we have continued with our lives.

And by the grace of God, I believe we shall see them again someday."

"I hope you are right, Lizzy. And I want you to know that I am mindful of your instructions. I will be perfectly well behaved tonight, and I will steer well clear of the wine!"

As laughter erupted between the two sisters, they fell into each other's arms. "I think that might be for the best, Kitty. Just focus on being Kitty Bennet and have confidence in yourself. I believe Mr. Bingley can hardly resist you, if you do that."

"Thank you, Lizzy," replied Kitty.

The sisters lapsed into silence as the carriage rolled along. It would be an interesting night, indeed.

Their arrival at Netherfield was met with cheerful greetings from Mr. Bingley, composure from Mrs. Hurst, and barely concealed contempt from Miss Bingley. Both sisters, knowing what a trial Miss Bingley could be, greeted her simply and moved along the line, not wishing to exchange false pleasantries with the bitter woman. Mr. Hurst merely grunted a greeting as they moved past him, but Elizabeth was certain that was simply his way, and not intended as a slight upon them. Of Mr. Darcy there was no sign—given the man's reticence, Elizabeth thought it likely that he had used his status as a guest of the estate to avoid the receiving line. She could not blame him.

The ballroom was a good size and was decked out with all manner of greenery and ribbons, and Elizabeth thought that Miss Bingley, whatever her faults, had managed to create an atmosphere which was both elegant and cheery. On the far side of the room, a string quartet which had been hired for the occasion had begun playing prelude music, as Elizabeth heard the strains of Mozart flowing out over the company. There were many already in attendance, including several of their close neighbors. Espying Charlotte, standing to the side of the ballroom with her mother, Elizabeth led her sister to their dearest friends.

"Lizzy, Kitty!" exclaimed Charlotte when she caught sight of them. "How well you both look tonight! Unless I miss my guess, are those not new dresses?"

"They are," said Kitty, looking shyly at Elizabeth. "Lizzy said that we might have them, since we have not had anything new since our mourning ended."

"And it becomes you very well, indeed, my dear," said Lady Lucas. "I am certain you shall be the belles of the ball tonight."

"Thank you," said Elizabeth. "But unless I miss my guess, are you not also wearing a new dress, Charlotte?"

Charlotte blushed and nodded, all while directing a significant look at Elizabeth. "Mama wished me to look my best this evening."

Well aware of the reason why Lady Lucas was so intent upon it, Elizabeth decided to simply ignore it. She had not the least suspicion that Charlotte would accept an offer from Mr. Collins, even could he be induced to turn his attention away from Elizabeth, so it did not signify.

"You look very well, indeed," said Elizabeth. "It shall be a wonderful evening, I am certain."

"Cousin Elizabeth!"

Almost cringing at the sound of her cousin's voice, Elizabeth turned and noted the hurried approach of Mr. Collins. He was, she reflected, dressed in his typical black attire, wearing his clerical collar as if it was a badge of honor. No doubt he thought it was.

"I am astounded, my dear cousin," said Mr. Collins. His dash across the dance floor had made him breathless, causing him to blow like a bellows as he attempted to speak. "I have never seen such a wonderful construction of fabric and lace as that which adorns you this evening. I would never try to put to words the vision you are, for I know that we mere mortals can never aspire to the language of the divine. I am simply awed."

Bemused, Elizabeth returned the parson's gaze, wondering if he had actually just inferred that she was a goddess. Not for the first time, Elizabeth wished her father was with her—Mr. Bennet's highly developed sense of the absurd would have found Mr. Collins to be an irresistible source of amusement, she was certain.

"Thank you, Mr. Collins. But you must confess that both Kitty and Charlotte are looking especially beautiful tonight."

A nudge in her ribs informed Elizabeth of Charlotte's displeasure, but she only turned a mischievous grin on her friend. Mr. Collins, of course, could not resist such a blatant invitation to wax poetic.

"Indeed, they do. Words cannot describe how enraptured I am to be in the presence of so many lovely young ladies." Mr. Collins then turned his attention back to Elizabeth, and with a sickly sort of smile, which he no doubt intended to be seductive, said: "I hope you are ready for our dance, my dear cousin, for I have thought of little else myself."

"I have promised them to you, sir, and I shall perform my obligation."

"Then shall we?" asked he, extending his hand.

"I believe the first dance is mine."

Elizabeth turned and saw Mr. Darcy looking at her, his countenance as unreadable as it ever was. Or at least it was until his eye flicked to the unfortunate Mr. Collins; then Elizabeth thought she detected more than a hint of disdain for the man, though it was hidden enough that Elizabeth did not think anyone else noted it.

"And I have the first dance with Miss Kitty," said Mr. Bingley from where he stood by Mr. Darcy's side. "Shall we?"

Kitty smiled and accepted his hand, and they moved away. Mr. Darcy extended his own hand to Elizabeth, which she accepted. But before they could move away, Mr. Collins's voice interrupted them.

"Mr. Darcy, sir, I wished to speak of your decision to claim my cousin's hand for the first set."

Mr. Darcy turned back and looked at Mr. Collins, and though his expression did not alter a jot, Elizabeth thought his eyes bored down on Mr. Collins like the blow of a hammer. Though perhaps it might have been best to remain silent, Mr. Collins forged on, even while he obviously felt the same thing Elizabeth did, if his pulling at his collar was any indication.

"Though I would not injure the nephew of my patroness by supposing that you have forgotten yourself, I would remind you of your arrangement with your cousin and your duty to your aunt. I know not how my cousin has induced you to forget yourself in such a manner, but should you feel it necessary to withdraw your application, I would happily consent to dance the first with her in your stead."

A sound of disgust drew Elizabeth's attention to Lady Lucas, and she noted that the congenial lady was looking at Mr. Collins. Had the lady had the power, Elizabeth was certain Mr. Collins would be writhing on the ground due to nothing more than the force of her glare.

"You promised the first to my Charlotte," said Lady Lucas, almost daring him to contradict her."

"So I did," said Mr. Collins, bowing deferentially to Charlotte. "But surely Miss Lucas can see that in a situation such as this, other considerations must take precedence, and arrangements must change. Though I am mortified to be the cause of any injury to your amiable daughter, I hope she will forgive me for this little lapse, and accept the offer of my hand for any other dance convenient."

"Mr. Collins," said Mr. Darcy. His countenance was forbidding and his tone firm, and even a dullard such as Mr. Collins had to see that he was seriously displeased. "Reneging on a request to dance is not only improper, but also insulting to the lady in question. I suggest you apologize to Miss Lucas for your poor manners. *Perhaps* she will be inclined to forgive you and still provide you with her company for the first sets."

"But—"

Mr. Darcy held up a hand, and Mr. Collins almost tripped over his tongue in his haste to cease speaking.

"I will not behave in such a manner, sir. I have requested Miss Bennet's hand for this dance in good faith, and I will not shame her by withdrawing. Furthermore, you should know that there is no engagement between myself and my cousin. Whatever my aunt says, it is her wish and her wish alone which leads her to speak in such a manner."

"But, Mr. Darcy!"

"Enough, Mr. Collins!" The cold look in Mr. Darcy's eyes brought Mr. Collins up short, and he turned pale. "You will not speak of this matter again, and you shall not censure Miss Bennet for accepting my hand for a dance. If you must have some solace, you should note that it is merely a dance—nothing more, nothing less. But if I hear of you speaking of the matter of my cousin again, I will not be responsible for my actions."

The rapidity at which Mr. Collins's head bobbed up and down would have been comical if Elizabeth was not already extremely vexed with the man. Luckily, Mr. Darcy led her away as the dancers were beginning to form up for the set.

Whatever Mr. Collins had said to Charlotte, it was clear his grovelling had been enough to induce her to keep their engagement to dance. A quick glance at Lady Lucas, however, informed Elizabeth that the lady was not amused by Mr. Collins's thoughtless words. Unless Elizabeth missed her guess, she thought that the days of Lady Lucas pushing her daughter in the parson's direction were now over.

"I hope you were not injured by your cousin's thoughtless actions, Miss Bennet," said Mr. Darcy.

"Indeed not, though I do thank you for the moderation in which you rebuked him, sir. I fear he is ridiculous and thoughtless, but there is no true harm in him. His upbringing, from what I understand, has left him with little knowledge of social graces."

"It is quite all right, Miss Bennet. Every family must have one such member. Ironically, the member of your family who is so afflicted is closely connected with my ridiculous family member!"

Feigning surprise, while fully realizing the effect was ruined by a persistent spate of giggles, Elizabeth said: "I am all astonishment, sir. I had understood that your aunt was the preeminent personage in all the land! Surely she cannot be ridiculous."

"I assure you, Miss Bennet, that Lady Catherine is quite as ridiculous as Mr. Collins, though in a completely different way. Should you ever have the good fortune to meet her, I am certain you will agree with me."

Though Elizabeth felt it unlikely she should ever be blessed with making the great lady's acquaintance, she gave her amicable agreement. They found their places in the dance, and glancing to the side, Elizabeth noted her sister across from Mr. Bingley in the first position. Smiling, Elizabeth turned her attention back to her companion, noting Mr. Darcy's scrutiny upon her. She thought he might say something to her, but the music began and the dancers started to move, necessitating his attention to the steps. It was not until their second pas that he addressed her again.

"I noticed you watching your sister and my friend, Miss Bennet," said he, when they had come close enough in the dance. "Can I infer, given your smile, that you approve?"

"Approval is not mine to give, Mr. Darcy. My uncle has the authority to approve or deny any requests by a potential suitor."

"Perhaps not, but unless I am very much mistaken, I suspect your opinion will hold a great deal of weight should such a thing come to pass."

Elizabeth sighed. "You are correct, of course. For my part I do not know whether to approve or not. Mr. Bingley is, of course, a good man, and I would be happy to have him as a brother. But I am not yet convinced that their feelings—either of them—extend beyond simple infatuation."

At that moment, Elizabeth's hand was taken by another gentleman, and she was led through the steps of the dance. It was several more moments before she came together again with Mr. Darcy.

"But surely you would wish for your sister to be well cared for, Miss Bennet. Given that my friend *is* a good man and would always take care of your sister, regardless of his feelings, would his suit not be a desirable one?"

"If one were to consider nothing more than prudence, you are correct. But I think you will find, Mr. Darcy, that I do not take a fashionable view of felicity in marriage. Yes, I want my sister to be protected. But of equal importance, I wish for her to be happy. If she can be happy with Mr. Bingley, then I would have no objection. But if there any doubts about their feelings, it would be better for them to just remain friends and attempt to find other partners in marriage."

It appeared Elizabeth had given Mr. Darcy food for thought, for he was silent for some time, moving through the steps by rote, while on his face rested a contemplative expression. Elizabeth continued to dance, knowing that he would speak when he had worked his way through her words. For her part, Elizabeth studied Mr. Darcy, though as unobtrusively as possible, thinking she had surprised him. He was of the upper echelons of society, which meant he had almost certainly been taught to put money and connections before anything else. Though there were many who would ultimately agree with him, Elizabeth could sense no censure in his manner toward her.

It was near the end of the set before Mr. Darcy once again spoke. "I commend you, Miss Bennet. There are few, I think, who would consider the matter in such a way."

"And what is your opinion, Mr. Darcy?"

Mr. Darcy smiled. "The Darcys are one of the few fashionable families who have always promoted love matches to their scions. My parents' marriage was a love match, and I hope for the same for my sister and myself." Mr. Darcy paused and smiled. "We like to think that it is this quirk, in a society consumed with status and money, which has allowed us to attain the level of success we have had as a family. I am certain it has never done us any harm."

"I dare say it has not," replied Elizabeth.

They finished the set in silence, but while no words were spoken, Elizabeth could not help but think that they had communed with more than mere words. There seemed to be some undefinable feeling which had passed between them, and though Elizabeth could not quite put her finger on it, that did not mean it did not exist.

Chapter XI

*F*itzwilliam Darcy was unhappy. Though he was not a sociable man, he could readily partake in the amusement of a ball with the right inducement. And Miss Elizabeth Bennet was most certainly the right inducement.

Though Darcy was ostensibly standing along the side of the dance floor, watching the dancers, he indulged in the memories of his dance with Miss Bennet. She was graceful and knew the dance steps well, seemingly moving about the dance floor as if she was floating on a cloud. When they had danced, he had felt her presence, sensed a kindred spirit close by, and the internal instincts that all men possessed were all afire with the knowledge that a potential mate was nearby, one who would make his days a joy, and his nights a pleasure. It had been all Darcy could do to keep his countenance.

But Darcy knew his duty and knew there could be no alliance with Miss Elizabeth Bennet. Though part of him rebelled at the thought, he knew that he would leave Hertfordshire and Miss Bennet behind, and that sometime in the future, he would find himself a wife of excellent dowry and connections and marry her. His words to Miss Bennet had not been mere bravado — he intended to find a woman he could love. But he was not concerned about that at present.

In fact, he had stayed in Hertfordshire too long, at least two weeks longer than he had intended. Bingley would have to fend for himself — Darcy was needed in London to collect his sister, and thereafter, they would retire to Pemberley for the Christmas season and the first month of the New Year. After that, it would be back to London. Perhaps this was the year he would meet the woman he would marry.

But while he fully intended to depart on the morrow, at present he was stuck at a country dance with his closest friend, and while Miss Bennet was a pleasure, there were others who were not so.

Of course, the first had been the fool to whom his aunt had gifted a living, completely unworthily, in Darcy's opinion. Though Mr. Collins had indeed danced the first with Miss Lucas, his haste to greet Darcy and Miss Bennet after the first sets had been unseemly, and he had almost tripped over Darcy in his haste to get to his cousin. Miss Bennet was mortified, of course, but so was Miss Lucas, who was forced to endure the man's abandonment without his even escorting her from the dance floor. Darcy was not going to stand for it.

As Mr. Collins attempted to move past Darcy to reach Miss Bennet, Darcy grasped his arm and turned the man around, walking him to a secluded location along the side of the room, ignoring Collins's squawking. By all rights, Darcy should not have been able to move him in this manner, as Collins was not a small man, but it seemed that he was not going to protest such treatment when faced with his patroness's nephew.

"How may I help you, sir?" asked Mr. Collins, bowing several times in succession while looking longingly in the direction from which they had just come. "I am to dance the next with my cousin, and I would not miss it."

"You will indeed miss it unless you begin to behave better."

For the briefest of moments, Mr. Collins gaped at him, his small brain clearly trying to comprehend Darcy's words. Then sudden anger came over him, and he appeared to forget he was speaking to the nephew of his patroness.

"How dare you attempt to take me to task! I am a clergyman and the nearest relation Miss Bennet has, and soon I am to be her husband!"

"You are a buffoon, Mr. Collins, and you have not the slightest inkling of how to act."

"I do not have to listen to this," replied Mr. Collins. "You are in no way connected to me, sir."

When Mr. Collins moved to brush past him, Darcy reached out and grasped his arm, hissing in his ear: "Mr. Collins, do you not remember who I am?"

A retort seemingly appeared on his lips before it died as his eyes widened. A curious transformation took place, for whereas Mr. Collins had been tall and haughty only a moment before, he seemed to shrink, his back bending, his shoulders drawing in until he was hunched over, once again bowing unremittingly to Darcy.

"Of course, Mr. Darcy. My most abject apologies. I fear I forgot myself. What may I do for you?"

"Stand up straight, Mr. Collins. My aunt may require a sycophant for a parson, but I prefer to speak to a man's face, not the back of his head."

By this time, the man clearly did not know what to do or how to act, but he straightened his spine, and though he had trouble looking Darcy in the eye, at least he was not hunched over.

"Now, Mr. Collins, I will give you some instruction on how to behave, and I expect you to follow it. It seems to me that you were not raised in a gentleman's house. Is that true?"

"Most regrettably, it is, Mr. Darcy. Though my father, God rest his soul, was a hard-working and industrious sort of man, he was not a gentleman."

"A simple yes or no will suffice, Mr. Collins."

Mr. Collins blinked, which Darcy took for an affirmative. In truth, he was beginning to acquire a headache from speaking with the man, and he wondered how Collins had ever managed to complete the requirements necessary to become a parson.

"A gentleman, Mr. Collins, escorts a lady from the dance floor, either to her family or another place of her choosing. He does not leave her standing on the floor, while he attempts to assault his next partner."

A guilty look at Miss Lucas, who was standing with Miss Bennet, told Darcy the man was indeed listening, and at least on some level, understanding.

"Second, a gentleman does not attempt to bowl over another gentleman in his haste to reach his next partner."

"I humbly apologize—"

The man halted mid-sentence when Darcy held up a hand. "I do not require your apologies, Mr. Collins, merely your attention. Third, a gentleman recognizes when a lady does not wish for his attentions, and he leaves the field with dignity and grace, refusing to make her feel uncomfortable."

A slack-jawed stare met Darcy's declaration. "But, Mr. Darcy!"

"I am not attempting to tell you what you should and should not do, nor do I know how the object of your affections feels about you. That is for you—and you alone—to decide. But I will tell you that you must not attempt to make her feel uncomfortable or monopolize her time or attention. Dance with her once, and attempt to judge for yourself how receptive she is to your overtures."

Mr. Collins licked his lips and his gaze darted in Miss Bennet's direction. "But I have come here, sir," said Mr. Collins, this time hesitantly and devoid of the pompous surety which usually filled his conversation, "for the express purpose of engaging myself to my cousin. I must—"

Blushing a little—and providing amusement for Darcy in the process—Mr. Collins looked away. Darcy was not certain what had embarrassed the man, but it was diverting nonetheless.

"What I mean to say, sir, is that I believe my cousin needs the guidance of a man, and her estate requires that same guidance. Since I am a relation and am single, I believe it a perfect match."

A sigh escaped Darcy's lips. "Mr. Collins, I know you mean well, but you must take Miss Bennet's feelings into account. *Your* goals in a marriage partner are clear, but you must attempt to understand *her* goals. If she does not agree, then she will reject your proposal, should you make it."

Mr. Collins gasped. "Surely she would not do such a thing!"

"I assure you, she will. Miss Bennet has impressed me as an independent soul, and one who would not take kindly to another attempting to direct or coerce her."

"Then I shall apply to her guardian!" sputtered Mr. Collins.

"Do you truly think her guardian will force her to marry?"

That brought Mr. Collins up short, and he did not reply.

"Her guardian loves her and wishes the best for her, and I doubt he will believe that forcing her to marry a man she does not wish to marry will be in her best interests. And you must remember, she will be of age next summer, and free to make her own choices."

For once, Mr. Collins remained speechless, a blessing, as Darcy was tiring of the man. As such, he made one last comment before sending Mr. Collins back to Miss Bennet.

"I advise you to return to Miss Bennet, as the next dance is about to start. Treat her with respect, dance with her, but do not hover over her, lest you ruin her enjoyment of the evening. Attempt to see whether she favors you. If she does not, you should not make the mistake of offering for her, for she will surely reject you."

With a bow, Darcy moved away, leaving the parson open-mouthed and speechless. He recovered quickly, however, and soon escorted Miss

Bennet to the dance floor, more was the pity. He was not a good dancer, and seemed to have only a rudimentary notion of the steps, moving wrong several times, and almost colliding with another dancer. And instead of attending and watching the other dancers in an attempt to move correctly the next time, he spent his time apologizing. It was the most disruptive dance Darcy had ever witnessed.

But if some good came from it, Mr. Collins led Miss Bennet to the side of hall once the dance was over, and after bowing, he left her there. For the rest of the evening, Mr. Collins watched Miss Bennet, and though he often frowned at some of her partners or muttered to himself as she danced, he did not stay by her side like a leech, as he might otherwise have done. Though Darcy doubted he had been successful in preventing the man from making her an offer, he had at least been able to make the evening more pleasant for Miss Bennet.

Unfortunately, when Mr. Collins left Miss Bennet, the second person in attendance who displeased Darcy made his presence known. A scowl settled over Darcy's face as he saw Wickham approach her, his typical expression of easy charm fixed upon her. Darcy was almost ready to give up on the woman in disgust when he happened to note her expression, which consisted of equal parts politeness and distaste. The sight lifted Darcy's spirits considerably; a woman could not reject a request to dance, lest she sit the rest of the night out, but it was apparent that she had believed him and was not appreciative of Wickham's particular brand of charm.

The libertine was not aware of it, but his wings had already been clipped with respect to Miss Bennet.

"Oh, Mr. Darcy, I have finally found you."

This time Darcy was not quite able to resist rolling his eyes as the dulcet tones of his hostess—and the third person whose presence was a trial—reached his ears. Darcy turned and greeted her politely, but he did not say anything else to her. He had already danced once with Miss Bingley, after he had opened with Miss Bennet, fulfilling his duty to his hostess. He would not do it again. Of course, it seemed she needed no such encouragement.

"Mr. Darcy, I am quite undone."

"Oh?" asked Darcy, turning his attention back to the dance, and to Miss Bennet in particular. "I cannot imagine why. It appears to me the ball is proceeding quite well, and the guests are enjoying themselves immensely."

An unladylike snort was her response. "Of course they enjoy themselves. It is unlikely any of them has ever experienced the like. I am not concerned with that, I assure you."

The inference, of course, was that Miss Bingley's ball that evening was the equal of anything that could be found during the season. Darcy was not a connoisseur of the season—in fact, he found it more of a trial, than a pleasure—but he knew that while Miss Bingley had arranged the evening's entertainment competently, there were many far grander events to be found in London.

"I am concerned for my brother," continued Miss Bingley. "It appears that he has once again lost his head to a pretty girl, and this one does not even have the benefit of being as beautiful as most of his paramours."

The mention of Miss Kitty Bennet prompted Darcy to search for the girl among the dancers, and he soon located her, down in the line on the other side of the room, dancing with one of the officers. She was smiling—laughing, actually—at something her partner said, and she appeared to be having a wonderful time. Every so often, however, her eyes would drift away from her partner, searching for Bingley, where he danced only a few couples away. Bingley, of course, was the fourth person with whom Darcy was annoyed. It was best not to think about that now, Darcy decided.

With a critical eye, Darcy watched Miss Kitty, noting that her joy made her almost glow. She was not, perhaps, classically beautiful, at least not what the ton would consider beautiful. Unlike her sister, she was tall and willowy, her hair a darker shade of blonde than what Bingley would usually prefer. But her features were pleasant, her eyes, a pretty brown, and her face, smooth and complexion, bright. Though Darcy preferred her sister, Miss Kitty Bennet, was a pretty girl indeed.

"I can see nothing wrong with Kitty Bennet," replied Darcy. "She seems to be a comely girl, and her behavior is proper and restrained."

"*That* is not the problem. The problem is that Charles seems to be on the verge of losing his head over her. It cannot be allowed."

Darcy's gaze swung to Miss Bingley, and he regarded her, wondering how a woman of her background could possibly think so highly of herself. Miss Bingley blushed a little at his scrutiny, no doubt thinking he was looking at her with admiration, before she raised her chin and watched him with a frank gaze. Whatever else the woman was, Darcy was forced to concede that she was not easily intimidated.

"I apologize, Miss Bingley," said Darcy, "but I do not understand. How can you, or anyone else, *allow* Bingley *anything*? By my reckoning, he is his own man, in control of his own fortune, and may choose his own path in life. Of what can you be speaking?"

"Of course Charles is his own man," replied Miss Bingley, her tone attempting to be soothing. "But often Charles does not know what is best for himself, and he requires guidance. That is why you are such a good friend to him. He listens to you, whereas he will often not give Louisa and me the same respect."

"I have advised him, Miss Bingley, but I take great care not to impose my opinion on him. I would not wish to direct him. He is a friend, not a subject."

"So he is. And what a good friend you are."

Darcy bowed, but he did not say anything further, preferring to let the subject drop. Unfortunately, Miss Bingley was not about to allow it.

"You must speak to him, Mr. Darcy. Convince him that it would be a mistake to offer for her."

"Are you not being a little precipitous?" asked Darcy. "He has only just begun to pay attention to her."

"I have seen this before, Mr. Darcy." Miss Bingley's eyes moved to her brother, and Darcy was certain he could see contempt in their depths. "Several times we have had to plead with him to keep him from throwing away all my parents' hopes and dreams. He cannot ascend society with such a woman as a wife."

"I will talk with him," replied Darcy shortly, more to induce her to depart than anything else.

"Oh, thank you, Mr. Darcy! I knew we could count on you!"

Repulsed, Darcy bowed and moved away, indicating a desire to have some punch. Miss Bingley had been called away at that moment, anyway, to deal with some matter of the ball. Of Miss Bingley's society, a little went a long way, and Darcy did not wish to endure her cloying attentions all evening.

So he walked the outside of the dance floor, watching the dancers. And time and time again, his eyes were drawn back to Miss Elizabeth Bennet. He watched as she danced and laughed, he applauded when she performed at dinner, and his eyes followed her wherever she went. She was the true jewel of this society, he decided. As an independent woman, he had no doubt she would have little difficulty in finding a husband. He only hoped she took care to choose someone who would suit her and treat her well.

Though Elizabeth could hardly have expected it, the evening proceeded rather well. She was able to dance most of the dances of the evening, share laughter and conversation with dear friends, and the embarrassment of the dinner at Longbourn was a distant memory. Furthermore, she had been able to escape Mr. Collins for most of the evening, as he had been content to simply watch her, rather than attempting to press his suit.

For this reprieve, Elizabeth knew that she had Mr. Darcy to thank, though the man did not approach her for the rest of the evening, and she was unable to voice her thanks. Under normal circumstances, Elizabeth might have been annoyed at the man's interference, which was not at all proper, but she decided, somewhat philosophically, that if Mr. Darcy was able to impart some measure of understanding of the social graces to Mr. Collins, she was not about to complain.

Mr. Wickham, of course, was another matter altogether. When the man had come to claim her for her dances, she had followed him readily enough, though with distaste. Their conversation was not at all what Elizabeth would have expected.

"You are ravishing tonight, Miss Bennet," began he, when they had taken their place in the line. "I almost lost my countenance when I saw you."

"Oh," replied Elizabeth, favoring him with an arch look, "I suppose that means my usual appearance is not at all attractive. You certainly understand how to wreak havoc with a girl's vanity, Mr. Wickham."

Laughing, Mr. Wickham assured her it was quite the opposite. "It is not the fact that I found you beautiful, but the fact that your beauty was so much enhanced tonight."

Elizabeth frowned at the man. It seemed he had either forgotten, or decided to ignore, the content of their previous discussion. His flattery was as thick as it had ever been, and he seemed to once again believe he could charm her with his smile and his pretty manners.

There was a certain part of Elizabeth which wished to once again disabuse the man of any such notion. The greater part, however, simply could not be bothered to concern herself with the man's expectations. Whatever Mr. Wickham chose to do, Elizabeth Bennet would not be affected. She was prepared to be perfectly indifferent and to ignore his attempts at flattery and courtship.

By the time her dance with Mr. Wickham ended, Elizabeth was happy to be rid of all three gentlemen—Mr. Darcy, who confused her; Mr. Collins, who annoyed her; and Mr. Wickham, who repulsed her.

At dinner, Elizabeth again had the opportunity to speak with Kitty, who she noticed had been engaged in dancing almost every set herself. And when Kitty had not been dancing, she had been the focus of all of Mr. Bingley's attention. Elizabeth was still cautious about this burgeoning relationship, but she was becoming cautiously optimistic for Kitty's sake. Mr. Bingley's actions suggested he was a man who admired a woman, and Kitty, Elizabeth thought, might be on her way to loving him, if he would only continue to encourage her. There still appeared to be a long way to go before such an eventuality was achieved, but Elizabeth was starting to feel like it might be attainable.

"Oh, Lizzy!" enthused Kitty as they came together for a few words. "Was there ever such a wonderful night? I almost feel as if I am walking on clouds."

"Yes, I can see that," said Elizabeth, regarding her sister fondly. "I am very happy for you, Kitty, though I would remind you to continue to behave properly. You are doing wonderfully, but I would not wish for your night—and the morning tomorrow—to be ruined by an excess of indulgence."

Kitty laughed. "I believe I have learned my lesson, and I have avoided the wine, just as I promised. You may count on my good behavior, Lizzy."

"I know I can, dearest," said Elizabeth, giving her sister an affectionate embrace. "Perhaps, if you continue on so charmingly, you might have your beau anyway."

"I can dream," said Kitty.

The two sisters parted, and as Kitty walked away, Elizabeth caught sight of Miss Bingley standing close by. She appeared to have swallowed a lemon whole, so sour was her expression as she regarded Kitty. When her eyes turned to Elizabeth herself, they went from cold to glacial. All at once, Elizabeth realized that the woman had been listening to her. Elizabeth had always known the woman possessed an unhealthy—and unwarranted—level of pride, and that she was not a friend of her brother's attentions to Kitty. But Elizabeth did not give three straws concerning the woman's opinion—her concern was for her sister's happiness and nothing more.

As Miss Bingley departed, however, she stopped at the sight of her brother and Mr. Darcy speaking animatedly on the other side of the room. Though it was difficult to tell, Elizabeth thought that Mr. Darcy was admonishing his friend. His expression, at least, was severe and disapproving, and Mr. Bingley appeared to be pleading, though at times his expression suggested sullenness.

After witnessing the sight for a few moments, Miss Bingley turned and directed a sly look at Elizabeth, who returned it blandly. Then the woman pushed her nose into the air far higher than was her usual wont, and she walked away, leaving Elizabeth behind. Clearly Miss Bingley had some knowledge of the subject of Mr. Darcy's conversation with Mr. Bingley, but Elizabeth decided it did not signify, so she put it from her mind.

Chapter XII

*I*t had often been a ritual for the ladies of Longbourn to meet with the ladies of Lucas Lodge the night after a ball or assembly, to discuss the evening, the fashions worn by the attendees, the partners of the various dancers, and whatever else caught their fancy. Such meetings were often held outside visiting hours, as a night such as the evening at Netherfield would often end quite late, and the two families often slept later than was usual.

Despite the late night, however, it had always been a custom for Elizabeth to rise early, as she was rarely able to sleep much past the early morning anyway. On those days, she would often indulge in a nap to help make up for the lack of sleep she had suffered the previous night. Within her family this was a well-known quirk, and she had often been teased by her sisters, and also by her friend Charlotte, who was privy to it.

On the night after the ball at Netherfield, however, Elizabeth had been feeling a little languid, and rather than awake with the sun, she was still in bed, just waking up from her night's sleep. It had indeed been an enjoyable evening. Elizabeth was happy that they had gone and that Kitty had been the continued focus of Mr. Bingley.

It was while she was in this attitude that a knock sounded on

Elizabeth's door. Instantly perplexed, as the staff was not in the habit of waking her, even on those rare occasions in which she slept later, Elizabeth called out permission to enter. To her surprise, Mrs. Whitmore appeared in the doorway.

"My apologies for disturbing your rest, Miss Bennet," said the housekeeper.

"It is no bother," replied Elizabeth. "I was already awake."

Familiar as she was with Elizabeth's habits, Mrs. Whitmore smiled briefly before her expression became serious once again. "Mr. Collins has come to the house, and he is insistent upon seeing you."

"Mr. Collins?" asked Elizabeth, frowning.

"Yes, miss. I attempted to inform him that you were not greeting visitors at present, but he was adamant you would wish to see him."

"I can well imagine it," said Elizabeth. She slipped her legs out from under the coverlet and sat up in bed, her legs dangling down the side. "I suppose there is nothing to do but greet him."

"Unless you wish for him to pace in front of the door or throw pebbles at your window all morning."

Elizabeth laughed at that portrayal of the man, knowing it was nothing but the complete truth.

"You may tell Mr. Collins that I will see him." Then a thought came to Elizabeth, and she turned a mischievous grin on her housekeeper. "I should greet him, but when I take into account his inconsiderate interference with my rest, early the morning after a late ball, I do not think I must be *too* quick in attending him."

The answering smile was all Elizabeth required. "I shall tell him, Miss Bennet, and I shall send Martha to you. Shall I have cook ready breakfast for you? Say, in about an hour's time?"

"That will do quite nicely."

A look passed between the two women, and Mrs. Whitmore departed. Elizabeth's mind was already on Mr. Collins, and given what she knew of his reasons for coming to Hertfordshire, as well as his comments and actions since arriving, she was certain she knew why he had come. And as much as she wished to avoid the pleasure of his company and addresses for as long as possible, Elizabeth knew it would be best to simply allow him to state his case and send him on his way. But she would not wait on him, as he obviously expected her to.

With Martha's help, Elizabeth was made presentable. The maid appeared perplexed when Elizabeth told her to take her time, but ever-dutiful, she did as she was asked. Choosing a dull muslin dress that Elizabeth had never truly liked and only wore when she knew she might get dirty, Elizabeth prepared, styling her hair into a simple bun. She would give her visitor no reason to feel his suit had any chance of success.

When Elizabeth thought she could delay no longer, she descended the stairs and made her way to the door, greeting Mrs. Whitmore, who was waiting, holding her pelisse, gloves and bonnet near the front door.

"He has tried to gain access to the house twice," said Mrs. Whitmore as she helped Elizabeth don her outerwear. "Mr. Whitmore is outside with him now."

Indeed, Elizabeth could hear the sound of raised voices from beyond the door. She shared an expressive look with Mrs. Whitmore, before the woman opened the door and allowed Elizabeth to slip out. There on the front portico, stood Mr. Whitmore, facing an obviously upset Mr. Collins.

"You will admit me to this house this instant, or I will see to it that you never work as a steward again!"

"This house is the residence of two young ladies, sir," replied Mr. Whitmore, seeming unperturbed by Mr. Collins's show of displeasure.

"And yet *you* enter it with impunity."

"I am the estate's steward. This is my place of employment. It is no more improper for me to be here than it is for the footman, or any of the others who make their livelihood here."

"Once *I* am master of this estate, *you* will not be welcome."

"*If* that eventuality ever comes to pass, I think I should be happy not to work here. But until it does, I will protect the Bennet sisters as I have been charged."

"Mr. Collins," said Elizabeth stepping forward to put an end to the argument, "why are you here this morning? And why are you accosting my steward?"

Eyeing Mr. Whitmore distastefully, Mr. Collins said: "The man is disobliging and disobedient. It will be necessary to replace him."

"Mr. Whitmore was hired by my uncle, not only because of his knowledge and expertise, but to see to the protection of my sister and me. He will not be replaced."

Perhaps speaking in such a manner was not the most diplomatic thing to do, but Mr. Collins's behavior already had Elizabeth wishing for his absence. The man seemed to hear her words with no less astonishment than resentment, but soon his expression turned patronizing, as if she were a little child and he was instructing her.

"That will be a matter for your husband to determine, my dear cousin."

"I have no husband, Mr. Collins, nor do I think I will enter that state in the near future."

Mr. Collins gaped at her momentarily, but he seemed to shake it off quickly.

"Of that, we shall see, my dear cousin. Now, if your *servants*," he directed a distasteful look at the Whitmores, who were standing on the portico watching him, "will give us a little privacy, we may discuss the business which brought me here."

"Mr. Whitmore will stay," said Elizabeth, before her steward could make a statement himself and rile Mr. Collins further. "His wife will provide a chaperone. Whatever you wish to say, sir, I suggest you say it now, so that I may return to the house."

"I can see your impertinence will need to be curbed."

"That is a matter for my future husband, should I ever marry, to discuss with me."

Suspicion was settled heavily over the parson by now, and Elizabeth wondered if she would be in danger if the Whitmores were not present. She had never considered her cousin to be anything other than an ineffectual twit, but he seemed determined to woo her, and indeed, almost desperate. There was no telling what a desperate man would do to achieve his ends.

"Very well. I have come here for the express purpose of engaging myself to you, my dear cousin, and as such make my proposal. Will you do me the honor of accepting my hand, and making me the happiest of men?"

It was all Elizabeth could do not to giggle at the silly man and his silly proposal. Though she might have expected a long-winded, flowery declaration of undying love and devotion, it appeared that Mr. Collins's pique suppressed his penchant for such language. The proposal was almost more of a demand than a request, and as such, Elizabeth possessed no qualms in refusing him. Of course, she had meant to do that anyway.

"I thank you for your kind proposal, Mr. Collins," said she, "but I cannot accept. I bid you good day, sir."

And with that, Elizabeth turned to go back into the house. As she had expected, however, Mr. Collins was not content to simply allow the matter to rest.

"You refuse?" said he, his tone strangled. "You *cannot* refuse."

"I certainly can, sir. It is a woman's prerogative, in situations such as this, to refuse or accept her suitor. I will not marry you, sir, so you had best redirect your attentions to some other, more welcoming woman."

"But—but . . ."

Elizabeth turned to look at the man, noting the utter stupefaction which had come over him. Another time it might have been amusing, but now, tired and hungry, she only wished he would leave.

"You cannot be serious in your refusal," said Mr. Collins at last.

"I cannot?"

"No." Mr. Collins stepped forward, seemingly gaining confidence. "You have marked my attentions these past days, I am certain. You cannot have been blind to them."

"What if I have? Just because you favor me with your attentions does not mean that I welcome them."

"I did not see any disinclination for my company in your manners."

"Must a woman necessarily object to a man's company if she does not mean to accept his proposal? I am happy to be in Mr. Bingley's company, though I cannot imagine ever accepting a proposal from him. Either way, I have not encouraged you, nor have I welcomed you. In fact, I have done everything in my power to inform you that I was not interested. If you did misunderstand my meaning, sir, that is *your* error."

Mr. Collins sucked in a deep breath, visibly calming himself. When he fixed his gaze on Elizabeth once again, his tone moved to one more conciliatory, and he showed her a half smile.

"Miss Bennet, I have come to Hertfordshire with the express resolution of engaging myself to you, and I shall not be moved from my purpose. I am in need of an estate, and you are in need of a husband. I cannot tolerate the conditions at my parsonage any longer, and the most logical solution is for us to marry. I will have your agreement before I leave this morning. You *must* agree."

"The conditions at the parsonage?" asked Elizabeth, uncertain to what the daft man was now referring. "I am afraid I do not understand."

"It does not matter," replied Mr. Collins. "You are my cousin, you are young and available, and in possession of an estate, and are quite comely besides. I intend to have you."

"I am sorry, Mr. Collins," said Elizabeth. "*You* might intend to have *me*, but *I* will not have *you*."

"But you *must* marry me!" exclaimed Mr. Collins. "Longbourn should be mine. I should already be the master of the estate."

Puzzled, Elizabeth looked at him, wondering what he was about. Her expression must have been question enough, for he scowled and spoke again, this time his tone angry.

"The entail on the estate, instituted by your great-grandfather, was to extend into the next generation. By those terms, I should already be the master."

"Perhaps that is so, Mr. Collins," said Elizabeth, already familiar with this matter, "but my grandfather and my father, as was their right, decided to terminate the entail."

"After your father produced his first two daughters!" snapped Mr. Collins.

"The reasons are irrelevant, sir," replied Elizabeth, though she knew he was correct.

Her grandfather had already been an old man when she was young, and her father, fearing for his wife and children and already with two young daughters, had persuaded his father to agree to end the entail, so he could leave it to any of his children. Not wishing to break up the estate, Mr. Bennet had subsequently willed Longbourn to the eldest daughter still living, which was why Elizabeth had inherited it.

"All that was required to break the entail on the estate was for the master and the heir to agree to it. My father and my grandfather so agreed, and they terminated it, allowing my father to leave it where he chose."

"They did so specifically to deny my father the opportunity to inherit," spat Mr. Collins. All semblance of the subservient fawning man was now gone, replaced with this vengeful, jealous creature.

"Again, sir, it matters not as to their intentions, only that the legalities were met. I will say, however, that I believe my father's primary motivation was the provision for his children. My grandfather required his agreement that the estate would not be broken up, to which father readily agreed."

"I will sue you for ownership of Longbourn!" cried Mr. Collins. "Marrying me is the only way you will retain your home."

"If I may, Miss Bennet," interrupted Mr. Whitmore.

He stepped forward and put himself in between Elizabeth and the man who was accosting her, looking down on Mr. Collins as if he was a worm.

"Mr. Collins, you may attempt to bring suit against Miss Bennet, but all you will accomplish is to bankrupt yourself. The matter was decided many years ago, by the only two men who had any power to change it. Longbourn is not and will never be yours. As Miss Bennet has forcefully rejected your suit, there is nothing left for you but to depart."

"I will appeal to her guardian! Surely he will see that my proposal is for the best!"

"You are welcome to try. Mr. Gardiner wishes the best for Miss Bennet, and I doubt highly that he will force her into a marriage she does not wish."

"Mr. Collins," said Elizabeth, "I thank you for your proposal, but we do not suit, and I will not marry you. It is unfortunate that you feel you have been cheated, and I am sorry for your disappointment, but that will not make me change my mind. Good day, sir."

And with those final words, Elizabeth walked into the house with Mrs. Whitmore, who helped her divest herself of her outerwear. The two women avoided looking at each other, knowing what the result would be. Elizabeth, unfortunately, caught her eye as she handed off her gloves, and they both descended into giggles.

"He is a ridiculous man, is he not?" asked Elizabeth in between laughs.

"He is," said Mrs. Whitmore, but then she became sober once again. "But I sense something else. It is fortunate that you are able to reject him, for I pity the woman who marries him."

"You do not suspect him of violent tendencies, do you?"

Mrs. Whitmore shook her head. "Not that, precisely. It seems to me he is subservient to all whom he considers to be superior, but I doubt a wife would command such respect. He is a large man, for all that he is soft, and I suspect he might not be averse to enforcing his authority over a wife."

Unbidden, Elizabeth shivered at the mere thought. Though she was not certain of the truth of Mrs. Whitmore's suspicions, Elizabeth respected her intelligence. It was a benefit to have a woman in residence to whom she could speak so openly—Mrs. Whitmore had been at Longbourn many years, and Elizabeth almost considered her to be a dear older relation, one to be looked up to.

The door opened and Mr. Whitmore entered, shaking his head.

"Is he gone?" asked Mrs. Whitmore.

A smile for his wife crossed Mr. Whitmore's face, and he turned to her. "Most reluctantly, but yes, he has departed."

"Do you think he will actually make his ridiculous claim to the courts?" asked Elizabeth.

"I doubt it. He might be foolish enough to approach a solicitor concerning the matter, but I doubt very much that any solicitor worth his salt would have anything to do with such a claim."

"Let us hope he does not engage someone as foolish as himself," replied Elizabeth.

"Enough of such talk," said Mrs. Whitmore. "Cook has laid out breakfast, and it will become cold if you do not partake."

"Thank you, Mrs. Whitmore," replied Elizabeth. "Thank you both for the care you provide to my sister and I."

"I am simply glad to be of service," said Mr. Whitmore, "and that my employment has led me to my dear Susan."

Happy with the company of dear friends and good servants, Elizabeth excused herself to go into the dining room. She truly was blessed with such faithful friends.

Kitty's response to the story of Mr. Collins's failed proposal was not surprising, considering Elizabeth's sure knowledge of Kitty's opinion of him.

"I cannot believe such silliness can exist inside one man," said Kitty, shaking her head with disgust. "It is fortunate that I slept through the entire affair, for I would certainly have given Mr. Collins a piece of my mind."

"Yes, fortunate indeed," replied Elizabeth.

"And for him to act in such a manner. I am certain that Mr. Bingley would not act thus."

Elizabeth shook her head, amused at her sister's determination to attribute every perceived virtue to Mr. Bingley.

"I dare say he would not, Kitty."

Then Kitty directed a sly look at her sister. "Perhaps you should have married him, Lizzy. At least life would not have been dull."

Laughing, Elizabeth replied: "I am certain life with Mr. Collins could not be anything *but* dull!"

The sisters stayed quietly at home that day and the next, taking pleasure in each other's company. As the ball had ended late, they were assured there would not be much occurring in the neighborhood for at least a day or two after. Elizabeth dealt with a few matters of the estate, played the pianoforte, and read, while Kitty sketched, remade a bonnet, and did reading of her own. In all, it was an enjoyable time for the sisters.

On the third day after the dance, Charlotte came to call, with her sister Maria in tow. Elizabeth was happy to see her dearest friend and welcomed her with an affectionate embrace and an invitation to share whatever news she had come by, knowing her mother was one of the foremost gossips in the neighborhood. The news that Charlotte had come to impart both astonished and diverted Elizabeth.

"Mr. Collins has returned to Kent," said Charlotte, moving to the heart of the matter immediately.

"Good riddance!" cried Kitty, making a disgusted sound in the back of her throat. "I sincerely hope that odious man never returns."

"If he does, he will not find welcome at Lucas Lodge."

Elizabeth looked at her friend sharply. "Has he done something enough to offend even your father?"

"I rather suspect he offended *you* too, Lizzy."

"Did he return to your home, complaining of the treatment he received at Longbourn?"

"Not immediately," said Charlotte. "When he returned, he went to his room and stayed there for some time, though one of the maids did report Mr. Collins muttering something about recalcitrant young ladies and his intention to seek legal advice. My father decided it was best to leave him to his own devices.

"When he emerged for dinner that night, it appeared like he was his usual self at first, but I could easily sense there was an edge to the man I had never before seen. We went to bed that evening without incident, but I could not help but think something had happened."

Elizabeth returned Charlotte's gaze evenly. "I assume it did not stay that way."

"No, indeed," replied Charlotte. "The first indication any of us had of any trouble was the sound of raised voices the next afternoon. For you see, Mr. Collins had accosted my father after luncheon, demanding that he go to Longbourn and 'talk some sense into you,' as he put it."

Wincing, Elizabeth shook her head. "I cannot imagine Sir William accepted Mr. Collins's demands well at all."

"I believe, my dear Elizabeth, that is a rather large understatement."

The four girls laughed. Elizabeth now found the whole matter humorous. Mr. Collins was certainly as ridiculous a man as she had ever met.

"Papa refused to even listen to Mr. Collins's entreaties to help him work on you, and when Mr. Collins persisted, he was ordered from our home."

"You should have seen them, Lizzy," said Maria, shaking her head. "Mr. Collins and Papa confronted each other throughout the house, yelling at each other, standing toe to toe. I was afraid they would come to blows."

Well able to imagine such a scene—after all, the one at Longbourn had been similar—Elizabeth shook her head. "It is truly incomprehensible for a man to believe that others will simply appease him because he is a clergyman. So he returned to Kent yesterday?"

"I know not," said Charlotte, "for Papa threw him from the house yesterday afternoon. He may have stayed in Meryton for the night before returning to Kent, but I do not know."

"And so ends Mr. Collins's residence in Hertfordshire."

"What actually happened, Eliza?" asked Charlotte. "I apprehend the fact that he proposed to you, but I would never have imagined that someone would take such offense, especially when he had attempted to court you for fewer than two weeks."

And so Elizabeth imparted to her friends the exact events which had occurred at Longbourn. Though politeness might have dictated that she leave out or smooth over some of the worst of Mr. Collins's excesses, Elizabeth spared no detail, left out nothing, preferring to state the absolute truth. Much laughter was shared by them all, amid exclamations of wonder and shaken heads.

"I am surprised Mr. Collins thought he could work on my father," said Charlotte. "He is not truly your guardian, after all—he merely assists when necessary. Mr. Gardiner makes all the decisions."

"Mr. Whitmore told him that applying to my uncle would be fruitless," replied Elizabeth. "My supposition is that Mr. Collins knew this to be true and thought your father's role was larger than it actually is."

"Regardless," interjected Kitty, "he is a silly man, and one I would just as soon forget. Shall we not speak of something else?"

"I do have another matter of some interest to impart," said Charlotte, though her uneasy glance at Kitty puzzled Elizabeth. "It seems that Mr. Bingley returned to London the day after the ball, taking Mr. Darcy along with him. The very next day, Miss Bingley closed up Netherfield and followed her brother to London."

A frown came over Kitty's face, and she chewed her lip. "Mr. Bingley did say something about being required to return to London for a few days," said she, speaking slowly as she turned the matter over in her mind. "But I do not think he intended for his sisters to follow him. He did also say something about Mr. Darcy leaving Hertfordshire, as he is to spend Christmas at his estate in the north with his family."

"Perhaps the sisters were bored with Hertfordshire and wished to return to London," said Maria. "It does not mean that he will not come back."

"But what if he does not?" fretted Kitty. "He *must* return, for he paid me particular attentions."

"And return he shall," said Elizabeth, "if his feelings are true."

Kitty frowned at such a statement, but Elizabeth would not allow her to concern herself with it any longer.

"Remember, Kitty, if a man's feelings are enough to propose to you, he shall. I believe you should also take this time of his absence to determine the state of your own feelings."

"But I know my feelings"

"Kitty," said Elizabeth, her tone kind but firm, "you have not known Mr. Bingley for long and you are only just becoming acquainted with his character. Do not focus on those feelings of infatuation which are foremost in your mind. Instead, picture Mr. Bingley in your life as your husband, father of your children. Does it seem right to you? When you know that, you will know you are in love with the man. Use this time to discover that for yourself. It will go better when he returns if you already have that question answered in your mind."

Tentatively, Kitty nodded, and Elizabeth breathed a sigh of relief. If Elizabeth was honest with herself, she wondered if Mr. Bingley would come again, or if his sisters had persuaded him from his interest in Kitty.

And then there was Mr. Darcy to consider. Specifically, Elizabeth remembered seeing Mr. Darcy speaking closely with Mr. Bingley that night, and she wondered if he had been attempting to persuade him to return to town and give Kitty up. If so, it was a cruel act, taken against one so young, who was truly infatuated with the man's friend. Elizabeth would have preferred Kitty to avoid forming an attachment for Mr. Bingley, but it appeared, at least on some level, she had. If the man was gone for good, Elizabeth had no doubt Kitty would have difficulty coming to terms with his disappearance.

"I am sorry, Kitty," said Charlotte, her tone remorseful. "I had not meant to upset you, but I suspected you had not heard the news yet, and I thought it was something you should know."

A wan smile met Charlotte's apology. "You were right, Charlotte. I appreciate the information, and I know you did not mean me harm."

They separated soon after, the Lucas sisters returning to their home, leaving Elizabeth and Kitty at Longbourn. Elizabeth spent the rest of the afternoon with Kitty, trying to comfort her, raise her spirits so that she could cope with what seemed to be her abandonment by Mr. Bingley. But Kitty would have none of it, insisting instead that it was still possible that Mr. Bingley would return.

"We have heard nothing of a definitive nature, Lizzy," said she, asserting her position rationally. "I believe I shall hope for the best, rather than be cast down into despair."

"Good for you, Kitty," said Elizabeth with a warm smile for her sister. "I believe that is the best way to handle the situation.

And so, they waited, hoped, and prayed. Elizabeth did not know if her sister prayed for Mr. Bingley's return, as they did not speak of the matter. For Elizabeth herself, she rather prayed that her sister would be strong enough to endure should Mr. Bingley prove fickle, for she feared that the man would not come again.

Chapter XIII

*I*t was hard, decided Kitty Bennet, to keep one's spirits up when all hope seemed to be fading by the hour. For though Mr. Bingley's words, promising to return after a few days in town, left no room for interpretation, still, he did not come. The longer he stayed away, the more her dark thoughts fed on her mood, teasing her with thoughts of what would never be, of what had, in fact, never been.

In truth, when Kitty looked back on the brief days of Mr. Bingley's interest in her, she realized that more than anything else, she had enjoyed being the focus of a man's attention. At the age of seventeen, Kitty had not felt herself to be singled out for attention by anyone, though since she had been left with one sister, naturally Elizabeth would look to her before any others. But Lizzy was also busy with the operation of the estate, concerned with the needs of the tenants, and engaged in the welfare of others. Consequently, there were times when Kitty felt that she shared her sister with all others who required her care and attention.

Growing up in a family of five daughters, Kitty had often felt left out, though considering the matter after the fact, she realized that Mary could likely lay claim to being the most forgotten Bennet sister. Mrs. Bennet had favored Lydia—the most like her in temperament—and

Jane—who was most like her in looks. And as Mr. Bennet had favored Elizabeth, Kitty had been largely left to her own devices, with Lydia for companionship, often emulating her younger sister in an attempt to be noticed by her mother. Now, having grown older and benefitting from the instruction of her elder sister, Kitty was not proud of the way she had often misbehaved. But she thought that on some level it was understandable.

Regardless, Mr. Bingley's attentions, though short in nature, had given her a sense of worth, not just as a beloved sister, but as a person to one completely unconnected to her. She had liked that feeling, even while she could fully confess that she was not certain what she had felt was, in fact, love.

Now, she simply felt bereft, as if something she had come to think of as hers by right had been stolen, with no possibility of recovery. It was possible that Mr. Bingley might return, but as the days passed and Christmas approached, hope faded, leaving Kitty irritable and despondent.

"Come, Sister," said Elizabeth, a number of days after the ball at Netherfield. "I hate to see you pining over Mr. Bingley. Shall we not go to Meryton, browse some of the shops? I know it would cheer you up."

Kitty was tempted to simply beg off, claim some indisposition, but she knew that she should not. Lizzy had been wonderful, speaking to her, telling her amusing stories, attempting to bolster her flagging spirits. In fact, Kitty was not completely certain Elizabeth was upset concerning Mr. Bingley's failure to return. She knew that Elizabeth was offended for Kitty's sake, but though she had always championed Mr. Bingley as a good and amiable man, Kitty wondered if Elizabeth was truly approving of the relationship she had thought they were building. At times, she almost wondered if Elizabeth was more relieved that Mr. Bingley had gone and not returned.

"Perhaps we could visit Aunt Phillips?" asked Kitty.

"Of course, dearest," replied Elizabeth with a warm smile. "If it would make you happy."

They did visit the shops and took tea with Aunt Phillips, and for a time it made Kitty feel better. It did not last long, however, as when they returned to Longbourn, the remembrance of Mr. Bingley and his failure to return once again assailed Kitty, and she was forced back into her morose thoughts and vain hopes.

Life, however, went on around her. Since the winter season had set in, there was relatively little to do on the estate. She and her sister still visited the tenants at times, but the visits were fewer and shorter. They busied themselves with putting together some hampers for the tenant families which would be delivered around Christmas, and that did help her put off her morose thoughts.

As the colder season descended, there were also fewer events in society, though the Longbourn ladies still kept up visits with the Lucases almost every day. On those few occasions where they were in company, Kitty learned that she had become something of a subject of gossip. Luckily, however, Mr. Bingley's attentions had not been of a long enough duration to excite anything dreadful.

"Do not let it concern you, Miss Kitty," said Mrs. Goulding, one night at a dinner party at the Goulding estate. "Young men these days are always flitting from one place to the next, and it takes some time before they can be induced to settle."

Kitty was in actuality a little shocked. "You think Mr. Bingley is not constant?"

"I cannot rightfully say," replied Mrs. Goulding, reaching out and patting Kitty's hands. "But though he was always amiable and happy in company, and seemed to single you out, Mr. Goulding reported that it was Mr. Darcy who was the more serious of the two. Mr. Bingley was not thought to be a *bad* or frivolous man, mind you, but most of the gentlemen thought he was still a little wet behind the ears, so to speak, not quite ready for the responsibilities of being the master of an estate, especially one as extensive as Netherfield."

"I always thought he was a good man," said Kitty, feeling a little offended.

"I never said he was not," agreed Mrs. Goulding. "But it is not to be wondered that a man of his tender years would not stay in one place for long."

"You should not make yourself unhappy over him," said Maria, one day while they were visiting Lucas Lodge.

"But he was a particularly amiable man," complained Kitty, though she well realized her tone made her seem petulant. "I hold him in high regard, and I was sure he felt the same for me. Why should I not be distressed that he does not come?"

"Why, there are plenty of young men out there, and many must be as handsome as Mr. Bingley." Maria giggled. "I dare say you will find another man as handsome."

"What if I do not want another man?" demanded Kitty.

"Then you shall simply have to wait. Something else has likely caught his attention. At some point he will tire of it, and I dare say that you will see him once again at Longbourn."

But Kitty was not so certain that Maria's assertions were at all the truth. In fact, she was almost certain that whatever had distracted him would not lose its charm any time soon. But what she could do on the matter, she could not say. So, she muddled on, still feeling unhappy, as if some dreadful ennui had come over her, never to depart. She could not help but hope that Mr. Bingley was as unhappy as she was herself.

Caroline Bingley could not have been more annoyed with how matters had turned out. She had returned to town, in the end, unengaged, and that despicable harpy, Lady Marion Lampley, had been unrelenting whenever in company, and likely when Caroline was not present. Her only saving grace was that Mr. Darcy had departed immediately for Pemberley upon returning to town. Only a few well-placed words suggesting that he had wished to speak to his family — Caroline had been careful to insinuate that the subject of his conversation would be *her* — was all that stood against her absolute ruin.

Of course, that had not stopped the woman. At one event in which they were in company, Caroline's assertions concerning Mr. Darcy had prompted one elegant eyebrow to rise.

"If what you say is true, should he not have wished to keep you close? Should you not be at Pemberley even now?"

"How can one understand the minds of these great men?" asked Caroline.

The woman only smiled at her, a predatory sort of expression, and allowed the subject to drop. Fortunately, for Caroline's sanity, Lady Marion had returned to her father's estate in Nottinghamshire soon after the incident, leaving Caroline to plot how she was to induce Mr. Darcy to propose.

A scowl threatened, which Caroline was forced to conceal. The fact that Caroline had not been invited to Pemberley was still a matter which infuriated her. She was certain there would be nothing better, especially if she was invited as Mr. Darcy's particular guest. But though Caroline knew she had shown herself to her best advantage, had proven her taste, sophistication, and had managed her brother's home in Hertfordshire with flair, still Mr. Darcy resisted.

It must be the fault of that insignificant speck, thought Caroline to herself.

Though she had relished having Mr. Darcy close, a captive audience, as it were, she had felt dirty at the mere fact of having to live in that backwards society. Would that a better location had been chosen . . . and a more significant estate. Caroline knew that she could hardly have failed had the estate Charles leased been greater, had it approached the grandeur of Pemberley. For if it had, then Mr. Darcy could truly have seen her mastery of her abilities. And then there was the interference of those two little adventuresses . . .

The very thought of the Bennets sent a scowl once again to Caroline's face, requiring an effort to remove it. Clearly they had thought far too highly of themselves, overestimated their worthiness, as evidenced by the fact that Miss Kitty had thought to ensnare Charles, and Miss Bennet—Caroline still could hardly believe the effrontery!—had set her sights on Mr. Darcy. The audacity of their actions was still enough to put Caroline into a fury.

Well, they had not succeeded, and Caroline would ensure they never would. Never let it be said that Caroline Bingley was bested by a pair of country misses.

"I say, Caroline, you must be caught in the midst of weighty thoughts. I do declare that I have never seen your expression change with such rapidity and with a countenance so varying."

Forced to hide another frown, Caroline turned to her brother, noting his frivolous smile. If there was one thing Caroline could trust, it was Charles's malleable temperament and ability to find contentment anywhere. It had been all too easy to deflect him from Kitty Bennet, though he still voiced some intention of returning to Hertfordshire as soon as may be. Thus, as there was still some danger—though Caroline did not doubt her ability to control her brother—today was to be the masterstroke in ensuring that Charles was ensconced in London for the winter, with no desire whatsoever to return to Hertfordshire. If Caroline had her way, the only time she would ever even set foot in that accursed shire was when she journeyed between Pemberley and London, after her marriage.

"I was simply caught in remembrance, Charles," said Caroline, waving him off.

"You must have thought of the unpleasant, as well as the pleasant. I swear I saw a fearsome scowl several times."

"No memory is completely pleasant, Charles. There is evil as well as good in the world."

"Perhaps there is," replied Charles. "But I dare say we are able to create memories which bear no stain of unhappiness. My memories of Miss Kitty Bennet are untainted, I assure you."

It was only the greatest of resolve that prevented Caroline from lashing out at Charles for his stupidity. For even now, after he had mostly forgotten the girl, there were still times when he would mention her name, and all the progress that Caroline had made seemed to be undone.

That the girl had incited nothing more than infatuation was very fortunate indeed, though Caroline knew that most of his paramours in the past had been nothing more than the same fixation. Though Caroline considered herself practiced at deflecting her brother and good at manipulating him, she knew that when he truly wanted something, there was little she could do to stop him. If his feelings for Miss Kitty had been strong enough, he would have returned to Hertfordshire regardless of Caroline's machinations.

"And so they are," said Caroline, using a soothing tone with her brother. "I am certain she waits for your return. I would have you take care though, Charles. I am not convinced the girl is not fixed upon your fortune."

"We have discussed this before, Caroline," replied Charles, a hint of steel entering his voice. "Miss Kitty is a genuine young woman and not a fortune hunter."

Caroline nodded, but gave him no other indication that she agreed with him. In fact, to contradict and argue with him would have been akin to turning loose the mulish qualities her brother possessed and sent him back to Hertfordshire without delay. Caroline was careful to make her comments about Kitty Bennet, but she did not push her opinions. Simply sowing a little doubt, whether he truly believed it or not, was more than enough.

The door chime rang, and Caroline smiled to herself. The next phase her of plan was now underway.

After a few moments, a young lady was shown into the room. She was of moderate height, a little shorter than Caroline herself, and possessed of a wealth of flaxen tresses piled up on her head, clear cerulean eyes, and a pretty, flawless complexion. She was very much the epitome of what society considered to be a beautiful young woman, and after Caroline had made her acquaintance the previous week, she was eager for her to meet Charles.

"Thank you for visiting, Miss Herbert," said Caroline, rising and greeting the newcomer with pleasure. "Please allow me to introduce my brother."

Gesturing to Charles, who had risen by her side, Caroline performed the office. "Charles Bingley, this is Miss Ruth Herbert."

"I am happy to make your acquaintance," replied Charles.

They sat and Caroline directed the conversation for a few moments, but slowly, as if she were a horse, slowly pushed to the side by one larger, Charles began to lead more, taking control, speaking more animatedly to the young woman. Miss Herbert, for her part, responded with quiet returning comments, as was proper for a young woman meeting a young man for the first time. But over time, her own comments became livelier, and soon, they were conversing as if they had known each other for some time.

Caroline had seen this particular scene play out too many times to be mistaken about where it would end. Charles would speak with her exclusively, insist on accompanying Caroline when she returned the visit, dance with her, flirt with her, and within a week, he would declare her to be an angel, and the most perfect woman of his acquaintance. All thoughts of Miss Kitty Bennet would be forgotten, not that the girl had ever been more than a diversion, for his praise of her had never been anything but lukewarm.

Victory is sweet indeed, thought Caroline to herself as she watched her plans mature.

The fact that Miss Herbert was herself nothing more than minor gentry was irrelevant at this point. Eventually, Charles would either tire of her, or Caroline would introduce him to another "angel," and he would become enamored all over again. Eventually, when she found someone who would advance their position in society sufficiently, Caroline would allow the relationship to proceed to its logical conclusion. That was, of course, if she was not successful in brokering a marriage with Miss Darcy. Mr. Darcy had been stubbornly reluctant up to that point, which vexed Caroline, but though she thought she would ultimately be successful in that endeavor, it was only prudent to have a contingency in place. There were many young ladies of society who would be acceptable, of course—Miss Darcy was perfect, for she coincided with Caroline's own ambitions. But another would do.

The important matter now was that Charles was focused on a new woman, someone who was not Miss Kitty Bennet. The chances of Charles returning to Netherfield now were nearly nonexistent.

If the talk in Meryton was that Kitty was to be pitied for Mr. Bingley's abandonment, Elizabeth discovered that what was spoken concerning her and Mr. Collins was quite different in nature. Mr. Collins, it seemed, was not well thought of in Meryton, for he had alienated several of the families with his pompous speeches and superior ways, not to mention his constant homilies regarding his gracious patroness.

"It is well that you refused the man," said Aunt Phillips, one day when Elizabeth was visiting with her. "He is a most undeserving young man, and I am happy that you were intelligent enough to refuse him."

"I was not aware that you held him in such antipathy, Aunt," said Elizabeth.

Mrs. Phillips made a disgusted sound in the back of her throat. She was a good woman, but she had not had the benefit of moving much in the circles inhabited by gentlemen, and as such could sometimes be a little vulgar.

"I do not think there are many young men I think less of, I assure you. Do you know he compared my best armchair to a chair in the servants' quarters of his patroness's estate?"

Amused, Elizabeth owned that she had not known of the matter.

"He called the servant's chair finer," said Mrs. Phillips with an offended huff. "It is an insult not to be borne. I was ready to throw the man from the house, I assure you."

Knowing that Mr. Collins was nothing more than thoughtless, and had undoubtedly not intended a slight, Elizabeth only shook her head, while murmuring comfort to her aunt.

On another occasion, while speaking with Mrs. Long, Elizabeth had another opportunity to learn what others thought of the man.

"Do you know he slighted my Prudence?" said Mrs. Long, speaking of her eldest niece. "Prudence is not the most beautiful girl—she certainly has not the appearance of your eldest sister, God rest her soul— but she is pleasant and pretty, and very popular in the neighborhood.

"But Mr. Collins had no compunction in saying otherwise."

Elizabeth frowned; that certainly did not sound like Mr. Collins, who was more apt to flatter, than to insult.

"Perhaps you misunderstood him?"

"I assure you, I did not." Mrs. Long's anger was a palpable entity. "The man was standing by the side of the dance floor, watching the dancers—watching *you*, unless I am completely blind—when young master Lucas, seeing him standing around in a stupid manner, recommended Prudence as an available partner for a dance.

"And do you know what he said?"

Though Elizabeth was almost afraid to hear it, she knew she would. Mrs. Long had built up an impressive well of affront, and the woman was not about to be gainsaid now.

"He said, 'I thank you for your good intentions, sir, but the young miss, while tolerably featured, is not up to the standards demanded by my patroness, Lady Catherine de Bourgh. I am not in the habit of dancing with young ladies who are not capable of inducing other men to stand up with them. I bid you cease your attempts to persuade me to dance, as I have found a delicate and beauteous flower—and one much livelier—to observe. I shall not be moved from it.'"

It was even worse than Elizabeth had feared, and she winced at Mrs. Long's retelling. "I apologize on behalf of my cousin, Mrs. Long."

"*You* have no need to apologize, Miss Bennet," said Mrs. Long. "The Bennets have always been well thought of in the community, and you girls are no different. We all understand that you and your sisters have long been the most beautiful young ladies in the district, and I think none of us have envied that with which you have been blessed.

"But to dismiss my niece in such a manner—it is completely beyond the pale!"

"I cannot but agree with you, Mrs. Long," replied Elizabeth. "Prudence and Patience are very good girls, and quite pretty, I am certain."

Mrs. Long smiled, her good humor seemingly restored. "I thank you, Miss Bennet. You are a good girl, regardless of your unfortunate cousin."

Such sentiments were often spoken in Elizabeth's presence, and she found herself relieved. She had never thought her friends in the neighborhood would turn on her, but gossip could be started with far less. The fact that most of her friends thought her uncommonly sensible for refusing an engagement from such an odious specimen as Mr. William Collins heartened her, though she would not have concerned herself for an instant, should the opinions have been different.

But though the matter of Mr. Collins was one which brought her relief, the presence of Mr. Wickham did not. Elizabeth attempted to make clear to the man many times of her disinterest in his attentions, but he seemed incapable—or unwilling—to understand. He would approach her in Meryton, insist on speaking with her whenever they were in company, laughing at his own witticisms, and laying on his charm with all the precision of a man pouring molasses over pancakes. And perhaps, most disquieting, he often appeared on Longbourn's grounds, approaching her when she walked out, intent upon walking with her and further disrupting her peace of mind. Elizabeth began to wonder if he was neglecting his duties in order to watch the house in anticipation of her leaving it, so that he could impose upon her once again.

It finally came to a head about two weeks after the departure of the Netherfield party. Mr. Wickham had met her the previous two days, once on the streets of Meryton and once at a card party in which he had sat by her, speaking animatedly and monopolizing her attention. She had stepped out into the back yard of the house to sit in the sunshine, which was bright that morning, and read a few letters she had received.

She had not gone more than a few feet from the door, when he appeared, hat in hand, a luminous smile affixed to his face.

"Miss Bennet," called he, "how fortunate it is I happened to be passing by as you came out. Shall we not walk together?"

This time, after being forced to put up with this man's attentions for two weeks, Elizabeth did not even attempt to hide her displeasure.

"You were only 'passing by,' were you, Mr. Wickham?"

"I had an errand in Longbourn village," replied the man. "But I had not thought to see you here."

"I *live* here, Mr. Wickham. Where else should I be?"

Mr. Wickham laughed as if she had made some grand joke, ignoring the irony and asperity in her voice. "Touché, Miss Bennet. But for me to pass by at the exact moment you came out through the door suggests some sort of divine providence, do you not agree?"

"Divine providence," said Elizabeth, completely unamused. "That is an . . . *interesting* way to put it."

"I have always had a gift for words," replied Mr. Wickham with good-natured cheer.

Turning, Elizabeth walked back to the front door, with Mr. Wickham trailing behind. "Do you mean to invite me in, Miss Bennet?" asked he, a nonchalant tone entering his voice. "I would be happy to take tea with you, but I had understood Longbourn did not accept male visitors, due to your sole residence with your sister."

"Please wait here, Mr. Wickham," replied Elizabeth, as she stepped into the house.

Within a few moments, Elizabeth had returned to the front door, and she was forced to confess she rather enjoyed the startled look which came over his countenance at the sight of Mr. Whitmore accompanying her, as well as John, the burly footman.

"Mr. Whitmore," said Elizabeth, gesturing to Mr. Wickham, "I am certain you remember Mr. Wickham."

"Oh, I do, indeed," said Mr. Whitmore, glaring at Mr. Wickham.

For his part, Mr. Wickham seemed determined to play the amiable gentleman. "Whitmore. It is a pleasure to see you again, sir."

"I am certain it is."

Elizabeth almost giggled at the man's wry tone, but she forced herself to maintain her stern expression.

"Mr. Wickham," said Elizabeth, fixing a steely look at the man, "it seems as if I cannot go anywhere without tripping over you. No matter what I do, you insert yourself into my presence, when it is unwanted."

"Unwanted?" cried Mr. Wickham, seemingly injured at the

suggestion. "I had thought we were building a friendship, Miss Bennet."

"In your own mind, perhaps. Now, I cannot control your movements, nor can I dictate your actions. I dare say you and I will meet in the streets of Meryton on occasion, and there may be instances where we will attend the same functions.

"But I *can* control what happens at Longbourn, sir. I do not believe for an instant that you *happened* to pass by as I was leaving the house. I do not know what your commanding officer thinks of you neglecting your duties to spy on me, but I do not appreciate it."

"Miss Bennet!" exclaimed Wickham, but before he could continue further, Elizabeth held up a hand and John stepped forward, forestalling his outburst.

"Listen to the mistress, sir."

"As I was saying, I will not have my peace at Longbourn invaded. As such, I will ask you to kindly depart and do not return without an invitation, sir. In the town, I will politely greet you, should we meet, but no more; the same thing will happen at any function we both attend.

"The fact of the matter is that I am not taken in by your manners, and your flattery does not affect me. Perhaps you wish to gain access to Longbourn's coffers, but I can assure you that will never happen. You may ply your trade elsewhere, sir, for I wish to have no part of it."

"Miss Bennet," said Mr. Wickham, his manner affecting an injured air, "I have only ever desired your friendship."

"I am sorry, Mr. Wickham, but I am not inclined to offer it. We are acquainted, and I will behave as I would to any other acquaintance. But if you continue to press me, I shall have no choice but to cut you. Good day, sir. Please do not return."

Left with no other option, Mr. Wickham bowed and turned to leave. But as he did, he looked at Elizabeth, and though he wore a look of affected hurt, his eyes glittered, their depths hard as diamonds. He was clearly not amused at being thwarted.

A few days before Christmas, the Gardiners arrived, to the welcome and relief of the Bennet sisters—Kitty because they would provide a source of distraction from her gloomy thoughts, and Elizabeth because she welcomed an outside opinion of their situation. They pulled up to the front door of Longbourn and debarked from their carriage to the warm affection and greetings of the Bennet sisters, their four children greeting their beloved elder cousins cheerfully.

When they had been to their rooms and refreshed themselves, the Gardiners joined Elizabeth and Kitty in the sitting-room, with keen interest in their recent doings and probing questions. As Elizabeth—and to a lesser extent Kitty—kept up a regular correspondence with them, they were already aware of most of the news. But Elizabeth was certain they had been anxious to see for themselves how their younger relations were doing, and to provide support, if need be. Mr. Gardiner was, quite understandably, concerned for their physical needs, though they were both also concerned for their states of mind, considering the changes of the previous months.

"Now, Lizzy," said Mr. Gardiner, fixing her with his look of good humor, "I must ask you to clarify about this Mr. Collins of whom you have written so eloquently. Was that man truly as ridiculous as you made him out to be?"

"More, if anything," said Kitty, her lip wrinkled with disgust. "Always spouting his patroness's homilies, carrying on, speaking ten words when two would have been sufficient, stepping all over ladies' feet at the ball. If anything, Lizzy understated how ridiculous he was."

Mr. Gardiner watched Kitty with affectionate amusement and then turned back to Elizabeth, a hint of a challenge in his raised eyebrow.

"I understand your reasons for thinking I was portraying Mr. Collins as a caricature, but I assure you that in this case, the caricature breathes and walks among us."

"And he truly asked for your hand after little more than a week's acquaintance?" asked Aunt Gardiner.

"He did, and he would not accept my refusal. Mr. Whitmore has had a busy autumn chasing away my suitors."

Though both Gardiners appeared intrigued by Elizabeth's statements, they continued to focus on the subject at hand.

"I cannot understand the man's thinking. He actually thought your father and grandfather had cheated him out of the estate?"

"I know it is incomprehensible, Uncle, but there it is."

Mr. Gardiner shook his head. "Well, at least he is gone. Perhaps I should write to him—explain to him that I am your legal guardian and that I will not countenance another proposal of marriage from him. If he has taken your refusal with such ill grace, I would not put it past him to intrude upon your peace again."

"I beg you would not," said Elizabeth. "I doubt Mr. Collins possesses the means to make frequent journeys, and as I will be of age in only a few months, it is of little matter." Then Elizabeth grinned. "And if Mr. Collins should show his face here again, I will simply have Mr. Whitmore run him off."

"Very well, Lizzy," said Mr. Gardiner. "Now, what of this other matter? Have you had other suitors of which you have not written?"

"Only one, Uncle," replied Elizabeth with a laugh. "I did not write to you of this latest episode because it would not be long before you arrived."

And so Elizabeth began her tale of Mr. Wickham's attentions, including Mr. Darcy's warnings about the man. She ended with a description of the scene which had occurred only a few days before, in which she had ordered Mr. Wickham from the property and told him not to return.

"Has he returned?" asked Mr. Gardiner.

"We have not seen him since, even when we went into Meryton," replied Elizabeth.

Mr. Gardiner seemed inclined to pursue the matter with the young man, but he soon sighed and eased himself back into the cushions of the sofa. "This Mr. Wickham shows all the signs of being a fortune hunter. I cannot impress upon you enough the need to take care, especially with what your aunt has learned."

Turning to her aunt in surprise, Elizabeth asked: "What do you mean?"

"As you are aware, Lizzy, I am originally from Derbyshire. But what you likely did not know is that I am from a little town called Lambton, which is only five miles from Pemberley."

"Mr. Darcy's estate!" exclaimed Kitty.

"Indeed. I am not familiar with the family, as we moved in very different circles, but I am familiar with their reputations. I had also heard something of this Mr. Wickham, and though, again, I was not acquainted with him, I remembered something of his activities when he was young, where he was not well thought of.

"As I maintain several acquaintances in the area, when I read of him in one of your letters, I asked one of my friends for her opinion of the man. I received a response from her only days ago."

"And?" Asked Elizabeth, moving to the edge of her seat. "What did she say?"

"Mr. Wickham is not well thought of, and though his father was respected, most of Pemberley's residents do not hold him with any esteem. He is known to be wild, loose with ladies' reputations, fond of the gaming tables, and he left Lambton not long after the elder Mr. Darcy's death, leaving many debts with the local merchants. It is also known that the present Mr. Darcy discharged those debts after he departed."

"So it is true," said Elizabeth with a sigh.

"Did you doubt it?" asked Mrs. Gardiners sternly.

"No, Aunt, I did not. But whereas before I only had Mr. Darcy's words—which I believed, I might add—now I have certain information. I had not thought much of Mr. Wickham from my first meeting with him, but to know that such a viper exists in our community . . ."

"I understand your dismay, Lizzy," said Uncle Gardiner. "Now, I believe additional measures must be taken to ensure your safety."

"Mr. Whitmore and I have anticipated you. Whenever I walk the grounds, I stay close to the house, and if I roam further afield—to visit tenants or tour the fields—John accompanies me."

"Good. I do not think I need to tell you what would happen if this Wickham fellow were to achieve his goal of control over your estate."

Indeed, it was not required, and Elizabeth was quick to inform her uncle of that fact.

"Then I believe I should like to have a word with Mr. Whitmore before dinner. If you will excuse me."

When Mr. Gardiner had departed, Mrs. Gardiner turned to the Bennet sisters and opened the topic of Mr. Bingley's actions in the neighborhood, and though Kitty was little disposed to discuss the subject, Mrs. Gardiner was relentless. It was not long before she had the entire story, mostly told by Kitty, though Elizabeth contributed her impressions when requested. When the entire matter had been shared, Mrs. Gardiner sat back and regarded Kitty.

"How are you Kitty?"

"I am coping, Aunt," replied Kitty. "It is hard because I truly esteemed Mr. Bingley. Perhaps I am naught but a silly girl, but I truly thought he esteemed me too."

"I do not know what to tell you, Kitty." She turned to Elizabeth. "What was your opinion, Lizzy?"

"Mr. Bingley is an amiable man, handsome, and seemingly in possession of every virtue."

"That much I have apprehended, Lizzy. What of your opinions about Mr. Bingley's attentions to your sister?"

Though feeling a little uncomfortable, and shooting an apologetic glance at her sister, Elizabeth said: "I was never certain of the matter. When Mr. Bingley first arrived in Meryton, he did not immediately single Kitty out. It was only after we returned from our night at Netherfield that he seemed to take an interest in her."

"And from Kitty's side?" asked Mrs. Gardiner.

Kitty blushed and Elizabeth looked at her sister with compassion. But she answered as truthfully as she was able.

"I wondered from the beginning if Kitty was merely infatuated with him. If his attentions had been constant, I think it might have become a deeper affection, but I do not think Kitty knew him long enough to truly love him."

"I *am* sitting right here," said Kitty, her irritability showing. "I would thank you to speak to me, rather than about me."

"I had wondered when you would protest," said Mrs. Gardiner, smiling affectionately. "Please, Kitty, I would be interested to hear of your opinion on the matter."

Though she huffed again, soon Kitty shook her head. "I have thought of little else, aunt. At the time, I believed myself truly in love with Mr. Bingley, but I cannot say Lizzy is incorrect. But that does not make the hurt any less acute."

"Indeed it does not." Mrs. Gardiner pulled Kitty into a close embrace, providing the support and love of a mother, which is what she had become to both girls. "It *is* unfortunate, Kitty. I think, however, you will emerge from this experience stronger for having had it."

Kitty attempted a smile. "I sincerely hope so."

Favoring her niece with an affectionate smile, Mrs. Gardiner said: "Would you like to hear my opinion on the matter?"

"Please," was Kitty's reply.

"Very well." Mrs. Gardiner's expression became stern, though Elizabeth knew it was not directed at either of them. "It seems to me like this Mr. Bingley has been rather fickle in his attentions. If a man is in love with a woman, he will do anything to be by her side. That he did not return suggests that either his feelings were not serious, or that he was simply passing his time in the country with a pretty young woman with no other serious intentions."

Kitty appeared stricken by her aunt's blunt assessment, so Elizabeth was obliged to say: "But what of Mr. Bingley's sisters? I am convinced they were no friends of Mr. Bingley's attentions to my sister."

Though Elizabeth did not say so, she also remembered Mr. Darcy's conversation with Mr. Bingley the night of the ball, and she wondered if he had had a hand in Mr. Bingley's failure to return to the neighborhood.

"Then I am afraid his actions suggest a want of resolution." Mrs. Gardiner looked at her niece kindly. "I know it is hard, Kitty. But as much as you are able, I would ask you not to make yourself unhappy over Mr. Bingley. *If* he ever returns, then you may judge for yourself if he is worthy of your affections. You are still young. There is no need to rush your way to matrimony."

Though it was obviously difficult, Kitty managed a smile. "I shall try,

Aunt."

"That, my dear Kitty, is all anyone can ask."

Chapter XIV

*I*t is not the purpose of this work to describe the Bennet sisters' Christmas with their London relations. As with any holiday season, it was a time filled with the happiness of family, good friends, food and drink, and celebrations of the Savior's birth. And as with any such celebration, they were able to forget their troubles, and in the case of the younger sister, to begin to heal from her disappointment.

For Elizabeth, though she herself had no particular injuries to resent, she found her attention often wandering to the autumn when the Netherfield party had been in residence. Though Kitty had suffered disappointment, Elizabeth felt no particular antipathy for Mr. Bingley. She suspected that the situation was exactly what her aunt had suggested—that Mr. Bingley had not possessed any deep feelings for Kitty, and though, perhaps, he should have exercised more discretion in order to avoid raising her expectations, she did not hold any ill will toward the man.

More often, however, Elizabeth found her thoughts turning to the other gentleman of the party. Mr. Darcy, quite honestly, was the most gentlemanly man Elizabeth had ever met. He was proper, obviously took great care of his sister, and supported his friends, as evidenced by his willingness to help Mr. Bingley, when he was at leisure. There was much to like in the gentleman, Elizabeth decided.

She was not in love with the man, she decided. There was no opportunity for her to have developed such feelings. But she felt a warmth toward him, not only for the friendship he had offered while he had been in Hertfordshire, but also for his caring enough to extend the warning about Mr. Wickham. Elizabeth thought she had seen through Wickham enough to be wary, but she would not have known of the true depth of his depravity. And for that, Elizabeth could only be grateful.

In the back of Elizabeth's mind, however, the memory of Mr. Darcy speaking sternly with Mr. Bingley the night of the ball refused to leave her. If he had warned Mr. Bingley away from Kitty, the largest question in Elizabeth's mind was the reason for it. Given his comments when he had been in residence, not to mention his kindness, Elizabeth could not imagine he had thought a Kitty unsuitable. But then why would he do it?

It was puzzling and vexing to Elizabeth, who generally thought well of the man. But though it often entered her mind at diverse times, Elizabeth decided not to concern herself on the matter. She doubted she would ever see Mr. Darcy again, and if ever she did, she would not dream of demanding an accounting of his actions. Thus, it was better if she just left it alone and focused on the joy of being with her family.

Of particular import to Elizabeth's future, though she could not know it at the time, was a conversation shared with the Gardiners not long after their arrival in Hertfordshire. Kitty had retired early, leaving Elizabeth with her aunt and uncle, and it was then that Mrs. Gardiner made a suggestion.

"Lizzy, why do you and Kitty not return to London with us after Christmas for a visit?"

"Is there any particular reason for your invitation?" asked Elizabeth, though she was not at all opposed to the idea.

"I would have thought *you* would have been eager to leave Hertfordshire for a time, Lizzy. A time away from Meryton would assist in Kitty's recovery from her disappointment and would remove you from the presence of Mr. Wickham."

"That is true," agreed Elizabeth, "but I should not like to run away from my troubles."

"Come, Lizzy, it is not a matter of running from anything," said Mr. Gardiner. "It is merely a visit with your dearest relations, one I would have thought you eager to accept."

Elizabeth laughed at his reference to dearest relations. "Indeed, Uncle, I have no objections. In fact, I think a visit to London sounds heavenly, and I do think Kitty would welcome the opportunity to leave Longbourn for a while, as well.

"Of course, we should return for spring planting."

Mr. Gardiner smiled with warm affection and patted her hand. "It does my heart well to know what prodigious care you take for the estate. I think that you could easily be absent, as Mr. Whitmore handles the details, but I understand if you wish to be back. But would that not preclude your participation in the events of the season?"

"Oh, and you now rub shoulders with the highest of society?" asked Elizabeth archly.

A laugh was Mr. Gardiner's response. "No, Lizzy, I am still a tradesman, though I have dealings with many gentlemen. I cannot offer you the finest of society, though I think we can manage some events, including museums, art galleries, and even a play or opera, or two."

"Then that is all I could wish for, Uncle. I will speak to Kitty, but I am certain she will have no objection to the plan."

And thus, to London they were to go, as Kitty was not at all opposed to leaving Hertfordshire for a time.

"What is it, Brother?"

Darcy glanced up from his letter, noting Georgiana's curious gaze resting upon him. "It is nothing," said he, shaking his head."

"Are you certain it is not a letter from our Aunt Catherine?" Georgiana showed him a bit of a mischievous smile, one which had been, in recent months, few and far in between. "You usually reserve such fierce scowls for letters from Kent."

Though he knew he should reprimand her, Darcy could not resist the impulse to laugh. It was nothing less than the truth, after all.

"No, Georgiana, it is not from our aunt. In fact, it is from Bingley."

Georgiana looked up from her breakfast with surprise. "Mr. Bingley? Usually you are happy to receive missives from your friend, though I will own that you often walk about with it in your hands, shaking your head and speaking to yourself."

Once again Darcy was forced to laugh. "That is because Bingley's penmanship is atrocious and it is difficult to decipher his writing."

"But you have not yet begun to read it."

"No, and I will not until later when I find myself at leisure. I am merely surprised because Bingley's letter is postmarked from London. I had understood he was to return to Hertfordshire. As I have not heard from him since we have come to Derbyshire, I do not know what to make of this."

"Perhaps he did not find Hertfordshire to his liking?"

Darcy nodded slowly, though he was considering several other possibilities at the same time. Bingley had never been the most . . . dependable of friends, though Darcy truly valued him for those qualities he did possess, such as his amiable nature and his ability to pull Darcy from his more serious disposition. There was much to like in Bingley, if one could ignore his flaws.

Shaking his head, Darcy was forced to confess his thoughts smacked of pride. Who did not have faults, after all? That his faults were different from Bingley's made the other man such a good friend.

"I suppose I should read the letter before coming to any conclusions," said Darcy. "There was some question of his intentions to a lady in Hertfordshire, and I had thought he would return to continue the acquaintance."

Had Darcy not been looking at his sister at that moment, he might have missed the way she hesitated, the brief expression of aversion which crossed her features.

"Is aught amiss, Georgiana," asked he, thinking of how, over the past few moments, their roles had been reversed.

"I do not wish to say anything," said Georgiana. "Mr. Bingley is a good man, and I would not have you think I am censuring him."

"Censuring him?" asked Darcy, puzzled as to Georgiana's meaning. "I was under the impression you liked Bingley."

Georgiana was silent for several moments, and Darcy wondered if she would speak. At length, however, her words came slowly and with much thought as to their content.

"I *do* like Mr. Bingley, Brother," said Georgiana. "But I sometimes wonder . . . That is to say, I have often heard you mention his propensity to fall in and out of love, and your lamentations concerning his want of resolution. He does indeed possess the most engaging of manners, but is not a gentleman judged by more than simply these things?"

"They are," agreed Darcy, as he considered his sister's words. "By the strictest definition of the word, however, Bingley is not yet a gentleman, though he is attempting to rise to that state."

"But, Brother, is not the measure of a gentleman also the manner in which he acts? And if Mr. Bingley is indeed attempting to rise to that estate, should he not act in such a manner as to make him worthy of it?"

"Some of the most immoral men I know are gentlemen by birth," said Darcy.

"That simply illustrates my point," insisted Georgiana. "Though Mr. Bingley is a good man and a happy one, he does not strike me as a man who takes his responsibilities seriously. I am sorry, Brother, but I would not wish to be tied to such a man."

Darcy stared at his sister, astonished at her assertions. Only months before she had almost eloped with George Wickham, and though Darcy could readily acknowledge that he had often harbored concerns about Bingley's character, there was no question as to who was a better man, when Bingley and Wickham were compared.

She appeared, however, to have given the matter considerable thought, and the more Darcy chewed it over in his mind, the more he was proud of Georgiana. Yes, she had almost made a grave mistake, but it appeared she had learned and grown from it. He had no doubt that she would not make such a mistake again, and he was certain that she was now aware of what kind of man she should search for when considering a prospective husband. Little though Darcy wished to consider the possibility of Georgiana leaving him to make a life with another man, as she was already sixteen, he knew it would happen, likely in the near future.

"I am sorry to speak of your friend thus, William," said Georgiana after a moment. "I hope you are not angry with me for my candid words."

"Of course not, Georgiana," replied Darcy. "I would hope you would trust me with your thoughts. Bingley is *my* friend. I would expect you to be polite to my acquaintances, but I do not require you to like them. Dare I ask after your opinion of his sisters?"

Georgiana laughed. "I am not afraid of offending you, Brother, since you have often commented on them yourself. I cannot like them, though Mrs. Hurst is tolerable. Miss Bingley, however, looks about and covets everything she sees. She simpers and flatters, and I am certain her praise of my playing, my person, and everything else she can think of, is motivated by nothing more than the desire to be the next mistress of Pemberley."

"I am afraid you will receive no disagreement from me," said Darcy with a rueful shake of his head. "Miss Bingley is, unfortunately, the worst social climber to whom I have ever been introduced."

"And she has set her cap on you," replied Georgiana. "As I would not wish for such a woman to be my sister, I would abjure you to take care."

"You think she would attempt a compromise?"

"I think she would do anything short of murder to achieve her desires. She is desperate to ascend into the first circles, and she sees you as the means to accomplish that goal. Do not give her the opportunity."

Nodding slowly, Darcy thought on the matter. He had always known this about Miss Bingley, though perhaps he had never considered it in so blatant a manner. When at Netherfield, he had locked the door to his chambers, and his valet had slept on a cot in the adjacent chamber. Darcy was certainly not eager to have Caroline Bingley as his wife.

Her breakfast consumed, his sister rose from her chair and leaned over to kiss Darcy on the cheek. "I will be in the music room for a time, Brother. After that I will be with Mrs. Annesley practicing my French."

Darcy laughed at his sister's distaste; she had not a true talent for learning languages, though she could be judged proficient in French and Italian. That was due more to effort, than aptitude, Darcy was aware.

Then she exited the room, leaving Darcy to his thoughts. He had not known of Georgiana's concerns regarding Bingley, though he was happy she was confident enough to voice them. But while Darcy would like to believe the best of his friend, he could not help but acknowledge that Georgiana's concerns had merit.

Sighing, Darcy took his letter and departed from the room, intent upon reading his letter in the privacy of his own study. When he had attained the room, he sat behind his desk and opened the letter, taking a moment to peruse it before attempting to read what his friend had written. As usual, Bingley's letter was a mass of blots, carelessly written words, and half-formed ideas which often flitted from one subject to the next.

Though it was most difficult to decipher, Darcy made a valiant attempt. It was clear that Bingley was in London and would be for the foreseeable future. He wrote of escorting his sister to different places and events, though the season would not truly begin until at least March, almost two months away. There was also mention of an angel, a Miss Herbert by name, though Darcy could not make anything out about the woman other than that. Then it closed with a wish to see Darcy in London again when he returned.

Sitting back in his chair, Darcy looked down at the offending letter, thinking deeply about what he had been able to glean from his friend's words. In fact, Darcy was not certain what to think. As far as he had been aware, Bingley had been intending to return to Netherfield no more than a week after departing for London, and given the attentions he had paid to Miss Kitty Bennet, returning would have been the proper thing to do, even if he was not intending to propose to the girl. But had he done it? Had the situation with her cooled enough that Bingley had been able to withdraw honorably?

There were no answers to be had in the letter, so Darcy resigned himself to asking Bingley when he eventually returned to London. But when there, he would demand those answers. Bingley had far too often been less than concerned over the feelings of the young women he often singled out. Georgiana was correct—if he was to become a gentleman, it was time Bingley began to act like one.

To heal from the wounds inflected on her by Mr. Bingley's departure was one of the hardest things Kitty Bennet had ever done. And it was not something she would have wished on anyone, though she knew that such things were all too common.

Living with her sister and her aunt and uncle in London helped put things in perspective. Kitty was not one who was meant for heavy introspection or long and detailed consideration about her life. Such things were better left for Elizabeth, who was much better suited for them. But that was also not to say that Kitty was completely shallow.

The thinking she did over the course of those weeks led her to two inescapable conclusions. The first was that though Kitty had enjoyed Mr. Bingley's attentions and had felt a warm regard toward him, Elizabeth's words about her depth of feeling toward the man were the truth—Kitty Bennet had not been in love with Mr. Bingley, but she had felt a healthy measure of infatuation for him. It was a sobering realization and one which shamed Kitty, though she knew there was no reason for it.

The second realization was that Kitty Bennet truly did not know what sort of man for whom she should be searching. What kind of man made a good husband? Kitty did not know, beyond some vague thoughts concerning a man's ability to care for her and protect her.

In fact, the longer she thought on it, the more Kitty realized that she had been searching for something all her life without knowing exactly what she was searching for. Surely there was more than this aimless wandering, this walk through life which flitted from one place to another without any thought for the destination. Surely there must be some purpose.

Thus it was one morning, when Elizabeth had gone to the local park with the Gardiner children, that Kitty decided to see if she could find some answers with another's help. Elizabeth could certainly be of assistance, but sometimes Elizabeth had a tendency toward complicated answers to questions—she did not always explain herself well to one who was not as intelligent as she. Fortunately for Kitty, she knew another who was adept at explanation.

"Aunt Gardiner," said Kitty, feeling unaccountably diffident with her beloved relation, "might I speak with you for a moment?"

Though her aunt had been engaged in looking over her menus for the week, she readily put her work aside and regarded Kitty. "How can I help you, my dear?"

"I . . ."

Pausing, Kitty thought for a moment, realizing that she had little idea of exactly what she wished to ask. How did one take all the questions she had, roll them all in together and then reduce them down to one overarching question which would explain the mysteries of life?

Against her will, Kitty let out a bit of a giggle, which caused her aunt to raise one eyebrow in response. The thought of the mysteries of life being explained in one or two words had suddenly struck Kitty as being amusing.

"I am sorry, Aunt," said Kitty. "I know I wished to talk, but now that I am here, I am afraid I do not know what to ask."

"You seem to have been building to this discussion for some time."

A shake of her head and Kitty looked on her aunt with wonder. "I have always wondered how you and Lizzy do it. Sometimes you seem to know what I want to say before I have said it—before *I* know what I wish to say!"

"Observation, my dear," said Mrs. Gardiner. "You are not normally the quiet girl you have been since you returned to London with us. May I assume you wish to speak about your experiences with Mr. Bingley?"

"Not that, exactly," replied Kitty. "It . . . Well, I suppose I am healing from the feeling of abandonment, and though I will own it still hurts at times. I am resigned to the fact that it is not likely that Mr. Bingley will ever return, and to be honest, I am not sure I would wish for it, even if it were possible."

"Then you have grown and learned, Kitty," replied Aunt Gardiner.

Feeling a little abashed at the praise, Kitty smiled in thanks, but soon her thoughts became serious again.

"I am not actually certain I know what I wish to ask. I suppose, most of all, I wish to know how I know when I am actually in love with a man. I would not wish to experience this again, and I know that I must learn in order to avoid it."

"Oh, Kitty, my dear," said Mrs. Gardiner, pulling Kitty down on the sofa beside her. "I cannot promise that you will never feel sorrow or the pain of abandonment, even if you do know what it is to love. Unfortunately, we cannot predict what others will do, nor can we know that those we love will not change. There are simply too many variables in life for us to know everything."

"I understand that, Aunt. I wish . . . Well, I would very much like to know that if I do have occasion to feel love, that at least I feel it for a man who is worthy of it."

The smile that Mrs. Gardiner bestowed upon Kitty was the widest she had ever seen from her aunt directed toward her. "I believe that is the trick, Kitty. It means that whatever else has happened in your life, you have chosen to bestow your love on a man worthy of it. And given the uncertainties of life, what else can we mortals ask for?"

"What else, indeed," murmured Kitty.

"In answer to your question," continued her aunt, "I do not believe there is any one answer which will suffice for all. What I feel for my husband will likely be different from what you will eventually feel for yours. There is nothing to say that my love is any purer than yours, any more estimable, or any closer to what we humans would consider to be an 'ideal' of love. For that matter, who is to judge what that ideal is?"

"Then how will I know it?"

"The only advice I can give you is to take your time and to consider your heart carefully. Love is many parts—physical attraction, caring, wishing that person well, an interest in their doings, a wish for their wellbeing—it is all of these and more.

"But Kitty, if I may, I would like to advise you in two things."

Kitty nodded her head, and her aunt smiled at her.

"The first is to wait. You are full young at seventeen, and there is no reason you must find your mate immediately. Allow yourself to grow and mature and gain experience. With experience comes a better understanding of your own heart, which will be invaluable. The second is that you should always question—both yourself and the man in whom you have an interest. I do not mean espousing suspicion where it is not warranted. Rather, you should always try to think of the why, as well as the what. If you do that, you can achieve the clarity you wish for. Or at least, you can come as close to it as we mortals are ever able."

It was, Kitty thought, not the complete understanding she had wished for when she had brought the matter up with her aunt. But then again, such a wish was an idealistic sort of desire which did not exist in the world, she supposed.

But it was good advice nonetheless. And Kitty decided then that she would follow it. She would not allow her heart to be captured again by a man unworthy.

"Thank you, Aunt," said she, after thinking on the matter for some moments. "I will try to do as you suggest."

"I know you will, Kitty. You are a good girl, and I am excessively fond of you. Take it slowly and do not rush, and I am certain all will be well."

Near the end of February, the Darcys returned to London. Darcy had never truly found London to be enjoyable, and the events in which society as a whole was so interested, he considered tedious. He did enjoy the arts, and he enjoyed escorting Georgiana to all the sights London had to offer, which was enough of a draw to allow him to go to London every year.

Of course, Darcy knew that it was necessary for him to eventually find a wife and beget an heir to ensure the next generation of Darcys at Pemberley, but that had always seemed like a problem for another time, something to be considered in the future. It did not help, of course, that he had never found a woman to whom he wished to bind himself, one whom he could love and respect, and one who would be a partner in his life, not merely an ornament for his arm.

Liar, said a small, suppressed corner of his mind, telling him that he *had* met a woman who intrigued him enough to wish to explore whether she could be the companion he desired. It could not be considered, he knew, so he ignored the voice.

Once he and Georgiana were settled into their London home, Darcy began to venture out, visiting his club and meeting with old friends and acquaintances. And it was not long before he began to discover gossip concerning his closest friend.

Now, Bingley was not well enough known in London to set tongues wagging among the foremost gossips of society. Instead, Darcy heard comments from mutual acquaintances, those who had known both Darcy and Bingley in university and after. And what Darcy heard did not please him in the slightest.

"It appears your friend Bingley is at it again," said Walter Richards, a friend of Darcy's from university. Richards was two years older than Darcy, and as he had left Cambridge before Bingley had arrived, he had not become as close to the man as Darcy had.

"Oh?" asked Darcy. He had come to the club to acclimatize himself once again to London's atmosphere and have a bit of dinner. Richards was the third man already to mention Bingley, though the other two had been in passing and had not stayed long enough to elaborate. Richards was seated at the same table, set to partake of the same meal.

"He has been seen frequently in the company of a Miss Herbert, and they appear to be getting on famously."

"Miss Herbert?" asked Darcy. "I do not believe I have ever heard of a family by that name."

"Nor would you," replied Richards. "Miss Herbert's family estate is in Devon. They are naught but minor gentry, as I understand, though I have heard it said that they possess some ties to higher society from that area."

"And what kind of woman is she?"

Richards laughed. "I have only seen her from a distance, so I know nothing of her character, but if you think on the matter a little, I am certain you know Bingley's preferences. She is blonde, tall, beautiful, and statuesque, much the same as every other young lady with whom Bingley has ever been in love."

A shake of his head indicated Darcy's annoyance with his friend, though he would never say as much to Richards. There would never be any question of what the woman on Bingley's arm looked like, as they were all the same. Kitty Bennet had been of a similar type, after all, though Darcy attributed Bingley's interest in her to a lack of his preferred type in Meryton. But he still was not certain if Bingley had returned to Hertfordshire the previous December, and he meant to find out.

"How long has this been going on?"

"According to my Cecily, Bingley's shrew of a sister introduced them in early December, and they have been inseparable ever since."

"December? But he was to return to Hertfordshire, or so he informed me."

"Then he changed his mind, and given what I know of Bingley, that is unremarkable. To the best of my knowledge, he has not left town since then." Richards snorted with disgust. "I know you mourn your father, as is proper, but you have no idea how beneficial it is to have control over your estate. I still live at my father's sufferance, and the old man has become ever more irascible and difficult as he ages. It is much easier for me to live in town so that I may escape him."

Their conversation from that point devolved to a continual complaint about Richards's father, which Darcy had heard so many times that it had become tiresome. As a man who had inherited his estate at two and twenty, Darcy well knew the cares and concerns which beset the property owner who was properly engaged in his estate. The relationship between Richards and his father had never been good, but it had been further strained when his mother had passed three years before. Darcy could understand that, but he sometimes wished his friend could appreciate what he had, which was a carefree lifestyle in which he was not required to think about the best for his estate.

Of more concern to Darcy was Bingley's actions, and the words

Georgiana had spoken of the man returned to him, little though he wished to contemplate them. Bingley had always been a carefree sort of man himself, but in the least two years he had become frivolous, always looking for his next "angel," never thinking about the concerns of life and livelihood which should occupy an independent man.

He was not tied to Darcy's apron strings—in fact, Bingley could be mulish if he felt himself to be right, much though he tended to look to Darcy for advice. It was more his lack of seriousness which troubled Darcy. If he had not returned to Hertfordshire, as appeared to be the case, then he had left Miss Kitty Bennet after paying attention to her, exciting her expectations, and no doubt, leaving her in a state of hope, never certain if he would return. That was not the action of a gentleman.

Determined to discover for himself the truth of the matter, Darcy arranged to contact his friend, knowing that if Bingley's focus was on a young woman, it might be weeks after Darcy returning to town before his friend would finally visit. Thus, he sent his card around to Bingley, letting him know that he had returned and requesting a visit. If Darcy had not had weighty subjects to discuss, he might have simply visited Hurst's townhouse, where he knew Bingley would be staying, even though he had no real desire to see the ladies of the house. Darcy knew there would be no opportunity for private discourse there, which necessitated drawing his friend to him, rather than the reverse. Bingley was such a cheerful fellow; he would visit immediately.

True to form, it was the very next day when Bingley knocked on the door to Darcy house and was escorted into Darcy's study, a spring in his step and a smile on his face.

"Darcy! How are you, old man? I have missed you these past months."

"Very well, Bingley," said Darcy, rising to offer his hand to his friend.

Bingley accepted it with a broad smile and pumped it several times, as was his habit.

"Excellent! I had wondered when you would return, as I know you are not fond of society."

"I can handle society, Bingley," replied Darcy. "The succession of events can sometimes become tedious, but all in all, it can be tolerated."

A wide smile came over Bingley's face, which usually presaged a teasing comment. "Should you find yourself a woman to fancy, you might find such activities more tolerable."

Nodding, Darcy took the opening Bingley had just given him. "I understand you have managed to find one yourself. The lips of our acquaintances at White's are filled with rumors of a Miss Herbert.

Apparently you have not allowed yourself to be pried from her side for several months now."

Bingley laughed, but Darcy could instantly hear the rueful quality it contained. "Ah, yes, well . . . You see, Miss Herbert is a lovely young woman, but I do not think she is the one for me."

"Oh?" asked Darcy.

"She is visiting some friends in East Sussex at present, though I understand she will return before the end of the season. I . . . ah . . . Well, it seems like her family has higher aspirations for her future than I can offer. They are connected to the Suttons of Somerset, you understand."

Darcy nodded. He knew of them, though he was not acquainted with them, and knew they were much higher on the social scale than Bingley was himself.

"It does not signify, in any case," replied Bingley, making a dismissive motion with one hand. "I had found that I was growing tired of her anyway."

Dismayed, Darcy looked on his friend. Though it was understandable that people should grow apart, and perhaps lose interest in a person, the better they came to know them, this happened with Bingley with distressing regularity. Bingley was not callous, but he quickly lost interest in favor of the next pretty woman or the next activity in which he took pleasure. It seemed he was not able to keep his focus on one thing, one person, one activity for long. He was very much like a child in that respect.

"Now, I am not sure if you know her, but Miss Diana Colford is positively an angel."

"Miss Colford?" asked Darcy.

"Yes!" replied Bingley eagerly. "Her family is from Kent, where her father owns an estate."

"I am familiar with the Colfords," said Darcy a little shortly. "Rockborough, the Colford estate, is not far from my Aunt Catherine's estate."

"Excellent!" enthused Bingley. "I had not known of the connection, but it is good to know that you approve of them. Miss Colford is the epitome of grace, style, elegance, and beauty. Though I met her less than a week ago, I am convinced that there is no one her equal."

"And she is blonde, tall, and willowy?"

Bingley frowned, catching a hint of the sarcasm in Darcy's voice. "She is, though I am certain you must already have known that."

"In fact, I did not," said Darcy. "I know the Colfords' eldest son, but I have never been introduced to his sister. My aunt, as you know, prefers to maintain the distinction of rank, and as Miss Colford is a young lady of age to marry, my aunt does not approve of my knowing her. I would not concern myself over such a matter, except for the fact that the Colfords must live close to my aunt."

Laughing, Bingley shook his head. "I had not thought of that. You portray your aunt in a very droll manner, Darcy. I hope to someday be introduced to her."

"What of Miss Kitty Bennet?" asked Darcy, fixing his friend with a stern look. In fact, he had been getting angrier by the moment, provoked by his friend's frivolous manner.

"W-who?" asked Bingley, clearly taken aback by Darcy's seeming non-sequitur.

"Miss Kitty Bennet," Darcy enunciated clearly. "The young lady in Hertfordshire to whom you were paying such an inordinate amount of attention."

"What of her?" asked Bingley, clearly perplexed. "As far as I am aware, she must still be in Hertfordshire with her sister."

"I expect she is, but I was not asking about that. What I wish to know is whether you returned to Hertfordshire like you clearly told me you would."

"Ah, well . . ." Bingley paused, clearly embarrassed by Darcy's question. "You see, after I returned to town, I . . . ah . . . Well, Caroline did not wish to return to Hertfordshire, and I could not leave her unescorted."

"Of course, you could not," said Darcy.

Bingley beamed. "I am glad you understand."

"I do not understand, Bingley." Darcy stared at his friend as Bingley's face fell, and the man fidgeted the longer Darcy regarded him. "The Hursts are still in town, and presumably they were here throughout that time. Could they not have escorted Caroline?"

"Well . . . I suppose . . . Perhaps it might have been. . ."

Bingley paused, seemingly ordering his thoughts. "Well, you see, Darcy," said he after a few moments, "it turns out that I did not esteem Miss Kitty as much as I thought I did. A few weeks in town and I had forgotten all about her, and as Caroline does not like the Bennets, I thought it best to drop the acquaintance."

"You did not return to Netherfield at all?"

"No."

"You did not send word back that you would not return?"

A blank look came over Bingley's face. "Should I have?"

Passing a weary hand over his face, Darcy leaned back in his chair, wondering if he friend would ever achieve the maturity of an adult, if he would ever outgrow the selfishness that seemed to have become such an intrinsic part of his character. In fact, Darcy mused, though he had not seen it before, Bingley and his sister were truly two birds of a feather. Miss Bingley was much more overt in her selfishness, and much crueler in its application, but from a certain point of view, they were very much alike.

"Yes, Bingley, you most certainly should have." Darcy's eyes bored into those of his friend, who looked at him with surprise. "You paid Miss Kitty a great deal of attention, speaking to her, dancing the first *and* supper dances at Netherfield, inviting the Bennet sisters to your ball personally. In fact, had you kept at it for much longer than you did, I dare say your honor would have been engaged.

"Regardless, you paid her enough attentions to excite her expectations, and then left her with no word, *and* with every indication that you would return. You *did* inform her that you were only to be in town for a few days, did you not?"

Had it been another situation, Darcy might have almost found his friend's surprised stupefaction to be amusing. Darcy could see no humor in this situation, however, and he was most put out with his friend.

"I . . . Well, I think I might have intimated as much," replied Bingley at length. "But I never promised anything to her."

"No, you did not, but you allowed her to believe that you did. I am convinced that Miss Kitty was, at the very least, infatuated with you, Bingley. It was very poorly done to leave her expecting your return, to expose her to the gossip and pity of her neighbors. How do you think she felt when she waited, day after day, for your return, only to be disappointed all over again?"

"Now see here, Darcy," said Bingley after he sputtered incoherently for a few moments, "I cannot help it if the girl holds an infatuation for me. Should I concern myself for every girl who might see me and wish me to pay them my addresses?"

"Of course not, Bingley," replied Darcy, his implacable stare never wavering. "But when you behave in so unguarded a manner, you create hopes which you may not mean to fill. It would be better if you would not be so open, and in this instance, it would have been far preferable had you not singled Miss Kitty out for your particular attentions."

"Oh, so have you now appointed yourself as Miss Kitty's protector?" demanded Bingley. It was clear he was beginning to become angry.

"You know I have not. But they are acquaintances and respectable ladies, and they have the right to be treated with respect and dignity.

Furthermore, Miss Kitty reminds me of my sister. Had a man treated her in such a manner, I would be of mind to call him out."

"I cannot see that I have treated Miss Kitty any differently from how I have treated any other."

There was some heat in Bingley's tone, and Darcy thought his friend was trying to start an argument, something which was beyond Darcy's experience when it came to Bingley. But Darcy was not about to allow him to claim that he had done no wrong. He was convinced by now that if Bingley did not begin to take responsibility for his actions and exercise more care, he would go through life perpetually looking for something he could not find. Even worse, Darcy was certain that Bingley would always possess a wandering eye, even if he did marry.

"And that is the problem," said Darcy. "You find a pretty young woman, treat her as if she was Aphrodite, then after a few weeks you become tired of her, before moving on to the next angel you come across. Miss Kitty was just one in a long string of paramours. Even this Miss Herbert only caught your attention for a short time."

"If you recall," replied Bingley in an acid tone, "her family decided I was not high and mighty enough for their tastes."

"I remember you saying that quite well, Bingley. But I also remember you telling me you were beginning to grow weary of her."

Bingley looked away. "I am not trying to censure you unjustly, my friend. I am merely trying to illustrate the manner in which your behavior is perceived by others. I do not know for a fact that your young ladies have been hurt by your actions, but I am convinced that Miss Kitty *has* been affected. You must be more circumspect in your dealings with the fairer sex."

"Oh, spare me your lectures," said Bingley, rising to his feet. "Ever since we became acquainted, I have been subjected to the great Fitzwilliam Darcy's thoughts of how a man should conduct himself. I am not your child, that you may order me about."

"No, but you have relied on my sole advice these past years," snapped Darcy, rising to face his friend. "I believe it is time you stood on your own."

"I think that is a marvelous idea," said Bingley.

He turned to leave, snatching the door open with one hand, and then turning to look back at Darcy. "If you do not like the way I live my life, then I shall not bother you with my presence."

Then he exited, the echo of the door slamming behind him reverberating through the room.

Spent and annoyed by his argument with his friend, Darcy sat and rested his head in one hand. Though Darcy had not expected his friend to take the matter with complete sanguinity, he had not thought that Bingley would become angry. Perhaps he had not handled the matter correctly. Should he have attempted a more conciliatory tone?

Darcy shook his head. He had no answers. But he knew that he did not wish to associate with a man who went around, perpetually falling in and out of love, a man who could not live his life with the seriousness it deserved. Perhaps Bingley would come around and seek him out again.

A knock sounded on the door of Darcy's study, and he called out, smiling when his sister entered.

"I heard raised voices, brother. Is there aught amiss?"

"That was my conversation with Bingley," said Darcy, making a face. "He did not take kindly to my words."

Eyes wide, a shocked Georgiana said: "That was *Mr. Bingley* yelling?"

"I am afraid so," said Darcy. "He has been behaving most inappropriately, and I sought to remind him of how to conduct himself."

"Concerning that young lady in Hertfordshire?"

"Yes."

"Perhaps you should tell me all."

Though Darcy would have preferred to keep the matter to himself, he sighed and decided he needed another viewpoint on the matter. Since Georgiana had already seen the problems with how Bingley conducted himself, Darcy thought she would have a good perspective on the matter. Or perhaps he simply wanted vindication. Darcy was not certain himself.

"It seems to me that Mr. Bingley is unwilling to modify his behavior," said Georgiana, once Darcy had finished his explanation.

"You do not think that I was too harsh with him? Is it not officious of me to take him to task in such a manner?"

"If you will forgive me for being blunt, I think no such thing. Has Mr. Bingley not looked up to you for instruction and assistance in society? Why should he now become angry because your advice is not to his liking?"

"But he is a man full grown," replied Darcy, trying to see the matter objectively.

"He is, but he does not always act like it," insisted Georgiana. "You may have been a little more direct than you should have been, but that is your way. Mr. Bingley cannot suddenly decide your advice is no longer valid because it is critical of his behavior."

"Thank you, my dear," said Darcy, favoring her with a faint smile.

"You know, at one point I had thought that Bingley might be a good match for you. He is beneath us in society, but he is kind and happy, and I thought he would be a good protector."

Georgiana rolled her eyes. "Can I assume you never spoke of such things to Miss Bingley?"

"Of course not. The woman would have become more insufferable than she already is, if I had."

"I have no doubt of that," replied Georgiana with a smirk. "But as for Mr. Bingley, I do not think we would suit. I thought him to be an amiable man, but I have never felt anything for him other than the respect due to one of your friends. Mr. Bingley will need to look elsewhere for his high society wife."

"I dare say he shall. And I thank you for your words, Sister. Though I am still not convinced I handled the situation in the best manner, I feel a little more at ease."

Georgiana rose and she came around the desk, kissing him on the cheek. "You have a tendency to take things too much to heart and to bear the world's burdens by yourself, Brother. Allow Mr. Bingley to carry the weight of his own part of the blame."

And then she left, leaving Darcy to consider how his angelic little sister had become so wise. He would follow her advice. Bingley would not remain angry forever. Surely they would be able to affect a reconciliation before long.

Chapter XV

"What do you think, Lizzy? This is an invitation to a far finer event than we would normally receive. Shall we attend?"

Elizabeth shared a look with Kitty, who laughed and motioned for Elizabeth to answer for them.

"I believe neither Kitty nor I have any objection, Uncle. You may respond for us all if you like. We shall be happy to attend."

Chuckling, Mr. Gardiner nodded. "Then Madeline will send a note with our acceptance."

"I believe new gowns will be in order," said Mrs. Gardiner.

Elizabeth groaned, prompting smiles from her relations. Her aversion to shopping was well-known, and they had done a fair amount of it since their arrival in London.

"I am certain we have something that is adequate for the evening."

"For the types of events you are accustomed to attending, yes," said Mrs. Gardiner. "But you would feel plain and colorless next to the concoctions the ladies of London commonly wear to their events here."

"Trust me, Lizzy," added Mr. Gardiner, "you will thank us in time. And I think that this time, we shall pay for the gowns. You may think of it as our thanks to you for providing us such fine company these past months."

The matter was argued for some minutes, Elizabeth declaring that Longbourn's coffers were more than full enough to bear the expense, while Mr. Gardiner insisted that he wished to treat his nieces. In the end, Elizabeth was forced to give way with a laugh, and the three ladies began to make plans to go shopping on the morrow. And even Elizabeth, though she was not fond of shopping for the sake of buying items which she did not need, enjoyed wearing fine clothes and was more than happy to join in the laughter which accompanied their planning.

In truth, Elizabeth had enjoyed herself a great deal that winter in London. Her uncle was known to a great number of people, most of whom seemed to be on very friendly terms with him. As such, it had enabled Elizabeth to meet many interesting individuals. In addition, they had spent their time as they normally would, with nights at the theater, visits to London Tower, the menagerie, the museum, and many other places besides. Even her uncle had taken some time from work and escorted them around the city, though often it was the three ladies alone in search of amusement.

Kitty was not as much of a connoisseur of such things as was Elizabeth, leaning more toward balls and parties, events with social interaction, than dusty old art exhibits. But still, Elizabeth was certain Kitty had enjoyed her time in London as much as had Elizabeth herself. It had allowed her to forget Mr. Bingley to a great extent, for which Elizabeth was thankful.

Thoughts of Mr. Bingley necessarily brought thoughts of his friend, though Elizabeth immediately forced them aside. She could not determine if Mr. Darcy had had a hand in Mr. Bingley's continued absence, and she was aware that she likely would never know. As such, Elizabeth had decided she would not worry over the matter.

They spent the next day shopping and the modiste promised that the dresses would be completed the next week for their fitting. Thus, on the appointed day, the three ladies all had new dresses to wear, and ones far finer than anything they had owned before—or at least finer than the Bennet sisters had ever owned. Mrs. Gardiner had attended such events before, and was no stranger to such fine clothes.

"I do not think I have ever seen such a beautiful dress," said Elizabeth, as she admired the creation of lace and satin which hung before her on the closet door. "The highest ladies of society own many of these?"

"It is said that some never wear the same dress twice," said her aunt with a chuckle. "I cannot say if that is true, but the wardrobes of high society ladies no doubt groan with such dresses."

"I would not wish to be so wasteful," said Kitty, her tone reflecting a seriousness which was far from Kitty's habit.

"Nor would I," agree Mrs. Gardiner. "But where the means exist, eccentricities might also follow. Many of higher society would seem strange to you and me."

Almost of its own accord, Elizabeth's mind jumped to a man with whom both she and Kitty were familiar. That man was not strange—in fact, he was as good and conscientious a man as Elizabeth had ever met, in addition to being one of the handsomest.

Elizabeth said nothing. She did not wish to endure the teasing she would no doubt provoke from her aunt and sister. Still, in the back of her mind, Elizabeth was aware that though she had not met with Mr. Darcy for several months, he had become the ideal to whom she compared all other men.

Such thoughts were not uncommon to Elizabeth of late, so she shunted it aside, as she normally did, in favor of what was passing at the time. But she did not forget it. In fact, it was becoming more a part of her, something she could not simply shove to the side of the road of life or leave forgotten in some remote locale.

On the appointed night, the girls prepared for the event, dressed in their fairy gowns, and departed, feeling as if they were queens, if only for one night. The event was held at a massive town home, imposing as it stood by the side of a wide boulevard, and from the number of carriages lined up by the entrance—not to mention the quality of their design—it would be well attended, and by those of higher society than the Bennets were accustomed to meeting.

The man who had invited them—a Mr. Dunleavy—was a kind and bluff fellow, several years Mr. Gardiner's senior, with whom, their uncle informed them, he had done much business. He greeted them cheerfully and welcomed them to his home, though his wife was more aloof in her greetings. Elizabeth did not concern herself, as she knew that there were many at this event who would be disdainful of her if they knew of her origins.

The dancers were as fine as anything Elizabeth had ever experienced, the musicians consummate, their instruments clearly of the best quality, and the tables which were laden with all manner of delectable dishes, surely held something for everyone, even those possessed of the most fastidious tastes. Kitty and Elizabeth by no means danced every dance, but they were asked to stand up more often than not, often making others' acquaintance due to their uncle's business connections. All in all, it was a satisfying evening for them both.

However, other than the fact that they were attending a ball far finer than anything they had attended before—even the event at Netherfield had in no way compared—the evening might have been unremarkable but for a singular event. For it was not long before Elizabeth became aware of the fact that they were not unknown to everyone in attendance, for Elizabeth soon caught a glimpse of Mr. Darcy from across the room.

He was standing alongside the dance floor, watching the dancers as had been his wont the first time Elizabeth had seen him at the assembly in Meryton. Though it was at a distance and there were many others between them, Elizabeth thought he had never looked so handsome, in his dark jacket, his wavy hair combed neatly, his height marking him in a room filled to overflowing.

But the sight of Mr. Darcy brought a certain sense of disquiet, for where Mr. Darcy went, Elizabeth thought it likely that Mr. Bingley would be nearby. After a short time, when Elizabeth looked back at the location in which he had been standing, Mr. Darcy was no longer there, and for quite some time, though Elizabeth searched for him amongst the dancers, or those standing by the side of the floor conversing, she could find no further hint of the man, nor could she see his friend. There were, she had heard, some other rooms which had been set aside for other activities, such as cards and the like, so it was possible that Mr. Darcy had gone to one of them, though Elizabeth thought he was not the type for such activities.

Though Elizabeth thought that it might be best to depart in order to protect Kitty's sensibilities, her sister, who was enjoying herself, would hear nothing of it. Elizabeth could not tell her why she wished to leave, so her persuasions fell on deaf ears.

"We have indulged in many of *your* favorite activities, Lizzy," said Kitty, though her words were affectionate, rather than severe. "I am enjoying myself to a great degree and would not wish to depart until we must."

"And I would not curtail your fun for anything, Kitty," said Elizabeth, still fearful that Kitty would see Mr. Bingley and all the progress she had made in recovering from her disappointment would be undone."

"Then let us simply enjoy ourselves," said Kitty. Her partner for the next dance soon came and whisked her away, and Elizabeth was left watching.

In the end Elizabeth thought it would be well. The ballroom was large, and it was such a crush that she knew that Kitty might not see Mr. Bingley, even if he was present. Elizabeth saw no further evidence of Mr.

Darcy's presence, and she had some hope that the man had departed, even though for herself she would have liked nothing better than to see him, speak with him, be in his company and receive his attentions.

But it was not Elizabeth who caught sight of Mr. Bingley that night. Unfortunately, it was the one person she most hoped would not see him.

The first indication Elizabeth had that anything was amiss was the sudden stiffness she sensed in her sister as they stood by each other watching the dance. Curious, Elizabeth looked to her sister, noting her gaze fixed on the dancers, and when Elizabeth followed her sister's eyes, she saw, there on the dance floor, Mr. Bingley moving through the set with a young woman.

He appeared to be enjoying himself thoroughly, as he executed the steps with his partner, a tall, blonde woman, willowy and graceful, and in whom shone the light of a woman those of society would no doubt find beautiful. As they danced, they spoke with great animation, laughing and carrying on as if they had known each other for years. For all Elizabeth knew, perhaps they had.

A fearful look at Kitty revealed that Kitty was watching them to the exclusion of all else happening around them, but rather than a stricken yearning, which Elizabeth might have expected, instead Kitty's eyes, hard as flint, suggested an anger Elizabeth would not have expected.

"Kitty, are you well?" asked Elizabeth, attempting to divert her sister's attention.

"I am very well, Elizabeth," said Kitty. Elizabeth winced at the sound of her voice. Kitty had sounded as if all the hurt and frustration of the past several months had all gathered together again, settling within her sister's mind, waiting for the most opportune moment to ignite.

"Dearest, perhaps we should find aunt and uncle and take our leave."

At that moment, the dancers executed their bows and curtseys and the set came to an end. Elizabeth watched as Mr. Bingley led the young lady on his arm to the side of the hall not far from where Elizabeth and Kitty stood, and he stayed there with her. Elizabeth could see — and Kitty could hardly miss — the liveliness with which he spoke, and though his partner was not nearly so demonstrative, she was clearly pleased with his company. The sight set Kitty's jaw working, as the muscles flexed in her agitation.

Before Elizabeth could once again suggest that they had best leave, Kitty stepped forward, marching toward Mr. Bingley like a lioness stalking her prey. Elizabeth soon caught her sister, but all her pleas for Kitty to come away went for naught, for her sister was focused on her quarry.

Elizabeth, following behind her sister, was witness to the exact moment in which Mr. Bingley became aware of their presence. He happened to look up as he was speaking, and his words trailed off as he saw Kitty approaching like some vengeful angel. His countenance was overspread by a whiteness of shock — or embarrassment? — which clearly confused his companion. Then she looked up to see Kitty, and her face instantly assumed the wary expression of a woman sensing a rival. Then Kitty came to a stop in front of the pair, looking at Mr. Bingley with the most imperious expression Elizabeth had ever seen her sister wear.

There was a moment of silence in which Mr. Bingley did not know what to say, while Kitty appeared to be daring him to speak. Elizabeth had never seen her sister like this, and she was inordinately proud of Kitty, though somewhat fearful that her sister would draw undue attention to them.

When Mr. Bingley did not say anything, Kitty fixed him with a sardonic grin and said: "Hello, Mr. Bingley. You do remember us, do you not?"

"Uh . . . Of course," replied Mr. Bingley, though not coherently.

Though Elizabeth might almost have expected it, the woman by Mr. Bingley's side did not appear to be looking on them with the disdain of a truly high bred woman. Rather, she was watching them, clearly knowing there was some tension, though not quite understanding it.

"Will you not introduce me to your friends?" said the woman finally.

"Of course, how thoughtless of me!" exclaimed Mr. Bingley, seeming relieved to finally have some occupation. He looked back and forth between his companion and the Bennets, seemingly at a loss to understand who was higher in society, before he finally began the introductions. "Miss Bennet, Miss Kitty, I would like to present Miss Diana Colford to your acquaintance. Miss Colford, this is Miss Elizabeth Bennet and her younger sister, Miss Catherine. Miss Bennet has inherited an estate near the estate I leased in Hertfordshire in the autumn."

"I am happy to make your acquaintance," said Miss Colford, dropping into a curtsey, which was mirrored by Elizabeth and, only very reluctantly, by Kitty.

Elizabeth, feeling it incumbent upon her to ensure smooth conversation which would incite no gossip, favored the other woman with a smile and said: "Have you known Mr. Bingley for long, Miss Colford?"

"Only these past few weeks," replied the woman. She seemed taken aback by an indelicate snort from Kitty, but she gamely continued on. "I have only recently arrived in London from my father's estate in Kent."

"If you recall," said Mr. Bingley, looking—and sounding—a little awkward, "Darcy has an aunt who has an estate in Kent. Miss Colford's family lives not far away."

"Ah, yes," said Elizabeth. "How could I forget? The infamous Lady Catherine de Bourgh."

"You know Lady Catherine?" asked Miss Colford curiously.

"Not personally," said Elizabeth. "But I have heard so much about her, I feel as if I am already acquainted. I have a cousin who is installed as Lady Catherine's pastor."

"At Hunsford."

"Yes, that is the place."

"My family attends church in a different parish, but I am familiar with Hunsford. He must be newly installed, for old Martinson was the pastor for many years."

"I believe he is," said Elizabeth.

While she might have been pleased that the conversation was continuing so innocuously, Elizabeth did not miss the fact that her sister's gaze was fixed upon Mr. Bingley and was not at all pleasant. For his part, Mr. Bingley seemed to recognize that fact, if his heightened color was any indication. Knowing Kitty was having difficulty holding her temper and wary of her saying something she should not, Elizabeth thought to withdraw. Unfortunately, she was a little too late her in design.

"How wonderful that you should be together here," said Kitty. "Elizabeth and I were speaking of you the other day, Mr. Bingley."

Mr. Bingley reddened, and Miss Colford frowned, clearly hearing the sarcasm in Kitty's voice.

Then Kitty turned to Miss Colford. "It is fortunate that you have secured Mr. Bingley's attentions."

"Kitty," said Elizabeth in a warning tone, but Kitty was not to be denied.

"Mr. Bingley is such an amiable man. He quite charmed the entire neighborhood when he was in residence."

Once again, Kitty turned her attention back to Mr. Bingley. The poor man—if he could be called such—did not seem to know where to look or how to act.

"How suddenly you all quit the neighborhood last autumn, Mr. Bingley. We were unable to account for your sudden absence when it was made clear that you were only to be gone for a short time. It is a great pity, as there were several in the neighborhood who were quite anticipating your return.

"I wish you well, Miss Colford," said Kitty, directing her words toward the other woman. "I hope you have better luck in curbing Mr. Bingley's wandering than others have before you."

Miss Colford frowned, though Elizabeth was certain the woman had taken Kitty's meaning quite well indeed. For his part, Mr. Bingley appeared to become offended, and the muscles in his jaw twitched as if he wished to say something, though what he could possibly say in his own defense, Elizabeth was uncertain. It was clear that if Elizabeth did not extricate them from this situation soon, it might become unpleasant. Luckily, Kitty had said all she wished to say.

"Elizabeth, I believe I am fatigued. Let us find aunt and uncle and depart."

"Of course, Kitty," replied Elizabeth. "If you will excuse us."

Elizabeth smiled at Miss Colford and curtseyed, though both Bennet sisters paid Mr. Bingley only the barest of courtesies, and they turned to leave. That was when they came face to face with Miss Bingley and her sister.

The woman had been standing behind them and a little to the side, her sister a step or two behind her. It was clear that she was not happy to see them, as her sneer of contempt was clear for all to see.

Making a decision on impulse, Elizabeth looked at Miss Bingley and then, with great deliberation, turned her head and looked the other way.

"Come, Kitty, it is time for us to leave."

Though she heard Miss Bingley's shocked gasp, Elizabeth did not turn around, instead moving away without a single glance back. About her, she could hear the whispers of those who had witnessed the confrontation, knowing that though she and Kitty were not well known in London society, they had been introduced as gentlewomen, and that the gossip concerning Miss Bingley receiving the cut direct would be rampant by the end of the evening. Elizabeth smiled grimly, knowing it was nothing less than the woman deserved.

Within moments, they had found their aunt and uncle, who were actually not far away, and who had witnessed at least a part of the confrontation, Elizabeth was certain. They quickly made arrangements for the carriage to be brought around, and while they were waiting, Mr. Gardiner stepped close to Elizabeth, a questioning look directed at her.

"Can I assume that was Mr. Bingley?" asked he, in a soft enough voice that Kitty could not hear.

"And his sisters," replied Elizabeth.

Mr. Gardiner appeared concerned. "Are you sure of your actions?

There may be repercussions for cutting her like you did."

"I am certain it shall not be a problem, uncle. We are not exactly known here."

Holding her gaze for several moments, Uncle Gardiner turned away with a sigh. "I hope so," said he.

Then he moved away, to where Mr. Dunleavy stood nearby watching them all. They exchanged a few words, among which Elizabeth thought was the promise of an explanation, before their host wished them a good night and returned to his guests. Within moments, the Gardiners and their nieces were ensconced in the coach back to Gracechurch Street.

Of course, the moment the carriage door was closed behind them, Kitty was unable to maintain the façade she had held onto throughout the day, and her composure cracked. The first indication Elizabeth had of her sister's response was a stifled giggle accompanied by shaking shoulders and a hand in front of her mouth. That hand soon went into Kitty's mouth and she bit down, trying to stifle her laughter, but it was all for naught. It was not long before her sister threw her arms around Elizabeth and exclaimed:

"Oh, Lizzy, you were marvelous!"

"I must confess," said Elizabeth, infected with her sister's laughter, "I never thought to see such a look of shock on Miss Bingley's face!"

"May I assume, then, that you met Mr. Bingley and his family?" asked Aunt Gardiner in a droll tone.

"We did," agreed Kitty. "And I made certain that Mr. Bingley understood how vexed I am with him."

Their aunt frowned. "I hope you did not make a scene."

"Not so much, Aunt," replied Elizabeth. "I was afraid Kitty would say something injudicious to Mr. Bingley, but she handled it with aplomb, saying nothing overt. But if Mr. Bingley was able to read between the lines—and I am certain he understood everything Kitty said—he would be suitably chastened."

Exclamations for a full accounting of their confrontation were made, and the Bennet sisters soon obliged them, explaining the matter concisely. When they had finished the Gardiners were shaking their heads, but proud of the way their nieces had handled the matter.

"I simply hope that there are no repercussions because of your behavior," said Mr. Gardiner. "You are by no means established in London society. You were introduced to several people over the course of the evening, and it is not inconceivable that one of them might have witnessed the confrontation."

"We were speaking low enough that I doubt anyone else heard our conversation with Mr. Bingley," said Kitty. "Since I made no accusations, I would think that if anyone did overhear, they would have no understanding of what we were discussing."

"As for Miss Bingley," added Elizabeth, "I would think that the greater consequences would be for *her*. Not only is she the one that has designs of ascending to the heights of society where I have none, but she is also the daughter of a tradesman who has been cut by a gentlewoman. Though I am not the equal of the Duchess of Devonshire, I suspect that will carry consequences."

The Gardiners looked at each other and they too joined the laughter, apparently unable to resist. Though it was not precisely proper to be laughing at Miss Bingley, the woman was eminently deserving of it.

Of more importance to Elizabeth was the effect the confrontation had had on her sister. Though she would not have credited the notion before, it seemed like the effect it had on Kitty was a positive one. They had discussed the matter many times and had come to the conclusion that Mr. Bingley was fickle in his attentions at best, or callous at worst. Now that Kitty had seen the man for himself, she had a reason to put her time with him in the past where it belonged. Perhaps she could now heal fully from her heartbreak.

For Darcy, the Dunleavy ball was another tedious event of the season, an opportunity to be fawned over by young debutantes on the hunt for a wealthy husband. He passed the night as he usually did, dancing little—and then only with his younger Fitzwilliam cousins—and avoiding the ladies whenever he could, spending his time in conversation with the gentlemen of his acquaintance or watching the dancers as they moved through their steps.

Darcy was aware of Bingley's presence, but since their falling out he had not called on his friend, nor had Bingley called on him, and he was noticeably absent from the club. Of course, the rift between them came with an unexpected benefit; it allowed Darcy to avoid having to dance with Bingley's younger sister, which was a welcome relief from the woman's machinations. He remembered meeting her with fondness for once, instead of exasperation.

"Mr. Darcy!" the woman had exclaimed as she hurried up to him, the Hursts following behind more sedately. "We had wondered if you had actually returned to London, sir, as we have not yet seen you at the townhouse."

"Miss Bingley," replied Darcy with a short bow. He turned to her companions, prompting an ill-concealed frown of vexation from the woman. "Mr. and Mrs. Hurst. I am happy to see you."

Though Miss Bingley preened at his words, Hurst seemed to understand that his words did not include Miss Bingley, and he smiled at Darcy, turning a sardonic eye on his sister.

"You must come and visit us, Mr. Darcy," said Miss Bingley as if he had not spoken. "I have been busy in the townhouse this winter. I dare say you will not even recognize it."

"I am happy for you, Miss Bingley," replied Darcy, giving no indication of any intention to visit. It seemed that Bingley had not seen fit to inform his relations of their argument, and if it was a matter of such little consequence to Bingley, Darcy would not bring it up either.

The woman nattered on for some time, and she appeared perplexed that Darcy made very little response to her statements, though he did not think he was more reticent than he usually was in her presence. Her conversation was of matters he did not care to discuss, interspersed with little hints that a visit would be welcome, or even better, an invitation to Darcy house. Through it all Hurst seemed amused by his sister's attempts. Darcy had once thought that Hurst's manners toward Miss Bingley were not proper, but given what the man suffered with such a shrew as a sister-in-law, he supposed it was understandable.

"Has dear Georgiana come to town with you?" asked Miss Bingley after she had spoken for some time. "How I long to see her. I believe we should visit, as I would love to be delighted by her playing all over again!"

The change of topic to his sister produced a far different reaction from that which Miss Bingley had obviously intended, as Darcy decided that he had spent enough time in polite conversation. And so he bowed politely to the woman, and then to the Hursts, and excused himself. As he left, he noted Miss Bingley's expression of stupefaction, which quickly turned to annoyance. What an insufferable woman she was!

The rest of the even passed unremarkably, and it was only as Darcy was considering departing that he chanced to see someone he had not expected to see again, and the evening was changed because of it.

As he was watching the dancers from one end of the hall, he happened to notice a disturbance down at the other end. Not having any interest, Darcy made to turn away, when he was arrested by the sight of the Bennet sisters walking toward him. For a moment Darcy thought they had seen him and were coming to greet him, but when they quickly passed him by and exited the ballroom, he was surprised, and did not follow them. By the time he thought to do so, he was certain they were gone.

"It is not as if I wish to speak to them anyway," said Darcy to himself.

But when his traitorous mind refused to leave the subject of the ladies he had seen, he knew that it was nothing more than a lie, bravado designed to trick himself into thinking that he was unaffected by seeing them again.

In fact, nothing could be further from the truth. Darcy attempted to think of something—anything—else, but he kept seeing a dark head of curls, framing a lovely face, which contained the most beautiful eyes he had ever before seen.

All thoughts of departure left Darcy, and he stood there for some time, unseeing, lost in the memory of a young woman unlike any he had ever met before. And had Darcy been able to see himself, he might have been surprised to witness a smile on his face, one which, though understated, was far more than what he usually wore at such a function.

Chapter XVI

*A*fter the events of the previous evening, Elizabeth was not surprised when Kitty indicated her desire to return to Longbourn.

"Though I am thankful for aunt and uncle for hosting us and have enjoyed my time in London, I believe there is no reason for us to stay any longer."

Elizabeth looked at her sister shrewdly, knowing it was no accident that she was saying this only the day after meeting Mr. Bingley. The sisters had slept a little late that morning, given the lateness of the previous night, and it had not been long after they had descended that Kitty had raised the subject.

"Yes, Lizzy," said Kitty with a laugh, apparently reading Elizabeth's look correctly, "I will own to it. A part of me had hoped to see Mr. Bingley in London, and though I will say that part had been growing weaker the longer we were here. Now that I have seen Mr. Bingley and have put him in the past where he belongs, I am eager to return to Longbourn."

"Eager?" asked Elizabeth with raised eyebrows.

"I am. I long for the quiet of our lives there, the company of dear friends, the serenity of the country. Let us leave the season and all its trappings for those such as Miss Bingley, little though she will enjoy it after your actions last night."

The sisters shared a laugh at the remembrance. "I do not care enough to stay here and witness the results of our actions, even if it were possible. Shall we not return to Longbourn?"

"To be honest, Kitty, I should have been happy to go back last month." Elizabeth smiled. "You know I am more at home in the country. Though Mr. Whitmore is trustworthy, and I am certain the estate is running efficiently with his guidance, Longbourn needs its mistress."

"And its mistress's sister!" chimed in Kitty.

"Just so," said Elizabeth, drawing her sister close for a warm embrace. "I am happy to accede to your request, Kitty. Let us leave as soon as may be."

As Elizabeth was not surprised at Kitty's request, neither were the Gardiners. When told of the sisters' intentions, they accepted it and did not attempt to induce them to change their minds.

"We had actually expected you to wish to return to Longbourn before now," said Mr. Gardiner. "Especially you, Elizabeth, given your words to us when we first convinced you to come to London. I am surprised you have managed to restrain yourself this long."

"We shall be excessively saddened to see you go," said Mrs. Gardiner. "But I dare say you have fulfilled your purpose in coming to London." She fixed Kitty with a knowing gaze. "Am I not correct, Kitty?"

Though Kitty colored, she nodded her agreement. "I believe I have, Aunt. I wish to thank you for your wise counsel and your patience. I believe I am better able to judge for myself should I be put in such a position again."

"You are a good girl, Kitty. I am happy you have grown wiser because of your experiences."

"We have one more matter to discuss with you," said Mr. Gardiner. "Your aunt and I are planning a holiday to the north country, perhaps even as far as the lakes, should my business allow me enough time away. Would you girls care to accompany us?"

"I believe I would be happy to partake in such a venture," said Elizabeth, knowing that her uncle had expected such a response. "But I will defer to Kitty, for she might not appreciate the ability to tour dusty old houses and see nothing but rocks and trees."

Kitty laughed and slapped Elizabeth on the shoulder. "You know very well that I will go along if only to give *you* pleasure, Lizzy. I believe, Uncle, that we would be happy to accept your kind invitation."

"Excellent!" said Mr. Gardiner, laughing at the sisters' banter. "I shall send more details once we decide on them. Until then, I hope you enjoy the anticipation."

With that, the decision was made, and the Bennet sisters prepared to depart. Word was sent to Longbourn, and they arranged for the Bennet carriage to be dispatched to London. It was only two days after the decision had been made that the sisters were prepared to depart for their home. But they were not able to depart before a visitor arrived to speak to them—a most unexpected visitor indeed.

The ladies were sitting in Mrs. Gardiner's parlor, enjoying their final morning in one another's company, when the door chime was heard. Before long, the housekeeper entered and spoke quietly with Mrs. Gardiner, and then departed. Mrs. Gardiner turned to her two nieces.

"Well, girls, it seems you are about to receive the first fruits of your labors."

Elizabeth's question was poised on the tip of her tongue, when the door opened once again and the housekeeper led a visitor into the room.

"Miss Diana Colford to see you, mum."

Shocked, Elizabeth stood, noting that Kitty was in much the same position by her side. Mrs. Gardiner, having known the identity of the caller already, was better able to withstand the shock of the young woman's calling on them, and she nudged Elizabeth to make the introductions. Though Elizabeth felt like she was encased in some especially sticky tree sap, which prevented her from moving, or even thinking, she managed to perform the office with credible composure.

"I thank you for receiving me, Mrs. Gardiner," said Miss Colford once the introductions were complete. "I understand it is an impertinence, given our previous lack of an introduction."

"Nonsense, Miss Colford," replied Mrs. Gardiner, displaying her good breeding and kindness. "You have been introduced to my nieces, after all. You are welcome, of course."

"Yes, indeed, I was." Miss Colford eyed them as if she was sizing them up, attempting to see through to their hearts. Elizabeth returned her gaze, feeling her command of her faculties returning. Kitty still seemed too astonished. "I was very pleased to have made their acquaintance at the Dunleavy ball, I assure you."

"Excuse me, but how did you know where to find us?"

"Kitty!" exclaimed a shocked Mrs. Gardiner.

Miss Colford only raised a hand, though her manner was all amusement. "It is a fair question, Mrs. Gardiner. My father is a close friend to Mr. Dunleavy, who, I believe, is a business associate of your uncle. My father, knowing that Mr. Dunleavy is happy with his relationship with Mr. Gardiner, asked for your direction, and I was able to wheedle it from my father."

Elizabeth could not help but laugh. "That is a very unflattering portrayal of yourself, Miss Colford."

A grin was the other woman's response. "No, but it is entirely the truth, I assure you."

In an instant, Elizabeth decided she liked this young lady. She was unassuming and kind, yet she seemed to possess a keen wit and a pleasant sense of humor. Should circumstance permit it, she knew this young lady would become a valued friend.

"Now that we are all getting on so famously," said Mrs. Gardiner, injecting her dry wit into the conversation, "let us call for tea."

A pleasant fifteen minutes was spent with Miss Colford, as the ladies became acquainted. While Elizabeth informed her of their situation, she responded by telling her something of herself. In particular, she was the second of four children, her elder brother had finished Cambridge and had recently returned from a tour of the continent, while of her young brothers, the second was currently studying to become a parson, while the youngest had entered the navy at a young age.

"I must own that I am quite envious, Miss Colford," said Elizabeth upon hearing of the other woman's family. "Kitty and I have no brothers. I think I might have liked to have a brother to care for us."

"And I envy you, Miss Bennet. I have always longed for a sister. Brothers are useful for scaring off unwanted suitors, but one cannot share certain confidences with a brother. You and your sister are blessed to have each other."

Elizabeth looked at her only remaining sister, and she was forced to concede that she was fortunate indeed.

"I apologize, Mrs. Gardiner," said Miss Colford, redirecting the conversation, "but I must own that I had a purpose in imposing upon you today."

Sighing, Kitty said: "I suppose you wish to know of Mr. Bingley."

"Indeed, I do." Miss Colford sighed. "Mr. Bingley is an amiable man, but even before the night of the ball, I will confess I had some reservations about him. He is cheerful, handsome, and pays me particular attentions, but I wished to know more of him. I sense a . . . I do not know how to explain it. Perhaps a shallowness, I suppose. I do not know if he means to pay court to me, but I should like to have any information of him that I can should it come to such an eventuality."

"Then what would you have from us?" asked Elizabeth.

"The truth. Or at least your perception of Mr. Bingley so that I might judge for myself."

Kitty looked at Mrs. Gardiner, wishing for guidance. Mrs. Gardiner only smiled and gestured at their guest. "I believe you cannot refuse to speak now, Kitty, not after your performance the night of the ball."

Seeing the truth of the matter, Kitty began to speak, telling Miss Colford of her experiences with Mr. Bingley. Elizabeth endeavored to assist, giving her opinions and observations whenever she could, but for the most part, Kitty related the facts to Miss Colford, who responded with questions at times, though she largely simply listened.

At the end of Kitty's recital, Miss Colford shook her head, a rueful sort of resigned acceptance evident in her grimace. "I had suspected that Mr. Bingley was not as serious as I would have wished. I thank you for this information."

Miss Colford chuckled and looked at each of them in turn. "The reason for my questions is that I have been in society for three years now, and my parents wish for me to marry, saying that I have been too fastidious in my wishes for a husband. Though Mr. Bingley is not of the gentry, my parents have decided that if he purchases an estate, he would be acceptable as a husband due to his wealth. But they will not force me—indeed, as I am of age and possess my own fortune, I need not marry if I do not desire it."

"What will you do now?" asked Elizabeth, feeling some curiosity.

"I will continue to enjoy Mr. Bingley's attentions," said Miss Colford, giving them a half smile. "He *is* a handsome man, after all. But I will take great care to guard my heart, and should he ultimately propose, I will think very carefully on whether he will make a good husband."

"That is all one can do," agreed Mrs. Gardiner. "We wish you luck in it."

Soon, Miss Colford took her leave. Before she was gone, Elizabeth requested, and was granted, leave to exchange letters, and she accepted Miss Colford's directions, promising to write to her as soon as they arrived back in Hertfordshire. Then she was gone, leaving three bemused ladies behind, though Kitty was a little fretful.

"I do hope I have not ruined her relationship with Mr. Bingley."

"Actually, I think you have helped her approach him with a measure of caution," said Mrs. Gardiner. "She might still marry him, but only if she feels he has matured enough to be a good husband. I dare say she has come out better for the experience."

"I like her very much," said Elizabeth. "I hope we can become friends."

The subject was then dropped, and they began speaking again of their departure on the morrow. Elizabeth was content. Kitty was on the mend, and some good had come from the confrontation the night of the ball. She could not be happier.

Upon returning to Longbourn, the Bennet sisters once again settled into their routine, content to be quiet at home, busying themselves with matters of estate, house, and the doings of the neighborhood. One of their first actions when they had returned home was to call on the Lucas family.

They were welcomed at Lucas Lodge with all the happy greetings of friends long sundered and invited to sit and stay for dinner, which Elizabeth and Kitty were happy to accept. Their doings in London were discussed at length, with the Lucases' offering exclamations of delight over their stories of what they had experienced there. In return, all the gossip of the neighborhood was disseminated and dissected with the precision of a surgeon at his work.

Of particular note to the Bennets was a small mention of one they knew, but who had been barred from Longbourn, and unsurprisingly, Maria's comment led to the discussion. The young Lucas sister, though a good girl, was still romantic in her ideals, and she had apparently long suspected some partiality for Elizabeth from certain quarters.

"I have heard that Mr. Wickham has not been quite himself since you went away," said Maria, turning a sly glance on Elizabeth. "According to his good friend Denny, he has been quite out of sorts. He did not even appear at the last assembly!"

"That is interesting, indeed," said Elizabeth, returning Maria's slyness with blandness of her own. "What do you suppose could be bothering him?"

"I dare say it was the absence of a certain lady which has him out of sorts."

"It appears, however, that the lady does not favor Mr. Wickham in return." Charlotte's censuring glance at her sister spoke volumes, and Elizabeth was grateful to her friend for her assistance.

"I have no idea why Mr. Wickham might have pined after Kitty or me," said Elizabeth, affecting a nonchalant tone. "I am certain he is nothing to us."

Maria turned on Elizabeth, her eyes wide with dismay. "But he is ever so handsome. I am sure I would die if he were to speak his pretty words to me."

"You might *wish* you had died," muttered Elizabeth.

Apparently Elizabeth had not spoken quietly enough, for Charlotte turned a severe eye on her and arched a brow. Elizabeth was spared having to respond when the conversation continued on around them, but Charlotte's steely glare told Elizabeth her friend would be asking questions of her later.

As it turned out, there was no opportunity for Charlotte to raise the subject, and the Bennet sisters went home that evening, Kitty happy to once again be near her friends, while Elizabeth was pensive. An unpleasant thought had occurred to her, and she wondered why it had not come to mind before. While they had been in town these past months enjoying themselves, Mr. Wickham had been left in Hertfordshire to wreak his havoc on the people of the town. The Lucases had not made any mention of any specific gossip concerning Mr. Wickham, so at least she could take solace in that fact. Perhaps he had been so fixed upon Elizabeth that he had not had time to focus on his usual depravities.

The matter bothered Elizabeth all night, allowing her little sleep in the process, such that by the next morning she was quite worn out. It was then, of course, that Charlotte called. Elizabeth was in no doubt as to the reason for her friend's visit.

"Lizzy, I wish to ask you about your words concerning Mr. Wickham," were the first words out of Charlotte's mouth once their greetings were exchanged. "I always knew that you were no friend of the man, but it seems to me that perhaps there is something deeper than a simple disinclination for his company. Will you share it with me?"

Sighing, Elizabeth nodded her head. "I am afraid there is, Charlotte. Mr. Wickham is not a good man, and I am certain he has targeted me for his attentions, though I have rebuffed him."

"Tell me," said Charlotte, her tone leaving no room for argument, not that Elizabeth would have demurred.

"Very well." Then Elizabeth began her tale, telling Charlotte of Mr. Wickham's attentions to her, then moving to what she had heard from Mr. Darcy, though not mentioning the man by name. As she spoke, Charlotte's countenance darkened, though she did not interrupt. But Elizabeth was well aware of the fact that her friend was not at all happy with her.

"And you did not think to share this with us?" asked Charlotte, her pique clear in the tone of her voice.

"In truth, I never even considered it," said Elizabeth, "though I will own I should have."

"Of course you should have!" snapped Charlotte.

"In my defense, I noted Mr. Wickham's interest in me and thought that he had targeted an estate. Besides, I was not at liberty to say anything, as I had not been given leave. It never occurred to me that he might have other activities in mind."

"You might have at least made a warning," replied Charlotte, her exasperation showing in her countenance. "You are known in the area, whereas Wickham is new—you would have been believed, should it have come to a question of who was more trustworthy. And you do not need to protect his identity any longer, Lizzy, for the only one who could have made such a communication to you is Mr. Darcy."

Flushing, Elizabeth turned away, and she held one hand out, palm forward, a gesture of surrender.

Sighing, Charlotte reached out and grasped Elizabeth's hand. "I am quite vexed with you, Elizabeth, though I understand why you thought as you did."

"Has Mr. Wickham caused trouble in my absence?"

Shaking her head, Charlotte said: "Not that I am aware of. There are no injuries to the ladies of the area that are the subject of gossip, though it is possible that nothing has come to light yet. Mary King was the recipient of his attentions for a time, coincidentally after she inherited ten thousand pounds, though she has since been taken to Liverpool by an uncle.

"As for Mr. Wickham's conduct with the shopkeepers, who can tell? I have heard nothing, but it is quite possible he has run up debts and it has simply not been noted."

A distracted nod was Elizabeth's answer. "The question is, what do I do about it?"

"I cannot tell you how to behave, Lizzy," said Charlotte. "But I will be making my family aware of Mr. Wickham's conduct and warning Maria to stay away from him."

"That is the best," said Elizabeth as the door to the sitting room opened.

Mrs. Whitmore stepped into the room and approached them. "I am sorry, Miss Bennet, but Mr. Wickham has once again come, and he refuses to leave without seeing you."

A scowl came over Elizabeth's face, and she noted the grim line of Charlotte's mouth, mirroring her own.

"Speak of the devil," said Elizabeth to no one in particular.

Charlotte raised an eyebrow at her, clearly curious to see what she would do. Elizabeth responded with a decisive nod before she turned back to Mrs. Whitmore.

"Is John at hand?"

"He is already outside, Miss Bennet. My husband is away from the manor at present, seeing to the eastern field, but he may be summoned quickly if required."

After thinking on the matter for a moment, Elizabeth shook her head. "I do not think it will be necessary. I doubt Mr. Wickham is an overt threat at present; I think he is likely here to make an attempt to charm me. He would not attempt anything bold with witnesses close to hand."

"You should still take care, Lizzy," said Charlotte, while Mrs. Whitmore nodded. "You know not of what he is capable."

"Agreed. That is why I wish both of you to accompany me outside. I mean to make it very clear to Mr. Wickham that he is not to return."

Both ladies agreed, and soon they all trooped outside where they saw Mr. Wickham pacing back and forth, John standing apparently at ease by one of the front columns. He seemed little concerned with the pacing man, but Elizabeth, who had known John for many years, could see the tightness of his stance, as if he were ready to spring into action at a moment's notice.

When they emerged, Mr. Wickham turned to face Elizabeth with a smile on his face, though Elizabeth did not miss the tightness around his eyes at the sight of Charlotte and Mrs. Whitmore following her out the door. But he apparently decided it was best to ignore them as he directed his words to Elizabeth. He stepped forward to greet her, an eagerness about him which belied the charming, casual façade he put up for their benefit.

"Miss Bennet," said he, sketching a low bow, "I cannot tell you how happy I am to see you once again. I . . . ."

Mr. Wickham paused, seemingly caught in the grip of some great emotion. Elizabeth, however, caught a glimpse of the glimmer in his eyes, and she knew instantly it was false. The man was a chameleon, changing his colors at a moment's notice to suit his needs. He would have been perfect for the theater, so convincing was he.

"I missed you so, Miss Bennet, far more so than I had any right. I am pleased that you have returned."

"You are quite correct on one count, Mr. Wickham," said Elizabeth.

Mr. Wickham smiled, though Elizabeth was certain she was able to discern a certain predatory quality inherent in it. She smiled thinly.

"You had no right to miss me at all, Mr. Wickham," continued Elizabeth, feeling a certain savage glee at the sight of the smile sliding from his face. "I am nothing to you, after all."

"I would like you to become something," said Mr. Wickham.

"I think not, sir," said Elizabeth. "I have no interest in becoming better acquainted with you, as I have already informed you once. I would ask you to please cease coming here, and do not importune me any longer."

"But Miss Bennet," said Mr. Wickham, his desperation coming through in his voice, "I truly wish that we could *become* something more to each other. I feel . . . I feel a passionate regard for you that no time can ever erase. Please allow me the chance to prove my devotion!"

"Mr. Wickham," replied Elizabeth, allowing a hint of steel to enter her voice, "I do not wish for your attentions. I have made this clear before, yet you continue to attempt to force them on me."

"But—"

"No more! I do not wish to hear of it! I require you to leave Longbourn and to never return."

Elizabeth turned to her footman. "John, please ensure Mr. Wickham leaves."

"A pleasure, miss," said John, stepping forward.

And Mr. Wickham was forced to depart. But as he left, Elizabeth noted his dark look in her direction, seeming to pierce her completely through. It was as if all the hosts of hell had taken up residence, all their evil focused out through those orbs and fixed upon her. Elizabeth shivered; in that moment she would not have been surprised if his eyes had suddenly turned red.

"Elizabeth," said Charlotte, sidling closer to her and grasping her hand in a tight grip, "I am uneasy about this. That man . . . I was wrong; he is ten times the danger to *you* as he is to the rest of Meryton."

"He has his eye on Longbourn," said Elizabeth dispassionately. "He cares nothing for me."

"Exactly. And should he ever gain his design, I do not doubt his behavior toward you would be reprehensible. He hates you for defying him."

Elizabeth did not respond. She watched as John escorted the lieutenant from the grounds of Longbourn until they were no longer in sight, finally exhaling a breath she had not known she was holding.

"What will you do, Elizabeth?"

A sudden thought came to Elizabeth, and her path forward crystallized in her mind. She knew exactly what she needed to do.

After a quick conversation in which she persuaded Charlotte to her point of view—which was not difficult—the two ladies returned to the sitting-room to plot their strategy. Soon the carriage had been called, and they stepped into it for the short journey to Meryton. Elizabeth was forced to smile as the carriage driver gave her a strange look when she mentioned the destination—the Bennet sisters rarely went to Meryton on anything other than their own two feet.

Soon the carriage stopped in front of the militia headquarters, and the two ladies entered the building. They informed the colonel's assistant that they had come to see Colonel Forster, and after a moment they were admitted to his office, a utilitarian room containing a desk, a few chairs, and several maps hung up on the wall. The colonel himself greeted them with his typical friendliness and inquired after them, though his curiosity was evident in the way he regarded them. Not wishing to prolong the matter, Elizabeth quickly stated the reason for their visit.

"Colonel Forster, I have come today to inform you that one of your officers will not leave me in peace. I would like to ask you to control the man."

The colonel started, clearly not expecting such a communication. "One of my officers?"

"Yes, sir. Mr. Wickham has continued to pay his addresses to me, though I have informed him repeatedly that I do not wish for them. Before my sister and I left for London, I had him escorted away from my estate, telling him not to return. We returned to the area yesterday, and once again, today he disturbed my peace, and I was forced to have my footman remove him from the property."

"Wickham you say," said the colonel, his eyebrows scrunching up in a frown. "I am sorry, Miss Bennet, but this is the first I have heard of this matter."

"Of course it is, sir," replied Elizabeth. "I did not think it necessary to make an issue of it before. But now that he has once again forced me to act against him, I felt it best to warn you."

"The man scared me this morning, sir," added Charlotte. "His gaze as he departed was positively malevolent."

The colonel paused and considered what they were telling him, and he nodded once, as if confirming something to himself.

"I have had some . . . questions, concerning Wickham myself," said he, speaking slowly. "Perhaps I should not mention it, but Miss King's uncle came to me before he took his niece away, saying that Mr. Wickham had become aggressive with him when informed that he would not countenance an engagement between them."

Charlotte gasped. "I had not known their relationship had gone so far."

"It was unknown to most," said Colonel Forster. "My understanding is that Wickham rushed a proposal when he discovered the girl's uncle was coming for her. Mr. King mentioned that Wickham pressed for an elopement. Wickham denied it, and as the Kings left soon after, I could only have him watched. This new news that you bring is troubling."

Elizabeth nodded, knowing his behavior was exactly what Mr. Darcy had told her of the man. With Elizabeth away from the county in London, Mr. Wickham had obviously turned to the mark at hand rather than wait for her return. The man was an opportunist through and through. How fortunate that Mary King had a guardian who was attentive to her needs, denying Wickham his desires! Elizabeth knew she would have felt awful had she been hurt by Elizabeth's lack of action.

"I have heard some other . . . stories of Mr. Wickham," said Elizabeth, feeling all the hesitation of making a communication she knew was long overdue.

"You have?" asked the colonel, raising an eyebrow.

"Yes, sir. You have my apologies for not speaking of them before. But I wish to rectify that mistake."

"Then by all means, Miss Bennet."

And so Elizabeth told him what she had heard, though she kept her source quiet. She told him of the debts the man had run up at Cambridge and at certain towns in which he had been known in the past. She also told him of Mr. Wickham's propensity to treat ladies with less than respect, though on this she could not, for obvious reasons, be explicit. When she was done, Colonel Forster looked at her, clearly troubled by what she had related.

"Miss Bennet, I had never imagined to hear such things about one of my officers, even Wickham, whom I have long known is not possessed of a noble character. But you did not mention who it was who informed you of these things."

"I have not mentioned his name because he did not give me leave to make these things known to you, sir," said Elizabeth. "If not for what I believe to be dire circumstances, I would not have said anything at all."

"Your circumspection is admirable, Miss Bennet. But I cannot take action unless I have some proof of Wickham's conduct. To do so would be to invite complaints of singling the man out for ill treatment."

"Then investigate with the merchants of Meryton," said Charlotte. "If you find that Mr. Wickham has run up debts, then you have your proof, at least in part."

"Even that might be an improper attack."

"Then do not mention it to anyone else," said Elizabeth. "You can ask a few of the local shopkeepers, and if you find nothing, you can abandon it. Present it to them as merely being diligent in making certain there is nothing untoward with your officers' credit with the local shopkeepers."

"The regiment will be departing for the summer, will they not?" asked Charlotte. "You can tell the merchants you want to ensure all accounts are settled before the regiment departs."

Nodding slowly, the colonel turned a smile on them. "I think you have hit on it. I shall do so directly, Miss Bennet. Again, I thank you for bringing this to my attention. I cannot have the honor of the regiment questioned, and should Wickham be the scoundrel you claim, it would follow us."

"You are welcome, colonel," replied Elizabeth. "I hope that you will forgive me for waiting this long to make my communication."

"I completely understand," said the colonel. "Now, if you excuse me, I must see to my investigations."

The ladies said their farewells to the colonel, and they returned to the carriage for the short journey back to Longbourn. Between them there was silence, as they both concentrated on thoughts of what they had done and what events would now ensue. And though Elizabeth could not be certain that Mr. Wickham would not wriggle out of his troubles, she felt a little safer because of it. She would need to make certain that she took great care, as she was certain Mr. Wickham was vengeful.

"Lizzy," said Charlotte, when the carriage had almost arrived at Longbourn, "I am . . . concerned for you."

"You have voiced my own thoughts, Charlotte," said Elizabeth. "But I will take care. I already take John with me whenever I leave to ride the estate. Though I would not wish for our merchants to be cheated, hopefully the colonel finds enough evidence to warrant tighter restrictions on Mr. Wickham."

"Good," said Charlotte. "I am excessively fond of you, Lizzy. I would hate for something to happen to you."

Chapter XVII

$\mathcal{B}$ rooding was not something unknown to Fitzwilliam Darcy. In fact, it sometimes seemed like it was his natural state. Growing up the eldest son of the master of a great estate, he had always been serious, but it was especially since his father's passing and his ascension to become the master of said estate that his true reticent nature had come to the fore.

But reticence was one thing; more and more in previous years, he had found himself brooding, agonizing about the estate, his ability to look after it, the behavior of the debutantes who attempted to capture his notice—the list seemed to be endless. In the past months, his brooding had often been centered around his sister's near ruin, or the behavior of Miss Bingley, though his distance from the lady's brother now made that less of a concern. Georgiana was slowly recovering, and though Wickham still had not been called to account for his deeds, at least he had not ruined Georgiana's gentle heart.

Recently, however, the subject of his ruminations had changed, and though he had often thought of Miss Elizabeth Bennet in the past several months, since seeing her at the ball his thoughts had been consumed by her. Quite simply, Darcy had forgotten just how appealing the woman was, and though he had elevated her to almost mythical status in his own mind, it had been a fond remembrance to keep him company on cold Derbyshire nights.

After seeing her again, there was nothing fond about his remembrances. Instead, he was afire with thoughts of her teasing smile, the glint of the sunshine on the perfect mahogany of her hair. He could suddenly recall with a clarity of detail, almost as if she were standing in front of him, the lightness of her figure under her dress, the confident stride as she had visited her tenants, the grace with which she had glided through the steps of the dance they had shared, and the happiness which shone on the flawless smoothness of her countenance as she had mingled with friends and new acquaintances alike. And perhaps most of all, he remembered her intelligence, the way she had held her own with ease in any conversation, her kindness, and her absolute devotion to those she considered important to her.

There was much to like in the person of Miss Elizabeth Bennet, and though Darcy knew that her connections were not the best, he rationalized that her dowry—the estate of Longbourn itself—was more than enough to offset that lack. Furthermore, what did Darcy care of connections? He had more than he wished, more than he ever kept up with, and some that he actively despised. What need had he for more? For that matter, he did not truly have any need for more wealth, as he was well able to provide for a wife and twenty children. Darcy was quickly coming to the conviction that Elizabeth herself was worth more than all the diamonds, rubies, and emeralds in the Darcy vaults.

But Darcy remained in indecision. As the lady was not, by any definition, highly connected, he well knew he would receive some resistance from his family. The earl and countess would eventually come around, he thought, if only for the relief that he had finally decided to take a wife, though he was certain they would appreciate her for her own merits once they met her. The largest problem, of course, would be his Aunt Catherine, though Darcy was prepared to brave her displeasure. He had always been prepared to do so as, contrary to her wishes, he had never intended to marry Anne.

But would Miss Bennet fit into his sphere? He thought she would, but he also knew that she would be subject to the vitriol of many of the more mean-spirited of society, who would resent her for her "common origins." And though he had no doubt she would be able to parry whatever barbs were sent her way, the thought of her being subjected to them at all angered Darcy. He would only be able to do so much, as to protect her all the time would give her the reputation of requiring a protector, which would only make the contempt worse.

And so Darcy existed, vacillating from determination to seek her out to fear that she might not wish to leave her simple life. It was ironic that he was once again put to rights by his sister.

They were sitting in the music room one night after dinner. Georgiana had played a few pieces on the pianoforte for his pleasure, then she sat next to him when she had finished. Mrs. Annesley was sitting to one side, concentrating on some embroidery, though she exchanged a few words with her charge at intervals throughout the evening.

"You have been very quiet of late, Brother."

The sound of his sister's voice brought Darcy from his reverie, and he blinked and then stared at her in incomprehension for several moments. Georgiana giggled, prompting Darcy to focus and then smile.

"I am sorry, my dear, I was woolgathering. Might I trouble you to repeat what you said?"

"I merely said that you have been introspective recently."

"Is this different from my usual behavior?"

This time Georgiana laughed openly. "Touché, Brother, touché. I would agree with you—we are much alike, in that respect. But this quietness is much more profound. There seems to be some great weight pressing down upon you."

Shaking his head, Darcy said: "It is nothing, Georgiana. There is no need to concern yourself."

A brief pause ensued, in which Darcy thought his sister was contemplating her words carefully before speaking.

"There is no question you are able to manage your own affairs, Brother. But I would be happy to provide a sympathetic ear if you wish to speak of your troubles. Perhaps I might even help you determine what is best to be done."

It was the diffidence in Georgiana's tone which alerted Darcy to the fact that she was not certain of his reception. Furthermore, Darcy noted that not only had Georgiana recovered from her experience with Wickham, but she was maturing and was no longer the child she once was.

Had he brushed her off in the past? Darcy did not think he had ever been so overt as to inform her that her opinions were not needed. But she was now older, had learned much, and could possibly help him with his problem. Would it be right to simply tell her that she should mind her manners and not question him? Part of growing was gaining confidence, and he thought she would gain much more confidence if he showed her that he listened to her and valued her opinions, which was why he decided he could speak with her.

"I met a . . . lady in Hertfordshire," said Darcy, his decision to speak still at odds with his impulse to keep his own countenance.

Georgiana's eyes widened at his confession. "Miss Bennet, was it not?"

Astonished, Darcy could only look at her blankly, to which Georgiana responded with a giggle.

"Brother, you mentioned Miss Bennet in almost every letter you sent me. You have never done that before. Is it not logical to suppose that you were speaking of her?"

"You are becoming far too perceptive," replied Darcy with a shaken head. "What happened to my little sister?"

"I am still here, Brother. But I have decided that I will never again be taken in by one such as George Wickham, so I am endeavoring to be more perceptive."

"Oh, Georgiana," said Darcy, reaching out to grasp her hand.

"I am very much recovered, Brother," said Georgiana. "But my wisdom was dearly bought, and I would not put myself into such a position again."

"That is very wise," replied Darcy.

"Now," said Georgiana, returning the subject back to the previous discussion, "I wish to know of this Miss Bennet. And I wish to understand the connection to your recent inattention."

For a moment, Darcy wondered if he should stay silent. His sister was becoming far too perceptive of late, and Darcy found that he wished to keep *some* of his dignity intact. Then he remembered his decision and his reasons for it, and he found himself speaking again.

"Miss Bennet is the proprietor of an estate quite near where Bingley leased his estate. She is . . ." Darcy paused, searching for the right words to convey what he felt. "Well, quite simply, she is the best woman I have ever known. She is kind and considerate, loyal to her friends, a careful manager of her estate, committed to improving it for future generations, and delightfully intelligent. Add to that her beauty, grace, confidence, poise, intelligence, and a whole host of other qualities, and I think you can understand my dilemma."

"She sounds wonderful, Brother," enthused Georgiana. "When shall I meet this paragon of virtue?"

"I am not certain you ever shall, Georgiana."

The beaming smile ran away from his sister's face, leaving a perplexity behind. "Why ever not?"

"Because, Georgiana," said Darcy, "she is not of our sphere. Her estate is small and her family has lived in the area as minor gentry for many years. As you know, I am expected to marry a woman who will increase my holdings and bring new connections to build our standing in society."

"And is this what you want?"

His sister had truly hit on the crux of the matter, and Darcy was impressed yet again by her newfound maturity.

"What I want is not at issue, Georgiana. I must think about our family's place in society, and equally important, your future. I cannot abrogate those responsibilities for the sake of a pretty face."

"If you will excuse my saying so, I do not think that you have thought this through."

Darcy noted the slight frown Mrs. Annesley directed at her charge, but Darcy only smiled at the woman and shook his head. He was finding it quite interesting that his sister had found the confidence to speak to him in this frank manner.

"These past days I have thought of little else."

"That much is evident," replied Georgiana, turning a sly look on him. "But it seems to me that whatever you thought, your conclusions are in error."

"How so?"

Georgiana frowned at him. "This Miss Bennet, she is a gentlewoman, by your own admission. Is it not so?"

"She has inherited an estate from her father, it is true," said Darcy. "By all accounts, it has been in Bennet hands for generations."

"Then that requirement is met. Of course you could never marry a woman who was not gently born, but as you are a gentleman, and she a gentlewoman, you are equal in this respect."

"But what of her connections?" asked Darcy, very aware that he was fighting against his own heart.

"Are her connections in any way improper?"

Darcy considered that for a moment, before he confessed he did not know. "I have never met them. But I do know she has an aunt whose husband is a solicitor in Meryton, and an uncle in London who is a tradesman. Finally, she has a cousin who is, incidentally, our Aunt Catherine's clergyman, and is perhaps the most ridiculous person I have ever met."

"Perhaps he is, Brother. But you must recall that even if the Bennets have a ridiculous man for a cousin, at least they do not have Aunt Catherine. Surely that must count for something."

It was the droll way Georgiana spoke that struck Darcy as amusing, and he let loose a lusty guffaw. Georgiana joined him in a more restrained giggle, a look of smugness on her face at the success of her attempt to make him laugh.

"So, we have dealt with the cousin. The uncle who is a solicitor is not a high connection, but it *is* respectable. The tradesman uncle is unfortunate, but you have told me yourself several times how those in trade are rising in society, so as long as they are not openly improper, I do not think they would be a consideration.

"Now, she owns her estate, which as a dowry must be valuable, is it not so?"

"It is, indeed," said Darcy, feeling a little astonishment at how with so little effort, Georgiana was shredding his arguments like so much paper. "Though it is not a large estate, it is prosperous, and Miss Bennet is overseeing its growth."

Darcy paused and laughed, prompting a raised eyebrow from his sister. "I was just struck by a memory," said he. "Part of Longbourn's recent growth is at Netherfield's expense, as Miss Bennet recently purchased a large field from her neighbor. When she discovered the matter, Miss Bingley was almost offended that Miss Bennet possessed the temerity to purchase a field from the estate her brother was leasing."

Amid laughter and a shaken head, Georgiana said: "I can well believe it. That is so like Miss Bingley." Georgiana then turned a serious eye on her brother. "Then from the standpoint of fortune, though it may not be a stupendous match, it is at least a good one."

"Again, I would have to say you are correct."

"Then I do not see why you hesitate," said Georgiana. "You find society distasteful, and you find most young ladies of society less than stimulating. You have a good woman before you, who, by your own admission, is everything you would want in a companion, and you find her pretty enough to tempt you. Aunt Catherine will be upset whoever you marry, so long as it is not Anne, while Aunt and Uncle Fitzwilliam will perhaps be hesitant, but I cannot imagine they would not ultimately accept her, if only because you wish it. Our cousins will be accepting of her, though Rachel may require some convincing.

"Furthermore, Brother, she makes you happy." Georgiana's countenance darkened a little and she directed a stern look at him. "And did you not tell me you were contemplating a potential match between myself and Mr. Bingley, of all people?"

Darcy could only nod, dumbfounded by her manner. "Then if you were able to contemplate such a match for *me*, with a man who comes from a long line of tradesmen, I wonder at your inability to accept a match for yourself with a gentlewoman, one who is by all accounts proper, industrious, and beautiful."

"But a marriage with Miss Bennet might hamper your ability to find a good match," said Darcy, feeling as if he was fighting a losing battle. In fact, he was beginning to wonder why he was fighting at all.

"Really, William, I would not care to marry a man who is offended because your wife is not the daughter of a duke. And I think my dowry guarantees me much more attention than I would ever wish to receive. I cannot think my prospects will suffer much if you should marry her, and I would not care a jot if they did."

A slow smile spread over Darcy's face, and he regarded his sister with happiness. Why had he not spoken to her before? She had taken all his arguments against an attachment with Miss Bennet and dispatched them with as much effort as one would use to swat an insect. Why was he concerned for such things? In truth, now that he had heard her speak, Darcy had not the slightest inkling himself.

"So, I ask you again, Brother: when am I to be introduced to this wondrous creature?"

Shaking his head and chuckling, Darcy drew his sister in for a quick embrace and a kiss on the cheek. "I will arrange it as soon as may be, dearest. I believe you will like Miss Bennet and her sister very well indeed.'

"She has a sister?" said Georgiana, her mature gravitas of a moment before turning to girlish excitement.

"Yes, she does," replied Darcy lazily. "Miss Kitty Bennet is seventeen years of age, I believe."

"Oh, Brother! Then you simply must introduce us! I would love to have a sister my age!"

"I will do everything in my power to make it so, Georgiana, my dear. I could not bear to see you disappointed."

A few days after removing Mr. Wickham from Longbourn and speaking with the colonel, Elizabeth went into Meryton, and while she was there, she stopped in at the home of her aunt, Mrs. Phillips, for tea and to visit. Mrs. Phillips was, much like Elizabeth's mother had been, a silly woman, prone to histrionics and less than proper behavior. The Gardiner sisters had not been born to gentlemen—rather, their father had been the previous solicitor in Meryton, whose practice Uncle Phillips had assumed on the man's death, and as such, they had received little training in gentle manners.

However, Mrs. Phillips was a kind soul, one who did not have a malicious bone in her body. She was also childless, and as a result, she doted on her two remaining nieces who lived nearby, always visiting them with sweets from her kitchens, imparting the gossip of the area, and treating them as if they were her own daughters.

Gossip was her purpose in life, and eager as she was to hear anything new of note, there was rarely anything in the village that she did not know of within a few hours of it happening. Such was the efficiency of her network of gossips and, some might cynically say, the result of her own nosiness. Elizabeth had always felt that her aunt was best taken in limited doses, for her voice was high and shrill and always excited. But she was a dear lady, and Elizabeth loved her prodigiously.

On that morning when she was visiting with Mrs. Phillips, Elizabeth was gratified to hear that the first words out of her aunt's mouth—and the primary topic of discourse—was the discovery of one Mr. Wickham's less than savory activities.

"I have such a tale to tell you, Lizzy!" exclaimed Aunt Phillips almost the moment Elizabeth sat down."

"Do you?" replied Elizabeth, quite used to her aunt's ways. Nearly every visit began in a similar manner.

"I do, indeed! For you see, the gossip is all over town about one of the militia soldiers, a man who has been exposed as a viper, a demon sent to destroy us!"

Elizabeth smiled, enjoying Mrs. Phillips's penchant for hyperbole, though she had often wondered if the woman was only exaggerating, or speaking the exact truth as she believed it. "A member of the militia has been behaving badly?"

"Or so the story goes. You see, Mr. Wickham is the man, and I have it on good authority that he owes money to every reputable tradesman in Meryton." Mrs. Phillips leaned forward and spoke softly, as if imparting some great secret. "I understand that he owes over five pounds at the inn alone, and that the total of his debts approaches one hundred pounds."

Eyes wide, Elizabeth gazed at her aunt, her surprise not feigned in the slightest. "One hundred pounds?"

"That is what I have heard. The colonel has gathered his debts together and has issued orders that he is not to be extended any further credit. Mr. Wickham will be made to repay everything he owes, and the colonel has already docked half of his wages to begin repaying the deficit.

"In addition, he has issued a general order to all his men that all their outstanding debts are to be paid in full immediately, and no new debts are to be incurred."

"Then I am happy to hear it," said Elizabeth, though she was still stunned by the sheer amount of Mr. Wickham's perfidy. She had thought it likely that the man had amassed more than he could pay, but she had never expected it to amount to so much.

"Elizabeth," said Mrs. Phillips, drawing Elizabeth's attention back to her. The woman was looking at her with compassion, and for once, her voice was not shrill and loud. "Did Mr. Wickham not attempt to pay you his particular attentions?"

"Particular and persistent," said Elizabeth, showing her aunt a wry smile. "He attempted to do so, even after I told him repeatedly that I wished him gone, and even after I had ordered him from Longbourn."

"I can only assume he was looking for the income of a gentleman to fuel his habits," fretted Mrs. Phillips. "I ask you to take care, Elizabeth. I cannot imagine what life would be like with such a man for a husband."

Elizabeth smiled; it seemed like everyone of her acquaintance had abjured her to be careful of late. "Do not concern yourself, Aunt. I have already implemented measures to ensure my safety from the lieutenant. I no more wish to be his wife than I wish to move to the continent and join a nunnery."

"Oh, Elizabeth!" cried her aunt, though her lips were curved with affection. "You do try my nerves at times."

For the rest of the visit, Mrs. Phillips carried on about the evils of one Lieutenant George Wickham, both real and imagined. As was normally the case when Mrs. Phillips began to speak in earnest, her words came so rapidly and without pause that there was no need for Elizabeth to respond, and so Elizabeth spent the time politely listening, but at the same time she was considering what she should do concerning the matter. By the time she departed, she had decided on a course.

The Phillips abode was right on the main street of Meryton and not at all far from the headquarters of the militia, which Elizabeth had visited with Charlotte only a few days before. There she turned her steps, noting the presence of her faithful footman, John, and grateful for his protection. She was admitted at once, and soon she was seated with the colonel, though this time, his wife was in attendance for propriety's sake.

"I understand you have made discoveries concerning Mr. Wickham," said Elizabeth without preamble.

The colonel sighed and glanced at his wife. Mrs. Forster was a silly young thing, prone to gossip and giggling, and, Elizabeth suspected, with little ability for deep thought. At present, she was watching Elizabeth speak with her husband, a faint sense of astonishment upon her brow.

"I have indeed, Miss Bennet," replied the colonel. "Wickham has never been the most diligent of my officers, but I had not thought that he was this bad."

"You have my apologies, sir. I should have brought the matter to you long before I did."

Colonel Forster sighed. "Perhaps, but then we can never know. It seems, based on my investigations, that Wickham spent some time establishing himself in town before he began accumulating debts in earnest. Once he began, it was done so skillfully that none of the merchants gave any thought to the matter at all. A few pounds here and there, and he has created a debt he can never repay.

"In addition, I have discovered that he owes a large amount of gaming debts of honor as well, which makes the situation even worse. He had, it appears, attempted to charm several of the ladies of the area, though it seems he has not managed to compromise any of them yet." The colonel smiled, though it was particularly mirthless. "I believe I have you and Miss King to thank for that, Miss Bennet, for he focused the bulk of his attention where he was likely to benefit the most from it."

Elizabeth acknowledged his words, though inside her stomach was churning at the thought of being the focus of such a man's attention.

"What will you do now?"

"There are only two options," said the colonel with a sigh. "Debtors' prison is a possibility, though that would leave him owing the merchants of the town for many years yet, causing hardship. The militia does not receive ready welcome in many places like we have in Meryton, and I would not repay that kindness by leaving your shopkeepers without the funds to feed their families."

"And the other possibility?"

"Is even more difficult, but the right thing to do, I think," said the colonel. "The regiment will assume Mr. Wickham's debts and ensure the merchants are paid. Wickham's debts will then become ours, and he will slowly pay it back through his wages being withheld. It will near bankrupt some of my officers, but I cannot see any other way to do it. The regiment's honor is at stake."

"I see," said Elizabeth. "Colonel Forster, I cannot help but think that I am partially to blame for this situation. I believe that had I come to you earlier, your scrutiny at the very least would have served to slow Mr. Wickham's accumulation of debts."

The colonel smiled at her, and nodded. "I thank you for your words, Miss Bennet, but you cannot be held at fault. The only one who can be called to account is Wickham himself."

"Perhaps that is so, but I still believe I should have done more. And to that end, I would like to propose a resolution to your dilemma, sir, which will absolve your men of the responsibility."

Though it was clear the man was hesitant, he motioned for Elizabeth to continue.

"I propose that my estate assume Mr. Wickham's debts, sir, and that any repayment which is taken from his wages be returned to me. If, at any time in the future, he is not able to continue to draw salary from the militia, we will revisit the matter."

"Miss Bennet," said the colonel with a frown, "that is a very generous offer, but I do not believe it to be your problem to resolve."

"Perhaps it is not, colonel," replied Elizabeth, "but I would not see your men suffer due to no fault of their own. Many of your men are from poor families and would suffer unduly because of Mr. Wickham's profligacy. Longbourn is much better able to assume this debt. I will do nothing about the debts of honor—it might serve as a lesson for your men to avoid gambling their wages away—but I would assist with the matter of his debts with the merchants."

When the colonel hesitated further, Elizabeth smiled and leaned forward. "Colonel, I mean to have this responsibility—it is futile to attempt to change my mind. Please let me do this for you, if nothing else, to assuage my own guilt over my actions."

A slow smile spread over the colonel's face. "Miss Bennet, I have often heard it said that you are one of the jewels of the county, but never until this moment had I seen with my own eyes. I thank you for your kind offer, and I accept it, on the condition that you also allow *me* to assume some of his debts so that I may lessen *my* guilt. This has taught me a valuable lesson, I assure you. I shall not be so complacent in the future."

"Then shall we shake on it?" asked Elizabeth mischievously.

The colonel laughed and held out his hand, which Elizabeth took in her own, the sound of Mrs. Forster's giggling filling the room around them.

It was unfortunate that as Elizabeth was departing the militia headquarters she came face to face with Mr. Wickham. The man was entering the building as Elizabeth was leaving, and if his stride and the black thunder clouds gathered on his brow were any indication, he was in high dudgeon. He did not see Elizabeth at first and did not check his stride, but when he had come within a few feet of her, he espied her and jumped to the side with an oath, as Elizabeth herself moved to avoid a collision. If she had thought his anger was impressive before, that was nothing compared to the blazing eyes full of pure loathing he fixed on her after.

"Miss Elizabeth Bennet."

Her name sounded like nothing more than a curse.

"Mr. Wickham," said Elizabeth, ensuring her disdain for him was evident in her own voice.

"I might wonder why, with so little provocation, you would ruin my reputation in such a manner. Did I not pay the warmest of attention to you? Did I not attempt to love you?"

Elizabeth could do nothing other than laugh in his face. "Love me? Love my estate, you mean."

"I assure you, madam, I was in a fair way to falling deeply in love with you before this betrayal."

"Mr. Wickham," said Elizabeth, "there was no betrayal. I did not ruin your reputation—you did a masterful job of that yourself. I only took steps to protect myself from you."

"I have never behaved in anything but the most scrupulously proper manner toward you," hissed Mr. Wickham, leaning toward her, attempting intimidation. "You had no right to carry tales to Forster or anyone else."

"She had every right!" boomed the voice of the colonel as he stepped into the room.

Mr. Wickham only looked at the colonel, his disdain evident in his features.

"At attention, Wickham!"

Though Mr. Wickham appeared inclined to disobey the order, he straightened his posture, though with evident aversion. The colonel was not amused.

"Wickham, I have told you not to approach Miss Bennet in any way, and yet here you are, disobeying me within the confines of my own offices. What have you to say for yourself?"

"We met going through the door, sir," said Mr. Wickham, a sullen expression on his face. "I would remind you that *you* summoned me. I had no thought of seeing Miss Bennet."

"No, you would not, but you should have passed her by without a word. But now you are here, perhaps we should make a few matters clear to you." The colonel turned to Elizabeth, a question in his gaze. "Do you wish to inform Wickham of what we have decided here today?"

Elizabeth shook her head. "Be my guest, Colonel."

"What?" demanded Mr. Wickham, peering at Elizabeth. "What could *she* possibly have to do with regiment business?"

"This is also business which involves the town, and the estate owners in the area. Miss Bennet has, due to the goodness of her heart, taken responsibility for the greater part of your debts. You are looking at your new creditor, Wickham."

Surprise warred with calculation on the man's face. It was clear that he was trying to decide if there was any way he might use this information to his advantage. Elizabeth shook her head, disgusted with the man all over again.

"No, Mr. Wickham, you cannot use this to further ingratiate yourself with me and mine. All connection between us is hereby dissolved, other than the matter of your debts, which you will now owe to me."

"I will also own a portion of them, Wickham," said the colonel, "but you will repay Miss Bennet first, regardless of how long it takes. Should it become necessary, you may repay it from debtors' prison."

"You will not call them in at present?" asked Mr. Wickham. It was clear he was not certain whether to be relieved or horrified.

"Against my better judgment," said Elizabeth, "I will not. But I will tell you now, should you ever approach me or my sister again, should you engage in further theft from the merchants of Meryton, or should you set foot on my lands, I will call for payment in full, and you will be incarcerated. Am I clear?"

"Perfectly," said Mr. Wickham, though in a sullen tone.

"Excellent," said the colonel. "Now that you have been acquainted with the particulars of these transactions, you may return to your duties. And Wickham . . ."

The colonel stepped close to Mr. Wickham and looked him straight in the eye. "You are never to approach Miss Bennet again. I shall fully acquaint all your fellow officers with the details of your actions, and Miss Bennet's efforts to relieve our distress. The other men will not take kindly to any denigration of her reputation or person. If you are caught approaching her again, I will personally see you in Marshalsea, where I do not doubt it will be many years before you ever see the light of day."

With a salute—which even Elizabeth could see was clipped and sloppy—Mr. Wickham stalked from the room without a single glance back. Elizabeth was happy to see him go; would that she never was forced to be in his company again!

"I promise you, Miss Bennet," said the colonel, "Wickham will be controlled to the best of my abilities."

"Thank you, sir. I appreciate your concern."

"No, madam. It is the regiment which is in your debt. We will not forget it."

With that Elizabeth departed, making her way back toward Longbourn, John following behind. The man looked about them, his manner uneasy, but Elizabeth could see nothing to give any concern.

"What is it, John?"

The footman fixed his eyes on her, and after a brief pause, he spoke. "That Mr. Wickham. I could hear him muttering after he left the building, saying that he would avenge himself on you."

"Then we will have to be vigilant," said Elizabeth. "The militia will not be here much longer in any case. Once they are gone, we can all breathe easier."

"I hope so, Miss Bennet."

But Elizabeth noted that all the way back to Longbourn, his vigilance never lessened. And Elizabeth was glad for it, though she knew Wickham would not be out shadowing them at present. She had made an enemy today, and though she knew he was leashed for the moment, she also knew he would be looking for a way to shed his chains. He was also vindictive. She did not require John's testimony to inform her of that.

Chapter XVIII

*T*hough Darcy had decided, with Georgiana's urging, to seek out Miss Bennet again, the problem was how to find her. Darcy did not have the direction to the uncle with whom she was staying, and while he thought Dunleavy might be able to introduce him to the uncle, Darcy was not certain what excuse he could use to request such an introduction. He did not wish to incite rumors, after all, both because he was not inclined to endure gossip about himself, and because of the scrutiny which must necessarily attend his interest in any woman.

As he had no acquaintance with Miss Bennet's uncle, he was not comfortable knocking on the man's door with a request to see his beloved niece. And the more Darcy thought of it, he decided he was not certain they were even still in London. Though most of higher society would not even think of leaving London while the events of the season were still in progress, he knew that Miss Bennet was different, and while that did not necessarily mean she had returned to Hertfordshire, if she had gone, he could not visit her uncle's townhome without an invitation.

After a little thought on the matter, Darcy decided that the best place to gain information on Miss Bennet was near her home in Hertfordshire. While he certainly could not visit Longbourn to ask after her, he remembered that the Bennet sisters were close to the Lucases, and that Sir William would almost certainly be acquainted with the Bennet sisters' guardian.

Thus, on a bright morning in spring, Darcy mounted his horse and made his way through the streets of London. Though Darcy knew it was nothing but fancy, the city seemed quieter that day, as if it was holding its collective breath, somehow aware that great events were afoot. As Darcy rode, he noted the passage of carriages, both fine, family conveyances and smaller, hired coaches, wagons, laden with goods, watched as those on horseback picked their way through the congested thoroughfares, saw people walking, dodging others as they hurried on their business. For a time, he watched suspiciously, noting the faces of those he passed by, unaccountably suspicious that he was being watched, as if some writer for one of the gossip rags knew of his intention to offer for a young country miss.

After a time, he forced his attention back onto what he was doing, knowing that it was nothing less than silliness for him to be suspicious. No one other than Georgiana knew what he was about. And even if they did, what did it signify? Had he not determined to pay Miss Bennet his attentions, specifically disdaining the opinions of any of the London set? Darcy shrugged the matter off as not worth the effort of thinking about it; the opinions of society did not concern him in the slightest.

Outside the city, Darcy began to feel more at ease, and he settled his mount into a steady ground-eating stride, swiftly passing through the surrounding patchwork countryside, eager to have this short journey behind him. Though Darcy had ample time to consider what he was doing, he contented himself with concentrating on the road, deciding to avoid second-guessing himself.

When the buildings of Meryton came into view, Darcy was almost surprised, considering how he had focused on the journey, rather than the destination. Slowing to a walk, Darcy passed through the town to the inn on the far side where he stopped and engaged a room in order to refresh himself. Then soon after he was once again on the road, heading north. He pulled his horse up in front of Lucas Lodge and passed the reins to a stable boy, stepping to the front of the manor, where he produced his card and requested to see the master of the estate. Unsurprisingly, he was admitted in an instant.

"Mr. Darcy!" exclaimed Sir William, once Darcy had been led into the older man's study. "I am happy to see you, sir. I had no notion of your being in the area."

"I was just passing through and thought I would stop and pay a call," replied Darcy, feeling like his explanation was feeble at best.

Sir William, however, took no notice, and seemed to accept his explanation at face value. "I am happy you did. It has been far too long since you were in the area. Now, tell me—how are Mr. Bingley and his sisters?"

"All well," replied Darcy, though not truly wishing to discuss his friend. "Bingley is in London enjoying the season."

"Ah, I should have guessed. For a man as amiable as your Mr. Bingley, I cannot imagine he would wish to be anywhere else. Though you made your intention to depart clear, we all expected your friend to return. I am certain the delights of the season far outshine our small society here in Meryton."

Darcy watched the other man closely for signs of censure, but he found nothing. It appeared that Sir William was inclined to ascribe good intentions to those of his acquaintances, and it was possible that he had not even noticed the attentions Bingley had paid to Miss Kitty. Darcy was hopeful that no damage had been done to her reputation.

But he did not wish to discuss Bingley, so Darcy adroitly turned the conversation, asking about Sir William's neighbors, and the man did not disappoint. His ability to speak in a civil manner about the doings of the area seemed indefatigable, as he continued to speak for several moments. Unfortunately, he said nothing about Longbourn or its inhabitants.

He did, however, bring up a most interesting piece of news which astonished Darcy greatly. It also gratified him, as he had rarely seen a certain former friend of his suffer the richly deserved consequences of his actions.

"I understand you know Mr. Wickham," said Sir William, his manner turning to an uncharacteristic gravity. When Darcy acknowledged that he did, Sir William shook his head. "A bad business, that. It has been resolved, though I doubt Miss Bennet will ever see the return of the money she spent to spare the merchants of Meryton hardship."

Finally, the subject Darcy most wished to canvass, though not in the manner he had wished. "What has happened?"

"It was discovered that Mr. Wickham owed a great deal of debt to the shopkeepers of Meryton," explained Sir William. "I do not know the exact amount, though I understand that it was well in excess of fifty pounds."

Darcy nodded slowly. "I own some of Wickham's debts myself," replied Darcy. "But I do not understand what this has to do with Miss Bennet. I thought she was in town visiting her relations."

"She and her sister returned about a week ago, Mr. Darcy. And the timing could not have been more fortuitous. It seems that Mr. Wickham was insistent upon paying his addresses to Miss Bennet, even when she informed him he was not welcome."

Grip tightening upon the arms of his chair, Darcy looked at Sir William, noting the congenial man's face suggested that nothing untoward had happened. Reassured that she was not injured, he allowed himself to relax and listen to the man's recital of the situation.

"Miss Bennet spoke to the colonel about Mr. Wickham, seeking Colonel Forster's agreement to keep Mr. Wickham in line. I am not certain how it all came about, but during the course of the discussion, the colonel determined to check into Mr. Wickham's affairs. The debts were discovered, and Mr. Wickham brought before the colonel to make amends."

"And Miss Bennet?"

Seeming unaware of Darcy's fixation on Miss Bennet, Sir William continued. "It seems like she knew something of Mr. Wickham, though I know not where she obtained her knowledge. She spoke to the colonel again, insisting that she take on the expense of settling Wickham's debts in the town. *She* now owns the majority of them, though I understand Colonel Forster has assumed some of the expense himself." Sir William chuckled. "I was privy to the lively discussion between Miss Bennet and her steward, who was not at all happy about her expenditure in the matter. But she was firm. Nothing was to be done that she did not do herself, and even my offer to help bear some of the burden was rejected."

"But surely they did not act to spare Mr. Wickham the penalties of running up debts he could not pay."

"No, indeed, sir," replied Sir William. "They acted to spare the regiment the stain of dishonor. The bulk of Mr. Wickham's pay will be forfeit until his creditors are satisfied, and if he defaults or attempts to escape, the debts will come due and he will be incarcerated. If Miss Bennet had not stepped in, the militia would have been forced to make good on Mr. Wickham's debts, which would have near ruined many. As you can imagine, Miss Bennet is a heroine to our militia encampment."

"I can imagine that quite well indeed," replied Darcy.

Though Darcy was ashamed to acknowledge it, he had never thought about warning the shopkeepers of Meryton against Wickham's profligate ways. He had cleaned up after the man several times and had vowed not to do it again — at the time, it had seemed more important to ensure that Miss Bennet was protected with knowledge of the man's proclivities. Had he given it any real thought, he would have known there was no choice but to protect the townsfolk too. The entire economy of a small town could be ruined by one such as Wickham.

The greater part of Darcy's ruminations, however, were reserved for Miss Bennet, and he was proud of her, impressed by all she had taken on herself. Even though the fortunes of Longbourn estate were obviously on the rise, an expenditure of more than fifty pounds was no small matter, especially when weighed against what else she might have been able to do with that money. It was not a huge amount, but he knew it would set her back in at least some fashion, likely why Whitmore had argued with her as strenuously as he had.

A plan began to form in Darcy's mind. If, as he hoped, he was able to gain Miss Bennet's hand in marriage, her expenditures would become his, and he could easily replace that money from his own coffers. The colonel, however, would be living on his militia wages, which was nowhere near the amount his cousin Fitzwilliam made as a colonel in the regulars. Darcy did not know the man's situation, nor what support he had from his family, but as he was almost certainly a younger son, Darcy expected that it was not much. If all went as planned, he would once again control Mr. Wickham's debts, as he ought.

As for Wickham himself, though Darcy had been loath to act against the man because of how his father had esteemed him, he now wondered if the time had come to ensure Wickham could not prey on anyone else. There were many ways he could control Wickham—seeing him transported, sent to prison, or perhaps even transferred to the regulars would work. He only needed to determine if he needed to act now.

"And that is what has happened recently in our little neighborhood," said Sir William. Evidently he had continued to speak while Darcy was thinking about Wickham, though he had not heard a word of the other man's discourse. He was fortunate Sir William had not noticed his incivility.

"I thank you, Sir William," replied Darcy. "It appears you have had an interesting time of it."

Sir William smiled broadly. "Not at all, Mr. Darcy. It is unfortunate you are only passing through, for there is an assembly to be held tomorrow evening. We would be happy to have you there, I am sure."

Thinking quickly, Darcy replied: "Perhaps I might stay, if you would extend an invitation."

"Are you certain, sir?" asked Sir William, eyes wide. "I am sure you are a busy man. I am not offended at all, should you need to continue on to London."

It did not fit Darcy's purpose to correct Sir William's misapprehension, so he allowed it to pass. If he sent off a request immediately after he left Lucas Lodge, his man would have just enough time to journey to Meryton before the evening. "It is no trouble at all, sir. In fact, I would be very happy to attend your assembly and renew my acquaintances in the area."

"Excellent!" enthused Sir William. "You may consider yourself invited. Now, would you also accept an invitation to dinner tonight?"

Darcy demurred, for he doubted his man would arrive in time, and he had no dinner attire with him. "However, I will gladly accept your invitation another time, Sir William. Perhaps some time later this week?"

"Very good, Mr. Darcy. We shall be happy to have you."

Soon after the invitation to the assembly had been issued and accepted, Darcy departed from Lucas Lodge. He made his way back to the inn, where he engaged a set of rooms for himself and his valet. The inn at Meryton was small, but it was clean and well-maintained. It was not up to the standards Darcy usually required when traveling, but as it was close to Longbourn, he found there was little of which to complain.

His first stop that afternoon, once he had eaten a small meal at the inn, was to call on the colonel of the regiment, where he made his case to assume any debt of Wickham's that Colonel Forster held. As Darcy expected, the colonel was intent upon holding onto Wickham's debts, as he held himself responsible for the man's actions. It was, therefore, Darcy's task to convince him that he was not at fault.

"In fact, sir, if there is to be any blame apportioned which does not rest with Mr. Wickham himself, it must be *mine*. I have known what he is for many years, and I have cleaned up his messes before. Had I warned the merchants when I was in residence at Netherfield, Wickham could never have succeeded in amassing so much debt."

"Perhaps that is so, Mr. Darcy, but as his commanding officer, it is my responsibility to ensure he — and every other man in my command — behaves the way he ought. I have learned much from this situation, but I was still negligent in my duties, and I must take my share of the blame."

Back and forth they went, arguing the matter. Darcy was sensitive to the man's opinion, knowing as he did that Colonel Forster was a good officer, who held himself to a high standard. In the end, though, Darcy was able to carry his point, by a simple appeal to the economics of the matter.

"Colonel, excuse me for saying so, but as I have a cousin who is a colonel in the regulars, I believe I have an accurate notion of your situation. If you do not mind my saying, you can ill afford to assume Wickham's debts, especially if you are attempting to pool your money for something better once the war is finished."

The colonel's grimace told Darcy he had guessed the matter correctly.

"As you know, I am a wealthy man. I am well able to assume these debts with no hardship. Please allow me to do this for you, Colonel. Please allow me to be of use."

Though the colonel was ill inclined to accept charity, Darcy kept at it until the man finally agreed. When they had shaken on it, Colonel Forster sat back in his chair and regarded Darcy, a faintly considering expression on his face.

"Given that you have amply proved yourself to be a generous man," said the colonel, "I will assume the stories Wickham has been telling of you ever since he joined the regiment are not true."

Darcy nodded. "Though I do not know exactly what he has been saying, I can well imagine. It is unfortunate, but the truth and Mr. Wickham are not well acquainted with each other. Lies flow through his lips as water flows over rocks."

"I had thought so. Wickham's reputation in the regiment has fallen recently, but in this matter I will make certain the word gets out that his stories of you are not to be trusted."

"Thank you, Colonel."

"No. *Thank you*, Mr. Darcy. Though I would gladly have taken my share of the expense when it comes to that scoundrel, I will confess that it takes a burden off my mind. I thank you for that."

The rest of Darcy's time in Meryton passed slowly. He visited some of the shops, particularly the bookseller, in order to ensure he had some reading material for the night to come, and he mounted his steed and went for a long ride the following morning after he had broken his fast. Snell, his valet, had arrived late in the evening, as he had expected, and though the man regarded his master with questioning eyes, he did not ask, being far too well trained to inquire.

When the time finally came for Darcy to dress for the assembly, he bathed and allowed his man to prepare him for the evening. Snell was surprised at Darcy's interest in his attire, where he had rarely concerned himself before, but what the man thought of it he did not say. Darcy would have been surprised if his valet did not have some inkling of his intention to impress a young lady, as Darcy thought he was being rather transparent.

Darcy was one of the first to enter the assembly hall that evening, and as the local gentry trickled into the room, he was greeted by many he had met the previous autumn. He listened to them speaking with an absence of manner, though he attempted to disguise it. As no one seemed offended, he thought he did a credible job of it.

The world seemed to stop spinning when he saw Miss Bennet enter the room, her sister laughing by her side. Even his glimpse of her at the ball, only a short week ago, had not prepared him for the almost physical blow the sight of her seemed to deal to his equilibrium. She was dressed in a light green dress, which swayed about her as she moved, with little flowers woven into her hair and a simple gold chain adorning her throat. Her hair was swept up in an elegant chignon, some longer curls dangling down the left side of her face, where they bounced as she walked, tantalizing him with the thought of how soft they were. In that moment, Darcy wished for nothing more than to be allowed to run his hands through the silky softness of her hair.

She was beautiful, everything a man could ever wish for in a woman. And Darcy meant to make her his own.

There was some discussion between the Bennet sisters of not attending the assembly. They had just come from London where their schedule of events had been far busier than they were accustomed to, and they were not certain they wished to once again spend the night dancing.

"What comparison could there be between an assembly in Meryton and the ball we attended just before we came home?" asked Elizabeth. "Perhaps we should allow a little time for our memories of that night to fade, so we will not be disappointed with the simpler gatherings in Meryton."

But in the end, Elizabeth did not mind attending. And since Kitty was excited to see friends she had not met since they had left the neighborhood in December, Elizabeth found that she could not deny her sister. Thus, to Meryton they were to go.

"Does the assembly hall not seem smaller tonight, Lizzy?" asked Kitty as they stepped into the vestibule.

Elizabeth turned an amused eye on her sister, noting her glancing around at their surroundings. The hall was not precisely small, but Elizabeth could well understand how Kitty suddenly found it to be so.

"Perhaps it is rendered so because of the sights we have seen in London," replied Elizabeth. "I suppose we must accustom ourselves to such poor fare after the splendors to which we have been witness."

A smile came over Kitty's face, and she swatted at Elizabeth playfully. "One would almost think you have grown too proud for such humble surroundings, Lizzy."

"And yet I believe I am quite happy to be home."

"As am I, Lizzy."

They stepped into the ballroom where they saw that many of the local families had already gathered. It was a marked change from their recent time in London where it seemed like a competition to see who could be the most fashionably late. The antics of those who considered themselves high and mighty in society had been a source of amusement between them, and many had been the comments at the expense of some of the more ridiculous ones.

Kitty soon located some of her friends, and she left Elizabeth's side to go and greet them. For Elizabeth's part, she scanned the room quickly. Seeing Charlotte standing to one side with her mother, she made to move toward her. That was when she was arrested by the most astonishing sight of Mr. Darcy, tall and proud, walking toward her.

"Miss Bennet," said Mr. Darcy, bowing to her. "I am pleased to see you this evening. How do you do?"

His question seemed to free Elizabeth from her sudden stupor, and she curtseyed in response, her mind still reeling at the sight of him.

"Mr. Darcy!" managed she, once she had risen to face him. "I . . . I am surprised to see you here this evening, sir. I had not known you were in the area."

Seemingly unperturbed by her shock, Mr. Darcy smiled and responded: "I was passing through and thought to call on Sir William. He was kind enough to invite me tonight."

"And you decided to stay and attend our assembly?" asked Elizabeth, not even attempting to mask the skepticism in her voice. "Are you staying at Lucas Lodge?"

"No," replied Mr. Darcy. "I have taken rooms for myself and my valet at the inn."

The matter was becoming even more curious, but Elizabeth was given no time to consider the matter further. At that moment, Elizabeth noted that the musicians began to play the opening strains of the first set, and she espied young Samuel Lucas—Charlotte's brother—approaching, likely to ask for the first set.

"Miss Bennet," said Mr. Darcy, drawing her attention back to him, "would you do me the honor of dancing the first with me?"

Elizabeth's eyes widened in complete shock, and she wondered if she had heard him correctly. How was she to interpret, not only his presence, but his present request?

"Come, Miss Bennet," said he, leaning close and speaking in a wry tone, "we have danced the first before, if you recall? Will you leave me suffering the pains of uncertainty while you decide if I am respectable enough to share a dance?"

Realizing that he was teasing her—and wondering all over again, as

Mr. Darcy had not, in her experience, ever teased before—Elizabeth found her voice.

"I would be happy to dance the first with you."

Though Samuel was disappointed that he was too late to secure her first dances, Elizabeth promised him the second two when he strode up only a moment after Elizabeth had accepted Mr. Darcy's request. Mr. Darcy's response could not have been more different—the man actually *beamed* at her acceptance, and looked on her with a smoldering eye as he led her to the floor. Elizabeth did not know what to make of it.

They took their places, and Elizabeth noted that Kitty was situated a little further down the line. Her wide eyes fixed on Mr. Darcy showed her to be just as surprised as Elizabeth felt. But Elizabeth had no attention to spare for her sister. Her entire being was focused on the man standing across the line facing her.

When the first bars of the dance sounded and the dancers began to move, Elizabeth felt her hand being taken in Mr. Darcy's gentle grip, and she watched him as he glided around her, wondering at the intense sort of scrutiny with which he regarded her. The fluttering in her midsection began at the sight of his attention and only seemed to become worse as the dance wore on.

It was thus throughout the dance. When they moved away from each other, Elizabeth attempted to regain her equilibrium, only to have it destroyed when he so much as looked on her, and to the best of her knowledge, he never took his eyes *from* her. She would have wagered that the man had eyes in the back of his head, had she not known the notion to be completely silly! And when he touched her hand, Elizabeth thought she might swoon. The man had such an effect on her, she wondered what it would have been like had her hands been bare!

They spoke, though their words were brief, and spaced out by long periods of silence between them. The air about them seemed charged, though with what Elizabeth could not be certain. It was as if they were the only two in the room, that no one else existed. And for Elizabeth, she was not certain if anyone else existed *for her*.

What was this between them that it could upset her balance so?

Chapter XIX

Clarity did not come the morning after the dance any more than it had the previous evening. Thoughts of Mr. Darcy had not left Elizabeth the entire night; she had gone to bed, thinking about the man, her mind active long after she should have been at rest, and when her eyes opened the following morning, Elizabeth's thoughts once again focused on Mr. Darcy, as if she had not had a few hours of precious sleep in between.

The fact of the man's attentions had been obvious. After dancing the first with Elizabeth, Mr. Darcy had insisted upon requesting her last dance of the evening too. She could still remember the tingling she had felt in the bottom of her stomach at his request, the way in which he had regarded her to the exclusion of all else.

"Another dance, Mr. Darcy?" The question had caught her without warning, and though she was proud of herself for not giggling like a little girl, still she felt like her dearest, late mother, with her palpitations and nerves.

"Yes, Miss Bennet, if you will allow it."

The firmness of his voice left no doubt as to the seriousness of his request, and Elizabeth wondered what it could all mean.

"There will be talk, sir. Though you have acquitted yourself well tonight, before this assembly, you only danced with one local lady."

"What of it?" asked Mr. Darcy, clearly enjoying their banter.

"It just so happens that your request for the last dance would elevate that lady to the enviable position of having danced twice with you tonight, an honor you have extended to no other."

"I can think of no other lady on whom I would wish to bestow such an honor."

"There will be talk!" cried Elizabeth, forgetting she had already made such a point.

"Let them talk," replied Mr. Darcy. "There can be nothing in their words which does not approximate the reality of my attentions."

"Oh, you had better let him have it," said Kitty. She was standing nearby and enjoying Elizabeth's discomfort far too much, in Elizabeth's opinion. "Mr. Darcy strikes me as a man who knows what he wishes and is accustomed to having it."

"Those with the means to obtain what they desire often are, Miss Kitty," said Mr. Darcy, smiling kindly. "But I would not wish to take something your sister would not wish to give. I think, however, in this instance, she is not truly unwilling, so much as hesitant."

Kitty giggled with Maria, who was standing nearby, while Charlotte, who had been observing the scene with them, turned an expressive eye on Elizabeth. Her gaze seemed to suggest that she expected to hear wedding bells in the near future. Elizabeth only scowled at her friend — Charlotte was adept at seeing that which did not truly exist, and she was not shy about sharing it.

"Well, Miss Bennet?" asked Mr. Darcy, drawing her attention back to him. "Shall we dance? I shall withdraw my application, if you would really rather not, but I do hope you will accept."

"Very well, Mr. Darcy," said Elizabeth, bowing her head in uncharacteristic shyness.

That dance was no less charged with emotion than the first had been, and as Elizabeth lay in her bed thinking about it, she could not quite put her finger on it. Surely Mr. Darcy, master of a reputedly great estate in Derbyshire, possessing connections to the nobility, could not have any intentions toward Miss Elizabeth Bennet, mistress of a small estate in a backward county. Could he?

Though feeling a little cross due to the lack of sleep, Elizabeth forced her weary bones from her bed that morning and dressed with the assistance of the maid. Though it was a little later than usual, still it was early, and Kitty had not risen from her own bed. Taking a quick breakfast, she made her way into the study, where she met Mr. Whitmore looking over some books.

"Miss Bennet," said he, rising to his feet. He peered at her closely for a moment. "You do appear to be fatigued, Miss Bennet. Perhaps this morning you should allow yourself to rest, rather than working yourself into illness."

"There are things I should accomplish," said Elizabeth, though she was aware that she merely wished for occupation to prevent her from thinking on the situation with Mr. Darcy.

"There is nothing urgent that requires your attention." Mr. Whitmore's tone was all considerate compassion. "I think a morning, free of the cares of the estate, would do you good. Come, Miss Bennet, I insist."

The only reason Elizabeth allowed herself to be persuaded was because she knew that she would get precious little done, between her fatigue and the thoughts still running through her mind. So she thanked him and departed from the study, seeking occupation.

Unfortunately, finding such occupation was much more difficult than she imagined. At first she thought to lie down on her bed and nap for a while, but being a person who did not sleep at all well during the daylight hours, the only thing she accomplished was to allow her thoughts back into her head. Needlework, never a favorite, also allowed her mind to wander, and a book could not hold her attention. She was able to find some measure of relief when she sat down at the pianoforte, but her playing was poor, no doubt due to the lack of rest. Finally, in desperation, she donned a bonnet and stepped out into the morning sunshine.

It was a fine spring morning, the buzzing insects counterpoint to the trilling of birds and the rustle of the newly budded foliage in a slight morning breeze. Elizabeth could not help but be affected by the tranquility of the morning, and she took great breaths of the clean, crisp air, revelling in the newly awakened world. Spring had always been Elizabeth's favorite season, for the scents and sights of the new buds, bright green leaves, the return of the birds who traveled far to southern climes, all invigorated her. Though summer and autumn held their own charms as well, summer tended to be far too hot, while autumn, though lovely with its riot of colors, had always reminded her of the impending death of winter, which was the one season which had always been a true trial on her patience.

In the glory of nature all around her, Elizabeth was able to find some respite from the tumultuous thoughts still pressing against her, threatening to burst forth and consume her again. She did not go far from the house—the recent troubles with Mr. Wickham were still too fresh — but there was ample enjoyment to be found on Longbourn's back lawn. In it, she found peace once again.

When Elizabeth had walked for some time, she turned her steps back toward the house and a small, stone bench which sat in the shade just outside her father's study. Mr. Whitmore had left sometime earlier, as she had seen him astride a horse, no doubt to look in on portions of the home farm. Thus, she knew she would be reasonably unobserved on that bench, which was tucked along the side of the house, and thereby protected from the wind, which had risen a little while she walked.

Elizabeth had almost reached the sanctuary of the bench when a movement out of the corner of her eye caught her attention, and the figure of a man came around the side of the house. Startled by the man's sudden appearance, she stared at him with consternation. It was Mr. Darcy.

"Miss Bennet," greeted he, bowing low to her surprised curtsey. "How do you do this morning?"

"I am well, Mr. Darcy, merely a little tired."

Mr. Darcy gazed at her for a moment, seemingly taking in every inch of her, before a smile settled over his face. To Elizabeth, it seemed like he had guessed the reason for her lack of sleep the night before, and he was satisfied that she should be thinking about *him* enough to disturb her rest. All at once, Elizabeth was vexed with him.

"I can see naught amiss in your appearance," said Mr. Darcy. "To me you look as vibrant as ever you have."

Vexation suddenly turned to shyness, and Elizabeth regarded the man from behind downcast eyelashes, wondering at his meaning. Did he just express admiration for her?

As they were out in the park behind Longbourn and not concealed in a room, Elizabeth decided that the demands of propriety were met, regardless of the lack of a chaperone, and she invited Mr. Darcy to sit. He acquiesced with alacrity. They spoke of inconsequential topics for some moments, but though they both readily carried their parts of the conversation, it was clear to Elizabeth that Mr. Darcy was as ill at ease as she was herself. She could not account for it, feeling as if her mind was particularly slow that morning. His nearness and the stark reality of his masculine presence did not help at all.

Finally, Mr. Darcy seemed to be able to take the tension no longer, for he rose to his feet and began to pace. Elizabeth watched him, confused by his actions, feeling her head grow a little dizzy due to the rapidity of his pacing. Thus, when he spoke, Elizabeth found herself to be lightheaded, and she listened to him with growing astonishment.

"Miss Bennet," said he, approaching her and standing still for the first time in many minutes, "I can go no longer without expressing my love for you in the most fervent manner possible. Though I have struggled to know what I should do, I have come to the conclusion that I can no longer bear the thought of allowing you to slip away from me."

"Struggled?" asked Elizabeth, latching onto that one word.

"Yes, to my eternal shame. Your dowry, given that it consists of this estate itself, is adequate. For a man in my position, however, I would expect more from my future wife in the connections she would bring to the marriage. Your connections are, unfortunately, nothing to what I might expect, should I marry the daughter of a noble, as I have the right to aspire. But it cannot be helped. I no longer care, and as I have more connections than I know what to do with, it does not signify."

"I apologize for being so low as to affect your sensibilities, sir," said Elizabeth with some asperity.

Mr. Darcy's speech, though it was clear that he was attempting to speak properly and from the heart, was, in fact, a little insulting. She was well aware of her condition in life and did not require it to be pointed out to her in exhaustive detail by a man who appeared to be much more arrogant than she had ever thought. In temperament, he would be well suited for the conceited Miss Bingley.

It appeared that Darcy realized he had struck a nerve with his words, and he gazed at her, his eyes opening in consternation. "That is not what I have attempted to say, Miss Bennet."

"It seems that it was, sir. Though I am aware that you have spoken from your heart, the contents of your heart speak to what you value over all other things."

A frown came over his face. "I have not the pleasure of understanding you."

"You do not respect me, sir," said Elizabeth, feeling the sting of loss at saying so much. "You say you love me, which I am well able to believe, though I have no notion of how you have come to such a state. But when you speak of my connections, your lack of respect betrays you. I do not know precisely what you wish for in a marriage, but I wish for love. If I cannot have it, then I must still insist on respect.

"You never met my parents, sir, for they had passed on before you and Mr. Bingley had come to the neighborhood." The thought of her dearest parents and how they would have reacted to having such an elegant man propose to their daughter, filled Elizabeth with the longing to have her father's counsel at that moment. But Mr. Darcy, though he appeared to wish to contradict her, stayed silent, allowing her to speak, and Elizabeth managed to master herself.

"My father, Mr. Darcy, was a good man, though perhaps not as diligent as he should have been. He was an intelligent man, and much of what I am today I owe to his guidance. By contrast, my mother was a silly woman. She was also a good woman, as she loved her daughters and wished for the best for us all, and though her wishes did not always agree with my own, I loved her for her attentions and honored her as my mother."

Elizabeth sighed, immersing herself in her memories as she continued to speak. "I believe my parents loved each other in their own ways, though it was sometimes difficult. My father, erudite man though he was, had married her in a moment of passion and had become disillusioned after his marriage when he realized that all of his guidance would not make her into an sensible companion, one with whom he could converse on an intelligent, if not equal, basis. And though it shames me to confess that a beloved parent would behave in such a manner, he at times teased her, taking enjoyment in her nervous responses.

"My mother, though she never truly understood my father, was at least aware of the fact that he did not respect her capabilities to any great degree. I was my father's favorite, and as such, I was much closer to him than to my mother, but it always gave me pain to see them interact in such a manner. I apologize, sir, but I will not subject myself to a marriage where I am not respected, for whatever the reason. Love alone is not enough."

When Elizabeth fell silent, she felt a particular lethargy settle over her. She was very aware that though she did not love Mr. Darcy at that moment, if she allowed herself to fall, she would do so with ease. But she also knew that would set her up for misery of the acutest kind, when he realized what he had given up by agreeing to marry her. When the members of society ridiculed him for his choice, he would come to regret her. She would not live like that. Far better to remain a spinster than to live with her husband's contempt.

As for Mr. Darcy, he had listened to her with gravity, his visage never altering a jot. He appeared to consider the matter for some time, and though Elizabeth expected him to give her his regrets and depart, he did not. It was several minutes before he spoke again.

"Miss Bennet," said he, startling her with the sudden sound of his voice. "Would I be permitted to begin again? I fear I have not expressed myself very well, and I should like the opportunity to correct the misapprehension I have created by my lack of eloquence."

Mystified, Elizabeth nodded her head, not feeling herself equal to speaking. Mr. Darcy, smiled, and he approached her, kneeling down beside the bench on one knee, while taking her left hand between his own, gazing at her with an earnest sort of expression.

"Miss Bennet, you must allow me to tell you how ardently I admire, love, and respect you. I had always dreamed that when I proposed to a woman, the words of love and affection, the praises for my chosen partner in life, when coupled with our shared experiences, would convince the woman to accept me. I had always assumed, of course, that she would return my feelings in every particular, and express them in her turn. Unfortunately, it seems that I have gone about this wooing business in an inept fashion, and I must correct that which has given you pause."

Elizabeth felt a small curving of her lips, which she could not help, in response to the man's self-deprecating humor. This seemed to give him the confidence to continue.

"How might I make you understand the contents of my heart? I am not the most articulate of men. When I left Hertfordshire, intending to return to my estate with my sister, I held you in warm regard. How could I not? You are a bright light, Miss Bennet, and I cannot fathom any man not valuing you for the precious jewel you are.

"But before we proceed any further, I wish to make it clear, without any shadow of doubt, that I respected you long before I loved you. When I saw the care you took in managing the estate, the love you showed for your tenants, your enthusiasm with which you planned your improvements and designed the future prosperity of your estate, I could not help but respect you."

"And the matter of my connections?"

Mr. Darcy smiled, sending butterflies fluttering in Elizabeth's belly.

"I cannot but respect them as well. Your uncles are not of high society, but it is clear that they love you and care for your wellbeing, as evidenced by your uncle's hiring of Mr. Whitmore. He is the best of men, and I cannot speak highly enough of him.

"I will own, Miss Bennet," continued Mr. Darcy, "that I have been a proud being during the course of my life. I have always known that I could expect the best in connections and fortune of my future wife. But though there are women in London I have respected, I have never been tempted to join myself to any one of them.

"When I began to realize my feelings for you, I was not certain what I should do. I knew what I wished to do, but I struggled with my duty, which I have always known was to Pemberley and my family name.

With the timely intervention of a most beloved sister, I was able to see that in marrying you, I was in no way refusing to uphold my responsibilities. In fact, I cannot but rejoice, for I know that far from putting that legacy at risk, you would in fact enhance it, for there can be no objection to you."

"No objection?" asked Miss Bennet. "Will your family not object to me as your choice?"

"My Aunt Catherine will object to anyone who is not her daughter," replied Darcy. His thumb was caressing circles on the back of her hand, sending thrills up her arm and making it difficult for her to concentrate. "But I have never agreed to marry my cousin, and I know for a fact that my mother did not wish for it, regardless of my aunt's assertions to the contrary. And as for my uncle and aunt, I know they will be concerned, but I am convinced of your ability to charm them.

"Miss Bennet," said he, grasping her hands more tightly, "I would not have you think you are not worthy of accepting my attentions. In fact, I am the one who is unworthy of you. Not only are you an excellent woman, calm, poised, and elegant, but you are also at home in any kind of society, happy, articulate, and with a magnetism of personality I have never before encountered. I tend to be the opposite—aloof, reticent, and not at all comfortable speaking with those with whom I am not well acquainted.

"If I did not make the attempt to earn your regard, I cannot imagine it would be long before hordes of others saw for themselves what a gem you are. I would consider it a great honor if you would accept my proposal and make me the happiest of men."

When Mr. Darcy fell silent, Elizabeth gazed at him with awe. How could a woman possibly reject such incredible sentiments spoken by a man she esteemed greatly? And Elizabeth did esteem him—she esteemed him very much indeed. Could she say that she loved him? Perhaps she was closer than she had been before he had spoken, but even then she had known she *could* love him if she only allowed herself to do so. But now was not the time to lose herself in this man's eyes. There were still a few things that she needed to inquire of him.

"I thank you for your words, sir," said Elizabeth, drawing a deep breath to calm her nerves. "I am not insensible to the sentiments you have expressed. Might I ask a question or two?"

At first Mr. Darcy had frowned at her words, apparently thinking that she meant to refuse him. He seemed to exhale in relief slightly, and he nodded his consent,

"Would you tell me of Mr. Bingley, sir?"

Seemingly taken aback, Mr. Darcy blurted: "Bingley?"

Feeling more than a little embarrassed, Elizabeth still forged ahead. She needed to know what had happened with the young man.

"I wish to know of Mr. Bingley. I had thought . . . Well, there was some suggestion that it was in part due to your influence that Mr. Bingley did not return to Meryton."

"And what was your belief, Miss Bennet?"

Mr. Darcy's manner did not inspire confidence. He had retreated into his typically closed expression, and for a moment, Elizabeth wondered if it truly mattered. But then she decided that it was of import, because it spoke to his claims of respect for her.

"I do not know, Mr. Darcy, that is why I ask. I have some . . . reservations about Mr. Bingley—I had some reservations about his attentions to my sister from the start. I did not *think* you convinced him to stay away, but I should like to hear it from you all the same."

As Elizabeth spoke, she noted the softening of Mr. Darcy's countenance, and by the end he sighed and flashed her a rueful smile.

"I am sorry, Miss Bennet," said Mr. Darcy. "I am afraid Bingley is a bit of a difficult subject at present."

"Tell me," said Elizabeth, looking at him, her previous curiosity turning to compassion.

"The fact is that I do not believe Bingley behaved properly with regard to your sister," said Mr. Darcy. "But I did not keep him away. In fact, at the ball at Netherfield, I spoke to him and strongly reminded him of his duties as a gentleman. I felt that he had paid your sister marked attentions which were akin to engaging his honor. He assured me that he had no intention of abandoning her, and that he would return to Netherfield once his business in London was complete as he had always planned."

"I witnessed your discussion, sir," said Elizabeth speaking softly. "I remember you speaking animatedly while he listened, but I did not approach, as it was not proper."

Mr. Darcy nodded. "Unfortunately, he did not follow through with his word. In January, I received a letter from him. Though his writing is difficult at best, I understood the substance of his communication and realized that he was in London, paying attention to another one of his long line of angels. It was then that my sister pointed out that though Bingley is a good man, he has a tendency to be captivated by a pretty face. He is aspiring to be a gentleman; he should behave as one.

"Then when I returned to town in March, I sought him out, and we exchanged words." Mr. Darcy shook his head, apparently still feeling the effects of whatever had happened between them. "I chastised him for going back on his word and leaving your sister to wait for his return, and he took exception to my comments concerning his affairs. I have not spoken to him since, as he left my house in anger."

Nodding, Elizabeth could only look on the man with compassion. "I am sorry to hear it, Mr. Darcy."

"I am not a man who possesses a disposition which allows me to easily make friends, Miss Bennet. In fact, my reticence is such that I more often give offense without any intention of doing so. Falling out with Bingley is painful, as I truly do esteem him. I have few close friends, and the loss of one is keenly felt."

"I understand, sir."

"How is your sister, Miss Bennet?"

This time it was Elizabeth's turn to sigh. "Kitty is well. She *was* disappointed with Mr. Bingley's failure to return, and she suffered from it for some time, but even Kitty will now confess that her feelings were nothing but superficial infatuation. I believe that she has come out of the experience a little wiser." Elizabeth paused and then giggled. "And she left Mr. Bingley — and his paramour — in no doubt as to how she felt on the matter."

A curious look betrayed Mr. Darcy's interest, and Elizabeth recounted the confrontation at the Dunleavy ball, and the manner in which Kitty had informed Miss Colford of Mr. Bingley's character, how Elizabeth had cut Miss Bingley, and Miss Colford's visit the next day.

"So you see, Mr. Darcy," said Elizabeth once she had finished her explanation, "I believe that Kitty has acquitted herself very well in this matter. She is not yet eighteen years of age; I hope she will wait and attain more experience before she falls in love. I would not wish to lose her so soon, and I certainly not to a man who does not deserve her."

"You confronted Bingley at the Dunleavy ball?" asked Mr. Darcy, his tone incredulous.

"Yes, Mr. Darcy," said Elizabeth, wondering at his reaction.

Apparently Mr. Darcy noticed her confusion. "It was at the Dunleavy ball that I saw you and your sister, leaving the ballroom. It must have been immediately after your confrontation."

"Yes, we left after we had words with Mr. Bingley."

"I did not approach you there as I was so surprised to see you that you were gone before I could react. I had no notion that something of that nature had happened, though I do recall seeing some sort of disturbance." Mr. Darcy laughed. "I dare say Miss Bingley has had a rough time of it. It has become known throughout town that Bingley and

I are not as close as we once were. The Bingleys' social status was derived in large part due to Bingley's friendship with me, though his sister's marriage to Hurst does assist to a certain extent. I do not doubt that invitations have been less plentiful, and I cannot imagine your cut of her could have helped."

They laughed together, and though Elizabeth thought it less than admirable to enjoy another's discomfort, in Miss Bingley's case she was willing to make an exception. The woman was most deserving.

"Did you never happen to see me at the ball, Miss Bennet?" asked Mr. Darcy, pulling her from her thoughts.

A blush came over her. "I . . . did, sir."

Her stammering response provoked a steady gaze in response. "And did you not think to approach me?"

"I . . . It was from across the room," said Elizabeth quietly. "You were gone before long, and I knew not where you went. Besides, I was not certain if you wished to continue the acquaintance."

"Then why did you blush just now?"

"I . . . remember reflecting on how . . . handsome you were."

"Should I have hope, then, that my lack of physical repulsion is enough to allow you to consider my proposal?"

Elizabeth struggled to answer his question, but when she finally opened her mouth, it was to blurt out something completely different.

"Would your aunt and uncle truly accept me?"

The thumb resting on her hand, though it had stilled some time ago, began its torturous caressing of her own yet again, drawing Elizabeth's mind to the pleasurable sensations it evoked.

"They would come around. I do not suggest that they do not have ambitions for me, but they would be happy for my happiness. I completely believe that they would eventually come to love you."

Elizabeth drew a deep breath and looked at Mr. Darcy. "I do not believe that I am ready for an engagement. This has all come on so suddenly. I hardly know what to think."

"Then a courtship?" asked Darcy, hope coloring his voice.

The firmness of his tone and the steadiness of his gaze—not to mention that damnable thumb evoking such delightful sensations—taught Elizabeth that she was not indifferent to this man. And suddenly she very much wished to learn if she could love him. And since he so clearly adored her, she knew that it behooved her to allow him the opportunity to persuade her. Being loved like he loved her was no small matter. In the end, it was an easy choice.

"Very well, Mr. Darcy. A courtship."

Until the end of her days Elizabeth was to remember the expression of heartfelt delight which settled over Mr. Darcy's features, coupled with a determination—a determination, Elizabeth thought, to induce her to love him in return. She suddenly felt confident of his ability to do just that. At the very least, she would enjoy the discovery.

Chapter XX

A harried Caroline Bingley hurried through the streets of London toward her home, desperate to move her feet faster, without seeming that she was hurrying, of course. Unfortunately, she doubted anyone watching would mistake her gait for anything other than the scurrying it was. At present, however, speed was more important than image.

It had been a difficult few months, and Caroline could set the blame on her brother's decision to lease that horrible estate near that little speck of a town, subjecting her to the uncouth savages of Hertfordshire. Though Caroline had thought she had a captive audience in Mr. Darcy — and consequently, was certain her dreams would finally come true — nothing had gone correctly, including Mr. Darcy's ill-concealed interest in that improper woman, Miss *Eliza* Bennet. How Caroline hated that name, hating the woman above all others she had ever met!

Still, it should have been a victory. The man had left Hertfordshire without losing himself to the woman, and Caroline had followed her brother to town only a day after he left. Caroline had hoped that Mr. Darcy might invite them to Pemberley for Christmas, removing the need for her to turn Charles's attention away from Kitty Bennet, but no invitation had been forthcoming. But even though Mr. Darcy had been maddeningly reluctant to side with Caroline in the matter of Miss Kitty

Bennet, still Caroline had been successful in turning Charles's attention and keeping him away from Meryton.

But nothing from that point had gone as planned. Upon hearing of his return to London, Caroline had waited for Mr. Darcy to visit them, but he had not, and it had been weeks after before Caroline had learned that Mr. Darcy had actually had a falling out with her brother.

"What do you mean, Charles?" Caroline had asked when she had first heard of the matter. Since Mr. Darcy had not yet visited them, Caroline had determined that her brother should make the overture.

"Exactly what I said, Caroline," said Charles. Caroline seethed over his indifferent manner, though she would never show such temper to him. "Darcy attempted to take me to task for not returning to Hertfordshire and Miss Kitty. We had words, and have not spoken since."

"When did this happen?" shrieked Caroline.

"A few days after his arrival from Pemberley," said Charles with a shrug.

"And why did you not inform me?"

A mulish frown came over Charles's face, and Caroline felt like pulling out her hair. He could be so infuriatingly stubborn at times!

"Darcy is *my* friend, Caroline. I was not aware that I was required to inform you of all my dealings with him."

And with that, Charles had left the room, leaving Caroline to her angry thoughts. How like her brother to refuse to consider Caroline's point of view. He had never supported her pursuit of Mr. Darcy as he ought; in fact, the only tines he had given any indication that he recognized her ambitions at all was on those occasions when he had attempted to tell her that Mr. Darcy would never make her an offer. Caroline ignored his words as something akin to the bleating of a sheep, but inside she had fumed about them.

That Mr. Darcy had felt that Charles should return to Hertfordshire was something Caroline could not fathom. Who cared about such things as honor when dealing with savages? He had never given any indication to Caroline that he thought Charles's attentions overt. Had he done so, she would have put a stop to it much earlier.

It was not long before Caroline had realized the true effects of Charles's argument with Mr. Darcy. It had seemed to her like the number of invitations they had received for society events had fallen off that spring, and it was not until she knew of the argument that it all made sense; word had been carried on the wings of rumor that Mr. Darcy no longer counted Charles as a friend. It was a serious blow for their ambitions to ascend to higher strata of society. Furthermore, once Lady Marion had returned to town, she had caught wind of the situation, likely hearing of it before Caroline had herself. The snide comments and veiled remarks she had endured from many quarters suddenly made sense.

And then the scene at the Dunleavy ball had further ruined their standing. Even now, the mere thought of Miss Bennet, looking at her with something akin to contempt, and then deliberately looking past her as if she was not there, was enough to make Caroline's blood boil in her veins. To think that chit possessed the audacity to give her — Caroline Bingley — the cut direct, was unfathomable. And worse, the whispers that had ensued after the event had followed and plagued Caroline wherever she went. Not a day went by when she was not asked about it, and it seemed that enough of the ball's attendees had been introduced to Miss Bennet and knew that she was a gentleman's daughter and gentlewoman in her own right. The cut had been all over London in a matter of days, and their invitations had dried up even more.

Finally, after desperation had set in, Caroline had determined to go to see Mr. Darcy herself in an attempt to regain her lost standing. Though it was not proper to call on a man, Caroline had a way to get to him — her acquaintance with his insipid sister. This was why she was walking, rather than traveling in the Bingley carriage — to be seen walking through the fashionable streets and calling on the Darcy townhouse could only improve Caroline's standing.

But that had also been a disaster. Even Georgiana, who at times seemed as timid and fearful as a mouse, had seemed to have grown some teeth in recent weeks, to say nothing of the news she had imparted.

"I have not seen your brother in some time, dear Georgiana," said Caroline when she had been visiting with the young woman for some minutes. Though Georgiana had never given her leave to address her so informally, Caroline knew that the girl was far too timid to object, and Caroline used that to her advantage.

"Is Mr. Darcy well?"

"Oh, yes, Miss Bingley. My brother is quite well indeed."

"I suppose he is hard at work dealing with his business matters," said Miss Bingley. In truth she knew no such thing, but as Georgiana had not yet made any comment concerning her brother's whereabouts, it was up to Caroline to pull the information from the girl.

"Not at present," was Georgiana's cheerful reply. "William works too hard at times, but at present he is at his leisure."

"Then I would be happy to greet him," said Caroline hopefully.

"I am afraid that is impossible, Miss Bingley, for William is not home at present."

"Then you must give him my warmest regards," said Caroline, hiding her disappointment.

"I will surely do so when I see him next. But he is out of town."

"Do you know when he will return?"

"Oh, not for some time." Georgiana regarded Caroline with that look of earnest innocence which Caroline had always found intolerable. "He is attending to *personal matters*."

Georgiana's emphasis on the final two words perked Caroline's interest, not to mention her dread. Could the man have something more than business in mind, wherever he was?

"That is very good, my dear Georgiana," said Miss Bingley. "Mr. Darcy is so busy. I cannot but think he should take some time to himself on occasion."

"Then you will be happy, Miss Bingley, for that is exactly what he is doing. I could not be happier for him."

Fear rose up in Caroline's breast, threatening to choke her with its icy fingers. Though she could hardly breathe, she found herself saying. "Oh? Your words seem to suggest something particular. Is he attending to the courtship with your cousin your aunt speaks of?"

A giggle was Georgiana's response, followed by a quickly spoken: "Oh, no, Miss Bingley. William will never marry Anne. They are not compatible, and I doubt she is capable of managing a manor, much less providing William an heir. No, Anne will not be William's wife. But he has spoken to me of the woman in whom he has expressed an interest, and I do not doubt she will be a wonderful sister. She is intelligent, witty, beautiful, and by all accounts, she makes him happy."

And then Caroline knew. She would never know how she made it through the rest of the visit, but she was not so far immersed in her panicked thoughts that she could not see that little Georgiana—who was as shy and fearful a creature as Miss Bingley had ever met—was in fact laughing at her. But it would not do to consider that at present—far better to deal with the matter at hand and arrange for the girl's punishment when Caroline was the mistress of Pemberley.

This all led to her race through the London streets toward the Hurst townhouse. Once she gained entrance to the house, she opened the door and rushed in unceremoniously, screaming for the butler to attend her.

"Find my brother, and inform him I wish to speak to him at once!"

"I am sorry, Miss Bingley," said Harris, the butler. "Mr. Bingley left this morning before you departed."

"Where has he gone?"

"I was not informed of his destination, nor did he say when he would return."

Caroline scowled at the man, swallowing the question which had been poised at the tip of her tongue. "What of the carriage driver?"

"The carriage has not returned, Miss Bingley. I do not expect it until Mr. Bingley himself returns."

"Very well," said Caroline. "The instant my brother steps from the carriage, you will inform him that I wish to speak to him at once."

Not waiting for a response, Caroline climbed the stairs in haste, making her way to the top and from thence to her rooms. Once there, she called her maid and instructed her to pack her things for an immediate departure.

"I hope we shall be gone by this afternoon," said Caroline, "so you had best get to it."

But even that was not to be, for Caroline spent a long afternoon pacing her room, simmering in her anger as her brother failed to appear. The servants all felt the effects of her pique, as she snapped at them, demanding information concerning her brother and his whereabouts and refusing any refreshment, knowing she would not be able to eat it anyway.

If only Louisa were here! Unfortunately, the Hursts had departed two days before for Mr. Hurst's estate. Caroline snorted. What an unfashionable man her sister had married; anyone who was anyone refused to leave London before the season was concluded!

It was fortuitous indeed that Caroline had possessed the presence of mind to send an express to Netherfield to ensure the house was opened and ready to receive its master and mistress. She did not expect much of the servants at that insignificant estate, but at least they would not have the excuse of having had no word of their arrival.

When Charles finally arrived, Caroline had managed to work herself into a state. "Charles! Where have you been?"

Her loud voice startled her brother as he was pouring a glass of port, sloshing some of it onto the floor. Caroline took no notice; after hearing from the servants concerning her brother's return, she had immediately rushed to the sitting-room to confront him.

"Hello, Caroline," said Charles, taking a nearby cloth and drying his hand, before he tossed back his drink. "How are you this fine day?"

Caroline ignored her brother's sardonic tone. "I am most distressed, and I must insist that you prepare for departure on the morrow."

That pierced her brother's insouciant demeanor, and he turned to peer at her as if she was fit for bedlam. "Depart on the morrow? I have not the pleasure of understanding you."

"Mr. Darcy has returned to Hertfordshire. We must follow him there and prevent him from making a serious mistake."

"There is nothing for me in Hertfordshire," replied her brother. "I had much rather stay in London where I can call on Miss Cranston."

"Miss Cranston?" asked Caroline, completely bewildered. "Who is Miss Cranston?"

"She is the eldest daughter of a landowner from Essex," said Charles. His face took on a familiar dreamy quality with which Caroline was intimately familiar. "She is demure and unpretentious, hair the color of corn, and eyes as bright as the most perfect sapphire. I met her at the Grangers' card party that we attended three nights ago."

Caroline could not remember being introduced to any Cranstons. "What of Miss Colford?"

"She returned to her father's estate not long after the Dunleavy ball," said Charles, shrugging as if it did not signify. "I suppose Miss Kitty's words concerning me were too much for her to ignore. It is of little matter, for Miss Cranston is Miss Colford's superior in every respect."

Dismayed, Caroline glared at her brother. Would he ever cease this unseemly habit of having his face turned by every pretty woman he saw? He was like a child!

"Brother," said Caroline, steeling herself and enunciating her words carefully, "I care not what you do. You may pay attention to every woman in the kingdom, and it would not bother me a jot. But I have it on very good authority that Mr. Darcy has returned to Hertfordshire for the express purpose of paying his addresses to Miss Eliza Bennet. I will not allow it! I have invested too much time in my efforts to claim Mr. Darcy as my own to be prevented by an upstart without fashion or fortune."

"And yet you are here, while she is in Hertfordshire with her own estate and apparently receiving Darcy's addresses. It seems there is little to be done on the matter."

Charles's casual words and mocking tone infuriated Caroline. She stepped forward, situating herself directly in front of him, looking him in the eye.

"I will thank you not to say such a thing ever again. I am certain she has used her wiles to infatuate him and lower his resistance. I will not allow it! Be ready to depart, for we shall leave London by seven in the morning!"

Spinning on her heel, Caroline stalked from the room. Whatever Miss

Bennet had done, Caroline would counter it. If she must, she would see the Bennets ruined, their names blackened, forever shunned from polite society, or the pale facsimile that passed for it in that town. Caroline meant to have what she deserved, and nothing would stop her.

When Miss Bingley returned from her visit to Darcy house, little did she know that not long after she arrived home, the master—and her quarry—had in fact returned to London. Having received Miss Bennet's acceptance of a courtship, he had informed her of his intention to ride for London in order to receive her uncle's permission. Thus, while Miss Bingley was pacing her rooms, muttering curses and abusing her servants, Darcy was washing off the dust of the road and preparing to depart again to visit her uncle. Though Darcy knew it would be a slight imposition to visit that afternoon, he was assured by Miss Bennet— Elizabeth—that Mr. Gardiner would be happy to receive him, especially given the note she had written to him, which Darcy carried on his person.

He was less than happy, however, to know that Miss Bingley had called in his absence, though Georgiana's giggling concerning the woman's state *was* amusing.

"She left as if the very hounds of hell were hard upon her heels, Brother!" exclaimed Georgiana once she had recited the matter to him. "I dare say, she understood my message quite well indeed."

In truth, Darcy wondered what the woman would do with the information. In the end, he decided it did not signify. Given the current state of Darcy's friendship with Bingley, there was little she could do, as he thought Bingley would prove mulish, focused, as he was, on his latest lady friend. It was a problem for another time, for he needed to depart immediately, lest he not have any time at all to call on Mr. Gardiner.

Thus, it was some thirty minutes later that Darcy alighted from his coach in front of a modest townhouse in an unfashionable area of town. Cheapside was an area with which he was familiar, though not intimately so. The houses in this section of the city were small, but they were neat and tidy, and if not quite fashionably appointed, at least they were well-maintained.

When Darcy had knocked on the door and passed his card to the housekeeper, he took the opportunity to look around in interest. The modest exterior of the house in no way suggested the elegance he witnessed on the inside. The furnishings were fine, but not needlessly ostentatious, the décor seemed to have been chosen with some taste, and the atmosphere was welcoming, but gave off a homey sort of feel. It did not seem so much the home of a tradesman, as that of a man of fashion.

The woman who greeted him was perhaps a few years older than Darcy himself, but she was attractive and dressed finely, with an air of grace and good humor, and a keen eye which suggested intelligence.

"I apologize, sir," said the woman, smoothly ignoring the fact that he had appeared on her doorstep without warning. "My husband has not yet returned from his offices."

"I regret disturbing your peace, madam," replied Darcy, "but I have business with your husband. If the time is inconvenient, I will be happy to call another time."

In truth, Darcy was anything but happy to call another time, for he wished to return to Hertfordshire the following morning. But he also wished to make a good impression on these people, who were so important to Elizabeth. Thus, he would accede to whatever they required.

"It is no bother, sir. I shall have a footman summon him at once."

The look with which she favored him suggested that she was well aware of what his business consisted, but she said nothing.

"Will it take long for Mr. Gardiner to arrive?" asked Darcy. "I would not wish to impose upon you for long."

"It will not be long at all, sir. My husband's warehouses are not far. He prefers it that way, as it is quite convenient."

Nodding, Darcy filed that bit of information away. Given what he was seeing, Darcy had no doubt that Mr. Gardiner could afford to live in a much more affluent and fashionable neighborhood, but chose his current location for its convenience. It showed a pragmatism which Darcy found appealing—this was a man who was unconcerned about society's opinion of his profession. In other words, he was about as far from the Miss Bingleys of the world as it was possible to be.

For the next fifteen minutes, Darcy sat with Mrs. Gardiner, and he continued to be impressed by her manners. She could easily have passed herself off as a gentlewoman had she cared to make the attempt, and her opinions were thoughtful and stated with confidence. Soon, Darcy realized that there was nothing to be lamented over concerning Miss Bennet's relations. The wife, at least, was one he could introduce to almost anyone without any need to blush. Furthermore, she had something of a connection to him, as he uncovered when they began to speak.

"I must own to having some knowledge of you, Mr. Darcy," said Mrs. Gardiner. Though he might have thought it was an attempt to attach herself to him, as he had seen done so many times in the past, she spoke with ease, and no eagerness. "I was raised in the town of Lambton, which is, I am sure, quite near to your estate."

"Why, that is not five miles from Pemberley."

"It is," agreed Mrs. Gardiner. "I have seen your home on more than one occasion, and it always impressed me as beautiful and elegant."

"I am very proud of my estate. It has been in my family for generations." Darcy paused, thinking of what he had learned. "I beg your pardon, but might I inquire after the identity of your father?"

"My father was the parson there, sir. Before my marriage, I was known as Meredith Plumber."

"Reverend Plumber!" exclaimed Darcy, putting the pieces together. "I have some memory of your father, though I will own I have little memory of you."

Mrs. Gardiner smiled. "I suppose you would not, sir. You were still young when my family departed Derbyshire for Shropshire, where my father took another living to be closer to his family. You see, he was a third son of a gentleman there."

"And Mr. Lansdown took his place in Lambton," replied Darcy. It was truly an odd thing to have such a connection exposed. Darcy could not truly remember Mr. Plumber, but he clearly recalled his father's high opinion of the man, and his regret when he had made his decision to move to a new parish.

Darcy spent several more minutes speaking with Mrs. Gardiner, and he was impressed with her gentility, the amiable way in which she spoke, and the unpretentious manner and lack of fawning which was so prevalent in those with whom he was acquainted. She reminded him of Elizabeth, though they truly did not resemble each other.

When Mr. Gardiner returned and stepped into the room, Darcy immediately understood why, for the familial resemblance between Mr. Gardiner and his nieces was striking. He was a happy, jovial sort of man, greeting Darcy with cheerfulness, and without the exaggerated deference which was also absent from his good wife's manners. He was perhaps some four or five years older than Mrs. Gardiner, though he was obviously fit and in good health.

The introductions were completed, and Mr. Gardiner invited Darcy into his study, which Darcy accepted. He said farewell to Mrs. Gardiner, certain he would see her again in the future. Given how she had impressed him, Darcy was quite happy at the prospect.

"Could I interest you in some port, Mr. Darcy?" asked Mr. Gardiner when they had taken their seats.

"No thank you, sir," said Darcy, determined to keep his wits about him.

"Very well. I understand you have some business with me."

"Yes sir." Darcy pulled Miss Bennet's letter from an inside pocket of his coat. "I have, this morning, asked for a courtship with your niece, Miss Bennet, and she has been gracious enough to accept. I have come this morning to request your permission and blessing, sir."

Far from being slow of thought, it appeared Mr. Gardiner had suspected something of this nature, as he nodded his head slowly, digesting the information. When he fixed his eyes on Darcy, there was a curious quality in his looks.

"I am not surprised, as a man does not come in all this state to ask investment advice. But I must own to a little surprise over the timing of this request, sir. I was not aware that you had been paying attention to my niece. She and her sister were visiting until recently and we saw nothing of you, and her letters since have made no mention of the matter."

"First, Mr. Gardiner, perhaps I should allow you to read your niece's thoughts on the subject before we proceed."

Though Darcy thought that Mr. Gardiner would prefer to discuss instead of reading the letter, he readily accepted and perused it quickly. Darcy noted the man's expressions gave nothing away — he might have been reading a report on the recent weather in London, for all the response he made.

When he was finished reading, Mr. Gardiner refolded the letter and placed it on the desk. He sat back in his chair and clasped his hands in front of him, peering at Darcy as if trying to puzzle him out.

"It seems that Lizzy is determined to have you."

"I would rather say that she anticipates the season of our courtship and wishes to discover the possibility of loving me as much as I love her."

Mr. Gardiner smiled and a slight chuckle issued forth from his mouth. "Indeed, Mr. Darcy. I shall remember not to try to trade words with you, for you are entirely too quick. In fact, you must have spoken of the matter at some length, for you have repeated in one sentence the gist of what Elizabeth has written to me."

"I believe I simply understand her, Mr. Gardiner."

A small pause ensued, during which Mr. Gardiner seemed to be studying him. Then he spoke, his tone was authoritative.

"I believe that had my brother Bennet still been alive to grant his permission, he would have claimed you are the kind of man to whom he could never deny anything. I, however, am not impressed with titles and connections, and so I shall speak plainly. I wish to know, from your own mouth, of your intentions. I must say that the performance of your friend does not inspire confidence, sir."

"I am not my friend," replied Darcy, keeping a tight rein on his annoyance. "I do not suffer from a wont of resolution—once I have determined my course, I follow through with it."

"No, you are not your friend. But given how I witnessed the lowness of spirits of my young niece, I do not wish to experience the same with her sister.

"Mr. Darcy," said Mr. Gardiner, as he leaned forward and regarded Darcy with an air of utmost gravity, "I do not know how much my niece has told you, but she was her father's favorite. Though Mr. Bennet was not able to inform me of his wishes for his daughters before his passing, I am convinced he would have charged me to take the greatest care of Elizabeth."

"I had expected as much, sir," said Darcy, knowing that he must make this man understand his feelings. "Though I have only recently come to the decision to court your niece, I have long known of my attraction to her, my respect for her, and my love for her. She is simply the best woman of my acquaintance, and would make an excellent mistress of my estate."

"And Longbourn?" asked Gardiner. "It will become your property, should you marry."

Darcy shook his head. "I am quite happy to leave it in her capable hands. She has done better than many gentlemen I know in seeing to the estate's prosperity. I am certain she knows it better than any other."

A laugh was Mr. Gardiner's response, and he said: "In that you would be correct. Lizzy takes a prodigious deal of care of Longbourn."

"Then let it remain hers in the marriage articles," said Darcy with a shrug. "She is far more precious to me than any amount of wealth. I shall settle a goodly income upon her so that she need never depend on Longbourn alone. I am more than prepared to do whatever you deem necessary in order to procure your blessing."

"That is generous. But I think you may be putting the cart before the horse."

"I merely wish to illustrate how serious I am. My intentions are that this courtship proceed to its natural conclusion. I would not have you think otherwise."

"And if Elizabeth ultimately decides against you?"

"Let us all hope she does not," said Darcy, trying desperately not to grimace at the mere thought. "But I will, of course, bow out if she cannot commit to me."

Mr. Gardiner looked at Darcy, and in a voice laced with humor and resignation, said: "I do not doubt that her answer will be in the affirmative. When Lizzy gives her heart, she does it without reservation, and I have no doubt, given the tone of her voice in her letter, that she is well on her way already."

Feeling a measure of euphoria come over him, Darcy nevertheless attempted to hold in his reaction. The opinion of a most beloved relation was no small matter, and it gave Darcy more hope than he could say.

But he still needed to gain her agreement. He would do anything to obtain it.

Given Mr. Darcy's attentions to Elizabeth at the assembly, the Lucases were not surprised when Elizabeth visited Lucas Lodge the following morning with news of her courtship. Lady Lucas was, of course, ecstatic at Elizabeth's ability to attract such an important man, and she was not hesitant about sharing it.

"Your mother would be so proud of you, my dear," said the woman, as she embraced Elizabeth fondly. "She wished for nothing but the best for you girls.

"But, oh! You must allow me to assist in planning the wedding, the breakfast, and all the other details! Your mother would have wished for a celebration which the entire town would speak of for months after, particularly given the status of the man you shall be marrying."

"I am sure that is an accurate portrayal of my mother, indeed!" exclaimed Elizabeth with a laugh. "But I beg you to remember that I have not yet accepted a proposal, Lady Lucas. At present it is nothing more than a courtship."

"So you say, my dear. But I have no doubt that it will not be long before you have Mr. Darcy completely in your thrall. He will propose ere long, I dare say."

Elizabeth said nothing of the fact of Mr. Darcy's already having proposed to her, knowing Lady Lucas as she did. Much as her mother would have protested against Elizabeth answering such a proposal with anything other than a hearty "Yes!" she knew that Lady Lucas's response would be similar, though likely more restrained. As such, she allowed Lady Lucas to drift off in thoughts and plans for Elizabeth's eventual wedding, though the looks she directed at her eldest daughter left no doubt as to the subject of her thoughts. Charlotte did not miss it either, though she tactfully ignored it.

In fact, Charlotte was the one person whose approval meant the most to Elizabeth, outside that of her own family, of course. It was not long before Charlotte contrived to speak with Elizabeth in low voices so as to avoid being overheard by the others in the room.

"I see you have managed to attract Mr. Darcy's attention, Eliza," said Charlotte. She flashed Elizabeth a teasing grin, saying: "Well done, I might add. Now, you should leave him in no doubt of your affections, if you are to secure him."

Laughing, Elizabeth reached out with a playful swat to her friend's shoulder. "You are well aware that I have no intention of behaving in such a manner."

"Lizzy, you know that for women, protection lies in marriage."

"And *you* know I have no need of it," said Elizabeth. "I will always have Longbourn should I never marry."

"And now you have the attentions of a good man. I hope you realize your good fortune."

Charlotte's words were spoken with such an air of melancholy that Elizabeth reached over and grasped her hand in an attempt to comfort her. "I do, Charlotte. But you should know that if you should never marry, if the situation in your own home becomes difficult, you will always have a home with me at Longbourn. We shall be the spinster ladies, befuddling the neighborhood with our ways"

Such a silly statement could only provoke her friend to laugh, which she did quietly. "Perhaps we shall, Lizzy. But since you are now receiving the attentions of Mr. Darcy, I doubt you will reside at Longbourn for much longer."

"It is still only a courtship, Charlotte."

"But Mr. Darcy strikes me as a man who would not enter into such an arrangement if he did not intend to pursue it to its natural conclusion."

To that Elizabeth could only agree—she had told no one of the fact that Mr. Darcy had actually proposed to her, preferring to keep that to herself. And even without such a sure knowledge of his intentions, Elizabeth thought she would have expected it of him.

"Lizzy," said Charlotte, the mirth of a few moments earlier forgotten, "you have thus far spoken of your courtship and Mr. Darcy, but you have not said anything concerning your feelings on the matter."

"You have often been privy to my feelings, Charlotte."

"I have. Knowing of your opinions of the marriage estate, I suspect I already know the answer, but I would hear it from your lips all the same."

"Then you may rest easy, Charlotte. I do not love Mr. Darcy at present, but I am well aware of the power he would possess over me, were I to allow him entrance into my heart."

Charlotte cocked her head to the side. "And what of Mr. Darcy's feelings? I am sure you could never be content with loving a man without your feelings being returned."

Though a little uncomfortable, Elizabeth decided to tell her friend so that she could rest easy concerning the matter.

"In fact, the situation is the opposite to what you have stated. Mr. Darcy has already declared his love for me—it is I who must now confirm the contents of my heart."

"Then I am happy for you," said Charlotte, drawing Elizabeth close to her. "With such a man's focus on you, I doubt it will be long before you are ready to return his feelings in every respect. I have no more fears for your future."

Having obtained her friend's approval, Elizabeth basked in the intimacy of their relationship. Perhaps she could take some thought as to Charlotte's situation; Charlotte was intelligent, pretty, level-headed, and possessed of every virtue to make her a wonderful wife. Surely there must be someone among William's acquaintance who was in need of a sensible wife. Should she accept William's proposal, Elizabeth would make certain Charlotte was thrown into the path of as many of William's friends as possible.

Chapter XXI

When Darcy returned to Meryton the day after obtaining Mr. Gardiner's permission for his courtship with Miss Bennet, he was confronted by a most unwelcome surprise. As he had left after breakfast, and after indulging his sister in her raptures concerning his courtship, he had arrived at Meryton soon after luncheon. Georgiana had been wild to accompany him, but as Darcy was staying in the inn at present, he was hesitant to include her, not knowing how long he would be staying there.

Taking the opportunity to refresh himself after his journey, Darcy was preparing to go to Longbourn to acquaint Elizabeth with the results of his interview with Mr. Gardiner, when a visitor of a most unexpected nature arrived and greeted him.

"Bingley!" exclaimed Darcy, eyes widened at the sight of his friend entering the inn. "What are you doing here?"

"I . . . ah . . ." Bingley paused, and Darcy was instantly suspicious. Bingley had never been able to dissemble.

"I have come to see to the estate, Darcy. I *have* leased it, after all, and I possess the lease for several more months."

"Bingley, you were not precisely diligent concerning the estate when you were here last autumn. I am at a loss to understand why it is of such great concern to you now."

"Should it not be?" demanded Bingley, seeming cross. "I have spent money on the lease, and I must recoup that money in the estate's profits, after all."

Darcy nodded slowly, certain this was not the reason for Bingley's return. In fact, he had an uncomfortable suspicion of why Bingley had returned, and his friend confirmed his suspicions with his next words.

"Now that I am again in the neighborhood, you should come and stay at Netherfield. Surely it will be more comfortable than this inn."

Privately, Darcy thought that the presence of a certain young woman would more than make up for the additional comforts the estate boasted.

"You could even invite Georgiana to come and stay with us too."

Darcy raised an eyebrow. "What of Miss Bingley?"

"She has accompanied me, of course," replied Bingley, though with a hint of a blush.

Considering the matter, Darcy motioned his friend to take a nearby seat. He *had* dreaded staying in the inn for a long period of time and had taken some thought to seeing if he could lease a house or smaller estate for some time while he was in residence. Netherfield would be an attractive option, were it not for the presence of one Caroline Bingley. Darcy did not begrudge his sister the pleasure of tweaking Miss Bingley's nose, but it was now clear that this information had caused the woman to rush to Hertfordshire in an attempt to stave off her ignominious defeat at the hands of Miss Bennet.

The question was, could he stay under the same roof as Miss Bingley and not strangle the woman with her own feathers? Perhaps he should take Bingley up on his offer and invite Georgiana—his sister would not particularly appreciate being in close quarters with Miss Bingley, but she could spend time at Longbourn, coming to know the Miss Bennets. She would provide a measure of protection for him from Miss Bingley's excesses, a boon which was not to be overestimated. If only Wickham were not present.

Darcy's thoughts turned to his sister and how she had changed over the past few months. Gone was the almost crippling shyness, replaced with a quiet confidence, no doubt fueled by the learning and growing she had been forced to endure due to the actions of the libertine. Perhaps Darcy should send her a letter, informing her of the situation. She was not in danger from Wickham any longer. So it was really a matter of whether she was comfortable being in such close proximity to Miss Bingley.

"What of Miss Kitty Bennet?" asked Darcy.

Taken completely by surprise, Bingley asked: "What of her?"

"I thought the question was quite obvious, Bingley. Miss Kitty expected your return and you did not come. How do you intend to behave around her?"

Bingley appeared at a loss for a moment, but soon he shook his head. "I have no intention of paying Miss Kitty any further attentions."

"That is for the best, Bingley," said Darcy. "No need to confuse the girl. Perhaps an apology for your failure to return would also be warranted?"

Though Bingley was not pleased at the suggestion, he nodded his head curtly, before returning to the matter had hand.

"Well, Darcy? What do you say? Shall you stay at Netherfield with us?"

In the end, Darcy decided that he could not refuse his friend, as it would be rude to do so.

"Very well, Bingley. I thank you for your invitation."

Darcy turned a stern expression on his friend. "I would appreciate it, however, if you would have a word with your sister. I am accepting your invitation in the spirit with which you offered it, and *not* as a compliment to Miss Bingley. She is not to expect anything from my agreement to stay at Netherfield."

"Of course, Darcy. I . . . I would not have thought it to mean any such thing."

"Perhaps not, Bingley, but I know your sister, and I am well aware of the fact that she *would*."

Though he looked affronted for a brief moment, Bingley nodded his head in a curt motion and indicated his intention to return to Netherfield. Darcy watched him go, wondering at his friend's actions. It was obvious that Bingley had only come to Meryton due to his sister's insistence on the matter, but what Darcy could not be certain of was Bingley's feelings on the matter. For a moment Darcy regretted accepting the invitation. He would need to take very great care when at Netherfield.

It was not long before Darcy was prepared to go to Netherfield. His valet, Mr. Snell, had quite clearly not been impressed with the accommodations at the inn, though he had confined himself to a contemptuous sniff on occasion. Still, Snell was no fool, and he immediately questioned Darcy's reasons for wishing to go to Netherfield.

"Are you certain it is wise, sir?" asked the man. "In the servants' quarters, it is well known that Miss Bingley intends to snare herself a wealthy husband."

"No, Snell, I am not certain at all of the wisdom of staying at Netherfield. I suppose I hope, at least in part, to restore some part of my friendship with Bingley."

"Surely that is not enough to put yourself at such risk."

"Perhaps. But I mean to request my sister's presence as well in order to assist in deflecting Miss Bingley's attentions."

Though it was clear Snell was still not convinced, he made no other comment, instead contenting himself with preparing for their removal to Netherfield. Darcy watched him go, thinking to himself that Snell was likely right. But Darcy had made the decision, and the die was cast. There was nothing to be done about it now.

In preparation for his departure, Darcy prepared two letters—one a short note to Miss Bennet, informing her that he would be delayed, but would visit her that afternoon, while the other he sent off with an express rider to Georgiana. In his own mind, Darcy warred with concern for his sister, hoping that she would accept, while not wishing to subject her to the likes of either Miss Bingley or Wickham. In the end, it would be her decision.

Once the preparations had been complete, Darcy boarded his carriage along with his man, and they sat back for the short two-mile journey to Netherfield. Snell made no secret of his disapproval, though he said nothing, allowing Darcy to lean back and watch the scenery out the window while he brooded.

It was fortunate the journey was not long, or Darcy thought he might have worked himself into quite a state because of it. Soon the carriage entered the drive in front of Netherfield and pulled to a stop. There, waiting on the front steps, were two people, a woman he would just as soon never see again and the person of his friend. Time would only tell if Bingley retained that title.

"Mr. Darcy," said Miss Bingley, attempting, Darcy thought, to display a sophisticated restraint. "How good of you to join us at Netherfield."

The polite man in Darcy could only reply: "I thank you and your brother for inviting me, Miss Bingley."

"Of course we must invite you, sir. A man of your consequence cannot stay in such rough accommodations as this *town's* small inn."

"On the contrary, Miss Bingley, I was quite comfortable at the inn, though I will, of course, concede that Netherfield possesses far finer appointments."

Feeling a savage sense of glee at the woman's brief look of annoyance,

Darcy nevertheless avoided baiting her any further. She was, after all, the mistress at the house at which he was to reside, and proper behavior demanded respect, even when it was undeserved.

"I have assigned you to the same room as you stayed in last autumn."

"Thank you, Miss Bingley. I shall ensure all is settled in my rooms and then join you in the sitting-room."

With a bow, Darcy departed. As he had only come from Meryton, there was no need to refresh himself, so after taking a few moments to compose himself, Darcy departed for the sitting-room. Before he left, however, he took a few moments to instruct Snell to maintain his vigilance.

"Of course, sir," replied Snell, his tone faintly annoyed that Darcy had thought it necessary to remind him.

Darcy smiled at the man and then made his way down the stairs. He took a fortifying breath before he entered the sitting-room, and he stood for some moments, wondering if he was truly in his right mind to be accepting this invitation. But there was nothing to be done, so he opened the door and stepped inside.

"Oh, Mr. Darcy!" exclaimed Miss Bingley on seeing him. "How happy we are to see you, sir! Please, come and sit with us."

Complying, though not sitting near the woman, as she obviously wished, Darcy thanked them once again for their invitation.

"We are quite happy to have you stay here, Mr. Darcy. I am certain that Charles welcomes your advice regarding the estate."

"Does he?" asked Darcy, turning his focus on Bingley. "I am, of course, happy to assist whenever I am at leisure to do so, but you did not mention that when you invited me."

"Well . . ." said Bingley. "If you recall, that was one of the reasons you accompanied me in the autumn."

"True," replied Darcy, deciding to leave the subject.

"And a better teacher he could not find, I dare say," enthused Miss Bingley. "The prosperity of Pemberley amply demonstrates what a consummate master you are, Mr. Darcy. Though I do not think that Charles intends to settle at Netherfield, I am certain the advice you dispense during our stay here will help in in his future endeavors."

"All I have learned has been through my father's instruction and, perhaps more importantly, through my own experience. There is no great secret to the proper management of an estate, Miss Bingley."

"I find your modesty refreshing, Mr. Darcy. There is a myriad of details which must be considered, and your ability to keep them all straight must indicate that you are the most accomplished master in all the land."

The flattery was thick, even for Caroline Bingley, but Darcy was surprised that she had chosen to eschew her typical hateful comments directed at the location in which Netherfield was situated. That, of course, would change once she was informed of Darcy's courtship with Miss Bennet, and he did not doubt he would be required to inform her that he would not allow any disparagement of the lady. He was curious, however, of Miss Bingley taking control of the conversation; usually, Bingley could not be silenced, but on this occasion, he sat back and allowed his sister to speak her piece. In fact, Bingley almost appeared to be nursing some petulance, though over what Darcy could not be certain.

"Now, I have spoken with the cook and have ensured that supper will be ready at the usual time." A sneer of distaste crossed Miss Bingley's face. "The servants are adequate, I suppose, though this is a rustic locale. But I assure you that everything will be up to my exacting standards quickly."

There was the haughty Miss Bingley that Darcy knew and detested; he had known it was only a matter of time before she could no longer hold her vitriol in check.

"I am sure you have everything in hand, Miss Bingley," said Darcy rising to his feet. "I wish you and Bingley a pleasant day, but you should not go to any trouble on my account, as I am to Longbourn for dinner."

Again, Darcy was almost forced to laugh due to the sudden consternation of his hostess. Then a cunning slant came over her features.

"Mr. Darcy," said she, "surely you do not mean to abandon us on your first night in residence at Netherfield? I am certain that the Netherfield kitchens can supply fare which is far superior to anything you might find at Longbourn."

"You have my apologies, Miss Bingley," said Darcy, ignoring her second statement. "This dinner at Longbourn was planned before I knew of your return and certainly before Bingley invited me to stay here."

"But Mr. Darcy!" exclaimed Miss Bingley, a note of desperation entering her voice. "Surely there is nothing for you at Longbourn. Do you not think it would be best for you to stay close to your own kind?"

Darcy frowned, as if in thought. "I am not certain of your meaning, Miss Bingley. Miss Bennet and her family have owned Longbourn for more than two centuries, and are well established as gentlefolk, and though the Lucases are much newer to their estate, at least they *own* Lucas lodge."

It was clear Miss Bingley did not miss Darcy's meaning, if her pinched look was any indication.

"Now, if you will excuse me, I should have departed some time ago."

Darcy strode toward the door and opened it, but before he departed, he looked back at the woman and said in a voice laced with steel: "And as for your assertion of there being nothing for me at Longbourn, you could not be more incorrect. I have been granted permission for a courtship with Miss Bennet. So you see, Miss Bingley, there is plenty of reason for me to go to Longbourn."

Bowing, Darcy closed the door and made his way to the entrance hall and thence to his carriage, which was waiting outside. As he entered and gave the command to depart, Darcy thought back on the confrontation—for there was no better word for what had just happened—with the Bingley siblings. And he reflected as he watched the passing scenery that he had enjoyed confounding the woman far too much. But he could not repine his actions. If anyone was deserving of such treatment, it was Caroline Bingley.

"Miss Bingley is once again in Hertfordshire?"

"I am afraid so," replied Mr. Darcy, as he continued walking about the grounds behind Longbourn. Though Elizabeth could not yet claim to be capable of deciphering all of his moods, she had never had any difficulty understanding what he felt about Miss Bingley. It was unfortunate the woman in question had never known; or perhaps it was more correct to say that she was wilfully obtuse in the matter. Either way, Elizabeth was not happy to hear of the woman's return to Hertfordshire.

"How did she know you were here?" asked Elizabeth.

Mr. Darcy put a hand over Elizabeth's where it lay in the crook of his arm, and shook his head. "I believe I must lay the blame on my dear sister." Elizabeth was intrigued by his tone, which seemed to be equal parts exasperation and fondness. "Miss Bingley visited Georgiana yesterday and Georgiana, who has often been forced to endure the woman's flattering attentions, enjoyed tweaking Miss Bingley's nose. While she did not speak of my attentions outright, she said enough to allow Miss Bingley to guess them."

Taking her lower lip in between her teeth—a nervous habit her mother used to despair of—Elizabeth chewed it as she thought deeply. "I assume the woman is now well aware of your reasons for being here."

A snort was Mr. Darcy's response. "I took great pleasure in ensuring she was well aware of it."

"I doubt that will end her machinations."

"I cannot imagine it will," replied Mr. Darcy. "But I am certain I am able to deal with the woman. I have been dealing with far more devious fortune hunters than Miss Caroline Bingley for my entire adult life."

"But now she is desperate, Mr. Darcy," said Elizabeth. "You do not know what she will attempt."

A pained look came over Mr. Darcy's face. "Miss Bennet, since we are now courting, I believe a certain familiarity of manner is permitted. Shall we not address each other by our given names?"

Feeling suddenly shy, Elizabeth glanced away, but her sense of the mischievous soon took over. "I do not know if I can do that, Mr. Darcy." At his pained look, Elizabeth responded with a light: "Your name, sir, is impossibly long and more than a mouthful for one such as I. Besides, do you not find it rather dreary to be continually addressed with such a pompous name?"

For a moment Mr. Darcy gazed at her through widened eyes, and Elizabeth thought she might have gone too far in her teasing. But just when she was about to offer her apologies, Mr. Darcy threw back his head and let out a guffaw.

"I suppose I must become accustomed to your teasing," said he, wiping the traces of his mirth from his eyes.

"And you did not know this about me when you asked for a courtship?" asked Elizabeth, her confidence restored.

"In fact, it is one of the qualities I most admire about you. The ability to laugh at life is not to be underestimated. I simply have not had the pleasure yet of you turning your wit upon *me!*"

They laughed together for a moment, before Mr. Darcy drew himself up tall and proud.

"I will have you know, Miss Bennet, that 'Fitzwilliam' is an old and very respectable name. I was named in such a way to honor my mother's family, who, as you know, are in possession of an earldom."

"I dare say your name *is* very distinguished, Mr. Darcy," said Elizabeth. "But it is also too pretentious for everyday use."

Shaking his head and still chuckling, Mr. Darcy said: "You may be correct. If you prefer something a little less formal, then my sister always calls me 'William.' It would please me if you would do the same."

"William," said Elizabeth, testing the name out and finding it suited him. "Very well, William. To please you, I shall do so."

"And I shall call you Elizabeth."

Startled by the way in which his use of her name was almost a caress, Elizabeth shyly nodded. "My friends will often call me Lizzy, and

Charlotte Lucas has the privilege of referring to me as Eliza. If you wish to shorten my moniker, I would prefer the first."

"And refrain from using such a beautiful name in its entirety?" Mr. Darcy—William—shook his head. "Your name is the name of monarchs, Elizabeth, and I cannot consider you to be any less than any of them. For my part, 'Elizabeth' you shall be."

Though his words thrilled her, they also caused some measure of embarrassment. She ducked her head, feeling shy, and said: "I assume you will take care in your interactions with Miss Bingley?"

William scowled, no doubt annoyed by the reminder of the woman. "I have already discussed it with Snell, my valet. I do not doubt that he is having a cot set up in front of the door to my room, so as to foil any attempt by Miss Bingley to gain entrance."

"I would laugh, if I did not consider her capable of such behavior."

A mischievous smile came over William's face. "You must understand, Elizabeth, that those in my employ have a vested interest in ensuring Miss Bingley does not achieve her designs. For if I was to marry the woman, she would become *their* mistress, and given her performance in Bingley's house—not to mention the liberties she took when she visited Pemberley—I am certain none of *them* wish to have her as a mistress!"

Though she could see the humor in his words, Elizabeth was only able to shake her head. "I pity the woman. She does not see how others view her behavior."

"She would not care for their opinions if she did."

"I know. That makes it all the more pitiable."

"There is one potential benefit to my staying at Netherfield," said William, changing the subject slightly. "At Bingley's request, I have dispatched a letter to my sister, asking her if she would like to stay at Netherfield."

"Oh, that is excellent news!" said Elizabeth. "I am looking forward to making her acquaintance."

"And she has expressed the same about you and your sister. While I would not subject her to Miss Bingley—and I will keep her from Wickham, if at all possible—I believe her presence will help to ease the situation. At the very least, she will provide a chaperone to ensure Miss Bingley does not attempt to claim a compromise."

Elizabeth nodded, though curious about his specific design to keep his sister from Mr. Wickham. "I hope she accepts. Kitty and I would love to make her acquaintance."

After walking for some more minutes, Elizabeth and William

returned to the house and entered. Sir William and his family were present, as well as Uncle and Aunt Phillips, and greetings were exchanged all around. Elizabeth was happy to have those closest to her in attendance, though she truly wished the Gardiners were more at liberty to join them.

But Elizabeth had an important communication to make, and she left William speaking with the other two men. Taking her sister to the side of the room, she informed Kitty of Mr. and Miss Bingley's arrival in the neighborhood.

"I thank you for informing me of their residence, Lizzy," said Kitty. "But I assure you that it does not affect me."

"I am happy to hear it, Kitty. But I would not have wished for you to suddenly come upon Mr. Bingley unaware."

Kitty nodded, though her responding tone was firm. "Thank you for that, but your concern is not necessary. I have put Mr. Bingley and his attentions in the past where they belong. He may come and go as he likes, and should he attempt to pay particular attention to me, I will respond accordingly."

"Good girl," said Elizabeth, and the sisters embraced and returned to their company.

The evening was a success, filled, as it was, with excellent food, good conversation, and the blessing of beloved companions. There was none of the awkwardness or impropriety of the first time Mr. Darcy had dined at Longbourn, and for that Elizabeth could be only grateful.

On more than one occasion, thoughts of the other two people who attended the last dinner came to Elizabeth's mind, but she shook them off. Mr. and Miss Bingley were truly nothing to her now, and though she would never dictate to William who he might have as friends, she thought he was cooling to Mr. Bingley, and she hoped he would not wish for the man's company much in the future. Regardless, Elizabeth would not allow them to affect her. She hoped Miss Bingley had the stomach for her dinner that evening without William in attendance. Miss Bingley would never have William's regard, no matter what ultimately happened between Elizabeth and the gentleman.

Chapter XXII

$\mathcal{I}$t should be noted that the cut direct was more than simply a social tool, used for embarrassing a disliked person or indicating a measure of disgust for a rival. In fact, its reach was far more profound. It could be used to destroy the social standing of a lesser ranked person, or to convey disapproval for another's behavior. But its central meaning, however, was almost always an indication of an intention to sever an acquaintance without possibility of reconciliation.

As Elizabeth had delivered the cut direct to one Miss Caroline Bingley, the usual form would have been for the woman to avoid her, and Elizabeth knew that Miss Bingley wished for nothing more. However, as she and her brother had returned to the neighborhood, and — more importantly — William was currently staying at the estate the woman's brother was leasing, Elizabeth decided that it would be more diplomatic to allow her entrance and ignore her. Thus, when the woman was led into the room, Elizabeth greeted her with a slight curtsey and a barely murmured "Miss Bingley" before she proceeded to ignore the woman completely. That seemed to suit Miss Bingley well indeed, for she did not even deign to respond with that much. Elizabeth looked on, amused, as Miss Bingley claimed a straight-backed chair and proceeded to watch them all as they interacted.

As there were much more interesting persons in attendance,

Elizabeth put the unpleasant woman from her mind. Mr. Bingley had, of course, joined his sister and Mr. Darcy in visiting that morning, but as he paid no particular attention to Kitty, and Kitty seemed to be unaffected by his presence, Elizabeth put the matter from her mind. Besides, there was one other whose presence was far more welcome.

"Miss Bennet, Miss Catherine," said Mr. Darcy, guiding a young lady forward, "may I present my sister to your acquaintance? Georgiana, this is Miss Elizabeth Bennet and Miss Catherine Bennet. Miss Bennet, Miss Catherine, this is my sister, Georgiana. Georgiana arrived from London this morning and insisted on accompanying us to be introduced to you."

Out of the corner of her eye Elizabeth saw the sour look of discontent which spread over Miss Bingley's face, but she turned her attention back to the young girl in front of her. Miss Darcy was tall—as tall as Kitty and slightly taller than Elizabeth—and she possessed a wealth of luxurious blonde hair. Where she was fair and Mr. Darcy was dark, their family resemblance was easy to mark, but in the sister, his strong jaw was softer, her features finer, like delicate china. As she was only sixteen, there were, no doubt, still two years before her debut into society, but Elizabeth thought she would be in demand as much for her beauty, as for her dowry and family name.

The three ladies curtseyed to one another, and Georgiana eyed them with perfect composure, though also with a hint of shyness in her eyes.

"Kitty and I have been so eager to make your acquaintance, Miss Darcy," said Elizabeth extending her hands to grasp the other girl's and make her feel welcome. "But I must own that I am rather surprised at your coming this morning."

"It seems Georgiana could not wait to make your acquaintance," said Mr. Darcy.

"I dare say she could not," replied Elizabeth, fixing the girl with a playful smile. "In fact, for her to have arrived early this morning, I dare say she must have been sitting by the door with her trunks already packed!"

"Surely you overstate the matter," interjected Miss Bingley, apparently unable to keep her silence and forgetting she had been cut. She pierced Elizabeth with a sneering sort of scowl. "Those brought up in illustrious families such as our dear Georgiana would never behave in so reprehensible a manner."

"Actually, it is not far from the truth," said Miss Darcy, ignoring Miss Bingley's outburst. "I had instructed my maid to make some preparations in the hope of William relenting and allowing me to come. When his letter came, I was eager to depart, I assure you."

"I can see that, Miss Darcy."

"Miss Bennet, since I very much hope that we will one day be sisters, shall we not call each other by our given names?"

"I would like that very much indeed," said Elizabeth. "Most of my friends call me Elizabeth or Lizzy, and I would be happy with either."

Miss Darcy darted a look at her brother, who was watching and apparently enjoying their interaction. "My cousin—who is also my guardian—has, at times, called me Georgie, but everyone else calls me Georgiana."

"Then Georgiana it is."

Beaming, Georgiana turned her attention to Kitty, saying: "Miss Catherine, is it? Might I be afforded the same privilege with you as well?"

"Of course," said Kitty, seeming to be a little in awe of the elegant younger girl. "But I have been called Kitty since my earliest memories, so it may be better if you use it as well." A nervous giggle escaped Kitty's lips. "If you refer to me as Catherine, it is very possible I will not respond!"

The two girls laughed, and soon they were seated together. It was not long before Kitty's uncertainty and Georgiana's shyness were shed, and they were speaking together as friends who had known each other many years.

"I believe you mentioned your sister to me as one who is excessively shy, Mr. Darcy," said Elizabeth in a low tone to her suitor. "I must question your assertions, as she appears amiable and open, though perhaps a little reticent at first."

"She has always been a shy creature," replied William, "but she has changed much these past months, grown in confidence and easiness in company. She had a . . ." William paused and a shadow came over his face. "Last summer was trying for her, but she has recovered remarkably."

Something in William's face told Elizabeth there was more to this story than a trying summer. As it was not truly her concern at present, Elizabeth adroitly changed the subject, knowing that as they grew closer, he would be more willing to confide in her.

"Miss Bennet," said Mr. Bingley for the first time, "I am happy to renew our acquaintance."

Though something in Elizabeth willed her to cut the silly man, she decided that he was truly not a bad sort, so she curtseyed and plastered a pleasant smile on her face.

"As am I, Mr. Bingley."

"I must own that I was surprised to hear of your courtship with Darcy." Mr. Bingley turned a teasing eye on his friend. "Darcy here is most reticent with his private affairs, and I had no suspicion at all of his interest."

Laughing, Elizabeth replied: "I am certain *I* had no notion of his feelings until he made his application to me."

"Indeed?" said Mr. Bingley, clearly surprised. "I should have thought this courtship has come out of interactions in which both parties were aware of the intentions of the other."

"Perhaps some couples come together in such circumstances, but we did not. I have always esteemed Mr. Darcy as an intelligent, rational man, but I did not know of his attraction for me until he applied for a courtship.

"But is that not the purpose of a courtship? Now I may discover more of Mr. Darcy's character, and see if we are compatible and if there is a chance of love growing between us."

"I am sure you must be correct, Miss Bennet," replied Mr. Bingley. "Well, you will not find a better man than Darcy here. When he makes a decision, it is set in stone, but he only arrives at it with careful deliberation."

"Of that, I am aware, Mr. Bingley."

The company sat down and Elizabeth ordered tea. The conversation was pleasant, Elizabeth speaking in a group which included William and Mr. Bingley, while Kitty and Georgiana giggled together. Only Miss Bingley held herself aloof, which was no loss, in Elizabeth's opinion.

"So tell me how this all came about," said Mr. Bingley, when they had settled in with their tea. "As I stated, I had no indication of Darcy's interest in you, Miss Bennet."

"Perhaps you should ask the man in question to account for himself, Mr. Bingley," said Elizabeth with a laugh. "I am certain I cannot read minds."

Mr. Bingley returned Elizabeth's laugh. "I suppose that is the case." Turning to William, he arched an eyebrow. "Well, Darcy? How can you account for this?"

"I must own to some curiosity myself," interjected Miss Bingley. She turned a superior eye on Elizabeth and continued: "In fact, I had thought Mr. Darcy did not care for your brand of impertinence. I remember our first assembly in the area and particularly hearing of Mr. Darcy referred to you as a bluestocking."

Elizabeth exchanged a glance with William, and they descended into laughter, a highly affronted Miss Bingley looking on.

"Now that you mention it, Caroline, I do remember something of that nature myself."

"As do both Miss Bennet and I," replied William. "However, Miss Bennet understood what I was saying at the time, and we both had a good laugh about it."

"I am not certain I take your meaning," said Mr. Bingley with a frown.

"Only that Mr. Darcy was attempting to put you off by making a seemingly rude statement," said Elizabeth. "He knew I could hear, and he deliberately said it, suspecting that I would be diverted because of it, and he was correct."

A clearly disgruntled Miss Bingley only snorted, foiled in her attempt to incite Elizabeth's anger by pointing out a perceived insult. It was all Elizabeth could do not to roll her eyes at the woman—Miss Bingley truly was a pathetic creature.

"In fact, Bingley," continued William, fixing his attention back on his friend, "I believe my attraction to Miss Bennet stems from those early days of our acquaintance. Certainly, my respect for her intelligence and how she managed her estate was borne almost from the beginning of our acquaintance."

"As were mine for *your* abilities, William," said Elizabeth, turning her smile on her suitor. "Though your application was not expected, I knew almost from the start that you were a man of honor and one capable and attentive to all matters within your purview."

The two shared a tender glance, which was broken by the strident tones of Miss Bingley's voice. "Miss Bennet, I would not have been able to believe even *you* capable of such effrontery."

Elizabeth's eyes found Miss Bingley, and she noted the woman's expression was not only outraged, but also wildly displeased.

"Mr. Darcy is the scion of an earl; do you not know? For you to refer to him as anything other than 'Mr. Darcy' when you possess only a tenuous connection is improper in the extreme. Perhaps you have not moved in polite company enough, but your behavior would shock Mr. Darcy's nearest relations."

"Actually, Miss Bingley," said William, turning a hard glare on the woman, "she uses my name at my particular request, as I do hers. As we are courting—and I am uncertain how you could consider such a connection to be 'tenuous'—a certain degree of familiarity is permitted."

Silenced, Miss Bingley only looked away, Mr. Bingley looking uncomfortably at his sister. For the rest of the visit, the woman made no attempt to continue her paltry attacks, which was just as well, as Elizabeth was not certain Miss Bingley could have withstood the constant set-downs she was experiencing.

As they continued to speak, Elizabeth took part in the conversation, but she also watched and endeavored to compare the two men before her. She had never possessed any feelings of a romantic nature for Mr. Bingley, so comparing them from that perspective was difficult. But as the conversation continued, she was struck by how William, though relaxed in her company, still appeared to be mindful of the situation, was still proper and serious and speaking of topics of some substance. Mr. Bingley, by contrast was completely at ease and spoke with animation, his ideas flitting from subject to subject without any seeming forethought or plan, much like a young child.

Furthermore, though it was evident within moments of meeting William's sister that she was the dearest creature in the world, still Elizabeth could not imagine William tolerating a sister who behaved as Miss Bingley did. Mr. Bingley, on the other hand, had listened to his sister speaking, sometimes with a blush, sometimes with annoyance or mortification, but never calling her to order or otherwise demanding her good behavior. Part of that could, perhaps, be due to their upbringing— Elizabeth had no idea as to the elder Bingley's character, of course, but as William had had a hand in his sister's rearing, it was easy to see that it had been a success, considering how the girl conducted herself. But even if he had not had such an influence in his sister's upbringing, Mr. Bingley was responsible for her *now* and was in a position to control her when necessary. That he chose not to do so was not a mark in his favor. As she considered the matter further, Elizabeth decided that it was fortunate that Mr. Bingley had not continued with his attentions to Kitty; she certainly would not wish for Kitty to have such a relation, especially when her husband's ability to protect her was in question.

When the time for a visit had elapsed, Miss Bingley stood, and with a smug sneer directed at Elizabeth, said: "I believe the time has come for us to depart. Thank you, *Miss Bennet*, for your hospitality."

William turned and regarded Miss Bingley, his gaze flat, knowing she expected to have a captive audience at Netherfield once they had departed. Elizabeth, however, merely responded to the woman's paltry attack with good cheer.

"I thank you for coming, Mr. Bingley, Miss Bingley. Since I assume you will be in the neighborhood for some time, I hope to see you both again soon."

"Oh, you do not mean to farewell your suitor?"

The venom in Miss Bingleys' voice only produced a smile from Elizabeth, which further soured her expression.

"I shall farewell *William*, when the time comes, of course."

"Georgiana and I will stay to spend the day with the Miss Bennets, Miss Bingley," said William. "I believe we shall return to Netherfield for dinner tonight."

"But Mr. Darcy!" exclaimed a shocked Miss Bingley. "Miss Bennet does not have a father present. You could not possibly stay here the entire day."

"Miss Bingley," said Darcy, the sternness in his voice bringing a pale hue to her skin, "I am not certain why you wish to take it upon yourself to determine the propriety of my actions, but I would ask you to keep your opinions to yourself. My sister is present, as is Miss Kitty—that should be sufficient to meet the demands of propriety."

"Of course it is," said Mr. Bingley, rising abruptly to prevent his sister from saying anything further. It was the first time Elizabeth had ever seen the man act in the face of his sister's rudeness. "Come, Caroline. Let us leave, as I am certain we both have some tasks which require our attention."

Though it was with evident ill-grace, Caroline Bingley managed to spit out a farewell, and the Bingleys departed, to the regret of none of those remaining behind. Once they had entered their carriage, and it drove away, William and Elizabeth returned to the sitting-room, where they rejoined their sisters. When they entered, Georgiana and Kitty looked up from where they were engaged in a whispered conversation and, catching sight of their siblings, broke out into giggles.

Elizabeth laughed along with them, knowing exactly what so diverted them, and after a moment, even William joined in the laughter.

"I have never liked Miss Bingley," said Kitty, shaking her head, "but I have never known her to be quite so mean-spirited."

"That is because you are not well acquainted with her," replied William, though it appeared he did not wish to speak ill of another. It was another reason to esteem the man—he did not disparage others when he could avoid it, regardless of how much they deserved it.

"I only hope you will take care, William," said Georgiana. "She is desperate, and I believe would do anything at this point to secure you, whether you wished it or not."

"I shall do whatever I must to defend myself," replied William. "It does not matter what she tries, or whether she succeeds; I shall not marry her, so it is of little matter."

"I believe I would prefer to leave the subject of Miss Bingley and turn to those more pleasurable," said Elizabeth. "What say you to a walk? Kitty and I can show you the view from Oakham Mount."

Kitty laughed. "Lizzy, only you would suggest a walk of over two miles. I do not know about Georgiana, but I believe it is too much for me!"

"I am not a great walker, though I would love to see it," said Georgiana.

"Shall we not go on horseback then?" asked William. "We could make a day of it—take a picnic lunch along." Then he paused and looked at Kitty. "I am sorry, Miss Kitty, but I should have ascertained whether you ride before suggesting such a thing."

"I am only offended by your reluctance to simply use my name, William," said Kitty, inducing them all to laugh. "As for riding, I am not as accomplished as Elizabeth, but I am conversant enough to ride such a short distance."

"And Longbourn has an excellent gentle mare in our stables that Kitty has ridden before," said Elizabeth, enthusiastic about the idea. "I believe I should like such a plan very well, William."

"Then let us plan to do so," said William.

They all agreed on the plan and decided to walk out anyway, but staying closer to Longbourn. For, as Elizabeth stated: "I wish to show you more of the neighborhood, so you will see my love of this land for yourself."

"I am quite happy to witness it through your eyes," said Mr. Darcy. "I only hope to be able to show you my home some time in the near future."

Though still unsure of her feelings, Elizabeth very much wished to see his home and understand his own love for it. She had no doubt it would prove instructional and provide her with more insight into his character.

In the end though, she could not help but suppose that it would not truly matter. The more time she spent in his company, the more she esteemed him. It was only a matter of time before he renewed his addresses, and Elizabeth was coming to the conclusion that she would be a fool to reject him.

As the carriage pulled away from Longbourn, Caroline Bingley cast a look back at the detested estate, fuming over the way she had been unable to keep Mr. Darcy away from the little adventuress. The more she saw of the man in Miss Bennet's company, the more she saw that he was indeed infatuated with her; it was the only possible explanation for his continued attentions to her, when Caroline, who was so obviously superior to her in every way, was before him.

The carriage traveled through the countryside, but as was her wont, Caroline did not see anything of it; what did she care for rocks and trees and fields? It was for those who worked the land to care for such things, not those such as she, who were destined for much greater things. And Caroline would rule over an estate—she would rule over the greatest of estates. She only needed to find a way to discredit her rival.

"Are you convinced now, Caroline?"

Scowling at her brother, Caroline refused to answer him, preferring to brood in silence. Charles, however, would not take the hint.

"I have told you many times that Darcy would not make you an offer, but you would not believe me. You must give up this doomed pursuit before you make a fool of yourself."

A baleful glare, directed at her brother, settled on Caroline's face, but Charles only sighed and looked away. Caroline's glare did not abate in the slightest, regardless of her brother's inattention. If only he would support her, like a proper brother would; instead, he flitted from one pretty girl to the next, engaging in frivolous conversation and mooning after his paramours. Caroline had spent her entire adult life endeavoring to raise the family fortune, and all Charles had done was to have the good fortune to come to the attention of a wealthy man! The least he could do is assist her to secure him!

"Our future is here, Charles," snapped Caroline, after she watched him for several moments. "At least it is here until Mr. Darcy proposes to me."

Charles sighed again, but Caroline would not allow him to insert his opinion. "I will not allow some trumped-up little tart to take my place as mistress of Pemberley."

"It is not your choice to make," replied Charles. "Or have you forgotten that it is a man's burden to propose?"

"Of course I have not forgotten!" Caroline felt like screaming. "But the man often requires guidance."

"I have rarely met a man less in need of guidance than Darcy. The fact that he is paying attention to that . . . that . . ."

"Have a care, Caroline!" exclaimed Charles. "Miss Bennet is a respectable woman, and I will not have you debasing yourself by using language the likes of which I am certain you were contemplating."

"I am a lady, Charles. I might wish to say such things about that *woman*, but I assure you I will not forget my own gentility."

A soft snort met Caroline's ears, and though she was immediately infuriated, she managed to maintain control of her temper.

"There is nothing for either of us here, Caroline," said Charles while

Caroline was controlling her reaction. "Come, let us return to London. We shall find you a husband, while I may once again see Miss Cranston."

"Let me be rightly understood," hissed Caroline from between clenched teeth, "*my* husband is here, and I will not depart until I have secured him."

The carriage stopped in front of Netherfield, and Caroline alighted before Charles could hand her down. She marched into the house, not looking back, seething over her brother's lack of foresight and weak-willed nature. In a few moments, she had reached her rooms, and she slammed the door behind her, and proceeded to pace the room, thinking furiously, trying to decide what stratagem she should utilize to achieve her designs.

The possibility of compromising Mr. Darcy and forcing him to marry her she discarded, almost without thought. Gaining access to his rooms was not likely to succeed, as she heard from the housekeeper that Mr. Darcy's man had requested a cot in order to sleep in his master's rooms. She would not put it past Mr. Snell to set it up in front of Mr. Darcy's door. And while the possibility existed that she might engineer a compromise in one of the main rooms of the house, timid little Georgiana was likely to stay close to him, making it difficult. Besides, Caroline doubted he would marry her, even if she did compromise him. And if he refused, his standing in society would no doubt protect him, leaving Caroline ruined.

No, a compromise was not an answer. In fact, Caroline did not think that working on the man himself was the answer at all. He had shown such a distressing level of affection for Miss Bennet and such a lack of concern for Caroline herself that she thought it might be difficult to get him to marry her at all. Though she had not thought it possible, it was becoming quite clear that he clung to quaint notions of love, and Caroline was not blind enough to think that she could ever make the man love her. Nor did she want his love, to be honest—she preferred a marriage to a man of fortune, where she could rule over his house and entertain the highest of society. Love was not required.

Throwing herself in a nearby chair, Caroline sat for some time brooding about the situation. If it had been a normal situation, she would simply have engineered a compromise, but she had already determined it would not work.

Or perhaps it *would* work. If it was done correctly it might work. The more Caroline mused on the subject, the more she thought that if done properly, a compromise might still get her what she wished for. But she would need to handle it properly. She did not now have all the pieces in place to ensure success, but Caroline was certain something would present itself.

Chapter XXIII

$\mathcal{M}$uch though the season of courtship should have been one of joy for Elizabeth and Darcy, they were instead forced to endure the interference of one Miss Caroline Bingley. And while they could often escape from the woman by simply planning on the Darcys visiting Longbourn and staying the entire day, still Miss Bingley would insist upon accompanying the Darcys — along with her brother — for a morning visit, even though they were required to return to Netherfield thereafter.

Worse than the woman's presence, however, was the conviction that she had not yet given up the fight. When she visited, she was quiet and rarely ventured an opinion, seeming to content herself with keeping a close watch on Darcy and Elizabeth's interactions. The matter was discussed at some length between them, but they were never able to come to any consensus about what the woman had planned, if indeed she planned anything. But Darcy insisted that, as much as he was taking precautions, Elizabeth must do the same.

"I would not put it past the woman to attempt something where you are concerned," said Darcy.

"What could she possibly do?" asked Elizabeth, feeling nothing but disdain for Caroline Bingley.

"I will own that I do not know," replied Darcy. "But it costs nothing to be prudent.

"Then it is fortunate that I am already being prudent. Mr. Whitmore insisted some time ago that I take care, since Mr. Wickham was showing a great deal of interest in me. Whenever I go out on the estate, John — my footman — accompanies me."

"And Kitty? If Miss Bingley were to somehow succeed in ruining your sister, that would likely be sufficient, in her mind."

"Kitty also is protected, William. If I accept protection for myself, you can hardly think that I would allow Kitty to remain at risk."

"No, I could not have thought that of you," murmured William.

"I must say," said Elizabeth with a mischievous smile, "I had not known a courtship with you would complicate my life in such a manner. I might wonder if it is all worth it."

"Perhaps you should have thought of that before, Miss Bennet. Now that I have you, I am not likely to allow you to slip through my fingers."

They laughed together. Indeed, by this time, Elizabeth was not disposed to allow the man to escape her either, though she decided that as of yet his ego did not require such a boost as telling him would constitute.

"Can I assume the situation has not changed at Netherfield?"

William scowled. "You may so assume. Miss Bingley continues to act as if I am there solely for her pleasure, and nothing I say or do can convince her otherwise. Georgiana and I have taken to staying in the sitting-room between our bedchambers for as long as we can manage, though we must pay her some attention in politeness to our hosts."

"Personally, I believe that Miss Bingley forfeits her claim to such attentions, given her behavior."

"I cannot disagree with you," said William. "But Bingley is a good fellow, and though I am still not completely happy with his conduct, I would keep him as a friend, if I can. Thus, I must be polite to his sister."

Elizabeth did not like it, but she could raise no dispute.

As they had planned, the two Darcys and two Bennets rode to Oakham Mount one fine morning, taking along with them a picnic lunch. The Darcys were duly impressed with the view, and many exclamations proceeded forth from their mouths. Of course, William could not allow the event to pass without once again speaking of his home, and if his manner was overly proud, Elizabeth could forgive him for it.

"This is a pretty location, indeed," said William as they looked out over the brilliant greens of the trees, the more muted greens of the fields, and blues of the streams and cool, clear pools of water.

He looked around with interest. "Unless I am very much mistaken, it seems to me as if this is the highest hill in the vicinity."

"It is," confirmed Elizabeth. "There are some low hills further to the north, but as that side is wooded, they cannot be seen from here."

Nodding, William said: "It is much different from my home. If you were to come to Pemberley, you would be able to see the peaks in the distance, quite clearly on a sunny day."

"Oh, you must come!" said Georgiana. "The peaks are so pretty, and there is plenty to be seen in the vicinity of Pemberley too."

"In fact," said William, as if speaking of the most casual matter, "I was informed by your uncle that you plan to visit the north this summer."

"Yes, indeed," said Elizabeth. "We are to depart in late June and spend several weeks, with our ultimate destination being the lakes."

"Ah," said Darcy, and Elizabeth thought he looked insufferably smug. "But, unfortunately, your uncle told me that his business will not allow him so much time away, and that you will not be able to travel so far as the lakes."

Elizabeth could not suppress the feeling of disappointment upon hearing such news, but her eye was soon caught by William's continuing expression of self-satisfaction.

"I am of the distinct impression that you are not sharing everything with me, William," said Elizabeth, feeling a little cross at his manner.

"Since your visit must be curtailed, and since Mrs. Gardiner has fond memories of living in Lambton, they have decided to content themselves with Derbyshire."

"Oh, William!" exclaimed Georgiana. "Lambton is not five miles from Pemberley. They should stay at Pemberley while they are in the neighborhood!"

"Indeed, my dear," said Darcy with a lazy sort of insouciance. "In fact, I thought so myself."

"Mr. Darcy!" cried Elizabeth. "I do not know that I wish to continue this courtship, for I am finding that you are quite incorrigible!"

"I own it without disguise, and I do not apologize for it, Elizabeth," replied William. "Particularly if it allows me to see you at Pemberley before I might otherwise have been able to arrange."

There was nothing Elizabeth could say to that. She had known from the beginning that Mr. Darcy's feelings for her were real and true. If her aunt and uncle could not travel all the way to the lakes, Elizabeth was, in fact, quite happy to spend the holiday in Derbyshire. And she was not above owning to more than a little curiosity about her suitor's estate.

They began to remove their lunch from the baskets, strapped to the backs of their horses, and Kitty and Georgiana spread out a blanket for their use, while Elizabeth and William began to prepare their lunch. While they were thus engaged, William drew up close to Elizabeth, and, looking at their younger sisters to see if they were being observed, said:

"Do not distress yourself about not going to the lakes, Elizabeth. If you accept my proposal, I promise we shall go there next summer."

Taken aback a little, Elizabeth drew back, and fixed him with an imperious glare. "Bribery, Mr. Darcy?"

"If I must." William's grin was positively roguish. "I own a small lodge there that we may use. I assure you, Miss Bennet, I am well aware of your appreciation for all nature has to offer, and I know you would love it there."

"We shall see, Mr. Darcy."

Throughout those weeks, Elizabeth became more familiar with William's character. But even more than his character — which Elizabeth thought she already trusted — she came to know the man, his likes and dislikes, how he behaved when he was annoyed, the cold flame which burned in his eyes when caught in anger, and the special smile he would often bestow on Elizabeth, one he used with no one else.

In fact, Elizabeth thought that a woman could not help but fall for a man who looked at her in such a manner, especially when the man was as handsome as William. But she was determined not to allow such things to rule her.

Life, of course, did not cease while being courted, and there were still tasks which needed to be completed. Elizabeth kept to her schedule of visiting the tenants and overseeing the operation of the estate, only now she was accompanied by her suitor, who cheerfully insisted that he would be honored to assist. Her need to manage her estate brought to mind the fact that William did indeed possess his own, and one which required his attention. But his response when she asked on the matter showed his dedication to her and his commitment to the courtship.

"There is nothing more important at present than you," replied William, his eyes smoldering with intensity. "I can manage Pemberley very well from where I currently am."

Elizabeth raised an eyebrow, happy for his dedication, but wondering as to his meaning.

"You forget, my dear," replied William, "that I own several estates. I correspond with my stewards at each location extensively. Though I will own that Pemberley is far more complex and diverse than the others, still the principle is the same. When we are married, you will manage Longbourn in the same fashion. Though I know Mr. Whitmore is well able to care for the estate himself, you, as the owner, need to be involved, for it is your livelihood which the steward only manages."

"*When* we marry?" asked Elizabeth. "And *I* will manage it?"

A predatory smile came over William's face at her conflicting questions, but he only ignored the first. "Yes, *you* will manage it, Elizabeth. Not only do I have complete confidence in your abilities, but you are much more familiar with Longbourn than I. I will, of course, assist wherever required."

Elizabeth decided against saying anything further, knowing the man was looking for any reason to tease her with the inevitability of their future union. It spoke to his wish for her to become an equal partner in a marriage. Elizabeth thought that few gentlemen would wish to leave the running of an estate to his wife, even if that wife brought it with her into the marriage.

They built an easy camaraderie through their shared endeavors, and when Elizabeth saw his interactions with the tenants, she was impressed all over again. She was even forced to laugh when Jenny induced William to lift her up, where she proceeded to plant a wet, sloppy kiss on his cheek.

Their interactions persisted for some time, with Elizabeth enjoying William's attentions, while he waited patiently as she accustomed herself to his presence and tried to make out her feelings. Unfortunately, Elizabeth remained uncertain of her feelings the entire time, knowing that while she liked him very well indeed, she could not be sure she loved him.

How long they might have continued in the same fashion, Elizabeth could not tell. She knew she esteemed him, but though she was waiting for something more, an understanding of the contents of her heart, a conversation with her sister helped Elizabeth further bring her feelings into focus. On a day, once again spent with the Darcys, and after they had returned to Netherfield, Elizabeth and Kitty were sitting down to dinner when Kitty began speaking.

"I must say, I truly esteem the Darcys. There is something completely without artifice about them both, which is quite appealing, and so unexpected from those of their social situation."

"Oh?" asked Elizabeth. In truth, she had not been attending her sister, so fixed her thoughts had been on William.

"I understand that William at times seems a little proud," said Kitty, "but can you honestly say you have seen anything of such behavior since his proposal?"

"No," replied Elizabeth, deep in thought. "I suppose I cannot claim any such thing."

"And Georgiana," said Kitty, oblivious to Elizabeth's introspection, "she is unpretentious and soft-spoken. In a way, she reminds me very much of Jane."

"Yes, she does," said Elizabeth, feeling a little melancholic nostalgia at the thought of her dearest sister. Jane would have liked Georgiana exceedingly well; Elizabeth was absolutely certain.

Of course, with Jane present, Elizabeth wondered if William would have even looked in her direction. Jane had had that effect on men.

"Do you think that you will accept William?"

Startled by the question, Elizabeth turned to her sister, wondering what she was about.

"I do not mean to rush or influence you in any way, Lizzy," said Kitty. "But I have to own that I wonder what you are searching for. If you are not disposed to accept William, is there any man out there who will meet your approval?"

"What do you mean?" asked Elizabeth. Though she was a little mollified by Kitty's words, she could not help but question Kitty's purpose.

"Lizzy," said Kitty, her tone admonishing, such as Elizabeth had never before heard her sister direct at her, "surely you can see that William worships the very ground you walk upon. If a man loved me that much, I could not imagine refusing him."

"What about my own regard for him?" asked Elizabeth, feeling a little cross with her sister.

"Can a woman not respond to a man's blatant regard? Can you not begin to love a man because he loves you?"

In truth Elizabeth had never thought of it that way. Ever since William's return and his surprising proposal, Elizabeth had attempted to divine the nature of her own feelings without respect to William's feelings for her. She felt she had owed it to him.

"Perhaps a man's regard can cause a woman's feelings to increase in response," said Elizabeth slowly. "But does the woman not have an obligation to endeavor to develop her own feelings without reference to his?"

At these words, Kitty actually rolled her eyes. "How can you do such a thing, Lizzy? How can you state with any surety that what you feel for another does not depend on what they feel for you? And is not love, at its heart, a taking and giving? Does not a person's love for another feed that person's love for them in return? It seems to me, Lizzy, that you cannot have one without the other.

"In fact, I must think you a simpleton if you cannot love William. He is kind, considerate, he clearly considers you to be deity in the flesh. He is temperate, rational, diligent, intelligent, he cares for all those in the sphere of his influence, and if he at times seems a little officious, I believe it is because he is intent upon ensuring their safety and happiness. With such qualities, what more could you want? You shall not find a perfect man, Lizzy, but I think the perfect man *for you* might have found you."

"I . . ."

Elizabeth fell silent, surprised as she was by Kitty's words. Could it truly be as easy as Kitty had said? Was it really nothing more than respecting and admiring his good qualities, basking in the love he obviously had for her, and allowing her own feelings to grow in response? Could Elizabeth actually have been hoping or searching for something beyond this simple exchange of regard?

"You have my apologies if I have spoken out of turn," said Kitty, once again breaking Elizabeth's contemplations. "But it seems to me you are on the precipice of a very special relationship with a truly special man, and I would not wish for you to throw it away."

At last, Elizabeth felt herself capable of responding, and she exerted herself to speak. "Kitty, I am not offended. Indeed, you give very good advice, and I am happy that you have determined to speak to me today. I . . . I do not know what my feelings consist of, but I was not on the verge of throwing it away, as you say. I *do* know that William is a very good man, and though I am not completely certain at present, I believe I am leaning more toward accepting him, than the reverse."

"That is wonderful news," said Kitty. Then her smile became teasing, and she continued: "William has said that Georgiana will come out in two seasons, and that I might have a season alongside her. Therefore, you simply must marry him!"

Feeling at ease, Elizabeth allowed herself to laugh in response to her sister's jest, though she knew that Kitty was, at least in part, hoping that Elizabeth *would* accept William, so that she might savor the promised delights.

"Then I suppose there is nothing else to say," said Elizabeth. "If you must have a season with Georgiana, I have no choice but to marry William. I dare say I will muddle through somehow."

"Oh, Lizzy!" exclaimed Kitty, shaking her head. "Only you could say such a thing. Allow yourself to love William. I dare say you will be surprised at how easy it is for you to do so."

Kitty's words kept Elizabeth up late into the night, and throughout that long night, Elizabeth endeavored to determine exactly how she had approached this courtship, and whether she had indeed been complicating the matter unduly. Though she did not think she had tried to make it more difficult, either on herself or on William, there was certainly some merit to Kitty's words. The question was, of course, what was Elizabeth to do with the information she now possessed.

Though sleep had not been plentiful, Elizabeth did not feel like she had just endured an unsettled night when she awoke the next morning. In fact, she was somewhat more invigorated than usual. While a casual observer might not notice any difference and might have attributed it to her normal liveliness if they had, Elizabeth knew that something had changed in her. She knew that Kitty was to thank for her words the previous day.

When William and Georgiana arrived for their usual visit that morning, Elizabeth was surprised, yet gratified, that they came without the Bingley siblings. It seemed an auspicious beginning to a new courtship with William.

It was also clear that William noticed something different about Elizabeth's demeanor, for though he greeted her with perfect ease, and they spoke in much the same manner as they ever had, her openness, where she had always been somewhat guarded, seemed to give him greater courage and hope. And if Elizabeth was honest with herself, she knew she wished for him to hope.

Unfortunately, their newfound felicity did not last long. William and Georgiana had only been at Longbourn for fifteen minutes before the sounds of raised voices penetrated the closed door to the sitting-room. Elizabeth rose to determine what it was, when the door was suddenly flung open and the tall, portly figure of Mr. Collins strode in, closely followed by Mrs. Whitmore.

The sight of the man shocked Elizabeth, and she stood stock still for a moment, trying to understand why he was here. Mr. Collins, for his part, bestowed one of his unctuous smiles upon her, until his own countenance turned to surprise at the sight of William.

"Mr. Darcy!" exclaimed he. "What do you do here, sir?"

"I am visiting with the Miss Bennets," replied William, though his tight jaw spoke to his annoyance at being questioned by Mr. Collins.

"But . . . but . . ." Clearly Mr. Collins was at a loss, though Elizabeth could not hope that the man would remain speechless.

"I am shocked at your behavior, Cousin," said Mr. Collins, finally finding his voice. "Did you not refuse to house *me* when I came to visit you?"

"You arrived without invitation and proposed to stay the night with only my sister and me in residence," reminded Elizabeth, remembering how much this man annoyed her.

"But I am your relation," snapped Mr. Collins. "Surely it was much more proper for *me* to stay here than for you to accommodate Mr. Darcy."

"I agree that Mr. Darcy's staying here *would* be improper, sir. But he is only visiting today with his sister."

"There is ample chaperonage with my sister and Miss Bennet's sister present," added William. "Of course, all of this should mean nothing to you."

The hard look with which he regarded Mr. Collins seemed to suggest that he was not at all amused by the man's presence.

"Yes, well," said Mr. Collins with a disdainful sniff. "Perhaps matters of propriety are served at present. I apologize most profusely, sir, but I have business with Miss Bennet, and I must ask you to leave."

"Mr. Collins," said William, his hard gaze turning into a steely glare, "I believe you have no say as to who visits Longbourn. It would be best if you would stop making demands."

"I shall be responsible for it soon enough," replied Mr. Collins. "When I am wedded to Miss Bennet."

"Mr. Collins!" snapped Elizabeth, her confusion over his presence giving way to annoyance over his continued presumption. "I believe you have already extended your proposal once, and should you choose to renew it, my answer will be the same."

"He proposed to you?" asked William, a strangled sort of exclamation, while at the same time, Mr. Collins said: "Cousin! Surely you cannot mean it!"

Elizabeth directed a curt nod at William, but it was to Mr. Collins that she responded. "I do mean it, sir. I have not changed my opinion that we will not suit."

"Besides, I am already courting Miss Bennet, sir," said William. "There can be no engagement to you."

The shock this pronouncement engendered was enough to render William Collins completely immobile for some moments, as he gazed at them with uncomprehending eyes. But though Elizabeth expected the man to deny it and continue to press his suit, his reaction could not have surprised Elizabeth more.

"Courtship?" growled Mr. Collins, an expression of utter fury coming over his face. Then he rounded on William, and in a voice positively dripping with rage, said: "I cannot comprehend this, sir. Such greed! Such avarice! I suppose I could not have expected the most proper of behavior from *your* family, but I never thought you capable of this!"

"Explain yourself, Mr. Collins!" thundered William. "I have half a mind to call you out, sir!"

But though the man was still the same ineffectual dolt he had been before, Elizabeth was forced to own that he had pluck—certainly much more than he had shown when he had visited before.

"This grasping for another estate, to the detriment of my young cousin. Surely you have enough wealth now, Mr. Darcy, without needing to secure my cousin's estate. Do you not recall that the Lord has said that it is easier for a camel to fit through the eye of a needle than for a rich man to enter into the kingdom of God?"

"Enough!" roared William, and this time his displeasure seemed to pierce Mr. Collins's haughty demeanor, and he almost crumbled in response, though he was not finished speaking.

"I have it on very good authority that you own a large estate and several smaller. Can you not leave this one for me? I have nothing."

"By what convoluted means do you suppose Longbourn should be yours?" demanded William, his disgust for the man evident in his tone.

"My father and grandfather decided to end the entailment," said Elizabeth, not wishing to hear Mr. Collins's grievances on the subject any longer. "In doing so, they cut Mr. Collins's father from the inheritance of the estate."

"Then there is nothing illegal about it, Mr. Collins. It is unfortunate in your case, but for you to importune the Miss Bennets about it is not the mark of good behavior."

There was nothing for Mr. Collins to say to that, though he made a valiant attempt. Unfortunately, no coherent words passed his lips, and soon he descended to muttering.

"It appears you have wasted this journey, sir," said William. "I believe it would be best if you returned to Hunsford at once."

It was a curious sight indeed to see Mr. Collins's countenance turn completely crimson, and it almost induced Elizabeth to laugh at the man, not that he would have appreciated the humor inherent in the situation.

"I cannot return to Hunsford," said Mr. Collins in a small voice. "I have given the Hunsford living up."

Shocked, the occupants of the room looked at Mr. Collins.

"You have given up Hunsford?" asked Mr. Darcy, raising an eyebrow at such a ludicrous statement.

"I have," replied Mr. Collins, apparently understanding Mr. Darcy's tone and taking offense.

"Why?" was William's response.

"Because of your aunt, sir," replied Mr. Collins.

Mr. Darcy frowned. "But I thought you venerated my aunt? Hunsford is a valuable living. I doubt there are many in all of England that are its equal."

A snort escaped Mr. Collins's mouth. "Perhaps the bonds of familial affection have hidden the truth from you, sir, but your aunt is perhaps the most domineering, meddling, officious woman I have ever met. When she instructed me to put shelves in the closets and demanded to know the contents of several confessionals I had recently received, I came to my wits' end and resigned the position. No worldly reward is worth having to put up with her as a mistress."

Elizabeth and William exchanged a glance, which turned out to be a mistake, as neither was able to hold their laughter. Soon, they were laughing openly, tears rolling down their cheeks, ignoring the affronted scowl which adorned Mr. Collins's face.

"I am very sorry, Mr. Collins," said William as soon as he controlled his laughter, his natural politeness coming to the fore. "I apologize for my response, but I am laughing at the situation, not at you. I have rarely heard anyone speak of my aunt in such a fashion, and I doubt I will again. But you truly have discovered the measure of the woman; even those of us in the family only tolerate her, for her moods and meddling are enough to drive a man to drink."

For Elizabeth, though she was still amused with the man's words, she had to own to a large amount of surprise. Mr. Collins had spoken concerning his patroness in such glowing terms that Elizabeth had thought him incapable of seeing her faults, let alone censuring her. This was the most diverted Elizabeth could remember being in quite some time!

"Now, if I understand you correctly, you left because my aunt is officious," said William.

"I did, sir. And now I have no means of supporting myself, and I doubt the little money I saved will go far. My cousin is my only hope, so I journeyed here in the hope of persuading her."

"Only to find she is already in a courtship with me."

Though a scowl came over Mr. Collins's countenance again, he only nodded his head curtly.

"Surely you might find another parish, Mr. Collins," said Elizabeth.

The man shook his head with apparent despondency. "I am not long graduated from the seminary, Cousin. Though I have confidence in my knowledge and abilities, such livings are not easily obtained, for almost every patron in the kingdom seems to have a relation to provide for."

"That is not far from the truth," said William, clearly deep in thought.

"Then how did you obtain this one?" asked Elizabeth. She had to own to a little curiosity. Having not known her cousin at all before his arrival in the autumn, she had no idea as to his connections or anything of his past life.

Mr. Collins sniffed with disdain. "When the previous occupant of the living passed away, Lady Catherine asked for the seminary to send three candidates for her to interview. I was one of them. At the time I thought I was being favored for my knowledge and ability to care for the spiritual wellbeing of her parishioners, but I can now see that she thought me malleable and easily influenced."

"You have my apologies, Mr. Collins," said Elizabeth. "I would gift you Longbourn church's living, though it is not nearly so valuable as Hunsford, I am sure. But my pastor has not been in his position for long."

"I thank you for the sentiment, Cousin," said Mr. Collins, bowing.

"Perhaps there is something that can be done," said William. "How long have you been out of the seminary?"

"Almost a year now, Mr. Darcy," a hint of his previous deference again entering his manner. "In fact, I learned from Lady Catherine that I missed your visit in the spring by only a matter of weeks."

"That is still very new indeed, but you might do."

"Sir?" asked Mr. Collins, hope blooming in his eyes.

"I have a friend who was in search of a parson for his parish, though the last I heard on the matter was some days ago. I could ask him if he is still searching."

"Truly?" cried Mr. Collins. "Mr. Darcy, words cannot express my appreciation for your kindly bestowed benevolence. I had not expected to find such attention, such condescension as this. I heartily thank you!"

Though he made no visible reaction, Elizabeth fancied she could see how William had almost winced at the return of the servile Mr. Collins. It was not a surprise, therefore, when his expression turned firm and he gazed back at her cousin, saying:

"A simple 'thank you' will do, Mr. Collins. Such behavior is almost certainly why my aunt thought you were easily led."

A frown settled over the parson's face. "But should I not show my deference to those who are so far above me in society?"

"Deference and respect is well," said William. "But on occasion your behavior dips to grovelling servility. You are a man, sir—have some confidence in yourself and pride in your abilities, and do not assume another is a better person because they have been born with a title. I do not require such visible displays from those with whom I interact."

Though Elizabeth might not have believed it possible, Mr. Collins actually straightened, and though he was not quite able to look William in the eye—which was rendered all the more amusing because of his anger and accusations only moments before—he appeared to take heart from William's words.

"I understand, Mr. Darcy. I thank you for your instruction."

William replied with a curt nod. "Now, as I was saying, I do not know if my friend has already filled his position, but since you seem to have some integrity, given your refusal to bend to my aunt's will, I would be willing to put you forward as a candidate. Of course, from that point you would need to secure the position on your own merits."

"Of course," said Mr. Collins, and though he was outwardly calm, Elizabeth thought he was almost bouncing with excitement.

"Now, I must warn you, Mr. Collins, that the living is not so large or valuable as my aunt's."

"That does not concern me, Mr. Darcy."

"Very well, I will dispatch a letter as soon as may be. If my friend has already chosen a new parson, I can send word to my parson at a living under my control in the village of Kympton near my home. My parson is only newly appointed to his position less than three years prior, but he has no curate. As the parish is large, he might appreciate the additional assistance."

"Mr. Darcy!" exclaimed Mr. Collins. Then he seemed to remember himself, and after taking a breath and composing himself, Mr. Collins continued: "I do thank you, sir. I had not thought to receive such a boon, I assure you."

"I am happy to do it, Mr. Collins. Unless Mr. Peters receives a promotion, I cannot think it likely that you will ascend to his position, but it will allow you to support yourself, and as long as you perform your duties well, it should lead to another opportunity at a later date."

"That is quite acceptable. I am well aware of the fact that I became a parson long before most of those in my profession. I do thank you for your care. I had no idea I would find such assistance."

William nodded. "Where will you stay until I may receive an answer, Mr. Collins?"

A grimace settled over Mr. Collins's face. "I have no living relations other than the Bennet sisters, Mr. Darcy. I can support myself for a time at the inn in Meryton, but my funds will not be sufficient for a long stay."

Pausing, William seemed to consider this for a moment before a devilish smile settled over his face. "I am currently staying at Netherfield Park with the Bingleys. It is a large estate, and I am certain that Mr.

Bingley would be happy to host you for a few days."

"That would be very much appreciated."

With a nod for the parson, William turned to Elizabeth. "If you would excuse me for a time, Elizabeth, I will escort Mr. Collins to Netherfield and ensure Bingley is agreeable to extending an invitation."

"Of course, William. Kitty and I shall enjoy our visit with Georgiana while you are gone." Elizabeth turned to Mr. Collins. "I am glad matters have worked out for you, Mr. Collins."

"I thank you, Cousin," said Mr. Collins, bowing low. "I am certain we shall see much of each other, especially if I am installed at the curate at Kympton in accordance with your future husband's infinite condescension. I will look forward to our next meeting most eagerly."

With those words, Mr. Collins bowed, indicating his intention to see to his possessions which had been left in Longbourn's front hallway. Elizabeth shared a knowing look with William, and she broke into giggles while he chuckled in response.

"I suppose we should not expect him to change his ways in an instant," said Elizabeth.

"No. But should he become the curate of Kympton, I am certain Peters will take him in hand. He is a good man, and he tolerates no nonsense."

"Then I hope, for Mr. Collins's sake, that Kympton is his destination. I think he would be well-served to function as a curate for some time."

"Of that, Miss Bennet, we are in perfect agreement."

Chapter XXIV

$\mathcal{M}$r. Collins's stay at Netherfield Park contained some unforeseen benefits, though the man was only in residence for a few days. For one, he was another person who provided a buffer between Darcy and Caroline Bingley, and for that Darcy could only be grateful. The woman remained intent upon him, and nothing Darcy could say, short of being completely rude, would induce her to leave off her pursuit. Darcy suspected that she would not desist even if he *was* rude.

Bingley agreed to host Mr. Collins without question as Darcy had known he would, and the man was installed in one of the bedrooms near to where Darcy and Georgiana were staying. Miss Bingley greeted the news of Mr. Collins's residence with the same indifference she displayed to any subject which was not Darcy himself, Georgiana (though her interest in Georgiana was solely a function of her wish to become mistress of Pemberley), society, or fashion. Unfortunately, the woman was to become exasperated with Mr. Collins very quickly.

The first Darcy was able to inform Elizabeth of the matter was the next day when he returned to Longbourn. He walked into the room displaying a grin which he knew Elizabeth, given her perceptive nature, would know indicated something more than simply a happiness to see her.

"Is there some joke to which I am not privy?" said Elizabeth as Darcy bent over and kissed her hand.

"Perhaps," said Darcy. "Of course, the joke is on Miss Bingley, so I must say that I find it all that much more amusing as a result."

"Miss Bingley?" asked Elizabeth, seemingly confused.

"Indeed. For you see, your cousin, Mr. Collins, appears to be completely disrupting Miss Bingley's plans."

"Though perhaps it is not precisely admirable, I believe I can be happy with anything that vexes Miss Bingley."

Darcy felt his grin becoming even wider. "That is certainly something on which we can agree, my dear. For you see, Mr. Collins appears to be so grateful for my assistance with his profession, that he has taken it upon himself to be my advocate at Netherfield."

Laughing, Elizabeth shook her head. "He has seen through Miss Bingley's intentions, has he?"

"Actually, of that I cannot be certain. But he has not been shy about sharing his opinion about the proper behavior of a woman, and as he was present in the sitting-room after dinner last night, and was eager to question me concerning the village in which he will potentially be serving as curate, Miss Bingley was not to able continue on her campaign. In fact, I am considering keeping Mr. Collins in Hertfordshire as long as possible, for he serves as an excellent buffer."

Peals of laughter issued forth from Elizabeth's mouth, and Darcy reveled in the beautiful sound. "Though I cannot find Mr. Collins tolerable in a general sense, I cannot but suppose him to be preferable to Miss Bingley."

"You might think that, but Mr. Collins may in fact improve upon acquaintance."

"I am certain Miss Bingley does not think so."

They laughed together and moved on to other subjects. When he had left with Georgiana that morning, they had suggested that Mr. Collins accompany them, but the man had indicated his desire to rest after his journey the day before. He had retired to his room before the Darcys departed, but Darcy was certain he would return to the sitting-room soon after. The thought of Mr. Collins continually bedeviling Miss Bingley filled him with mirth.

But though Mr. Collins provided them with much amusement, his true worth only became apparent a few days later. As Darcy had thought, his friend had already filled the position which was in his power to give, so with that option unavailable, and with Mr. Peters indicating that he would be happy to have a curate to assist him in his duties, Mr. Collins was to depart for Derbyshire to take up his position.

As Bingley's guest was to depart, he decided to hold a dinner, inviting the Bennet sisters to farewell their cousin. Miss Bingley was not best pleased to be inviting her rival to Netherfield, but Darcy suspected she came to look on the event as an opportunity to show her superiority as a hostess. Darcy could only chuckle and shake his head.

On the appointed day, the Bennet sisters arrived and were shown into the family sitting-room where they were greeted by Bingley with his typical enthusiasm, Mr. Collins with his own brand of civility, and Miss Bingley with indifference. Of course, Darcy and Georgiana were present, but as they had spent the morning and a good part of the afternoon at Longbourn with the sisters, as was their habit, their greetings were more subdued, though almost certainly happier.

Though Darcy had seen Mr. Collins speak to Miss Bingley of her behavior throughout the man's time at Netherfield, the sharpness with which he viewed her when she claimed Darcy's arm as they had been called into dinner was unmistakeable. The man readily did his duty and escorted Kitty and Georgiana in to dinner—Bingley, as the host, walked with Elizabeth—but Mr. Collins's eyes rarely left Miss Bingley's face, a fact to which the woman herself seemed oblivious.

Throughout the meal, Miss Bingley kept up a constant chatter, monopolizing Darcy's attention. As Darcy was seated across and down the table from Elizabeth, who was, of course, seated beside Bingley, and it was difficult to carry on a conversation exclusively with her, he took the simple expedient of saying little and allowing Miss Bingley to continue to speak. The conversation was subdued by the other diners, partially because of Miss Bingley's constant flow of words and the smallness of the table, but also because Mr. Collins spoke little, though Darcy could hardly have fathomed such behavior from the man.

They were already into the main courses of the meal when Mr. Collins, seated to Miss Bingley's other side, cleared his throat, causing Miss Bingley to stop in surprise at the sound.

"Perhaps, Miss Bingley," said he, in a voice clearly heard by everyone in the room, "it would be proper to allow others a share in the conversation."

Miss Bingley's eyes widened, and she seemed to have little notion of what her reply should be.

"I believe the benefits of hearing others' opinions cannot be overstated, for it is through the exchange of ideas, thoughts, and opinions we become truly enlightened. And though I would recommend that all be active participants, as far as their individual natures and knowledge of the subject allow, the benefits of listening to another cannot be overstated."

A stifled giggle drew Darcy's attention and he noted Kitty and Georgiana sitting with their heads together whispering, and apparently attempting not to laugh out loud. For her part, Miss Bingley's surprise turned to disdain, and her nose rose perceptively higher.

"What . . . fascinating relations you possess, Miss Bennet," said Miss Bingley, as she lifted her fork to her mouth.

No one—even Mr. Collins—could have missed the scornful quality in her tone. But the man surprised Darcy once again by smiling at Miss Bingley and saying, in a clear voice:

"I thank you, Miss Bingley, for your kind words. I assure you that I am quite happy with my relations, the Bennets, and I wish them all the best as they walk the paths of life. I hope that we have many years of communion and happiness in each other's company."

"And we are quite happy to be reunited with you, Mr. Collins," said Elizabeth, favoring the man with a smile, though her tone was all amusement. "Our branches of the family have been sundered far too long."

Nodding instead of replying, Mr. Collins soon turned back to Miss Bingley. "I am proud of my cousin, I assure you. Though perhaps my own experience with certain other members of his family was not all I hoped it to be, I have come to see Mr. Darcy as the best of men. He will take prodigious care of Miss Bennet, I am certain."

Darcy almost thought his jaw would drop to the floor; he had not even known that Mr. Collins understood irony, much less that he would make use of it. For her part, Miss Bingley glared back at the man with distaste written upon her brow, and Darcy was certain he saw her nostrils actually flare in her anger and disgust.

"I am afraid I do not see the matter in the same way, Mr. Collins," said Miss Bingley. "It is evident that Mr. Darcy's present course will only result in him marrying beneath him. I believe Mr. Darcy's family expects him to wed someone of a much higher standing."

"My cousin is mistress of Longbourn, her family has lived on the land for generations." Mr. Collins's gaze bored into Miss Bingley, and the woman actually looked away. "There is no disparity of rank, though Mr. Darcy's family *is* much wealthier. Furthermore, I am convinced that in matters of compatibility, similarity of opinion, and true depth of affection, my cousin and Mr. Darcy are almost perfectly matched."

"Here, here!" cried Bingley from the other end of the table. "I cannot agree with you more, Mr. Collins. Perhaps we should all focus on our dinner and allow them to come to a resolution on their own."

"Very well," said Mr. Collins, and he raised his glass to his host.

For the rest of the meal, Miss Bingley was blessedly silent, though she attended to any words spoken between Elizabeth and Darcy. When anyone else spoke, she tended to regard them with contempt, though she never contradicted anything which was said. It was a much more pleasant meal after that, needless to say.

When they had retired to the sitting-room after dinner, having eschewed the separation between the sexes, the entertainment only continued, for Mr. Collins did not appreciate Miss Bingley's continued attempts to single Darcy out, nor was he impressed with her snide comments toward Elizabeth. Miss Bingley had stopped to speak with the housekeeper for a moment, and Elizabeth and Darcy were allowed to proceed to the sitting-room unmolested, where they stood together to the side of the room, speaking in low voices.

"I believe I am coming to understand your comments about my cousin," said Elizabeth. "He truly appears to possess unplumbed depths. I never would have suspected him of it."

"He is not a gifted intellectual," replied Darcy, "but he is not a dullard either." Darcy paused and thought on the matter for a moment, wondering what he should say. Miss Bennet looked on curiously, prompting him to ask her: "Have you any knowledge of your cousin?"

"Nothing other than my own observations. My father confined his comments to Mr. Collins's father, with whom, I believe, he had a falling out."

Darcy nodded. "I should, perhaps, say little, as I have nothing more than conjecture, but I suspect Mr. Collins's childhood was not happy. From a few comments he has made, I suspect his father was a mingy man, and quite likely a little harsh in his discipline. It seems he left Mr. Collins with little upon his death, and everything he has managed to obtain since has been by his own diligence. Though I cannot expect he would be a great orator or give sermons which will inspire the masses, I believe Mr. Collins will actually be a passable clergyman, at least when Peters has had a chance to tutor him."

"Then I am happy for him," said Elizabeth, looking at her cousin with a sad smile. Darcy was filled with warmth—during the course of their acquaintance, Mr. Collins had given Elizabeth little reason to feel esteem for him, but her natural empathy overcame her feelings for the man. She truly was too good.

"Mr. Darcy! I am sorry to keep you waiting, sir."

The sound of Miss Bingley's voice prompted a cringe from Darcy, though, as he was facing away from her, he knew she would not be able to see it. He doubted the woman would care even if she had, so fixed was she on having him for a husband.

"Now, shall we retire to the sofas so that we may continue our conversation from dinner?"

"Excellent idea, Miss Bingley," said Darcy, and he turned to Elizabeth, offered his arm, and led her to a nearby love seat, where he sat her and took the seat next to her.

Miss Bingley followed close behind, and her poisonous glare at Elizabeth told the story of her annoyance. That was when the fun truly began.

"Mr. Bingley," said Mr. Collins, speaking as Miss Bingley was opening her mouth for the same purpose, "I am generally judged to have a good voice, which most of my compatriots at the seminary agreed was easy to listen to. Shall I read for the company tonight?"

Though Bingley was clearly surprised by the offer, he was not of mind to deny it, so he readily gave his permission.

"Excellent, sir. I have just the material here which I believe will be of relevance to the company."

Mr. Collins's eyes alighted on Miss Bingley, his eyes speaking volumes as to whom he was directing his comments. The man produced a book from a pocket in his jacket, and he opened it to a page near the front and began to read.

"Having mentioned wit, let me proceed to warn you against the affectation and the abuse of it. Here our text from the Colossians comes in with propriety, 'Let your Speech be always with Grace, seasoned with Salt.' These remarkable words were addressed to Christians in general. They are considered by the best commentators, as an exhortation to that kind of converse, which, both for matter and manner, shall appear most graceful, and prove most acceptable; being tempered by courteousness and modesty, seasoned with wisdom and discretion, that like salt will serve at the same instant, to prevent its corruption and heighten its flavour. How beautiful this precept in itself!"

When Darcy recognized the passages Mr. Collins was reading from, it was all he could do not to laugh out loud, and he was certain, if her overly bland demeanor was anything to go by, that Elizabeth was in the same straits. Though Darcy had never read any of Dr. Fordyce's works himself, he had heard enough about them to recognize them instantly. Indeed, those works had been much quoted and ridiculed when Darcy went to Cambridge, and often they had been used to mock another.

What followed was a selection of Fordyce's quotes on the proper behavior of young women, all recited in Mr. Collins's surprisingly well modulated voice. Mr. Collins did not read each sermon in its entirety, rather, choosing to devote specific attention to certain passages he no doubt thought would be instructional to Miss Bingley. As each quote proceeded forth from the man's mouth, Darcy found the trial on his composure to be sore indeed.

"At any rate, the faculty termed Wit is commonly looked upon with a suspicious eye, as a two-edged sword, from which not even the sacredness of friendship can secure. It is especially, I think, dreaded in women.

"Who is not shocked by the flippant impertinence of a self-conceited woman that wants to dazzle by the supposed superiority of her powers?

"It is not gold, nor emeralds, nor purple, but modesty, gravity, and decent deportment, that can truly adorn a woman."

And the final quote, which caused Darcy to come closest to losing his composure:

"Only take care, my dear clients, not to hurt it yourselves. Remember how tender a thing a woman's reputation is, how hard to preserve, and when lost how impossible to recover; how frail many, and how dangerous most, of the gifts you have received; what misery and what shame have often been occasioned by abusing them! I tremble for your situation."

And though Mr. Collins was ostensibly reading to the company as a whole, the way his eyes frequently sought Miss Bingley's while he was reading told the true story of whom he thought would best benefit from his words.

This continued for some time, and though Mr. Collins's assertions about his abilities were, as far as Darcy could tell, well founded, there was at least one of the party who did not appreciate it. Of the rest of the party, Georgiana and Kitty appeared to be in an almost constant state of hilarity, and though they refrained from laughing out loud, Darcy thought it was a near thing indeed. Of course, he and Elizabeth, though they attempted to listen carefully, were in a similar situation themselves. Even Bingley, though he might have felt affront at the manner in which his guest was treating his sister, appeared to be attempting to hold back a smile. It was far and away the most amusing evening Darcy had ever spent in the company of Miss Bingley.

Finally, the woman's temper snapped, and she appeared to be able to withstand Mr. Collins's words no longer.

"Let us have some music, shall we?" said she as she shot to her feet as if she had been launched from a cannon. Not waiting for a reply, Miss Bingley stalked off in high dudgeon, wrenched open the cover on the pianoforte, and began playing a piece which almost seemed designed to mimic thunder, her fingers on the keyboard like rocks rolling down a hill.

Mr. Collins simply watched her go, and he closed his book and stowed it in a pocket in his jacket, accepting the thanks from the company for entertaining them with gracious magnanimity. And entertaining it had been! But Mr. Collins's eyes never left Miss Bingley, though she stayed at the pianoforte for some time. Moreover, unless Darcy missed his guess, he seemed to be considering how best to go about Miss Bingley's reclamation.

At length the evening did come to an end, and the Bennet sisters rose to leave Netherfield. Darcy escorted Elizabeth and Kitty to the front door of the estate, Georgiana walking with Kitty, while Bingley and Collins brought up the rear. Miss Bingley had claimed an indisposition and had marched off to her rooms, her stride showing her offense.

As Mr. Collins was to depart for Derbyshire the following morning, this was to be his parting from his cousins, though Darcy knew they would see him in a few weeks when they traveled north in their turn. The farewell was much more cordial than Darcy knew would have been the case, had it taken place only a week prior.

"I thank you, my fine cousins," said Mr. Collins, "for your kindness in allowing me to once again know you. As you are the last of my living family, words cannot express my happiness at our re-established ties. I wish you all the best, and shall anticipate seeing you in Derbyshire when you travel there in a few weeks' time."

"Thank you, Mr. Collins," replied Elizabeth. "I hope your situation in Kympton is to your liking and that you will find another parish very soon."

Mr. Collins bowed low. "I thank you, Cousin, though I am certain I shall be happy to stay in Derbyshire for some time. I do not think it necessary to make haste in order to secure a new parish. God will provide in due time."

"I am sure he will, sir," replied Elizabeth, though in a softer tone of voice.

Though it was dark on the front steps of Netherfield, Darcy thought he caught a glimpse of her gaze alighting on him as she spoke, her eyes sparkling in the light of the torches. The final farewells were said between the group, and Darcy escorted them to their waiting carriage, first handing Kitty in, Elizabeth following. Feeling an immense tenderness for this woman building within him, Darcy bowed over her hand, kissing it with every ounce of love he possessed, before handing her up.

"I shall anticipate seeing you on the morrow, Miss Bennet," said Darcy.

"As shall I," was her response.

The command was given and the carriage soon departed. And Darcy watched it as it moved off into the gloom. When the others turned to depart, Darcy stood, his eyes never leaving the vehicle. Within its confines rode his heart, and Darcy knew he would never be the same again.

When the carriage finally passed from his view, Darcy turned to enter the house, surprised that Bingley was still waiting inside. His expression—closed, whereas Bingley was always an open book— surprised Darcy. It also caused him to feel a little wary, wondering what had come over his friend.

"I will own that I was a little surprised over Mr. Collins's behavior tonight," said Bingley, without preamble.

Darcy nodded. "Perhaps he spoke when he would have best remained silent, but at least he will be gone tomorrow."

Bingley grunted and was silent for a moment. Though his friend had every right to be annoyed with Mr. Collins, Darcy knew he was not unaware of his own sister's behavior, and Darcy thought the matter was not what was dominating Bingley's thoughts.

"Has Georgiana returned to the sitting-room?" asked Darcy, though he thought it unlikely.

Seeming surprised at the sound of his voice, Bingley's eyes darted to Darcy's face, but he soon composed himself. "I believe she and Mr. Collins have already retired for the night. Shall we play a round of billiards, or have a bit of a nightcap?"

"I thank you for the offer, Bingley, but for my part, I think I shall decline. I think I prefer to retire and consider the great pleasure a pair of fine eyes set in the face of a pretty woman can bring." Darcy clapped his friend on the back. "You should have told me how rewarding it was to fall in love with a woman. But if you had, I might have tried it and not been at liberty to love Miss Bennet as I do."

With those words, Darcy made to pass by his friend and continue into the house, but the sound of Bingley's voice arrested his movement.

"The Miss Bennets are to travel to Derbyshire?"

Turning, Darcy regarded his friend, wondering what he was about. "Yes, and Georgiana and I are to travel with them."

Bingley frowned. "I should think that even with your sister, traveling with the Miss Bennets to the north would not be proper."

The note of censure in his friend's voice brought a similar reaction from Darcy. "I dare say you would be correct, but Mr. and Mrs. Gardiner—the Bennets' uncle and aunt—will be traveling with us. Mr. Gardiner is their guardian."

"And they are to stay at Pemberley?"

Though Darcy was beginning to feel quite cross at his friend's inquisition, he answered again with a curt: "Yes, they are. I am sorry, Bingley, but to what do these questions tend?"

"Nothing," replied Bingley, though his effort at nonchalance was a failure. "I merely heard Mr. Collins mention his upcoming meeting with his cousins and was curious for the details."

The explanation did not fool Darcy for an instant, and he fixed his friend with a firm glare. "I am aware that your sister will not be happy with the news, Bingley, but, forgive me if I am blunt, it is of no concern to her. If I am not engaged to Miss Bennet by the time we leave, I am hoping the engagement will be in place before they depart Pemberley."

"So you mean to go through with it."

"Did you doubt me?" Darcy looked at his friend, not certain he knew this Bingley.

But Bingley only waved him off. "Of course not." Bingley sighed and passed a hand through his hair. "Caroline will be impossible once she learns of it."

"I am not disposed to consider your sister's feelings. I am resolved to act with my own happiness in mind. I have told you and Miss Bingley time and again that I will not offer for her. If you would like, I will inform her of my plans tomorrow morning and ensure she understands the situation. If it becomes too uncomfortable, I will take Georgiana and remove to the inn for the remainder of our stay here."

"Of course you do not need to do such a thing," replied Bingley, making a cutting motion with his hand. "As for Caroline, you will forgive me if I wish to delay her fury for as long as possible."

"Very well."

Bowing, Darcy bid his friend good night and climbed the stairs to his room. That, in essence, was what was at fault with Bingley's relationship with his sister. Bingley was stubborn enough when it suited his purposes, but he almost always dealt with her by simply ignoring her. In other matters, such as her behavior, and anything which went contrary to her wishes, he took the path of avoidance.

Of course, to Darcy it mattered little when Miss Bingley was informed of his departure and in whose company he would be. The relative quiet which would be occasioned by leaving her ignorant of the matter was welcome, but the better course would be for Bingley to take his sister in hand, inform her of what would happen, and not allow her to vent her spleen, if necessary, treating her like the spoiled child she was.

But such would never happen with Bingley. He was far too interested in avoiding any unpleasantness to take such a stand. More was the pity.

Chapter XXV

Mr. Collins did indeed depart the morning after the dinner, and Darcy was surprised at how sorry he was to see the man go. With a little training in proper manners, Darcy thought he would be almost tolerable, and Mr. Collins had provided an effective barrier against Miss Bingley's excesses. The thought almost caused Darcy to laugh—perhaps the man should hire himself out to young men attempting to avoid young women who are intent upon snaring them. Maybe that was his calling in life!

Of course, Miss Bingley did not see matters in the same way as Darcy did, and more than once on the morning of Mr. Collins's departure, she was known to look about smugly and say: "How nice it is to have one's house to oneself again."

On the third such occasion, Darcy took the opportunity to have a little amusement at her expense, replying: "I am sorry, Miss Bingley, but I did not realize you wished for your company to be gone with such energy. If it would make you more comfortable, I would be happy to remove to the inn, or perhaps even Sir William might enjoy billeting us for a few weeks."

Eyes widening to an almost comical degree, Miss Bingley stammered out a denial. "I assure you I do not consider your presence to be an imposition." Her face took on a measure of cunning, and she continued:

"In fact, we are so close that I almost consider us to be family. You are welcome to stay at any time, Mr. Darcy. And your enchanting sister, of course."

"Thank you, Miss Bingley." Darcy turned to Georgiana. "Shall we go, my dear? I believe Elizabeth and Kitty are waiting for us."

"Of course, William," said Georgiana. "I must change into my riding habit, but I shall be ready in fewer than fifteen minutes."

Georgiana rose and departed with a word of farewell to Miss Bingley. For the woman herself, she looked at Darcy with barely concealed exasperation.

"Surely there is no call to go there every day, Mr. Darcy."

"We enjoy our time with the Bennets, Miss Bingley," said Darcy, rising to his feet. "I am confident it will not be much longer before Elizabeth and Kitty become part of *our family*. Of course, that is merely a formality, for we already consider them as such."

Bowing, Darcy left the room. But before he was able to escape, he caught a glimpse of a frown on Bingley's face, and he wondered as to its meaning. Surely he could not begrudge Darcy a response to his sister's rudeness; if he would take her in hand himself there would be no need for Darcy to continually remind her of the reality of the situation.

Putting it from his mind, Darcy soon met up with his sister, and thereafter they were mounted on their horses on the way to Longbourn. They did not speak much, for they were both eager to reach Longbourn as quickly as possible. When they arrived, they greeted the Bennet sisters with pleasure, and after a few preparations, they were once again astride their mounts and on their way north.

"This valley to which you are taking us," said Darcy as they rode, "I understand it is not far?"

"Five or six miles, by the path we must ride," replied Elizabeth. "It is on the north side of Oakham Mount, some ways around it. I believe it is actually a part of Mr. Pearce's lands, but as it has no real use, being heavily forested and somewhat rugged, he does not mind others taking in the location."

They rode on for some time, Darcy and Elizabeth in the lead, with Kitty and Georgiana following behind. Inevitably, the conversation turned to Mr. Collins and his departure.

"Mr. Collins left as planned this morning?" asked Elizabeth.

Darcy could not help the smile that came over his face. "He did. Miss Bingley was vocal in her happiness to have her house to herself and her *family* again. Curiously, however, she did not wish for Georgiana and me to leave, though we are most certainly *not* her family."

"I cannot make that woman out." Elizabeth shook her head. "She is so ambitious and haughty, and yet she behaves in such a crass way. Can she not see how others perceive her? Surely she must have realized by now that you are not impressed by her efforts."

"For as long as I have known Miss Bingley she has always believed what she wished to believe. I cannot explain it, but it is the way she is."

Elizabeth nodded and they rode on in silence for some minutes. Darcy's attention was once more drawn back to her when she put a hand in front of her mouth to stifle a giggle.

"Does something amuse you?"

"I was simply remembering last night," replied Elizabeth. She giggled again. "I have never seen such a spectacle, and considering my mother's character, that is almost unfathomable. There is something invariably diverting about Mr. Collins, and though I do not think much of his choice of reading material, somehow one knows when watching him that something of a ridiculous nature will occur."

"Actually, my dear, I must say that I rather esteem Mr. Collins. I had not known that he was such a discerning gentleman. You must own that he saw through Miss Bingley in an instant, and unlike my friend, he was not afraid to chastise her for her excesses."

Elizabeth shook her head. "I think Mr. Bingley is in want of some resolution and firmness of character. But I hope Mr. Collins does not take to quoting from Fordyce when he has occasion to preach. My sister Mary discovered Fordyce at a young age, and she took to quoting him wherever possible."

"Surely you must own that he gives some rather good advice," said Darcy. He smiled at her, an easy sort of amusement he knew she would recognize at once.

"On the contrary, sir," said Elizabeth, her tone prim and not at all amused, "I believe that Fordyce's words were outdated when he wrote them. Now they are positively antiquated."

"Well, for myself, I find that I rather like Fordyce now," replied William easily. "In the future, should Miss Bingley become too persistent in her attentions, I need only dredge up some musty quote from the good reverend, and I have no doubt she will leave me alone for the rest of the day!"

Elizabeth turned and looked sharply at Darcy, but he only fixed her with that easy expression. Elizabeth watched him, but it was not long before her composure cracked and she began to laugh gaily, Darcy joining in with a hearty chuckle.

"Poor Miss Bingley," said Elizabeth when she had managed to

control her giggles. "She was not best pleased last night. I thought her hair would combust from the fury coloring her face."

Darcy laughed. "But it could not happen to a more deserving person, you must agree."

Nodding her head, Elizabeth clucked her mount into a faster trot, pulling ahead of Darcy. He watched her go with some amusement. She was becoming easier in his company—Darcy was certain of it. Hopefully it would not be much longer now.

The feeling persisted and grew stronger. There was simply no doubt that Miss Bennet was becoming more and more attached to Darcy the longer they courted, and Darcy was impatient to secure her hand. He forced himself to wait, however, not wishing to unduly pressure her.

The days turned to weeks and they continued on in Hertfordshire. Regardless of what he had told Elizabeth, Darcy was fortunate that nothing of a serious nature had come up at Pemberley, for he would have been obliged to travel there should it be required, loath though he would have been to depart.

The time for them to all depart for Pemberley was swiftly approaching, and Darcy began to look forward to it with some impatience. He was certain that Miss Bennet was as much in love with him as he was with her, but he determined to give her all the time she required, Darcy had decided to wait until she gave him an unmistakable sign that she wished for him to renew his addresses. But he had all the time in the world. Though perhaps it would be preferable to be formally engaged before they departed for Pemberley, he was quite willing to make her another offer in the north as well. In fact, he could think of half a dozen locations which would serve the purpose admirably.

The situation at Netherfield, by contrast, had deteriorated steadily since the departure of Mr. Collins. Miss Bingley was becoming more desperate over time, and Darcy was careful to ensure that Georgiana was with him at all times in order to avoid any suggestion of impropriety or compromise. Of course, Darcy had seen no indication that Miss Bingley was contemplating such a drastic step, but her shrill pronouncements and almost constant venom toward the Bennet sisters ensured he understood that she was still intent upon having him.

Of more concern to Darcy, however, was the fact that Bingley seemed to be changing the longer the situation persisted. Darcy had never known his friend to be anything other than friendly, amiable, and open, and yet in recent weeks he had turned into a harried man, with a perpetually surprised expression on his face, coupled with a sullenness

Darcy had never before seen. Given several comments Bingley made, it was evident he wished to be back in town with his most recent angel, but his sister insisted on their staying in Hertfordshire. And Darcy had no doubt that the woman harped on him constantly when the Darcys were not present, though what she hoped to accomplish was beyond Darcy's understanding.

If only Miss Bingley would hold her tongue on the subject of the Bennet ladies, Darcy would gladly allow her displeasure without any concern. However, the woman was incapable of holding her tongue. Her comments were a patchwork of veiled criticism of Elizabeth's person, dress, comportment, and every other fault—real or perceived—that she could imagine. Before long, Darcy was at his wit's end, and he took to responding with more censure than he perhaps should. She infuriated him such that he found it difficult to refrain. If she had focused her criticism on *him*, he would have been better able to ignore it.

It all came to a head one day less than a week before the Darcys were scheduled to depart. After spending the day at Longbourn, as was their wont, they had returned to Netherfield in time for dinner and joined their hosts in the sitting-room. It took no great insight to see that Miss Bingley was in an especially poor frame of mind, for her expression was pinched, and she even glared at Georgiana when she made some comment of their day at Longbourn. Bingley too appeared much the same as he had recently, and if the near exhaustion etched on his countenance was any indication, his sister had been at him again all that day. Darcy wished he would just take her in hand and silence her. His predicament was his own doing.

"You walked out?" asked Miss Bingley, catching a comment Georgiana made about their activities that day.

"Yes, Miss Bingley," replied Georgiana. "Longbourn has many concealed delights. There is a pretty little pond hidden in the woods behind the house where we spent some time today, picnicking and enjoying the locale."

"A pond, is it?" The sneer on Miss Bingley's face was unmistakable. "Well, I hope you all enjoyed yourself, though I fear for Miss Eliza's petticoats. I have no doubt she would not give three straws if she should dip them in six inches of mud while walking alongside such a dirty place."

"Her skirts quite escaped the indignity, Miss Bingley," replied Georgiana. In her tone was something Darcy had rarely heard in the past—disgust for Miss Bingley's continued pettiness. Clearly Georgiana was tiring of the woman's constant criticism.

"Then perhaps she is fortunate that there has not been much rain of late," continued Miss Bingley. "Of course, I consider it likely that she would strip down to her chemise and swim in the water, given the chance. No doubt she is quite the wood nymph."

"Though, of course, I cannot speak to the past," said Georgiana, her tone becoming testier by the moment, "she could hardly do such a thing with William present. Should we have been alone, I might have done the same on such a hot day."

An indelicate snigger escaped Miss Bingley's lips. "Perhaps you should rethink your attentions to Miss Eliza, Mr. Darcy. I have the distinct impression that your dear sister is being unduly influenced by the woman. If she is corrupted much more, you may need to send her back to the schoolroom, a place which no doubt will be occupied by your *wife*."

The mean-spirited attack incensed Darcy, but he held his tongue with the greatest of difficulty, while looking at Bingley to see if he would censure his sister. Bingley, however, just shook his head and massaged his temples, lifting his hand and showing it, palm toward Darcy in a gesture of surrender.

The sight enraged Darcy, and he decided that he would not suffer Miss Bingley to continue on in such a fashion — propriety be damned!

"Perhaps you should send her to finishing school before you marry," said Miss Bingley, completely oblivious to Darcy's infuriated state. "If you polish a rock it still remains a rock, but I suppose you must make the attempt."

"Miss Bingley," said Darcy, barely keeping control of his tone of voice, "I have no qualms about Georgiana emulating Miss Bennet. Indeed, I do not believe she could find a better example. Miss Bennet is calm, poised, at ease in any company, and she is beautiful, witty, kind, and loves without reserve. Indeed, the world would be a much better place were there more ladies of Miss Bennet's calibre. She has never required a finishing school, as her disposition is such that confidence and competence comes with ease, lacking any artifice I see so much in many London ladies."

"Indeed?" scoffed Miss Bingley, bringing her hand to her mouth to hide a titter. "I can hardly believe we are speaking of the same woman, Mr. Darcy. I wonder if you are blinded by nothing more than infatuation."

"No, Miss Bingley, I am not. In fact, I see Miss Bennet and her sister clearly, through the eyes of one who has searched his whole life for one as good as she. And I should tell you that I feel quite fortunate to have met her. She is the best woman that I have ever known, and if she should favor me with her hand, I would be honored and humbled. It is not *she* who must live up to *me*—quite the reverse, I assure you."

"She even has you devaluing yourself, sir," said Miss Bingley. "I must question your sanity. To think that she, the mistress of an insignificant estate, a savage who has never even had a season, could be compared with the scion of an earl is completely beyond any comprehension."

"That is because you lack any such qualities yourself," said Darcy.

Shock appeared on the woman's face that he should speak to her so, but Darcy was implacable. "I apologize for speaking in such a way, Miss Bingley, but I cannot tolerate such undeserved, spiteful attacks against the woman I mean to make my wife. I understand you do not get on with her, but I would ask you to keep your vitriol in check when in my presence. I will no longer tolerate it."

Darcy turned to Bingley, glaring at him, challenging him to say something, but as he would not stand up to his sister, Bingley was not about to engage Darcy either. But his eyes told the story of his annoyance with the dispute which was being carried on in his sitting-room, though he was not disposed to put an end to it.

"Miss Bingley," said Darcy, turning his attention back to the woman, who was regarding him with an expression akin to terror, "again I would ask you to keep silent about your opinions, at least for another week. Then, we shall be gone and you will not be forced to endure our presence any longer."

A frown settled over the woman's face. "A week, sir? I had understood that you would stay here through the summer."

"I do not know where you obtained such intelligence," replied Darcy coldly, resisting the urge to glare at his friend, "but it is not true. Georgiana and I will be departing for Pemberley on Tuesday next. I apologize that we have trespassed so long, but I assure you that we shall not do so again."

A slow smile settled over Miss Bingley's face. "You are returning to Pemberley? I cannot but think that it is a good plan, sir. Leave this backwards community and return to your home, where you might gain some perspective.

"Oh, how I long to be at Pemberley! There is no better place in all the world. I remember how we were all there last summer. If only we could recreate the magic of that time."

"I am sorry, Miss Bingley, but I cannot accommodate you this summer. For you see, I will be hosting the woman whom I hope will be my fiancée by the time we depart, her sister, and her dearest aunt and uncle and their children. I am afraid you will need to content yourself with Netherfield."

Though Darcy could not understand how she could so misunderstand him, Miss Bingley became as white as chalk at his pronouncement.

"Surely not!" cried she.

"I assure you I am in earnest. Not only shall we host them, we will join them on the journey north, together take in the sights between Longbourn and Pemberley. I anticipate it very much, I assure you, as I know my sister, the Bennets, and the Gardiners do as well."

"And well they should!" snapped Miss Bingley. "For it appears they have succeeded in entrapping a wealthy man. Should they not find cause to celebrate such success?"

Darcy stood and looked down at Miss Bingley, every unfriendly feeling for this woman roiling through his mind at that moment. Miss Bingley was not a timid woman—in fact she was anything but. In that moment, however, he saw her blanch even whiter than she had before, and she looked away in the face of his fury.

"If anything, Miss Bingley, it is *I* who have insisted on joining *their* family. I have pursued Miss Bennet assiduously, and though she has been cautious in bestowing her affections on me, I believe my efforts are finally taking fruit. You should recall, Miss Bingley, that I am a member of the first circles, and my influence is profound, though I typically do not wield it. In addition, my uncle is an earl. We, neither of us, will tolerate *anyone* speaking unkind and untrue words about a member of our family. I hope very much that Miss Bennet will soon be one of us."

Extending a hand to his sister, who was impaling Miss Bingley with an unfriendly glare, Darcy said: "Come, Georgiana. Let us retire for the night. I am finished listening to such attacks against the woman I love."

Georgiana rose and put her hand in his readily, and he led her from the room. Bingley, he noted, still appeared most unhappy, though he did not speak to anyone.

The moment the door closed behind them, Darcy could hear the sound of raised voices—or a raised voice, to be more precise—and he knew that Miss Bingley was venting her frustration, not only of the failure of her plans, but likely also because of the information Darcy had dropped concerning their imminent departure.

"I cannot make Miss Bingley out," said Georgiana. She was shaking her head and appearing more than a little confused. "Why would a woman want a man who is so set against her?"

"She blinds herself," replied William. "She sees only what she wants to see; what she sees is the Darcy fortune, our standing in society, and others looking up to her as their superior should she become my wife. She does not understand the power a man has over his wife, and how he could make her life miserable."

Georgiana's eyes darted to his. "You would never behave in such a manner, William. Perhaps that is why she ignores such thoughts."

"It is impossible to say that I would not behave in such a way. But it will never happen regardless of what she might do, so we will never find out."

"I hope so, William. Miss Bingley would be a most reprehensible sister. I much prefer the one you are courting now."

"As do I, Sister dear. As do I."

The next morning, Darcy thought to leave Netherfield before either Bingley descended, so as to escape the constant sense of misery which seemed to have descended on the house, especially when Miss Bingley was present. Before entering their separate bedchambers the previous evening, Darcy had arranged with his sister to meet early and depart for Longbourn so that they might take breakfast with the Bennets. As soon as he had awoken, Darcy sent Snell with a short letter down to the servants' quarters, where one of his coachmen was engaged to ride to Longbourn with the missive—at this juncture, Darcy did not even wish to send one of his friend's footmen on the task, so noxious had the environment at Netherfield become.

The response soon came back that of course they were welcome, so Darcy informed his sister, and they completed their preparations for an imminent departure. Unfortunately, all did not work out as Darcy had planned, for as he was escorting his sister down to the entrance, they were confronted by Bingley.

Surprised, Darcy regarded his friend. Bingley's expression that morning was positively stony, and he fidgeted with his cravat, which looked as if it was a little askew, no doubt because of being hurriedly tied. Though he greeted them, it was mumbled and entirely incoherent, and it seemed he could not quite look Darcy in the eye. Darcy had never seen his friend in such a state before.

"Bingley," greeted Darcy. "I am surprised to see you. I have not known you to descend quite this early."

"I . . . Well, that is to say . . ." Bingley stopped, swallowed thickly, and attempted a sickly smile. "I had thought to take breakfast with you this morning. I have not been the best host during your time here."

"It is civil of you I am sure," replied Darcy, "but entirely unnecessary.

In fact, Georgiana and I are to Longbourn for breakfast with the Bennets."

His face falling, Bingley gaped at them. "To Longbourn?" said he, his tone bordering on petulance.

"Yes," replied Darcy. "If you would prefer, perhaps you could accompany us. I am certain Miss Bennet would not mind."

"No thank you," was Bingley's short reply. He almost seemed offended by their intentions.

"Very well," said Darcy. "If you would excuse us."

"Darcy, before you go, might I have a word?"

The sudden application was not a surprise—Darcy had suspected his friend had a specific reason for being there that morning, and it almost certainly had to do with his sister. The tension of the past weeks had frayed Darcy's temper to the point of snapping, and it seemed Bingley was in no better shape. Perhaps it was best that a confrontation take place now.

Darcy turned to his sister, but she anticipated him. "I hope you do not require much of my brother's time, Mr. Bingley, for our friends are waiting for us."

A murmur suggested Bingley's assurances of being brief, but it was largely unintelligible. Darcy looked at his sister with pride—perhaps her words had been a little short, but she was truly coming into her own due to her association with the Bennets. She would never have spoken in such a manner before making their acquaintance.

"Then I shall wait for you in the music room, Brother," said Georgiana.

Agreeing, Darcy turned back to Bingley as his sister walked away. "You have my attention, Bingley. Of what did you wish to speak?"

Eyes darting around the hall, Bingley motioned with his hand. "Perhaps we should take this to the study."

"Of course," replied Darcy, following his friend when he began to walk away."

Soon they had gained the room and Darcy shut the door behind him. It was bright and airy, overlooking the front drive of Netherfield, with shelves along the walls—pitifully understocked as was Bingley's custom—and a large desk in the center. Even had he not been staying at Netherfield, Darcy would have known just from seeing the desk that his friend spent little time there, for all his assurances of wanting to see to his investment. It might have been the room of some anonymous man, for all the effort Bingley had made to make it his own.

Bingley did not sit when they entered the room; rather, he began to pace, muttering under his breath as he did so. Though Darcy could not understand him, he thought he heard Bingley say his sister's name once. It was unsurprising—Darcy was ready to cut the woman himself.

"Well, Bingley? I hope you did not ask me to accompany you simply to watch you pace. The Bennets are waiting for our arrival, so I would prefer to complete whatever business you have in mind quickly so that we may depart."

"Of course you wish to depart," replied Bingley, his tone oozing sarcasm. "You may leave any time you wish, leaving me to endure my sister."

"If you will pardon my saying, Bingley, that is of your own doing. Take her in hand and insist that she cease this objectionable behavior."

"I have tried, but it has little effect. She will not listen."

"Then make her listen, man!" Darcy growled, the frustration of the previous weeks finding its way into his voice. "As her brother, you control her dowry, and as she lives in your house, you have authority over her, regardless of her being of age. Use it to bring her under control! And if she will not desist, then eject her from your house, send her to live with the Hursts, or form her own establishment for her."

Bingley shook his head. "The letters I have received from Hurst indicate that they are happy that Caroline is not present. Louisa has hardly been parted from her since her marriage, and Caroline has been a trial on Hurst's patience. Furthermore, I have also heard that Louisa is with child, and Hurst has decreed that he will not have Caroline upsetting her in such a delicate time. They will not have her."

"Then set up her own establishment, if you cannot control her." Darcy stared at his friend coldly. "I am sorry to be frank, Bingley, but I will not bear the responsibility or the blame for your sister's inability to behave as she ought."

A frown settled over Bingley's face. "Caroline is not so very bad."

Incredulous, Darcy glared at his friend. "She is not? I suppose the constant cruel and spiteful attacks against the woman I am courting are the mark of elegant behavior? It is clear your sister thinks so, as she will not desist, no matter how many times I chastise her."

"You said moments ago that you were not responsible for my sister, and you speak of chastising her?"

"It appears I must, since you will not." Bingley appeared offended, but Darcy just shook his head and shrugged. "Bingley, I have informed you of my willingness to leave Netherfield if the situation becomes too difficult, and it is clear to me that it has. I believe Georgiana and I should have left long ago. Perhaps you might have induced your sister to leave

Hertfordshire altogether, if I was not present."

"Where would you stay?" scoffed Bingley.

"The inn is quite sufficient for us," replied Darcy, "as I told your sister last night. We could also have stayed at Lucas Lodge. Truly it does not signify, as it is obvious we should not have stayed so long. You have my apologies."

"But . . . But . . ." stammered Bingley. "You *cannot* simply leave."

"I assure you that we can. I believe it is for the best, Bingley. I shall make the arrangements directly."

Favoring his friend with a short bow and wondering if their friendship could be salvaged, Darcy turned to leave when he was prevented by the sound of Bingley's desperate voice.

"Darcy, I think you should give serious consideration to Caroline as a prospective bride."

Shocked Darcy turned back to his friend, noting the almost frantic wildness in Bingley's eyes.

"I am sorry, but I must assume I did not hear you properly. Did you just suggest that I should marry your sister?"

Apparently Bingley missed the dangerous undertone in Darcy's voice, for he nodded his head in a vigorous fashion, and for the first time since this infernal interview began, he actually looked Darcy in the eye.

"Caroline has much to offer as a wife. She is intelligent, capable, and manages a house with an adept hand. She is a consummate hostess, a talented entertainer, and she is attractive to look upon. Furthermore, she possesses a fine dowry, which I would be willing to augment should an agreement be reached.

"What can Miss Bennet give you? The headache of another estate—when my sister's dowry has the benefit of being in ready funds—unfashionable manners, and I dare say that she cannot hold a candle to Caroline's beauty."

"If you think *that*, I must think you blind, Bingley," said Darcy, his anger overcoming his good manners."

"That was uncalled for, Darcy," said Bingley, his own countenance darkening in response to Darcy's rudeness.

"Perhaps it was, but given what Georgiana and I have endured since we arrived, it is little enough response."

"What *you* have endured?" cried Bingley. "What of what *I* have endured? You are able to leave the house for hours at a time, visiting with your *paramour*, while I must stay with my sister, listening to her harangues."

"Then control her if you do not wish to listen to her."

Bingley turned away and visibly calmed himself. "I do not wish to fight, Darcy. But I do not believe that you have ever given serious thought to the prospect of my sister as a wife. I believe you should, for she has everything a man could desire."

"I do not love her, Bingley. In fact, given her behavior these past weeks, I believe I am closer to detesting her than the reverse. I will not marry her—not if she was the last woman on earth.

"Furthermore," said Darcy, regarding his friend with a feeling akin to contempt, "your eagerness to marry her off to me smacks of a desperate attempt to rid yourself of her so that you may resume your attentions to the next pretty girl to catch your fancy."

"I am not sure I like your insinuation," said Bingley, though his desperate tone belied his apparent affront.

"And I do not appreciate your attempt to induce me to marry your shrew of a sister."

Turning, Darcy stalked to the door, which he wrenched open with some force. "My first instinct was correct, Bingley," said he as he exited. "Georgiana and I will make immediate arrangements to depart from your house. I only wish that we had done it sooner."

Feeling betrayed, Darcy strode from the room, intent upon finding Georgiana and departing Netherfield as soon as may be. In the fury of his mind, Darcy wondered if he had ever truly known his friend. He had always known Bingley to be somewhat weak-willed and easily led, but he had thought his friend's stubborn streak would serve him in the end to blunt his sister's excesses. Unfortunately, Darcy had underestimated the woman's ability to dominate him. It was unfortunate, but at present, Darcy was not even certain he wished to keep Bingley's friendship. As long as the man refused to deal with his sister, she was a liability to any friendship, and Darcy was becoming convinced he could not ignore that liability any longer.

His sister was soon found in the music room as she had indicated, but Darcy was so caught up in his thoughts and his anger that he did not note the lack of any music emanating from the room. He opened the door and strode in, calling out to her.

"Georgiana, I—"

Darcy's words died in his mouth as he beheld his sister sitting on a sofa with Miss Bingley sitting close by. If Georgiana's expression was any indication, it appeared that she was not happy with the topic, and Darcy could well imagine of what it consisted.

"Oh, Mr. Darcy," said Miss Bingley, favoring him with a calculating smile, "dear Georgiana and I were just discussing what we should do today. Perhaps a little exercise would be beneficial? Netherfield has a quaint little wilderness behind the formal gardens which would be perfect for a picnic."

"You should refer to her as 'Miss Darcy,'" snapped Darcy. "To the best of my knowledge, Georgiana has never given you leave to address her by her given name. To do so without permission is presumptuous and insulting."

The woman's eyes widened, and her mouth opened, but no sound issued forth. Darcy was aware that he was allowing his anger free rein, but he no longer cared. Regardless of the state of his friendship with Bingley, he would no longer endure the man's sister.

"Come, Georgiana," said Darcy, extending his hand to his sister, which she readily took. "It is high time we left Netherfield."

"Oh, but I have planned many events for your amusement today, sir," said Miss Bingley, rising to her feet. "You cannot go to *Longbourn*. I am certain what we have here will be finer than anything you will find *there*."

"We *can* depart and we will," replied Darcy.

It seemed, belatedly, that Miss Bingley understood that he was seriously displeased, but though she opened her mouth, no doubt to continue to spew her venom, Darcy would not allow it.

"Perhaps you have not understood me when I attempted to speak with kindness, Miss Bingley, so let me speak clearly now so there is no misunderstanding. I will not marry you. I do not even like you. You are all that I despise in society. You are grasping, artful, you care not whom you injure in your ambition to ascend society's heights, and you malign the good names of others in your petulance and disappointment. You are the last woman in the world to whom I would ever make an offer of marriage.

"Now, if you will excuse us, Georgiana and I will depart from Netherfield and we will not return—not tonight for the decadent dinner you no doubt have planned in your continued attempts to entice me to offer for you, nor at any time in the future. I am done with you, Miss Bingley. I declaim all acquaintance with you and I will not recognize you if we should meet again."

With those words, Darcy turned and led his sister from the room, leaving Miss Bingley staring at their retreating backs in open-mouthed astonishment.

Chapter XXVI

"*I* cannot comprehend such behavior! Has there ever been anyone as reprehensible as Caroline Bingley?"

Elizabeth was fuming. First, she had received William's letter early that morning, and she had been thrilled to write back inviting them to take breakfast at Longbourn, even while she had felt giddy about the prospect of his coming early. Then, not an hour later, another letter had arrived with an apology, stating that something had occurred which made their attendance impossible, but promising that they would arrive a little later in the morning. Elizabeth had been perplexed but encouraged by the great pains he had taken to reassure her. Thus, Elizabeth and Kitty had continued about their morning as they ever would, confident that the Darcys would arrive before long.

It had taken more time than Elizabeth had expected, but when they finally arrived, they came with the story of the events of the previous evening and that morning. Her good mood of the morning had disappeared, replaced with a fury the likes of which she had rarely felt.

"While I agree with you," said William, who was walking by her side, "it would be best to calm yourself, Elizabeth. I have handled the matter. Georgiana and I are now removed to the inn, and we will not put ourselves in her company again."

"Perhaps you have, William," said Elizabeth. Her anger had not abated a jot. "But that woman is trying to affect *my* happiness. I have half a mind to go to Netherfield and inform her exactly what I think of her."

The sound of William chuckling drew Elizabeth's attention and she turned to him, piercing him with a scowl. Soon, however, she felt the pull of his contagious mirth, and she smiled, however unwillingly.

"I suppose you *did* handle the matter," said Elizabeth, her best efforts at maintaining a serious demeanor failing. "She is now in no doubt as to your exact opinion of her."

"She should have been in no doubt before," said William. "The most galling part of the confrontation this morning is that she goaded me into behaving in an ungentlemanly manner. I have always prided myself on my restraint, but the woman provokes me beyond all endurance."

"William," said Elizabeth, looking him full in the eye, "you should not censure yourself so. You have possessed the patience of a saint with Miss Bingley. Let her assume the blame for her own behavior."

A curt nod was William's response, and Elizabeth put her hand on his arm once again and they continued walking. They were in the back garden where William was telling her of what had occurred, leaving the younger girls inside to their own conversation. Elizabeth had no doubt they were giggling over the matter incessantly, and she thought she would be able to laugh at Miss Bingley at a later date; at present she felt little of the humor of the situation.

"Will you be comfortable at the inn?" asked Elizabeth after they had walked a few moments. "I am certain Sir William would be happy to host you if I asked. In fact, I do not doubt you would be far more welcome guests than the one he previously housed at my request."

The light jest had the desired effect, as William smiled in response. "I do not doubt it, though I will continue to assert that Mr. Collins will make a good sort of man when he has been properly schooled in how to conduct himself.

"As for your comments about our accommodations, let us refrain from imposing on Sir William. Though I know he would be happy to do it, we are quite comfortable staying at the inn. It is only a matter of days before we depart for the north, and I imagine we will do little more than sleep there regardless."

Feeling unaccountably shy, Elizabeth ducked her head and nodded.

"Now, I have something else to discuss with you, Elizabeth."

Looking up, Elizabeth felt almost overcome by the intensity with which he gazed at her. Her heart fluttered in response to his scrutiny, and she wondered with idle inattention how his eyes could have become so impossibly blue. Did such a shade exist anywhere else in creation?

"It seems your feelings have undergone a remarkable change these past weeks, and your comment concerning Miss Bingley affecting *your* happiness has given me reason to hope that you might have another answer if I possessed enough courage to ask for your hand again."

Her breath stilling with anticipation, Elizabeth found it impossible to look away from him. "I would not say that my feelings have changed, William."

"Oh?" was his lazy reply. "That does not seem correct to me."

"That is because you cannot read my mind. In fact, my feelings have not changed at all. They have only deepened, akin to an ocean compared with the small pond in Longbourn's wilderness."

William watched her, his whole being focused in this single, sublime moment. "Tell me, Elizabeth."

"What, shall I say the words first?" asked Elizabeth, feeling a hint of her impish nature coming to the fore.

"If you recall, I have already said them, and I received a rejection for my troubles."

"A rejection?" asked Elizabeth, arching her brow. "You entered into a courtship for your troubles. I do not believe that constituted a rejection."

"But I have said them all the same. I would hear them from you."

"Then you shall. I love you, Fitzwilliam Darcy. I love you completely, utterly, and without reservation. There, will that do?"

"Minx!" exclaimed William, delighted laughter bubbling up from his breast.

"You received what you wished. Now, do you not have something to say to me?"

"I do," replied William. "Miss Elizabeth Bennet, I love you completely, utterly, and without reservation. Would you do me the honor of joining our fates together and accepting my proposal of marriage?"

"Of course I will," said Elizabeth, laughing at how he echoed her words.

The expression of delight which came over William's face became him and rendered him handsomer than ever before. But Elizabeth was not able to contemplate the matter, as William's head descended and he claimed her lips in a first, sweet kiss.

The sound of giggling interrupted the moment, and William and Elizabeth separated, noting the presence of their sisters standing nearby. The two girls flew to them, extending their congratulations, amid embraces and delighted laughter.

"I had wondered when you would come to the point, William!" exclaimed Kitty as the four celebrated together.

"I came to the point some time ago, Kitty," replied William with good humor. "It seems your sister required more time to determine whether I was a good risk. For all she knew, I might have been a pauper intent upon gaining her fortune."

Laughter erupted all around, and Elizabeth turned a mock glare on her fiancé. "Perhaps I should have waited longer before accepting, sir, if I am to be teased in this fashion."

"Perhaps you should have," said William, "but since you have now accepted, I think I shall insist upon your keeping your word."

"And so you should!" exclaimed Georgiana. "You have gifted me with two fine sisters, and I do not think I will allow them to slip away."

They soon entered the house, and the mood continued to be euphoric. The Whitmores were apprised of their situation and their congratulations were sincere and heartfelt. And as the company were invited to Lucas Lodge for dinner that night, Elizabeth did not doubt that the news would be all over Meryton by the following day.

As she watched the man who was to be her husband, Elizabeth could not help reflect that Miss Bingley had paid a role in their current happiness. Though she knew it would have come at some time, likely in the near future, the woman's behavior in inducing William and Georgiana's departure from Netherfield had undoubtedly sped their reaching an understanding. Elizabeth felt almost grateful to the spiteful woman, though she rather suspected Miss Bingley would not appreciate the sentiment.

While the mood at Longbourn was joyous, that at Netherfield could not be more different. With the Darcys' departure and all that had preceded it, the blackest of moods settled over the two left in residence. While Charles blamed Caroline for the straining and possible dissolution of his friendship with Mr. Darcy, Caroline felt nothing but contempt for her brother. Though she had insisted upon his speaking to Mr. Darcy to remind the man of her eligibility and qualifications to be his wife, she had no doubt that he had made a hash of it.

From her earliest childhood, Caroline had always been blessed with confidence. The youngest child in a family of three, she had been the beloved child, the one who could do no wrong. She had always known that she was destined for great things, the one who would pull her family up from their despised ties to trade to a much higher sphere of society. Caroline Bingley had always known she would be greater than her humble beginnings suggested.

Her confidence had only been reinforced when she had learned of her brother's friendship with Mr. Darcy. There were few anywhere in any level of society that mattered who had not heard of the Darcys of Pemberley. For Caroline to secure the master of Pemberley would cement forever the Bingleys into their new sphere, and would make Caroline one of the leading ladies of society. And she had never doubted her ultimate success, regardless of Mr. Darcy's seeming caution and his hesitance in offering for her. The time in Hertfordshire had been meant to ensure that she left an engaged woman, engaged to the only man who mattered to her.

To be prevented from achieving her goal by the upstart machinations of Eliza Bennet was a difficult pill to swallow. How Caroline despised the woman! But given how Mr. Darcy had spoken to her when he departed, Caroline began to understand that he was unlikely to offer for her. Bile filled her throat whenever she thought of the man carrying on with that *woman*. It was clear to Caroline that breeding did not necessarily guarantee discernment.

No, there was nothing left to be done concerning Mr. Darcy. He had made his choice, and though Caroline railed against it, she knew that despite all that she could do, Mr. Darcy was lost to her. There must be more discriminating men in London who would recognize her qualities. Perhaps she could even snare an earl, or even better! Caroline was eager to get on with her search.

But it was not in Caroline's character to forget the slights of others. Mr. Darcy had slighted her, shunted her to the side in favor of an improper, fortuneless, adventuress without style or fashion, and that could not be forgotten. Caroline had business in Meryton with Mr. Darcy and Miss Eliza Bennet, and if she could, she would make his life miserable—well, more miserable than it was already destined to be, since he was to marry the trollop. She only needed to determine how it was to be done.

The day after the Darcys had left Netherfield, Caroline, in a fit of restlessness, decided she simply must get out of the house and further think on the matter at hand. Charles was less than useless—his time had been spent moaning about the strain on his friendship with Mr. Darcy and how he wished to return to town and Miss Cranston. Since Caroline had not the slightest idea of who this Miss Cranston was, she knew the woman was not of significance in the ton, so she was keen to keep Charles from her. Now, more than ever, he would need to be guided to a woman who would meet the Bingleys' needs for advancement in society.

Having nowhere else to go, Caroline went to Meryton, and she was disgusted all over again. The shops were all small, dingy, and dirty, the locals would not know high fashion if it was waved in front of their noses, and the streets were dusty and narrow. Caroline could not wait to leave this mortifying place behind!

However, while she was looking at a hideous bolt of cloth through a shop window, she happened to notice a reflection in the window. When Caroline turned, there in all her glory, stood the bane of Caroline's existence. The woman stood some ways away to the side of the road, next to a shop, speaking with several other women, like a queen looking down on the masses, no doubt crowing to all and sundry about her *conquest*. Mr. Darcy stood watching with an indulgent smile on his face.

Caroline felt the bile rise in her mouth at the very sight—Mr. Darcy had never looked at Caroline in such a fashion in all the time she had known him. For a moment she saw red, and she took a step toward them, intent upon giving them a richly deserved stinging set-down.

But then she noticed something else. Beyond their party at some distance, stood a man in a red coat watching them, and though he was too far away to be seen clearly, Caroline thought he looked on them with even more loathing than Caroline. Thinking quickly, and seeing a potential opportunity, Caroline turned her back on Mr. Darcy's party and made her way across the street, walking slowly so as to avoid drawing notice. Once that was done, she walked down the street toward the officer, and when she chanced a glance back, she noted that they had continued on in the other direction.

Laughing to herself concerning her good fortune, she strolled up to the officer, watching his wary surprise at seeing her.

"Yes?" was his gruff question.

"Pardon me, sir, but given your expression, I would guess that you have something against Miss Eliza Bennet?"

A snort was his response. He turned back to his scrutiny of the party, but when Caroline turned to look herself, she noted that they had gone into one of the shops. All the better.

"If you will excuse me," said the man. He bowed and turned to march away when Caroline called out to him.

"You have my apologies, sir; I had no wish to anger you. Obviously you have been ill-used by the woman, and as one who has had the same experience, I had thought to condole with you."

"Miss Bingley," said he, "you have obviously not been in town long enough to know what I hold against Darcy and Miss Bennet. I am sorry, but I have no wish to enlighten you."

"I do not need to know it, sir. I am more interested in vengeance."

The man stopped, looked at her, appraising her, she thought, clearly uncertain. Then he bowed slightly and said: "George Wickham, at your service."

The woman was handsome enough, Wickham supposed, but he fancied he could see a perpetual sneer about her mouth, as if it were her natural expression. Yes, Wickham had heard of Miss Bingley. She was thought to be haughty, proud, and above her company without reason, if the talk of her ties to trade were accurate. Wickham, of course, did not care about such things. She was rumored to have a twenty-thousand pound dowry, which was certainly enough to tempt him, but his own observation of a few moments told him she was a shrew, and one who would make a man miserable within fifteen minutes of marriage.

This talk of vengeance, however . . . Retaliation for what Darcy and Miss Eliza had done to him was all Wickham had thought about these past weeks, but he had never had the opportunity to do anything about it. His duties had become onerous and he was usually watched. In addition, the regiment was to depart in only a few days, leaving him short on time to do what was needed. And the woman was always protected by that blasted mountain of a footman! He had heard about their engagement—idly he wondered if this Miss Bingley had herself—but there were ways to break an engagement, if one were resourceful enough. But time was becoming an enemy.

"Caroline Bingley, though it seems you already have the advantage of me."

Wickham shrugged. "I will own I have heard your name. Now, what is it you propose?"

"What is it that you wish, Mr. Wickham?"

"What is it that *you* wish?"

"Vengeance, nothing more, and nothing less, as I have already said."

"The talk was that you wished to be mistress of Pemberley."

A grimace settled over the woman's face, and Wickham smiled to himself. It seemed like she had been disabused of the notion that Darcy would ever stoop to marry one from a line of tradesmen. No doubt the lesson had been delivered with Darcy's usual form of tact. The vicious man in Wickham enjoyed her discomfort.

"Perhaps I did have designs on that front," said Miss Bingley. "But I have realized that I should aspire to a man much higher than Mr. Darcy. I wish to leave this town, but before I do, I wish for Mr. Darcy—and particularly *Eliza Bennet*—to share in my misery. I wish for them both to know that I will not be used in such an infamous manner. I wish for them to lose the opportunity to marry each other, and if they go against the gossip of society, I wish for them to be completely shunned because of it. In short, I wish them ruined.

"Now, I ask again, Mr. Wickham—what is it that *you* require?"

Though Wickham was well aware of his character, and knew some men would call him libertine, rogue, or villain, what he was not was stupid. A stupid man did not go far when he engaged in the activities in which Wickham had; the chances of paying for his crimes were great. Wickham was well aware that the woman was not interested in *him*, and did not care if he was adversely affected by her stratagems. In fact, he knew she would set it up so that whatever blame was to be apportioned would be borne solely by him if she could manage it.

She also seemed to be unaware of what had happened between Wickham and Miss Bennet, else she likely would have approached him in a different manner. It had been made abundantly clear to Wickham that should he accost Miss Bennet, even to pass her on the street, his debts would immediately be called in and he would be sent to Marshalsea, after, of course, being court-martialed. Wickham was not about to risk that.

Then again, it may be that there was another way to get what he wanted—and what he wanted was Elizabeth Bennet and the money she possessed. He would take her in the middle of the street, if necessary, and laugh at her mortification. Miss Bingley might present him that opportunity, but she did not need to know of what his ultimate goal consisted.

"What did you have in mind?" asked Wickham.

"To make her unmarriageable. I want her shunned and despised as she should be. I want her name to become one of ridicule, and for Mr. Darcy to feel the worst sort of misery imaginable."

It was easy to smile at the woman, for Wickham could see that they were kindred spirits. Indeed, they would have made a good pair, had his thoughts tended in that direction. And as she spoke more, Wickham's heart lightened considerably. Here was the opportunity for which he had been waiting. He would finally have his revenge on Darcy.

Chapter XXVII

The transition from courting couple to one engaged saw few real changes for William and Elizabeth, though the few that Elizabeth noticed were rather profound. For one, the couple was afforded a little more latitude than they were before, which meant they were not always trailed by dutiful sisters, especially when they walked out of doors. The second change was that William was much freer with his affections, telling Elizabeth he loved her whenever the chance presented itself, and Elizabeth, not to be outdone, she said teasingly, responded with much vigor and affection.

The final change was in part brought about by the greater freedom which they possessed, and though it might not have been scrupulously proper, it was the part of their closer relationship that Elizabeth liked best. Whereas before, William had been attentive to the appearance of propriety, touching Elizabeth only when bowing to kiss her hand, when her hand rested lightly upon his arm, or, on occasion, when he reached out and touched a hand gently to her arm when making a point during conversation, now he was more demonstrative. Much more demonstrative, in fact.

Though their first kiss in the gardens behind Longbourn—and its rather injudicious interruption by their sisters—had been short and sweet and left Elizabeth feeling breathless for more, their subsequent encounters always left Elizabeth feeling there was more to intimacy to come, but they oddly satisfied her nonetheless. The first such occasion happened later the afternoon of their engagement when they had occasion to escape from the house before they were to depart to join the Lucas family for dinner at Lucas Lodge.

When they had reached the end of the park, Elizabeth had thought to head back toward the house, when William paused and said, gesturing to the left: "This trail leads off through the trees?"

"Yes," replied Elizabeth, not quite understanding why he was asking. "It loops around to the west, before it turns and eventually leads to the pond."

"Come," said William, and he began striding into the trees, pulling Elizabeth along with him.

"William!" cried Elizabeth. "We must depart before long."

But William did not slow his pace. He walked for several moments, looking back through the trees. It seemed like he was satisfied after a few moments when he stopped, glanced around and, after seeing no one, turned to her, his eyes burning with desire, as he once again lowered his lips to hers.

A surprised squeak escaped Elizabeth's lips, but it soon turned to a moan of delight as the tantalizing feeling of his lips on hers, his hot breath filling her mouth overtook her senses, and she lost herself in the kiss.

If the kiss behind the house was soft and sweet, this one was a raging torrent of desire, and Elizabeth felt as if she were on a rowboat passing through a hurricane. If the pure need in his kiss was not enough, the pleasurable sensations it engendered made Elizabeth feel as if she were about to expire from the sheer ecstasy. It was the most sublime moment Elizabeth had ever experienced.

At length, though Elizabeth could never be certain how long they had stood there in that attitude, William softened the kiss, allowing her to breathe, which she did, drawing in great gulps of air. He continued to kiss her, nipping at the corners of her mouth, her eyes, cheeks, and the side of her neck, but with a more playful quality than the pure desire he had displayed before. And though Elizabeth knew not how, she had ended with her arms around his neck while his were around her back, the tips of her toes barely reaching the ground.

Feeling almost overwhelmed, Elizabeth sighed and allowed her heels to touch the ground again, while she buried her head in his chest.

"I am sorry, Elizabeth," said William, his voice husky, as if the emotion of the moment had stolen his ability to speak. "You know not how long I've wished to do that."

"I had no notion a kiss could be so . . ."

"Passionate?"

Elizabeth giggled. "Lethal."

The full throated sound of William's laugh reverberated through his chest, and Elizabeth laughed along with him, certain she could stay this close to him for the rest of her life.

"I suppose we shall be required to refrain from doing this again," said William. "I cannot have you expire before I have even met you at the altar."

"Oh, I am certain I can stave off the reaper now, William. Perhaps it is a matter of practicing often."

"If that be all that is required, then I shall be happy to oblige."

They stayed that way for several moments, until, knowing they would need to depart soon, they separated in order to return to the house. It was at that moment Elizabeth remembered what they had been doing and she pinked with embarrassment.

"I cannot return to the house!" cried she. "I am certain I look a fright!"

"In fact, there is little damage to your appearance," replied William. "Your lips are, perhaps, a little pink, but there is naught else amiss."

That was the first lesson Elizabeth received about the more passionate Fitzwilliam Darcy. Though they indulged in such activities as often as they had occasion to, William was always careful that no boundary that should not be crossed was ever approached. Furthermore, though Elizabeth often wondered if their activities led to damage to her appearance, she always emerged from them with perfectly coiffed hair, and with her dress always in the same state in which she entered. It was gratifying, to say the least, that William cared enough about her and her reputation that he never attempted to go beyond that which was acceptable.

Though Elizabeth was an innocent in the manner of young women of her time, she was also worldly enough—and more importantly had lived her life on a farm—to have a good notion of what the marriage act entailed. She was also aware that young men in love with their young women could often become impatient, leading to liberties taken. With William, Elizabeth was not required to keep him under good regulation, as he maintained that himself. She loved him all the more because of it.

Their arrival back at Longbourn was, indeed, little commented on, and their sisters did not seem to have any indication of what had happened between them. Of course, the worldlier Whitmores were not fooled, but as Elizabeth had returned in perfect order, Mr. Whitmore only raised an eyebrow at Mr. Darcy, which was returned with a steady look of his own. An understanding seemed to pass between the two men—Mr. Whitmore would allow such liberties, and Mr. Darcy promised he would not abuse the man's trust.

When they entered Lucas Lodge, William instantly requested a moment of Sir William's time and gained his approval for the engagement in lieu of Mr. Gardiner's agreement, which they had decided would be sought only after they had arrived the following Monday, the day before they were scheduled to depart for the north. Sir William, of course, bestowed his permission with hearty congratulations and exclamations concerning their ultimate felicity and his happiness.

"There!" said Lady Lucas as she engulfed Elizabeth in an embrace. "I knew your young man would not take any such step without the goal being firmly in mind. I cannot be happier for you, my dear."

The family sat down to a boisterous dinner, as was the wont at the Lucas home, and many toasts were raised to the happy couple, and many exclamations of happiness and expectations for their future felicity as friends. But Charlotte, Elizabeth's closest friend throughout her life, gave her own congratulations in a more subdued manner, though no less happy.

"It seems you are to be a grand lady indeed, Lizzy," said Charlotte.

"Oh, Charlotte, you know that is not my character. It is not William's to be so puffed up either. Given the choice, I am certain he would sequester us at Pemberley, never to go into society."

"Perhaps he would, but he also knows his duty. And you will be part of that duty, for a wife's abilities as a hostess must be important to a man of Mr. Darcy's stature."

"You must come and stay with us, when we have settled in," said Elizabeth. "I would love to have my dearest friend with me when I take such steps."

"Shall you throw me in the paths of other rich men?"

The two friends laughed together. "Oh, Charlotte! If you wish, that is indeed what I shall do."

"Thank you, Lizzy. But I believe I would be happy with a man who simply esteems me, regardless of his consequence."

"Then we shall find that for you too," replied Elizabeth.

Since it was only a few days before they were to depart, much of Elizabeth's time was spent ensuring that everything would be in hand for Mr. Whitmore while she was absent. The man proved his worth, however, by being aware of everything that was happening on the estate and assuring Elizabeth that he would have no trouble while she was away.

"You need not worry, Miss Bennet," said he. "You may enjoy yourself in the north without reference to the estate. I shall have everything in hand."

"I think you shall be required to have everything in hand for the foreseeable future," said Elizabeth. "Since I shall be living in the north, you will be entrusted with the day to day operation of the estate."

"And I am gratified with your trust. I will do my best to ensure the changes you have implemented are carried out and that the estate continues to prosper." Then he smiled and changed the subject: "As you know, I lived in the north for many years, and I was actually born in a neighboring shire. I believe you will not be disappointed with the sights you will see. It is truly a wonderful county."

"Is the Matlock estate also in Derbyshire?" asked Elizabeth, curious.

"Indeed, it is. Snowlock is some twenty miles south of Pemberley. I have visited on occasion with my mentor, who was an intimate of the elder Mr. Wickham."

"And which is the more beautiful estate, do you think?"

Laughing at the playful note in her voice, Mr. Whitmore was quick to answer. "Oh, Pemberley, without a doubt. Even the earl would allow Pemberley to be the superior estate in terms of beauty, though there has always been a friendly rivalry about which estate is the greater."

"And which one was, in your opinion?"

"Come now, Miss Bennet," replied Mr. Whitmore. "I was employed at Snowlock. Surely you cannot think I would be so disloyal as to suggest that Pemberley is the greater."

Elizabeth laughed along with him. "I assumed no such thing."

"Good." Then he leaned closer, as if to impart a secret. "The truth is the estates are very similar in income and size, though Pemberley is the more diverse. That, in my opinion, must give it the edge."

"Mr. Whitmore!" exclaimed Elizabeth. "I am shocked and appalled at your traitorous words!"

When informed of the matter, Mr. Darcy preened and strutted like a peacock, and Elizabeth laughed at his antics. It was gratifying to hear such an opinion from a man he respected so.

They continued on in this manner for the remaining days of their residence in Hertfordshire until the last day had arrived before they were to leave. The Gardiners were to come to Longbourn early that afternoon, and Elizabeth, wishing for some new reading material, proposed a walk in to Meryton. Kitty readily agreed, indicating a wish to procure a few small items for herself, and they departed with the ever-faithful John in attendance.

They stopped by the inn, where they met Georgiana, who indicated her intention to go with them, and they departed, promising to meet William later; he was seeing to some tasks in preparation for their departure. They perused a few shops in Meryton in high spirits, Elizabeth purchasing a few books to take with her to Derbyshire, while Kitty bought a new bonnet to wear on the morrow when they departed, and the sisters generally had a marvellous time in company with their future sister. And when they had finished, they turned their steps back toward the inn, where William had engaged a room for them to eat a light luncheon.

The street was busy that morning, carts laden with goods passing here and there, while those on foot hurried on their way, and even a few of the shopkeepers had stepped out onto the street to cry attention to their wares. In all, it was a typical Monday morning.

After, were Elizabeth to be asked, she would have said that it was the crowded streets which prevented her from seeing the trouble before it came upon them. In reality, it was almost certainly as much due to the fact that the three ladies were having so much fun and were, as a consequence, unaware of their surroundings. Thus, they were almost on Miss Bingley before they noticed that she stood there, blocking their way.

"Miss Eliza Bennet," said the woman, her name spoken as if it were an epithet. Miss Bingley was dressed, as she normally was, in a dress which would have been ostentatious for a ball in London, with a headdress of feathers standing high above her raven head.

"Miss Bingley," replied Elizabeth, unintimidated by the woman. "I might have thought you and your brother would have departed for London."

"What we do is no concern to one such as you," replied Miss Bingley, her tone faintly bored. "But I could not leave Meryton before congratulating you on your . . . conquest of the great Mr. Darcy."

"It was no conquest, Miss Bingley. If anything, *Mr. Darcy* won me over with his ardent manner of courting."

Looking down her nose at Elizabeth, who was only a little shorter than Miss Bingley, was no mean feat, but the woman somehow managed it. When she spoke, however, it was as if Elizabeth had not even spoken.

"You must tell me how you did it, my dear." Miss Bingley sidled in closer, as if eager to hear a confidence. "Mr. Darcy has been pursued by many, you know, and until you came along, none were successful in capturing him. It must have taken all of your allurement to succeed where many others have failed."

Elizabeth eyed the other woman, returning contempt for contempt. "In fact, it was Mr. Darcy who persuaded *me*. I did not need to attempt a compromise in order to induce Mr. Darcy to offer for me."

"William loves Elizabeth!" exclaimed Georgiana. She surged forward to confront Miss Bingley. "William could never have loved a woman such as you. You are everything he hates!"

Those words finally cracked Miss Bingley's façade, and she glared at Georgiana. "So says a timorous little girl who must rely on her brother for her courage. You must know, *dear Georgiana*, that no man will ever offer for you who does not covet your dowry and the connection to your brother."

"Miss Bingley," said Elizabeth stepping forward and pushing an incensed Georgiana behind her, "I do not know what you hope to accomplish here, but whatever it is, I suggest you leave and do not compel William to act against you."

"Perhaps if I respected Mr. Darcy I might fear him. But I have lost every ounce of the admiration I once possessed. Any man who cannot see *you* for what you are cannot be a man who commands any sort of respect."

"What I am?" asked Elizabeth, a harsh laugh impacting Miss Bingley. "I know *exactly* what I am, Miss Bingley. Do you know what you are?"

"She is the daughter of a tradesman giving herself airs," said Georgiana from behind Elizabeth.

At that moment, several things happened at once. First, Miss Bingley stiffened, feeling all the insult of Georgiana's words, and she stepped forward, a truly ugly expression on her face and lightning in her eyes.

At the same time, John stepped forward to put himself between his mistress and the enraged woman, saying: "You shall not harm the mistress!"

At nearly the same time as John spoke, Elizabeth felt her arm being grasped in a vise grip, and she was wrenched around to come face to face with George Wickham. Idly Elizabeth noted the crazed expression on his face, the way he leered at her, promising retribution, his hot putrid breath as he exhaled in her face.

"Finally, I have you, my *dear* Miss Bennet," said he, though his voice was more of an animalistic snarl than that of a man.

In a motion which seemed like it lasted forever, and one which would haunt Elizabeth's dreams for months, his hand rose to the top of her dress, and Elizabeth was powerless to stop him from ripping her dress asunder.

But a flurry of muslin and rage pushed past her and a hand appeared out of nowhere, impacting the man's face with a resounding slap. The impact forced Wickham's face to the side, and he released Elizabeth's arm involuntarily, but before he could even think of recovering, that bundle of muslin attacked him, kicking and punching, all the while screaming: "No! You shall not harm my sister!"

Still shielding his head with his arms, Wickham turned a murderous glare on Kitty, who was still assaulting him, screeching her fury. Elizabeth, by now, had begun to recover her wits, and she saw Mr. Wickham's intent, she rushed forward to protect her sister.

"How dare you touch me!" screamed Elizabeth as she confronted the man. Elizabeth grasped her sister and pulled her back.

Kitty, feeling her sister's arms around her, burst into tears and buried her face in Elizabeth's shoulder. "He was trying to take you away from me!"

With her sister on her shoulder, Elizabeth faced Mr. Wickham, seeing the scratches Kitty had inflicted on the man's face, and the purpling hand print on his left cheek.

"How dare you, sir!" growled Elizabeth. "I shall see you in prison for this."

"Not if I have you first," sneered Mr. Wickham.

He stalked forward, though what he meant to do, Elizabeth could not say, when John once again pushed past Elizabeth and intercepted Mr. Wickham, taking his upraised hand, and in a deft motion twisting it behind the man's back.

"I would not try anything else, if I were you," snarled John in Mr. Wickham's ear, though it was clearly audible to Elizabeth.

Several soldiers rushed up and they took control of Mr. Wickham from John. But the most welcome sight was William striding up, taking control of the situation as was his wont.

"It seems you have finally crossed the line, Wickham," said William, stepping up to Elizabeth and grasping her hand.

He brought her hand up and inspected it, and for the first time, Elizabeth noticed the bruising around her wrist where Mr. Wickham had grasped it.

"Are you in pain, Elizabeth?"

"No, William," replied Elizabeth, glaring at Mr. Wickham. "I believe his bark is worse than his bite. He is not nearly as smooth and charming as he likes to think."

William nodded, though he caressed her wrist gently as he looked back at the soldiers, and at Lieutenant Denny in particular, who appeared to be the highest ranking officer present.

"Mr. Denny, if you would be so good as to convey Mr. Wickham to Colonel Forster and see that he is confined. I will come to discuss the matter with the colonel after I have seen the ladies back to their home."

With a nod, Mr. Denny took control of the situation, fixing Mr. Wickham with a particularly dark look. Elizabeth understood in an instant—Mr. Denny was the one who had introduced Mr. Wickham to the colonel. The man's behavior was a poor reflection on him.

But before Mr. Wickham could be taken away, William stepped forward, and in a low voice, said: "With your debts, I doubt you will emerge from prison before you are old and grey. Think of that as you rot where you should have been all these years."

"Then perhaps there is nothing preventing me from ruining your precious sister," growled Mr. Wickham.

William only gave the man a slight smile. "Speak, if you wish. Your reputation is now such that no one will believe you. Your lies will only make it worse."

Stepping back, William motioned for the men to take him away, and Mr. Wickham was escorted from the area, screaming promises of vengeance the entire way. Once he was gone, William turned his attention back to the other player in the drama.

"Miss Bingley," said William, stepping toward the woman. Elizabeth almost laughed, for Miss Bingley was attempting to sidle away, a curious sight given her plumes waving in the air, proving such an ostentatious dress was not conducive to sneaking about.

When William spoke, Miss Bingley straightened and glared, haughty and proud, almost daring him to speak to her. To say William was unimpressed was a rather large understatement.

"What part have you played in this farce, Miss Bingley?" said William.

"I know nothing of what has happened."

"You confronted and distracted us!" cried Georgiana. "It was only when John's attention was on *you* that Mr. Wickham accosted Elizabeth."

Miss Bingley sneered at Georgiana. "You are nothing but a silly little girl. I do not even know the man who spoke with Miss Bennet." Then Miss Bingley turned her venomous gaze on Elizabeth. "Perhaps she has encouraged him. It would not surprise me."

A rumbling of discontent sounded all around them, and Elizabeth glanced around, seeing for the first time that they had drawn a crowd to see the spectacle. Shuddering, Elizabeth thought to end the confrontation; the situation had the potential to be ruinous for her reputation.

"She is lying," said a voice, and Mr. Dwyer, the butcher, stepped forward. "Why, only the other day I saw the two of them speaking right outside my shop. They was watching your party, Miss Bennet, as you walked down the street."

"This man does not know of what he speaks," said Miss Bingley. "Question Miss Bennet on her relationship with that man. I am innocent."

"As if we would believe the likes of you over Miss Bennet, who has lived in the neighborhood all her life," said Mr. Roberts, the bootmaker. "We all know what she has done for us. All you have ever given us is your contempt."

A murmur of agreement sounded throughout the crowd, and Elizabeth felt like weeping with relief. She well knew how a few idle reports could prove disastrous, but the good people of Meryton had just proved themselves to be true and loyal friends.

"Come, let us end this," said William. "I thank you all for your care of my betrothed."

As the crowd began to disperse, a gasp was heard, and Elizabeth looked over at Miss Bingley, noting the whiteness of her countenance. "Betrothed?" asked she, though it came out as a strangled whisper.

"That is the natural result of a courtship, is it not?" said William, his tone laced with irony.

Miss Bingley only gaped. Elizabeth was not disposed to pity the woman; she had reaped what she had sown, though she was much too prideful to accept, or even understand, the fact. It was also rather amusing to see the woman so surprised, though she must have known that it was likely they would eventually be engaged. For all of her bluster about having lost any respect for William, it appeared like the sure news of their engagement had caused her great pain. Had she truly still expected that she might secure him, even after all that had happened? It was unfathomable.

"Go home, Miss Bingley," said William. "I assume you have a carriage or a horse waiting somewhere?"

The woman only nodded her head mutely.

"Then go back to Netherfield. You may tell your brother that I will be there to speak to him this afternoon."

For a moment, Miss Bingley only stood there and looked at him. Then she turned on her heel without a word and strode off. Needless to say, no one was saddened at her departure.

"Come with me, Elizabeth," said William, taking her hand and putting it in his arm. "I believe we should have Mr. Jones look at your wrist."

"I am well, William," replied Elizabeth, looking down at the appendage. It had purpled already, but when Elizabeth flexed it experimentally, it gave her no pain.

"Indulge me, dearest," replied William. "Since we are to depart on the morrow, I would wish to ensure all is well."

What could one say to such concern? Elizabeth felt warm all over and she allowed herself to be led away. Soon, she, Georgiana, and Kitty had been installed in one of the small dining rooms the inn kept for the use of their customers, waiting for the apothecary to arrive. William, once he had seen to their comfort, had excused himself to ride to Netherfield to speak to Mr. Bingley about what had happened. Elizabeth would have loved to be a fly on the wall for that discussion.

By the time Darcy arrived at Netherfield, he had worked himself up to a state of constant anger. That Miss Bingley had been a part of the day's events had never been in question—Darcy had seen the guilt in Miss Bingley's eyes long before hearing the testimony from the butcher about her discussion with Wickham. He had no doubt that the two, at heart similar to each other in their vicious characters, had planned the day's events. Darcy was certain the goal had been to compromise Miss Bennet and make her unmarriageable to anyone other than Wickham, not that it would have worked, regardless of what had happened.

Still, to plot against a woman who had never done either of them any harm filled Darcy with rage. His opinion of Bingley, which had taken a beating lately, rendered Darcy uncertain his friend would act, but he hoped he could get his friend to do something with his sister. His decision to declaim all acquaintance with Miss Bingley, however, would not be changed. It would almost certainly destroy any ambitions she had to a marriage with any sort of highly placed gentleman.

When Darcy dismounted in front of the estate, he passed the reins off to a waiting stable hand with instructions to walk him in the vicinity of the door, as Darcy did not expect to be long. Then he climbed the front steps and rang the bell, where he was allowed into the manor by Fosset, the Netherfield butler.

"Has Miss Bingley returned, Fosset?" asked Darcy as he handed his gloves off to the man.

"Yes, Mr. Darcy. She returned not a half hour gone and went straight to her room."

"Good," said Darcy. "And Bingley?"

"In his study, I believe."

It was all Darcy could do not to snort. The man had never paid any special attention to the room in the past. Why he could be in there now, Darcy could not fathom. He should have taken his sister back to town when it became clear there was nothing here for either of them.

"Thank you, Fosset. I know the way, so there is no need to announce me."

The butler bowed, and he allowed Darcy to go into the estate on his own. It was a trick of the imagination, no doubt, but Darcy felt the atmosphere was oppressive, almost as if Netherfield had become a house of despair. Regardless, it *was* quiet, and of even the servants Darcy could see little sign. Perhaps they had let many of them go, due to an imminent return to town.

The door was closed when Darcy arrived, and though he would have preferred to simply walk in and confront his friend—though that designation was now in question—a lifetime of polite manners dictated he knock. When he heard the voice from inside bidding him to enter, he did so without hesitation.

The first thing that assaulted Darcy's senses was the scent of spirits, sweet and heavy in the room. Bingley sat on one of the sofas across from the fireplace, a glass of port in his hand, as he stared morosely into the cold hearth.

Shocked, for he had never seen Bingley like this before, he gaped at his friend, noting the way that Bingley's lifeless eyes found him, then widened in recognition.

"Darcy? What do you do here?"

At least it was clear that his friend was still somewhat sober. But Darcy still could not help but wonder what had affected Bingley so.

"Is it not a little early in the day for such things, Bingley?"

Grimacing, Bingley stood and walked toward the desk, setting the glass down upon it. Darcy was pleased to note there was nothing of a stagger in the man's gait; he had obviously not consumed as much as Darcy had feared.

"Trust me, my friend," said Bingley as he turned to face Darcy, "if you had been stuck in this house with Caroline's company these last days, you would have taken to drink too."

The reminder of why he had come returned to Darcy's mind, and he suppressed a scowl. He stepped fully into the room and closed the door behind him, though when Bingley offered him a seat, Darcy declined.

"Tell me, Bingley, are you aware of your sister's whereabouts?"

Bingley frowned. "Somewhere in the house, I would assume. I have not seen her since this morning, and for that, I can count myself fortunate."

"Then you have no knowledge of the fact that she went to Meryton?"

The frown on Bingley's face deepened. "Go to Meryton? Why ever would she do that? She has never made a secret of her disdain for Meryton."

"I shall tell you why she went there," said Darcy, almost shaking with suppressed rage. "She went there because of a plot she had cooked up with George Wickham to attempt to compromise *my betrothed* in the middle of Meryton's busiest street."

Aghast, Bingley looked on Darcy with horror, a fact which, in itself, told Darcy of his friend's innocence. "She did *what?*" asked Bingley. "And with whom? Is Wickham not that man who has given you trouble over the years?"

"He is," replied Darcy shortly. "Apparently they met on the street several days ago, and I strongly suspect the plot was born then, though I have no idea of the length of their acquaintance."

Bingley's knees suddenly seemed unable to support him, and he sat heavily on a nearby chair. "I swear, Darcy, I had no notion of such a plot. She has been almost unbearable since you left, and I have attempted to avoid her whenever possible."

"Why did you not take her back to London, man?" demanded Darcy. "I had made my sentiments clear to you both; why would you continue on when there was nothing here for you?"

A grimace was Bingley's initial response. "I attempted to induce her to leave, Darcy. London during the summer is difficult to endure, but I had thought to visit our relations in York. But Caroline was adamant that she did not wish to leave yet." Bingley shook his head. "I wished to return to Miss Cranston, but I know not if she is even still in town. York seemed like the best option."

Darcy neither knew nor cared who Miss Cranston was, though at this point he was relieved that Miss Colford had not succumbed to Bingley's charm; he did not know the young woman herself, but her brother was a good man. He might have been obliged to warn Colford concerning Bingley, given how affairs had turned out.

"Bingley," said Darcy, speaking slowly in order to control his anger, "you are responsible for Miss Bingley. Though I begin to sound as if I am repeating myself time and time again, you may make the decisions, and she has no choice but to go with you. You should have taken the initiative and removed her from the neighborhood."

"How could I have known she would try something like this?" cried

Bingley.

"Of course, you could not have known. But Bingley, you knew how fixated she was on me, how much she despised Elizabeth. Would it not have been better to have removed her from the area so she could have focused on her future?"

"You do not know what Caroline is like when she has been denied."

"Bingley, are you the man of the house, or is your sister?"

Stiffening at the insult, Bingley refused to respond. He only glared at Darcy.

"You may take offense, but you do not act in a manner which would suggest that you are the one who makes the decisions. I do not wish to cast aspersions on your character, so I will make no further accusations. What I wish to know now, is what you will do concerning this situation."

His glare did not abate for a moment, but soon Bingley turned away and grimaced. "I suppose we are for York then. I do not doubt that Caroline will wish to be as far away from you as possible, so it should not be difficult to persuade her to leave."

By the time his friend had finished speaking, Darcy felt like yelling at him, or shaking him until he was able to see sense. He controlled himself only by the slimmest margins and directed a baleful look at Bingley, which he knew the man could not see due to his refusal to return his gaze.

"What about her punishment, Bingley? Will you allow this attack on my betrothed to pass without reprisal?"

"Should I give my sister another reason to make my life miserable?" replied Bingley. "She has failed. Knowing that you and Miss Bennet will be happy will be punishment enough, I am sure."

"I am sorry, Bingley, but I disagree."

"What would you have me do?" demanded Bingley, this time standing and looking Darcy straight in the eye. "As you have eagerly pointed out several times, Caroline is *my* responsibility. Should I send her to Bedlam, to live in squalor and disease, opening myself up to whispers of having an insane sister? I will not do it."

"No, but you can bar her from society, ensure you knows of your wrath. You cannot simply allow it to pass without response. Bingley, if she is not checked, she will be a much heavier burden on you in society, if she is not already. Banish her to York, or send her to a convent—I care not. But ignoring the event does nothing, for she will not learn that her actions have consequences."

"You are keen to insert yourself in my affairs, are you not?" Bingley was as angry as Darcy had ever seen him. "Your assertions concerning

how my honor was engaged with Miss Kitty. The girl is obviously not
affected by my leaving—I am glad I left and did not come back. Ever
since we became friends, you are here with your advice and your
meddling. I believe it is time for you to step back and allow me to live
my life without your interference."

"Just because Kitty does not appear hurt by your actions *now* does
not mean she was not affected by your abandonment," replied Darcy, a
cold fury burning in his veins. "I have it on good authority that she was
infatuated with you and spent many months trying to overcome her
disappointment."

Bingley only waved his hand and picked up his forgotten glass of
port, swallowing it in one gulp. "So say you. But you have never been as
all-knowing or wise as you believe you are."

"I have faults, the same as any other man," replied Darcy, "but I hope
they do not consist of going from one comely young woman to another
without thought to their feelings or reputations. And I certainly hope
that I do not display my haughty manners for all to see, arrogantly
dismiss good people as beneath me when they are in fact above me in
society's eyes. And I have never actively attempted to ruin a good
woman's reputation, conspiring with a known rake and womanizer to
do so."

A glare was Bingley's only response, though the tightening around
his eyes told Darcy that his barbs had hit their marks. Oh, they had
scored—many times over, in fact.

"Very well, Bingley," said Darcy, when the other man said nothing
more. "I shall give you your wish. From this point, I am severing our
friendship. I will not cut you in public, but I shall no longer maintain a
friendship with a man who takes so little care of his reputation and so
little control over his affairs.

"On your sister, however, I will bring down the full force of my
displeasure. I will publish it far and wide that Miss Bingley's pretentions
of intimacy with my family are exactly that. She will receive no notice
from me or any of my family, and if she attempts to approach me, I will
cut her. She is dead to me, Bingley. Given how I have tolerated her airs
over the years due to nothing more than a desire to retain your
friendship, it is far less than I could do."

"Then you had best leave," was Bingley's cold reply.

"I believe I shall. Good bye, Bingley. I sincerely hope that one day
you find the strength of character within yourself to take control of your
life. At present, it is your sister who controls you."

With a curt bow, which was little more than a brief nod of his head,

Darcy strode from the room. The sound of his footsteps along the halls as he strode from Netherfield for the last time formed a strange counterpoint against the beating of his heart, which was elevated due to the emotion and anger of the moment. Darcy had never been so disappointed—Bingley had truly never been the man he had thought he was. If only his cousin was not in the fighting in Spain! Darcy wished he could consult with him, though he did not doubt he would be required to endure Fitzwilliam's smugness about the matter. Fitzwilliam had always maintained that Bingley was a puppy who would ever be ruled over by his shrewish sister. It seemed he was right.

As Darcy reached the main hall, he took his gloves and hat from Fosset, who had no doubt been alerted to his coming by the sounds of his boots on the tiles, and he thanked the man, eager to be gone from this place. As he turned to survey the hall one final time, Darcy saw the figure of Miss Bingley, standing two steps up the grand staircase, watching him as he readied to depart. For a brief moment, Darcy thought to give her a harsh set-down, tell her exactly what he thought of her.

But then he realized he had no interest in ever speaking with the woman again. No doubt Bingley would inform her, if he ever worked the courage up to do so. For Darcy's part, he cared not what the woman would do again. He was done with her.

So, he looked at her, and with a slow and deliberate action, he turned away from the woman, ignoring the gasp that, even at this late date, informed him of Miss Bingley's continued hope that he might be persuaded to relent. A moment later he was out the door and astride his horse once more, riding back toward Meryton and his future. He did not look back even once.

"I would ask you not to brood, William."

A slow smile settled over William's face, and he turned to regard Elizabeth. "I am not brooding, Elizabeth. I am merely thinking of all that has occurred."

"Simple thoughts for you are akin to brooding in others."

"That is a grave accusation indeed. Perhaps you should attempt to cheer me up."

Laughing, Elizabeth sidled closer to him, until they were seated side by side, and though it was perhaps not completely proper, she laid her head down on his shoulder, sighing in contentment. She supposed it would ever be thus; William's tendency toward excessive grave thought and bearing the burdens which were not his own was ingrained, and

Elizabeth supposed that she would never be able to completely induce him to leave it behind. But she was determined to make his life as light and happy as possible.

"I simply . . ." said William, after they had sat for some moments in silence. "Well, let us say that though I had known for some time that Bingley's friendship might be forfeit, actually breaking it off has affected me profoundly."

When he fell silent again, Elizabeth waited for him to speak, and when he did not, she decided to prompt him, knowing he would feel better if he unburdened himself.

"How did you even meet Mr. Bingley? Given his roots in trade, I doubt he ever would have found acceptance in London if you had not extended your friendship."

"You are correct about that." William paused and chuckled to himself. "I met Bingley in Cambridge. It was my last year of schooling when he arrived for his first. Our apartments were nearby, but what drew my attention was his perpetually sunny disposition and his penchant for laughing.

"As you know, I am much more inclined toward soberness. As we took some interest in the same activities, it was natural that we should form a friendship. I did indeed introduce him to others of my acquaintance, and though I do not think anyone became so close to him as I was, he was still able to acquit himself well and gain many friends."

"But there was something missing," said Elizabeth.

William sighed. "I knew almost from the start that he was not of a forceful disposition. This impression was further enforced when I met his sister." William's lip curled with contempt. "Even as a young woman only newly out in society, Miss Bingley's tempers controlled her brother. I tried for years to encourage him to control her, but it has all been for naught. It is unfortunate, as I believe Bingley has the ability to be a great man, but his inability to stand up to her and his propensity to wandering eyes robs from his character.

"And the elder sister?"

"Mrs. Hurst is actually the most serious of the lot of them. She is intelligent, I think, but much as Bingley has done, I think she has simply agreed with Miss Bingley over the years in order to prevent disagreements. But whereas her behavior is understandable, Bingley is the one who is in control of Miss Bingley's dowry and her living arrangements. Mrs. Hurst is not, yet she has suffered because of her sister for years.

"Hurst, as you are probably aware, dislikes his sister, but it was not until recently that he took steps to ensure Miss Bingley would not rule over them. He is a bit of a bore, but not truly a bad sort."

Lifting her head from his shoulder, Elizabeth turned and gazed into William's eyes. He had often told her of what he considered to be her fine eyes, but Elizabeth found his own equally mesmerizing. She had told him more than once, albeit in a joking fashion, that it was not fair that so handsome a man possessed eyes so deep, that it felt like she was looking into his very soul.

"I do not think you could have done anything else, William," said Elizabeth. "It sounds like Mr. Bingley is determined to continue on this course."

"That does not remove the hurt of losing a friend."

"No, it does not." Elizabeth leaned forward and pressed a light kiss to his lips. "But it does prove you to be an excellent man, one who demands excellence in his friends. Considering Miss Bingley's actions, you could not allow your friendship to continue unless Mr. Bingley acted to curb her. Since he did not, you were left with no choice."

Though his slumped shoulders told the story of his feelings at the moment, William nodded. "That is why I did it. I could not have you forever concerned about Miss Bingley, having to be on guard for her acid comments and overt contempt. Regardless of what Bingley decided, I would not have allowed his sister to continue to impose upon my generosity.

A snort escaped Darcy's lips. "In fact, I have known the woman has often used my name to gain entrance into higher society functions. I do not think she was aware of my knowledge, but though I never instructed her to stop in deference to my friendship with Bingley, whenever I became aware of her excesses, I quietly informed those involved that her claim of acquaintance was far less than what she intimated."

A shake of her head was all Elizabeth could muster in the face of such blatant social climbing. "She truly is a reprehensible creature. I believe she will soon be feeling the effects of her behavior."

"I believe she already has. London society is preternaturally aware of everything that happens, and I am certain there were some who knew of my estrangement from Bingley, if nothing else than through the fact that we were not often seen in each other's company this spring. Your cut of Miss Bingley did not help her cause, though you were a relative unknown at the time. Now, however, her ambitions are at an end, unless she can find another to sponsor her."

William's exasperated huff told Elizabeth his opinion of the chances of that ever happening. She was content, she decided. She had no need to seek vengeance on Miss Bingley, for the woman had already been punished harshly.

"And Mr. Wickham?" asked Elizabeth.

William shrugged. "My meeting with Colonel Forster was short and concise. Wickham will be court-martialed, and then sent to Marshalsea. Perhaps I might relent at some point, but I shall not do it for some time."

"I disagree, William."

The hint of a question in William's eyes prompted Elizabeth to explain herself.

"If you relent, he returns to his life. I understand you do not wish to take responsibility for him again, but he cannot be allowed to prey on the good people of England any longer."

An affectionate smile came over William's face. "My fierce Lizzy. You are correct, of course. No amount of respect for my father should affect my decisions regarding Wickham. I have allowed such sentiments to rule me for far too long."

"Then perhaps he should stay there for some time," said Elizabeth.

"Agreed. Then, once he has learned his lesson —"

This time it was Elizabeth's shaken head which told William what she thought of that possibility. He leaned forward and returned her kiss.

"Once he has had time enough for a better man to have learned his lesson, it might be best to have him transported."

Elizabeth nodded. "I would hate to be required to constantly watch to ensure Mr. Wickham is not trying to cause us harm."

Agreed in the particulars, they settled back into their positions. Elizabeth was content — she was marrying the best man of her acquaintance, and she could not be happier. There would no doubt be times of trial, and she thought they would eventually have some rather infamous disagreements. But in the end, she knew he would stand by her, as she would stand by him. Together they would face whatever challenges life put in their path.

"Elizabeth."

Starting, Elizabeth realized she had begun to drop off into slumber. She straightened and directed a smile at her betrothed. "You are entirely too comfortable to lean against, William."

"Be that as it may, it is now after noon, and I believe we should return to Longbourn to greet your uncle."

"And your trunks must be delivered as well," said Elizabeth. As her relations were to be in residence, they had decided that the Darcys would spend the night at Longbourn as well. Elizabeth was thrilled, for she knew they would not be parted again.

"Yes. Shall we depart, dearest?"

Allowing herself to be drawn up, Elizabeth looked about the small parlor, noting that Georgiana and Kitty were speaking quietly on the other side of the table, though their frequent looks in Elizabeth's direction betrayed the topic of their conversation. Their intention to depart was communicated, and the girls rose readily and accompanied them from the room.

But before they left, William's hand on her wrist halted Elizabeth's progress. She turned to him, wondering what he was about, when he lowered his lips to hers, kissing her sweetly and tenderly. He broke the kiss immediately, as their sisters were waiting outside for them, but even in that brief kiss, Elizabeth could tell his heart was engaged to its fullest extent.

"Thank you for accepting me, Elizabeth," said he, his voice husky with emotion. "I count myself the most fortunate of men."

"I dare say you are, William. Most fortunate indeed."

The sound of their laughter preceded them from the room, and they stepped out into their future. Never had it looked so bright.

Chapter XXVIII

As her uncle had said, laughter evident in his voice, Pemberley contained trees and woods enough for even Elizabeth's enthusiasm for them. Indeed, though Elizabeth had commented on the greatness of the park within moments of their passing through Pemberley's outer boundaries, even she had not expected to still be riding in the coach ten minutes later. And yet there seemed to be no end to the vast succession of rolling hills, trees, mantled with their verdant summer greenery, and even a brook or two in the distance. Already Elizabeth was almost watering at the mouth, anticipating the delights of the many pathways she was certain existed on the estate.

"Tell me, William," said Elizabeth, turning to her betrothed and favoring him with an impish sort of smile, "shall we reach the house before night has fallen, or are we doomed to continue to roam through the darkness?"

William grinned; Elizabeth knew that this was one of the things he loved about her best, so she endeavored bringing his laughter to voice as often as she could.

"It is possible," said he, though he looked out the window thoughtfully. "Though perhaps we should search for a campsite before we go too much longer. Traveling these woods at night can be dangerous, after all."

"Teasing man!" cried Elizabeth. "How dare you speak to me in such a manner?"

"Methinks that is a case of the pot calling the kettle black," said Mrs. Gardiner.

"Our Lizzy does have a way with words," agreed her husband.

Elizabeth only ignored them with a superior sniff, emulating quite exactly the behavior of a young lady who could not be forgotten soon enough. Though William still turned contemplative at times, thinking of his broken friendship with Mr. Bingley, Elizabeth often adopted Miss Bingley's superior tones, eliciting a laugh and turning his attention to a singular young lady whose society he was most certainly *not* unhappy to be without.

Their journey through the counties leading to Derbyshire had mostly been swift, though at times they had stopped to take in a sight or two. When they had crossed the border into the shire, however, their pace had slowed and they had taken more time to see what the county had to offer. Though the great houses, such as Blenheim and Chatsworth, had been well worth seeing, Elizabeth preferred to savor the hills and rocks, noting the proximity of the peak district in the distance when they had traveled close to Pemberley.

Kitty and Georgiana followed in the second carriage with Mrs. Annesley and the elder Gardiner children, which rolled along close behind the lead carriage, and as the girls had become close friends, they seemed to prefer it that way. It made sense as they were of age with each other and had much to discuss, and in general, were less interested in the sights their elder relations savored. This suited Elizabeth well indeed, as it allowed her to sit with her betrothed more often, along with her beloved relations who had done much for her.

One other thing the journey had accomplished—as they had been traveling for more than a week, Elizabeth's birthday had passed, which meant that she was now of age. It had not meant much in a general sense, as she had agreed to join her life to William's, still it had been an important milestone for her.

Now, only a few days later, she was about to see her new home for the first time, and Elizabeth found herself impatient to be savoring its delights.

"Patience, Elizabeth," said William, seemingly reading her eagerness. "We are almost there."

Eschewing a response, knowing it would likely come out a little caustic, Elizabeth instead concentrated her attention out the open window of the carriage. The woods through which they traveled had grown thicker and were obscuring any view of the surrounding countryside. Annoyed with the trees for their presumption, Elizabeth glared at them. The road ahead of them passed through a narrow passage between the encroaching trees, which seemed, despite the clear skies overhead, to be the whole of the world, so close had the woods grown to their path. A few moments later, however, the coach began to climb the side of a gentle rise, and some hints of the land beyond started to come into focus.

Soon the coach approached the crest of the hill, and at the highest point, just as Elizabeth was about to lose her patience entirely, the trees to the left gave way, allowing a clear view out into the valley beyond. And what a sight it was!

Situated some distance away stood a large, handsome stone building, looming like a sentinel over the surrounding county, watching over it like some squatting giant. The land about it had largely been cleared of the woods, which had been their constant company since entering the estate, and in the distance, Elizabeth could see crops growing, though she could not quite make out what they were. Closer to the house, she could see some hint of the gardens beyond, but in the front, there was a small lake, fed by a stream which meandered in from the distant hills. On the other end of the lake, another stream began its long journey to whatever river it joined, and thence to the ocean.

"Elizabeth?" a voice interrupted her contemplation of the sight before her, and she turned to see William regarding her with a knowing look. "There is a path which will take us to the front drive. Would you and Mr. and Mrs. Gardiner like to take the longer route? We shall arrive long before darkness, and I dare say you would appreciate the chance to see a little more of the estate today and stretch your legs."

"For our part, I think we will decline, Darcy," said Uncle Gardiner.

"I am unfortunately not a great walker, unlike my niece," said Mrs. Gardiner. "But I think it would be acceptable for you to walk, if you would prefer."

Though he had suggested the walk, it was clear to Elizabeth that William had intended the entire company to walk with them, and he hesitated, clearly torn between wishing to arrive at the house with them, and have Elizabeth to himself for a time.

"For myself, I would love to walk for a time," said Elizabeth. "Surely Georgiana can welcome Kitty and my aunt and uncle to Pemberley. You may show us the house at a later time."

That declaration resolved William's indecision, and he readily agreed. The two alighted from the carriage, and after a quick assurance to her aunt and uncle that they would not tarry, they departed.

The fields were fine and the late afternoon, pleasant, with a hint of a breeze to cool them from the heat of the day. Elizabeth looked about with interest as they walked, gasping in delight as each new sight made itself known to her, drawing her in with its beauty.

"What do you think, Elizabeth?" asked William, after they had walked some distance.

"Are you attempting to fish for compliments, Mr. Darcy?" asked Elizabeth teasingly.

"No," replied William. "But I would have your honest opinion. It means much to me."

"Then I shall tell you. It is simply the most breathtaking sight. Your home is happily situated, William, perhaps more so than any place I have ever seen."

"Better than Chatsworth?"

Laughing, Elizabeth said: "Chatsworth has its own appeal, to be certain. But I must say that it does not have the wild and authentic charm of your home."

"*Our home*, my Elizabeth."

Elizabeth nodded her head, allowing his comment, though turning her attention back to the conversation. "Chatsworth is very beautiful, of course, but I find I prefer the wild and untamed to the signs of man's influence on every rock and tree."

"My ancestors felt the same, as you can see," replied William. "Though there are formal gardens aplenty behind the house, we have always attempted to allow the greater part of the park to remain pristine and unspoiled."

"And it is simply marvelous!" exclaimed Elizabeth. "It speaks to the foresight of your ancestors."

"Yet some would disagree. Should you ever visit my aunt Lady Catherine's home, you will see the exact opposite."

"Then again, Kent is a much more tamed part of the kingdom," said Elizabeth.

"That is true, but her opinion is that man should be the lord of the land he owns, and nothing should be left to chance. The gardens at Rosings are almost sterile, though from a certain point of view, I suppose they are lovely."

Since William had not announced their engagement until they left Hertfordshire, it had been unknown to society in general, though it had been all over Meryton. An important consideration, however, was that it was still unknown to his aunt. When she did discover it, William had assured Elizabeth, she would no doubt fly into a rage, and he would not put it past her to journey all the way to Pemberley to make her sentiments known. When it happened, he doubted there was anyone in all of Derbyshire who would be ignorant of her explosion of anger.

"Then perhaps we shall have to persuade your aunt to allow a little of the randomness of nature into her estate."

William snorted, telling her what he thought the chances of that were. "I am glad you like it," said he, changing the subject back to Pemberley. "Since this is to be your home, I would have you love it as much as I do."

"I feel I do already, William." Elizabeth paused and fixed an arch look on him. "Of course, Pemberley is nothing to Longbourn, but I am impressed with what you have done."

They exchanged a glance and both broke out into laughter at once. It felt so good to laugh with him; for as he was not prone to an excess of mirth, when he did laugh, it was to be cherished all that much more.

"In fact," continued Elizabeth, "I think that had you simply brought me to Pemberley from the outset, I would have accepted your proposal immediately."

Still chuckling, William wiped a tear from his eyes. "You should have told me earlier, dearest. I would have done it straight off."

They continued to walk, and within moments, they had made the edge of the lake. From there, it was only a short journey to the front of the house. It was perhaps even more impressive close up than it had been from a distance. Close to the house, Elizabeth could see the fine workmanship which had gone into its construction, from the perfectly shaped stones which made up the walls of the edifice, to the care which had been taken to set the windows, to the fine greenery which lay at intervals around the building. Elizabeth was charmed all over again.

"I like it very much, William," said Elizabeth, her tone shy.

"I am glad you do, my dear," said William. "Welcome to your future home. I am certain we shall have many years of perfect felicity within its walls."

In future years, Elizabeth would joke that their felicity was not *quite* perfect, but feeling almost philosophical, she was known to state that two such confident individuals could hardly go through life without a disagreement or two marring their world. And they did disagree. But though they often held to their opinions with stubborn assurance of their own rightness, they took care for each other's feelings. Estrangements were short, and they generally reconciled with the force of passion shared by two people so completely devoted to each other.

As the Darcy family grew in the coming years, both William and Elizabeth took the opportunity to thank each other many times over for giving the other a chance. Though Elizabeth had been independent and not of mind to marry for anything other than the very deepest of love, she was aware that such a situation might have blinded her to the ability to eventually find such love, left her looking for something perfect, when perfection did not exist in an imperfect world.

Georgiana and Kitty were the closest of friends and sisters ever after, and both remained close with Elizabeth over the years. The girls came out together — Kitty, though she was a year older, declared herself quite content with waiting an extra year for London society — and for several years, they broke many hearts, determined as they were to emulate their elder siblings' example and marry for inclination alone. Their paths, however, led them in very different directions.

As was her right to expect, Georgiana caught the eye of an earl after her third season, and after a long courtship in which she took very great care to ensure her feelings were engaged, they married, settling at his estate in Northamptonshire, where they raised a small family, being blessed with two boys.

Kitty, for a time after her friend married, mourned the loss of her closest companion, though she was happy for Georgiana's good fortune. This all changed, however, when she — quite by chance — met an old acquaintance. Michael Denny — formerly known as Lieutenant Denny of the regiment which had stayed in Meryton that fateful winter — was the fourth son of a gentleman of modest means. After resigning his commission at the end of the war, Mr. Denny had thought to take up the law as a profession. That had all changed when he had met Kitty by chance on a street in London.

Theirs was a whirlwind courtship, which ended in marriage not two months after their meeting. Though he had not much to live on, Kitty's dowry by now was a handsome sum, and his intention to pursue the law, though a little later than most men, meant they would always have enough to live on.

That was when Elizabeth had conceived of an idea, and presented it to her husband, confident he could be brought to her way of thinking very quickly.

"My dear Elizabeth," William had said, "you know very well that on this subject yours is the only opinion that matters."

"Then you approve of my plan?"

"I cannot think of much you might propose that I would not approve of. It will make your sister happy, I think, so yes, I am quite in agreement."

And thus it was that the proposal was put before Kitty and the man she was soon to marry.

"Kitty, as you know, Longbourn stands empty for most of the year. I wish for you to have it. I want you and Michael to live at Longbourn."

Eyes widened in surprise, Kitty exclaimed: "But Elizabeth, Longbourn is yours! It is your dowry. I cannot take it from you."

Elizabeth only laughed. "Do you think I require it, Kitty? William's holdings are vast and my settlement is very large. I have been managing Longbourn these years, and I have done what I can, but only so much can be done from a distance, even with a good steward. I wish for you to have it. I want you and Michael to make it into the prosperous estate I always dreamed it could be.

"The only condition I have is that I wish for *Bennets* to once again hold Longbourn. Thus, as long as Michael is willing to take on our surname, Longbourn will be yours."

Michael Denny, having had no idea he would ever become master of an estate, was almost overcome by Elizabeth's generosity, and for a time he tried to tell her it was too much. But Elizabeth was firm, and soon, upon his marriage, Michael Denny became Michael Bennet, and a new dynasty of Bennets at Longbourn took residence. His parents, not at liberty to provide much for their younger sons, were simply happy that he had come into such good fortune, as their legacy and family name was adequately protected by Michael's three older brothers and their families.

And it proved to be a great boon to the estate to install the new Mr. Bennet there as master. Though Michael was not a gifted master of an estate, he was competent, and he knew when to rely on the expertise of Mr. Whitmore, who remained Longbourn's steward until he retired to a cottage on the estate with his beloved wife, who had given him several beautiful children. But though Michael was not gifted when it came to running the estate, he truly was when it came to horseflesh. Under his careful management, Longbourn's new stables soon thrived, and their equine stock became highly sought after. In this, the Bennets were able to raise their fortunes greatly.

With Michael and Kitty settled into their new home, there was much congress between the three branches of the family, and as Georgiana's estate was situated almost exactly in the middle between the two outlying estates, her home became a gathering place for the three couples for many years. Their children largely grew up with each other, and though none of them married cousins, they, by and large, remained close throughout all of their lives.

As William had intended, his estrangement with Mr. Bingley was of a permanent nature. Mr. Bingley, through his sister's marriage to a gentleman, maintained some measure of respectability in London. However, as Mr. Hurst was not of the first circles himself, Mr. Bingley's access to said circles was lost when Darcy severed their friendship. Mr. Bingley seemed to accept this change with an unusual philosophy, as he had never truly desired to climb the heights of society.

Miss Bingley, however, was not of the same stuff as her brother, and it was said that she bitterly railed against Mr. Darcy, and most especially *Miss Eliza Bennet*, who had ruined all her chances of happiness. Since it was known that she was no longer acquainted with the Darcys, her venom—on the rare occasions when it made its way to anyone of consequence—was wasted. In the end, she was presented with the choice between marrying a modest country gentleman and remaining a spinster, and perhaps surprisingly, she chose the first option. As that gentleman's estate was in Devonshire, and as a consequence at a great distance from London, she was rarely seen there. But she reportedly remained bitter throughout the rest of her life at how she had been treated, and Elizabeth suspected that there were not many in Devonshire who were unaware of the name *Eliza Bennet*, and had not heard of her perfidy.

Conversely, William retained his acquaintance with Hurst, and the two of them found an easy friendship, though William still laughingly told his wife on occasion that Hurst was still a bit of a bore. As for Louisa Hurst, her children, when they came, changed her priorities, and as she rarely saw her sister again, she was able to shed much of the reticence which had come of having such a sister. Elizabeth found, after meeting with the woman several times, that she could actually like Louisa Hurst a great deal. And though the two families were not the closest of friends, they kept in touch and often stayed with each other. Mr. Hurst, especially, was happy to maintain access to Pemberley and, more importantly, its wine cellars, and though Elizabeth grew to be somewhat fond of the man, she could readily agree with her husband about his character, particularly on the nights when he had been drinking. Since those nights were plentiful, Elizabeth typically could only tolerate Mr. Hurst during the day when he was sober.

As for Mr. Bingley, though he was aware of his sister's continued acquaintance with the Darcys', he never attempted a rapprochement. He eventually did marry one of his angels, and he purchased an estate in Norfolk. By Mr. Hurst's intelligence, the Darcys learned that the estate, though prosperous, was not made that way by the efforts of its master. Rather, Mr. Bingley was fortunate when William recommended a good man to Mr. Hurst to become Mr. Bingley's steward. Mr. Bingley, however, remained invariably unserious, his head often turned by a pretty face—though no dalliances were ever known to society—and apt to change his mind on a whim.

Of Mr. Wickham, Elizabeth never again saw a thing, a circumstance which was highly in the gentleman's favor—the only circumstance he had in his favor, in Elizabeth's opinion. Beginning two years after his incarceration, William would visit him periodically to see if he had learned his lesson. Mr. Wickham, however, continued to rail against his former friend, claiming ill-use, declaring that he would have his vengeance on them all.

In total, Mr. Wickham remained incarcerated in Marshalsea for more than five years, and when William had grown convinced that he would never change his ways—not that there had ever been much hope—he arranged to have Mr. Wickham transported. Of Mr. Wickham once he left England's shores, nothing beyond the fact of his safe arrival in Van Diemen's Land was ever heard. He never again preyed on the good people of England, and for that, the Darcys could only be grateful.

The one final member of Elizabeth's family—Mr. Collins—also found fulfillment and contentment in his life. Though he was never to inherit an estate, he found his true calling as a parson, and as William had claimed so many times, he became a tolerable man, though he remained less than gifted in intelligence, and was never quite able to suppress his obsequious streak.

By chance, the man holding the living at Lambton passed quite suddenly, leaving a vacancy to be filled. As Mr. Collins had performed his duties as curate for some years, he was offered the living, which he gratefully accepted. The parish was not quite as large, and as a consequence, the living was not quite so valuable, but Mr. Collins was only grateful that he had been given another chance to hold the sacred position. He eventually married a local woman, and they had two beautiful children who, it was said, took after their mother more than their father. Even Mr. Collins had been known to say, with pride and joy, that his children were very blessed indeed.

Elizabeth remained on the best of terms with those of the neighborhood of her birth, especially with the Lucases, to whom she was always grateful for providing support in the years after the deaths of the rest of her family. Charlotte was often invited to visit Pemberley and London with the Darcys, and it was during one of the latter times that she met a man of some consequence, an acquaintance of William's, who decided he could not live without her. Charlotte's wedding was one of true joy for Elizabeth, who was happy that someone had finally seen her friend for the jewel she was. Needless to say, Charlotte was happy with her situation, and ever after remained close to Elizabeth.

And what could be said of our couple? Pemberley was filled with the sounds of laughter, once again alive with the joy of children and the blessing of the love of a husband and wife. They lived to great ages, and when they passed, within weeks of each other, it was said that they could not be separated, even in death. Future generations all held to the same standards as their forebears, and the estate prospered for many generations to come. Indeed, they were all blessed.

The End

Please enjoy the following excerpt from the upcoming novel *On Lonely Paths*, book two of the *Earth and Sky* fantasy trilogy.

It was night in the sky realm. And what a night it was.

The sky was clear and the stars as visible as if there was nothing in between the firmament above and the earth below. The wind shifted and swirled about the settlements of the Skychildren, the area at once calm and peaceful, yet giving a hint of a world which, though not flush with youth, was alive and rich with life.

On the ground world below, the night was equally fine—warm, as dictated by the summer season yet calm and gentle, with no hint of the sometimes spectacular storms which plagued the area during the summer.

But the world below was of no concern to the two who lay upon the soft grasses of the sky realm. Here and there, hints of nearby foliage, though certainly not as lush and green as that found on the earth below, could be seen in the darkness. Heathers, brush, and even the occasional stunted trees covered the landscape, bringing life to what would otherwise be a blasted land.

The two people themselves were a study in contrast, and one which, not many months ago, would not have been seen anywhere in the world. The man was tall and slender, possessed of short locks of straight blond hair and cobalt-colored eyes. He was intelligent and kind, but quick to anger and lacking patience, something which his companion would often tease him about, though always with the utmost of affection.

By contrast, the woman was small in stature, though her determination and intelligence more than made up for her short height, and while she did not possess a particularly fiery personality, she was not one to be trifled with. As for her looks, they were the opposite of his, for she sported a mane of long, rich, chestnut hair and had a lovely face with amber-colored eyes.

The fact that their people were the bitterest and oldest of enemies had been all but forgotten by both of them, though their respective peoples were not as quick in embracing one another as the two lovers were. Still, with patience and persistence, they both believed that the change in the relations between their peoples would make their world a better place. This belief and their love for one another drove them to continue their course, no matter what obstacles arose before them. They were determined it would always be thus.

The woman shifted, gazing fondly at the man beside her for a moment before returning her eyes upward once more. She loved the look of peace and contentment upon her fiancé's face; there had been a lot to try their patience lately—much of it involving their impending wedding—yet these stolen moments were theirs to enjoy together in relative solitude. Right now, there was no need to worry about consulting with advisers and family members or handling the variety of problems that had cropped up as they attempted to facilitate peaceful trade relations between their peoples. This time was theirs. It was a period when they could afford to be selfish, if only for a brief time.

"One of the things I love most about the sky realm is how I can see the stars so clearly," Tierra said softly, breaking the comfortable silence between them.

"A Groundbreather who also fancies herself a stargazer? I fear you may soon be disowned by your people for heresy," Skye teased.

She elbowed him gently in the ribs. "I am not the only one demonstrating unusual qualities for one of a certain race. I seem to recall *you* admiring some of the flowers in the castle gardens down in the ground realm, which some of your people up here might view to be just as heretical."

Skye snorted but did not comment; Tierra knew he was well aware of the fact that his opinions of the ground realm had undergone an almost miraculous transformation. Somehow, she had broken through his barriers without even realizing she was doing it. And she was so glad that she had, for his soul had become irrevocably bound to hers in a way that she had never imagined possible.

They were quiet again for a few moments before Tierra asked, "Do you remember my constellation?"

His light chuckle brought a smile to her face. "Of course," he said, pointing. "That crass sword over there has your name written right on its hilt."

"And yours is that primitive old bow over there," Tierra responded in kind, nodding toward a small grouping of stars. "An absolutely useless weapon for a battle."

"I'd say it wasn't that useless when Cirrus used it to save your neck in our battle with the Fenik," Skye countered.

"Mmhmm," Tierra said. She was glad Skye could speak more lightly of the battle and her role in it now—he had admitted to having some nightmares about it after the fact which she suspected centered on losing her—but she was less than pleased that she owed something to Skye's friend.

While the man was all smiles and joviality when it came to Skye, Cirrus's expression always took on a disapproving cast when he focused on her. She had considered asking Skye to talk to his friend, but Skye seemed so glad Cirrus was alive that she did not want to cause his happiness to dim even a whit. So she held her tongue, hoping that Cirrus would eventually come to see that her motives were pure when it came to Skye. In marrying him, she was not seeking to be queen; she was seeking love and companionship. And she knew she would have it in ample measure.

"You know," Skye said, twisting and propping his head up on an elbow while he lazily draped an arm across Tierra's stomach, "I still can't believe you disguised yourself as a soldier so you could participate in a fight with a giant beast."

As he began to draw circles with his fingers on Tierra's side, she had to fight against the urge to shy away from the ticklish sensation. "I had no idea that was what I was going to face." "If you had known, would it have stopped you?"

"No."

Skye laughed, his amusement clearly seeping through their mental bond. "That's my little Groundbreather."

Tierra raised an eyebrow. "*Your* little Groundbreather?"

"That's right," he said, wrapping his arm tightly around her. "*Mine.*"

"I ought to imprison you in a ground cage for that one and teach you just what your place is."

"Probably. But then you wouldn't have someone to take you stargazing."

"I would just have to find another Skychild to serve as my personal form of transport. I imagine Mista would not protest."

"You're probably right. But I think her fear of insects and becoming dirty might hamper her willingness to partake in such outdoor activities as reclining on sky soil. And all that's not even taking into account her insipid personality, which I think would be the more important factor when considering whether to use her as your transportation."

"Skye," Tierra chided, "you know she has a good heart."

"I still don't know what you see in that woman," he grumbled, shaking his head.

"As I have told you before, I find her innocence refreshing. But come—you cannot tell me you brought me up here to complain about your stepmother, now, can you?" Her lip quirked. "I am certain you had something more interesting in mind if you were willing to brave my mother's wrath. She is still angry that I snuck away from the castle to help with the battle against the Seneschal. If she knew how often you snuck me away from the castle, she would have both of our hides hung up outside the castle walls for all the world to see what happens to those who bring about her displeasure."

"I think your mother would like my hide regardless. If it weren't for the water connecting us . . ."

"Yes, Terrain's water has indeed brought us great good," Tierra said with a smile, reaching up to touch his lips at the memory of their first kiss. "Because of his gift, our two peoples have been drawn together at last."

COMING IN 2016 FROM
ONE GOOD SONNET PUBLISHING

http://onegoodsonnet.com/

FOR READERS WHO LIKED THE MISTRESS OF LONGBOURN

A Life from the Ashes
A sequel to Jann Rowland's beloved first novel *Acting on Faith, A Life from the Ashes* chronicles Lydia's journey toward self-discovery, knowledge, and a future she never knew she wanted.

An Unlikely Friendship
Elizabeth Bennet has always possessed pride in her powers of discernment. She discovers, however, that first impressions are not always accurate.

Bound by Love
Lost as a young child, Elizabeth Bennet is found by the Darcys and raised by the family as a beloved daughter. Bound by love with the family of her adoption, she has no hint of what awaits her when she and Mr. Darcy join Mr. Bingley in Hertfordshire at his newly leased estate, Netherfield.

Cassandra
The pain of losing a beloved wife threatens to undo Darcy's very sanity, but the introduction of a young woman gives him reason to hope. Through her patient tutelage and love, Darcy learns to put the past behind him and comes to see the precious gift he has been given.

Obsession
Banished from her home at the age of seventeen for refusing a marriage proposal from an odious man, Elizabeth Bennet moves to London to live with her aunt and uncle Gardiner. But when she is approached by a mysterious stranger who wishes to know more of her, Elizabeth can only allow herself to be caught up in the excitement of the moment.

Shadows Over Longbourn
The approaching death of Mr. Bennet threatens to leave his five young daughters at the mercy of the vengeful Mr. Thaddeus Collins. But Mr. Bennet plays one final desperate card before he passes, calling on his distant relatives—the Darcys—to provide his children with a home.

For more details, visit
http://www.onegoodsonnet.com/genres/pride-and-prejudice-variations

ALSO BY ONE GOOD SONNET PUBLISHING

THE SMOTHERED ROSE TRILOGY

BOOK 1: THORNY

In this retelling of "Beauty and the Beast," a spoiled boy who is forced to watch over a flock of sheep finds himself more interested in catching the eye of a girl with lovely ground-trailing tresses than he is in protecting his charges. But when he cries "wolf" twice, a determined fairy decides to teach him a lesson once and for all.

BOOK 2: UNSOILED

When Elle finds herself practically enslaved by her stepmother, she scarcely has time to even clean the soot off her hands before she collapses in exhaustion. So when Thorny tries to convince her to go on a quest and leave her identity as Cinderbella behind her, she consents. Little does she know that she will face challenges such as a determined huntsman, hungry dwarves, and powerful curses . . . .

BOOK 3: ROSEBLOOD

Both Elle and Thorny are unhappy with the way their lives are going, and the revelations they have had about each other have only served to drive them apart. What is a mother to do? Reunite them, of course. Unfortunately, things are not quite so simple when a magical lettuce called "rapunzel" is involved.

If you're a fan of thieves with a heart of gold, then you don't want to Miss . . .

THE PRINCES AND THE PEAS
A TALE OF ROBIN HOOD

A NOVEL OF THIEVES, ROYALTY, AND
IRREPRESSIBLE LEGUMES

BY LELIA EYE

An infamous thief faces his greatest challenge yet when he is pitted against forty-nine princes and the queen of a kingdom with an unnatural obsession with legumes. Sleeping on top of a pea hidden beneath a pile of mattresses? Easy. Faking a singing contest? He could do that in his sleep. But stealing something precious out from under "Old Maid" Marian's nose . . . now that is a challenge that even the great Robin Hood might not be able to surmount.

When Robin Hood comes up with a scheme that involves disguising himself as a prince and participating in a series of contests for a queen's hand, his Merry Men provide him their support. Unfortunately, however, Prince John attends the contests with the Sheriff of Nottingham in tow, and as all of the Merry Men know, Robin Hood's pride will never let him remain inconspicuous. From sneaking peas onto his neighbors' plates to tweaking the noses of prideful men like the queen's chamberlain, Robin Hood is certain to make an impression on everyone attending the contests. But whether he can escape from the kingdom of Clorinda with his prize in hand before his true identity comes to light is another matter entirely.

About the Author

Jann Rowland

Jann Rowland is a Canadian. He enjoys reading and sports, and he also dabbles a little in music, taking pleasure in singing and playing the piano.

Though Jann did not start writing until his mid-twenties, writing has grown from a hobby to an all-consuming passion. His interest in Jane Austen stems from his university days when he took a class in which *Pride and Prejudice* was required reading. However, his first love is fantasy fiction, which he hopes to pursue writing in the future.

He now lives in Alberta with his wife of more than twenty years and his three children.

For more information on Jann Rowland, please visit:
http://onegoodsonnet.com.